The Face of the Waters

The Face of the Waters

Tony McKenna

PRESS

Published by Vulpine Press in the United Kingdom in 2022

ISBN: 978-1-83919-441-2

www.vulpine-press.com

For Joshua and Nathan Hudson

'In the beginning, God created the heavens and the earth.
The earth was without form, and void, and darkness was over the
face of the deep.
And the Spirit of God moved upon the face of the waters.'
Genesis 1:1

Prologue

Mexico 1957

When the flood arrived, it was like nothing he had known. They had been driving in her beat-up truck, its engine sputtering, choking. Somehow it continued down the old dirt road, which ran those many miles from Ciudad Puebla to their village. The air had been hot and clammy, though that was not unusual. But there was something different about it that day; it seemed to tingle with an electric charge. Even though it was early afternoon, there was a strange purple glow on the horizon.

He played with his fingers and thumbs, squirming in the front seat, his small seven-year-old body sinking into the torn, sweltering leather. He felt wrong – he was hungry, yes, but he was used to that. This was something else. Something that shone in his eyes. Shimmered in his head.

He looked up at his mother. Her eyes were dark and unwavering, focussed on the road ahead, the sides of her mouth pinched in sour determination. He wanted to say something, to somehow give voice to the strange feeling swirling inside of him, but he knew better than to speak to his mother when she looked that way.

Besides, he could never find the words.

It came first in a gentle *hiss*, like the rustle of long grass when the sun was high in the sky. The sound began to build.

'*Escucha, Mamá, escucha!* Listen, Mama, listen!' The words had slipped from his mouth.

'*Escucha, Mamá, escucha!*' she parroted back.

She made the middle word – 'Mama' – sound pleading and pathetic, as she always did, her voice laced with a bitterness he knew well but still could not fathom. Normally it would be enough, a warning, but now there was that feeling in the air – it seemed to crackle – and that strange purple hue on the horizon had deepened, throwing a shadow across the top of the truck.

The word slipped out again: '*Mamá, por favor.*'

This time, she didn't react straight away, but he saw her eyes tighten and knew it was bad. Nothing happened for a few moments. Then she took her right hand from the steering wheel and snapped it back, driving the knuckles into his nose. The pain was instantaneous. The soft cartilage in his nose had been damaged and split by her fists on many other occasions, so it didn't take much for it to reopen. And yet the pain was worse because the previous injuries had never entirely healed. He wasn't even able to scream. It was like being winded; all he could do was struggle for breath.

At the same moment, an almighty *screeching* sound almost caused his mother to swerve the truck off the road. Tens, maybe hundreds, of birds flocked across the near distance. One of them *cracked* the windscreen with a *thud*.

'*Puta madre!*' his mother spat.

But that *hissing* sound had grown now, and he looked past his mother and out through the window, in the direction from which those birds had come. The top of the nearest hill looked strange, as it began to shimmer and curl like it was not solid at all, and then he understood. His eyes made sense of it, as the dull brown tide of water – running as far as his eye could see – flowed over and spilt downwards in a long curling wave. On the one hand, it seemed like this was happening in slow motion; only when he blinked that wave of water was inexorably closer, and the sound had heightened. He went to say something to his mother again, only the blood had clogged his nose and drenched his mouth, and the fear he felt now was more than the whimpering, helpless fear he felt every day of his waking life. It was an absolute, paralysing sense of terror, for he was certain this was the end of the world.

She made a sound. When his mother finally caught sight of the water, she made a sound. An *ughh*. Not quite surprise. Not quite fear. Only a dull sense of bafflement.

And then the water hit.

All at once, it was as though the world was screaming. The rushing water, the *thudding* violence of the truck being upturned, the *shattering* of glass, and then all those sounds died as they were sucked under. The water flooded in, and the feeling of shock – the feeling of its cold – hit him, and the sense of the cold water, the blood from his nose, and the pounding of his temples all rolled into a series of shuddering images. He was choking and spluttering as the light from above dulled in a thick grey-blue.

He passed out momentarily. Then felt someone's hands on him, pulling him. He felt the moment when his head broke the surface, gasping for air. They were flowing forwards now, the thick muddy tide carrying branches and dead animals and pieces of debris from houses and cars. He could barely keep his head above the water.

His mother held him up, her face grim and determined, pulling him along in her wake. He heard her breathing in harsh rasps and was aware of the anger in her eyes, as though this indecipherable chaos was merely one more attempt to undo her on the part of some demented cosmological power.

He did not know how long he was in the water. Eventually, he felt himself hauled out onto a small island of rocks. The sun had fallen out of the sky, and the last rays of light illuminated the tawny water, which flowed all around them. It was colder now, and he shivered, wet and damp. He sat on one side. She sat on the other. She had limped towards her resting place, and before the light had died completely, he saw the gash on her leg. It looked as thick and prominent as her lips when she would go out at night in her best dress and put lipstick on, which was blood red. He had always liked that. For it was in those moments when she was nicest to him. Sometimes she would even kiss him on the forehead before she left. Afterwards, he would touch his finger to that spot and look miraculously at the impression of red left on its tip.

Only now, the red and the thickness was something else entirely. She saw him looking.

'What are you staring at?' she snapped, but her voice was weaker now.

He wanted to say something. Only he could never find the words.

He woke up in the night. He watched her. She was snoring softly.

The next day the water was still flowing. He looked out across it. He felt a moment's happiness because he was on an island, which meant he could go exploring. He looked out across the brown water and into the distance. The water seemed to flow and flow until, at some point, it reached the hazy blue of the firmament above.

He returned to his mother. She was lying by the same rock, looking up, glaring at him.

'Why don't you do something useful?' she said. Her voice sounded weaker still.

4

He thought about the question. He resolved to do something useful. He gathered up some moss and green plants and brought them to her. He didn't know exactly why. Perhaps they were magic. The shaman talked of such things. She looked at the offering contemptuously and closed her eyes. There was a strange smell coming from her. He thought it might be coming from her leg. Those red lips had now grown a scale of seeping yellow across them.

It was night again. He didn't know how that had happened. He heard a sound and peered up. Underneath the stars, he could just make out the shape of her face. He could see it moving. She was eating. He crawled forward, his swollen belly suddenly throbbing with hunger. He saw her eyes gleam the moment she caught sight of his movement. He could smell both her leg and the sodden burrito she was biting into. He couldn't say for sure, but somehow, he knew she was looking at him with that same bitter sharpness – 'Escucha, Mamá, escucha!'

From within the gloom, a small packet hit him. He picked it up, soft and meaty. He devoured it at once, panting in pleasure.

'I've always given you everything. And you have always just sucked it up. Like a little animal.' Her voice was strangely bereft; she was making a statement of fact.

Moments later, she was snoring again.

He could see she had shit herself. He didn't want to look. He had done his own business on the other side of the rocks; she could no longer move. His eyes were drawn to the trickle of her faeces dribbling down her diseased leg. She had not said anything for a while. But now, the grey film across her eyes seemed to disperse – she was conscious again, shrewd. She saw the moment of his realisation, his comprehension – the fact that she had soiled herself.

5

Her lips crinkled in a genuine smile. 'Doesn't pretty baby wanna give his mama a huggy wug?'

Sometime later, it was night again. In the darkness, crabs scuttled across the rocks; he could see their zigzagging shadows in the black.

He awoke suddenly when he felt the smooth sleekness of a snake sliding over his legs, its scales still damp with fluid. His beating, bursting heart felt as though it might break.

He felt her eyes on him again. The stench from her leg pervaded the air. She tried to sit up, but she couldn't quite do it. She reached out an arm. She stabbed her hand at him through the gloom. She belched and gurgled.

Finally, her voice arrived, low and subdued, yet filled with terminal poison. 'You ...' she rasped. 'Do you know what you are?'

He drew closer instinctively, but he did not know what he was. He did not say anything. But she continued as though triumphant, as though this was something she had waited a whole lifetime to say.

'You,' she said, 'are a ... *rape baby!*'

She giggled.

He blinked.

'Do you know what that is?'

There was a strange intensity to her voice, and part of him thought that she might actually be telling him something nice. Part of him wanted to cling onto that more than anything, for he had become so tired. He thought that neither of them might ever leave this place, and he desperately wanted her to tell him something nice because he felt so frightened.

At a deeper level, there was something wrong in that voice, in that word. 'Rape' – he did not know what it meant, but it sounded like something sharp and awful. The way she'd said it was both bitter and gleeful.

Again, he wanted to say something, needed to say something, only his voice died in his throat.

When he woke up, the sun was burning his eyes. Those small crabs were there again, but this time they were moving in and out of the wound in his mother's leg. Only, she was no longer moving. Her face was washed out and grey. He pulled himself up, swiped the crabs away, went to say something to her, one final time, and finally, the words arrived:

'*Te amo, Mamá!* I love you, Mama!'

He had heard other children say this to their mamas, so it seemed like something he should do.

The night came so quickly once more, and the hunger was unbearable. He tried to catch the crabs, but they moved too fast, and he was so slow and tired.

The following day he crawled towards his mother's corpse. He was crying, but there was no longer any moisture in his eyes. Her mouth was open, her teeth bared.

He pulled on her arm. '*Mamá, por favour! Ayudame.* Mama, please. Help me.'

Those grey eyes were dissolving. Creatures had worked on them in the night. The smell from her wound was less pungent now, even though her leg throbbed with activity.

He brought her palm to his face – she would never have touched him with such tenderness in reality. He pressed her fingers against his skin.

'*Ayudame, Mamá!*'

He smelt the tips of her fingers, the fragments of the burrito she had eaten days earlier. In desperation, he sucked those fingertips for the last scraps of flavour. He was so hungry. He was starving.

And that was when his teeth pushed into those fingertips a little harder.

One

Mexico 1991

It was raining. The hot summer shower fell on the parched concrete of downtown Puebla City, throwing up a vaporous mist. The nasal sounds of dry, angry horns from the traffic-clogged streets broke against the thick hot air. The water pattered against a large grey building, a monotonous lulling sound – something one wasn't quite aware of but at the same time couldn't quite tune out. Outside, the pall of the clouds threw a strange shadow onto the building. Though it was only a little past noon, the normal graduations of light to dark, which demarked the passing of the day, had been thrown out of kilter; it seemed as though time itself was not quite on its axis. The air was nervy, charged with static; it felt the way it did in the hours before the coming of a storm, only the clouds in the sky were sluggish and low-hanging, fissured with muted light.

The intermittent *buzz* of the stuttering air conditioning provided little relief against the stultifying air. In exasperation, some of the police officers threw open the large windows, while others pressed paper flannels soaked in tepid water against fissured sweaty brows. The weather was so close that it seemed to cling to bodies; clothes, hair, skin. The moisture slickened beards and eyebrows. Squeaked in the smalls of backs. Nestled in the crevices behind knees.

There was no respite. Phones at the desks *shrilled* incessantly, and nerves frayed. Commands were uttered in taut toneless voices, and pulses in temples quickened and throbbed. One young man, though, seemed impervious to it all. Brown eyes shining with lively anticipation, he came bounding up to an older, heavier set man whose stocky frame was compressed into a cheap, faded, and ill-fitting suit.

'*Hombre!* You have to check it out. This fucking woman! You have to see it for yourself, man! Can you second me?' the younger man said.

Armando looked at him. José Luis was twenty years his junior, and sometimes he felt the age difference. Today, even more so.

'What have you caught? What's the case?'

The young man *whistled* through his teeth, his lips crinkled in a crooked smile. He peered at the other shrewdly.

Armando's voice came in a murmur. '*Por favor, chico*, it's not the weather for games. You expect me to go in there cold?'

'I'm just bustin' your balls. It's a domestic, a bullshit complaint, that's all. No tech, no prep. But this woman, *Jesús Cristo*, you gotta take a look at her.'

When Armando arrived at the interview room, two women were sitting at the desk.

One was small and young with a pale white peach-shaped face, pretty but fragile. The silk black of her dress hung thinly over an androgynous body, and her whole physical bearing was turned inwards in a perpetual flinch.

The other woman had the same colouration, the same dark, moist eyes, but the resemblance ended there. It was like seeing a moon on the far side of a planet; this woman was vast – reams of billowing fat staggered in layers of undulating flesh, out of which pushed a head festooned with thick, greying hair and jowls of soft doughy skin. She had been marked up – one eye was swollen purple and black, and a big yellow bruise marred the side of her face. The nostrils of her reddened puggish nose flared, indignant but mournful.

'I'd like to present you with my colleague, Detective Armando José Maria. He is an expert on … social and domestic issues, having spent many years in Mexico City University doing various case studies …' José Luis looked at Armando knowingly. His eyes twinkled at this piece of ridiculous fiction. No one in the lower ranks of the police force had a degree.

But the larger woman sniffed and drew herself up as though mollified by the seriousness with which the police were treating her case – a detective no less.

José Luis gave a supercilious smile. 'So, if you will just tell him what you told me, from the start.'

'I … I … the motherfucker, this sordid *hijo de puta* … that I call my son-in-law …' Her voice came out in a claxon blast, which seemed to reverberate the air and echo in their ears. It was almost cartoonish – nasal and husky before building to its whiny crescendo.

Armando inwardly winced; he had knocked back the best part of a bottle of whisky the night before, the heat making it hard to sleep. The hard, bright light of morning had arrived early and remorseless, his sweat-soaked sheets still clinging to him. His hangover, coupled with the *screech* of her voice, made the interview difficult to sit through.

But she continued. 'He has been insulting my daughter. He calls her all the names, *muy grosero*, and hits her too. But she is my blood, and I will not stand for it. So, I tell him as much. And when I am not expecting it, the *cabron* clocks me with an iron!'

José Luis turned his eyes to Armando, struggling to fight off laughter.

But Armando couldn't feel the humour in it. Her voice was like a rake being pulled across his head. He rubbed his eyes and looked at her again. The sheer bulk of her – she was more beast than woman, a hulking, sagging cow who had birthed a weak, pallid calf and was now trembling with instinctive maternal rage. Eyes wide, tongue lolling, her whole body drenched with sweat and fury.

Armando felt a sudden sense of profound sympathy for the son-in-law; it must have felt satisfying to bludgeon this great ox with the iron. He was only surprised it hadn't happened sooner.

'I tell you something,' she added, pointing at some invisible spot in the darkness. Her piggy eyes narrowed into slits. 'You had better do something. Because I am going to cut off the *cabron's* balls and fucking feed them to him, I'm gonna—

In an attempt to curtail that horrific voice, Armando turned to the other woman. '*Señorita*, do you have anything to say about this? He is, after all, your husband.'

The young woman raised her eyes to him momentarily. She spoke softly, carefully, but with conviction. 'It is as my mother says. I think … it is very wrong what Fernand did. I was very frightened. For my mother.'

Her mother snorted. 'You don't have to worry about me, *querida*! I've had my share of hard knocks, and that little shit doesn't even qualify. And when I get my hands on him.' She looked at José Luis and Armando accusingly. 'What are you going to do?'

Armando went to give the normal spiel, but José Luis cut across him smoothly.

12

'Well, *Señora*,' he said, the ghost of a smile playing on his lips, 'there are a few things we can do. We will need to take your details in full, and of the person you are making this complaint against. However, it may take some time because our list of complainants …' His gaze floated over the proportions of her body. '… is rather *large*.'

He winked at Armando.

'We could ask the Chief for more manpower, of course, but the answer is always the same. A *big fat* "No!"' José Luis went on.

Her eyes crinkled momentarily, a slight flinch.

Armando caught the gesture.

'Of course, we always try to change the minds of the top brass – we try to get them on our side so that they see how understaffed we are. How difficult it is on the ground. But we are just lowly policemen. We don't have … the *heft,* the *weight,* the *girth* which is required.' José Luis grinned.

The large woman blinked as her body began to tremble.

Armando braced himself for another shrieking onslaught.

But she didn't say a word. Instead, ever so gently, she started to cry.

The smaller woman got up from her seat and put her hands on her mother's head, gently turning her so that she was looking into her mother's eyes.

She spoke with such softness, but the words were implacable. 'I love you very much, but it is time to go.'

Her mother gave a small nod.

Armando felt something inside him catch.

Slowly, the two women got to their feet and shuffled out of the room, not even bothering to glance at the men.

The detective and the junior officer sat there in silence for a few moments.

Then, José Luis burst out laughing. 'My God. Did you see her? Well, it wasn't like you could miss her, the fat bitch! Imagine living with that – having that as your mother-in-law! That voice, oh *hermano,* no wonder he gave her a slap.'

Armando grunted noncommittally before getting up and leaving the room.

The younger man caught up with him in the corridor. 'You wanna know something?'

'Mhmm.'

'Not once have I hit my wife – or any of the girls I used to poke before her. You know why?'

'Why?'

The younger man's eyes shone with confidence. 'One thing I know in this life is women. I grew up with six sisters. I had my first girl when I was twelve years old.'

'One of your sisters?' Armando inquired politely.

'Fuck you, *cabron!*' José Luis grinned.

'I will tell you this about women. They all have the same nature, especially the Latin kind. They are passionate – hot one moment and vengeful the next. Once you learn the rhythms of those moods, it's a piece of cake. I have never hit a woman because I never needed to. That big momma out there? For all her noise and drama, I made her quiet with just a few words.'

Armando felt his gaze, but any type of response seemed like too much work. He thought about the whisky bottle. His apartment. His bed.

José Luis looked ahead, the traces of a smile still lingering on his face.

'I know women,' he murmured, almost to himself.

*****

The time passed like the rays of the withering sun. You felt every moment beat against you until, finally, the hour arrived, and you got to walk out into the evening.

The thick fumes of petrol and noise from cars were combined with the voices of vendors and their makeshift carts. These offered the Yankee promise of 'hot dogs' – the faded image of Bruce Springsteen, Madonna, or Marilyn Monroe etched out in charcoal and glitter on their weathered wooden panels. On the road, men would rush up to car windows gibbering happily and incoherently before throwing a handful of soapy dirt across the windscreen and causing the drivers to honk even more. It was a hustle, of course, but Mexico was the holy land of the hustler, the corrupt politician, the bribed cop.

Armando had a pale-blue Chevy sedan, at least fifteen years old, with rust creeping over its emaciated grill and wheel arches. He left work and got into the car. But he didn't drive all the way home. Instead, he pulled over at a side street. That evening the heat was particularly intense. Even this late, it sat upon the city like a warm swollen cloud with the strange clamminess that lingered before a storm.

He walked down the back alley, taking refuge in a side-street bar, waiting things out until the heat broke. He sat down, his large frame leaning across the thick weight of the bar's black wooden surface.

The bartender came over.

'Whisky, double!'

'Coming right up.'

He noted how the guy loaded the ice into the glass before pouring the bottle over it with a dramatic flourish. The result was that the same amount of liquid which went in spilt out. Underneath, the countertop was gridlocked with a metal webbing. Armando knew that there were compartments for each drink – whisky, tequila, vodka, and so on. At the end of the evening, the bartender would scoop up the contents of each box and refill the bottles with the correct liquid. Armando had seen this done too many times.

He glared at the barman. 'Try pouring a little more into the glass and less outside, eh?'

The guy withered under his gaze but tried to make his voice sound strong. 'Why the fuck are you questioning how I pour, *cabrón*? Who the hell are you?'

Armando looked at him a little longer and kept his voice civil enough. 'Just a concerned customer.' He pulled out his badge.

The guy paled. 'I'll get you another, sir.'

He dribbled more liquid into Armando's glass.

Armando knocked it back and set it down. 'Again.'

The barman poured.

Armando drank. 'Again.'

The man hesitated but poured once more.

Armando drank. 'Again.'

The guy who had looked so shifty at first was now powerless.

Armando liked seeing the bartender reduced to that. The detective would never have taken advantage of a working man – he put stock in a good, hardworking man – but this guy was a petty crook.

'Again.'

Armando almost chuckled. The creep looked like he was about to cry.

He knocked back a fifth generous double whisky and watched the bartender for a few moments. Slowly, he extended his arm and allowed the glass to slip from his hand. It fell onto the floor with a satisfying *tinkle*.

'You should get that cleaned up. Health and safety,' Armando told him and left.

He wandered outside. The air was still thick and hot, but the clouds above reverberated in a shuddering *rumble*. The rain came as a deluge, which splashed the streets and rendered everything murky, while rivulets of water rushed along the inseams of the road like mini floods.

Armando got into the car and drove off. The whisky still swirling in his belly, he smiled ruefully as the rain *pattered* against the roof. He was thinking about his ex, Cynthia. The rain always made him think of her. She had lectured at a community college and penned some articles for a local paper. She used to tell him he was bright, but he knew there was a gulf between her education and his. He had left his small village school at thirteen; she'd gone all the way to university – but she had never been pretentious about it.

They would tease each other, though. He would laugh at her about being an academic and not being in touch with the real world, and she would just throw him a wry smile. Mock him. When they were out, she would say something about Confucius. It was nearly always a response to something he'd raised, a gripe he had. If he was angry about the latest riot, she – who was something of a leftie – would come out with some Confucian proverb.

'Confucius had a very profound saying in around 500 BC,' she would say, 'which related to rioting. He said those who hated the rioters were very possibly anally repressive authoritarians who were frightened to think for themselves.'

He would go to argue and catch the gleam in her eye, and it would hit him that Confucius really probably hadn't said anything of the sort. She'd always been … very quick that way. And when Armando banged on about the rain, she would put on an Eastern accent, press her fingers to her eyes, stretch them in an Oriental slant, and say, 'Confucius say, wise man like the feel of nature on his face!'

Despite himself, he would grin. It was a joke between just them – something no one else would have found funny. And that was what made it precious.

He was smiling now as the clouds opened up and the thunder pealed. He reached his *barrio, Chulavista la Puebla*. Further out from the centre, the houses became much more ramshackle and rough. A few layered flats, many one-floor residences, slapped with corrugated iron across the roofs. Aerials stuck out of them, wires unearthed, writhing across the small concrete spaces that passed as gardens.

The lightning rippled across the sky. In the background of the raffish haphazard buildings, he caught the image of the mountain belt whose dark ridges loomed up into the fading grey of the evening sky. The lightning tapered away, and the horizon became dull and indistinct again.

He parked the car and made his way into his building, one of the better ones in the *barrio*. He used his key, which *clicked* open a door that led into a lobby. There was even an old rickety elevator, but it didn't work.

He went up the stairs. Just before he arrived at his own door, another door burst open. His neighbour's teenage son ran out.

The boy pushed past Armando, bouncing off the bulk of him as though he didn't register the older man's presence.

Then, the teenager stopped and looked back. His eyes were wide and irate, and he was trembling with rage.

'Why do you have to be such a dried-up cunt all the time?' he screamed at his mum.

Armando turned to the mother, standing in the other apartment's doorway. Her arm was slightly extended, eyes desperate and beautiful.

The boy turned and ran down the stairs.

'*Estas bien, Celia? Que pasa? Are you okay? What happened?*'

She spat on the ground and muttered something.

There was something unbearably erotic in that gesture for him. Through the haze of whisky, he felt himself twitch. He imagined that a woman who could spit like that, so casually, would be just as confident when it came to sucking dick. Not like a whore – who does it because she has to – but like she was really into it. But there was also pain in her face, which she fought down. He liked that about her too.

'Hey, Armandito,' she said, addressing him diminutively, even though they were around the same age. 'How you doin', pal?'

'Overworked, tipsy and old, but more to the point ... What the hell just happened?'

Her opaque eyes narrowed, the gesture causing crow's feet to fissure from their sides. Her whole face looked weary – high cheekbones pushed up against the skin – and yet to him, she was beautiful.

Her voice was low. 'Armando. He ... Cristóbal ... he's finding it hard to fit into his own skin. He doesn't know who he is or what he wants to be, and because of that, he's lashing out. But he is a kind boy. Whatever you might think, he is good-natured underneath it all.'

19

She was looking at him, those eyes wide again, something pleading in them.

'Yeah … I'm sure, Celia.'

His voice sounded limp even to himself. He didn't know what else to say, but she looked somewhat cheerier.

'Perhaps he just needs a good fuck,' she added. 'Let's face it – that's the answer to every boy's problem at that age, right? Though a mother doesn't like to dwell on such issues, I do believe my son is still a virgin.' She chuckled. 'At seventeen, I had fucked several boys.'

Armando, who had worked in Vice, and seen virtually every sexual perversion humanity could offer, felt his face reddening.

Celia's expression became serious again. 'You must come over for dinner some time. I know Cristóbal would like you if he got the chance to talk to you properly. And besides … I'd like to see you too.' She gave a suggestive smile.

Despite the whisky in his belly, he struggled for words.

He watched as she slipped back into her apartment, closing the door behind her.

He went into his own and was greeted by the tinny odour of takeaway food. In the darkness, he went straight to the fridge and swung it open. Its light revealed the unwashed cups and plates on the front room coffee table and the beer bottles arranged on the unfolded plastic table in the small kitchen. There was no divider between one room and the other.

He took the whisky bottle out of the fridge. He enjoyed the taste of whisky. Cynthia had even coaxed him into going to a whisky convention once. He hadn't really been aware that such things existed. He'd drunk loads. Made a fool of himself. You were supposed to sip slightly to attain the aroma, not knock it back like there was no tomorrow. But that wasn't the world he had grown up in. He didn't know how to sip that little bit and then delicately put it down. He'd told her that. Screamed it at her, in fact. His hands on her clothing, shaking her soft, slight frame. For she had seemed so irrational, so impervious to what he was trying to tell her, that the only solution had been to shake her, so she finally woke up to it. Woke up to the ugliness of who he was and where he had come from.

But she hadn't left him that night. She'd continued to love him – or at least he felt that was true.

One thing he remembered from that convention was that they had advised everyone *never* to put the whisky in the fridge.

From that day on, he had liked it cold.

***

Armando lay on his back, sipping the whisky. He turned on his TV. There was some old documentary on about the Lusitania. He was familiar with the subject and enjoyed watching documentaries late at night. The Lusitania was an ocean liner sunk by a German U-boat in the later stages of World War I. War promoted every type of violence, and the sinking of a boat – with the kind of technology the Germans had – was hardly unusual. But it had been a passenger boat, the largest ship of its kind. The civilian losses were high. Armando wasn't interested in it because of the violence – the deaths seemed merely another statistic to him. What he found compelling was how this one incident had changed the course of history. The United States, shocked by such an attack, had entered the war on the Allies' side, and the forces of Germany were defeated.

Everything that had happened since – the power of England, France and the US, the development of communism in Russia, and maybe even the fascism of the Hitler period – would never have happened, or happened in the same way, had the US not entered the war and secured the victory for the Allies. If the Lusitania had not chosen to embark on its voyage that fateful day, the world would have been a very different place.

That was what fascinated him. The way a single, almost arbitrary event – small in the scheme of things – could shape the destinies of so many people many years after it had happened.

Cynthia would talk about history a lot. Usually, a left-wing rant on how the revolution of 1910 had been betrayed or how Zapata had come undone – and how everything would have been so different had this battle gone the other way or that assassination not taken place. Armando had resisted the idealistic thrust of her politics with his own world-weary exasperation; his experience as *police* dealing with the actual Mexican working class on the street, who were less concerned with freedom and equality and more concerned with fighting, fucking, and killing.

Nevertheless, when Cynthia talked about history, Armando was drawn in. She represented a world that he was fascinated by but was very alien. His own mother and father had been taciturn and insular. Second generation peasants, living on the city's outskirts, suspicious of its debauchery and stench, the promise of its atheism, the hatred of God. They never had discussions about politics or history. For them, there was no history; there was only birth, death, the seasons, the sun, and the floods.

The voice *crackled* out from the TV, emitting its sharp Yankee tone:

22

'And then Germany's forces, and its cruel and ancient need for world domination, threw it against the vibrant, youthful, and democratic strength of a different type of superpower, and the USA at once …'

The voice elongated into a drone as the image on the TV – of ships and planes – suddenly fissured before dissolving into static.

'*Puta madre!*' Armando cursed, but he couldn't summon the energy to give the TV a hard *whack*, which usually revived the image.

The heat wasn't letting up, either, as the time crept towards 11.00 pm. The TV was *hissing*, and his shirt clung to him. He felt tired but not so tired that sleep was coming any time soon. He took a longer drag of the whisky and gazed at the ceiling. A door slammed outside, the aftermath of it resonating off his walls. He heard the muffled voice of Celia and the lower rumble of her pubescent son. Armando could not make out the words. He felt a dull throb of aggression. If he was that boy's father, he would have slapped the taste straight out of his mouth.

He raised himself up. His vision of the room jarred, shimmering on its axis, but now that he was vertical, he realised he couldn't stay indoors. He took another long drag of the whisky bottle, put on his trousers, and headed out into the night.

He headed three blocks down, and even before he came to the place, he heard the throb of its music. 'Septimecielo' – one of the more hard-core joints, a club which doubled as a strip bar. When he got there, it was still early. The place didn't get going until about one in the morning. He looked through the small secreted door and into a bigger room with a dance floor, across which crept reams of artificial smoke, illuminated momentarily by the flashing of winking pink and green lights. Past it was a stage and six poles, which reached the ceiling, but there were no strippers. The whole place was empty.

A large man moved into the space of the door. He was dressed in a black jacket with a loose white shirt – the vulgar nod to some form of respectability.

The large man was also fat, like the mother-in-law that Armando had encountered at the station. But despite her bluster, she had the reek of powerlessness and helplessness emanating from her. This man was at home in his own body and self-satisfied. Upon seeing Armando, he creaked his face open, his blubbery lips forming a wide shit-eating grin.

'*Armando, Armandito, La Armada es muy peligrosa!*'

Armando grunted. 'I want to speak with *el pequeño jefe!*'

Armando was there for the payoff, which many detectives got from the heads of clubs in the local area. The club owner or pimp or dealer watered the local police with money to overlook their activities.

The bouncer's name was Filippo. He looked at Armando with that same grin but was a little hesitant now.

'The boss isn't expecting you until tomorrow.'

'Yeah, only I am here today!'

At that moment, a woman came sweeping through the door. Armando caught sight of her face, half in shadow – young, mid-twenties perhaps – but she was already on the turn, already pinched and sour. From the fabric of her dark jacket, he could see the full globes of her breasts, the way they pushed together at the point where the material parted above the last and highest button.

The bouncer shot out one hand, pushing the woman against the side of the door, her small body ricocheting backwards under the impact, but her expression remained tight and immobile.

'*Puta*! How many times do I have to tell you? You give eighty per cent to the house, and I get my dick sucked every third night. How fucking difficult is that for you to understand?' Filippo snapped.

She raised her head to him. In the gloom, her eyes were little more than slits of white, emotionless and dull. She didn't register the presence of Armando. She nodded slightly, and the bouncer moved back.

She went to walk forward, but his arm shot out again, barring her path.

'Stupid bitch!' He shoved his fingers into her pocket and retrieved a small bag of white powder. 'So fucking predictable!'

He slapped her on the ass hard, the impact causing her to shudder, but those eyes never changed; she just continued to stare right ahead.

Filippo withdrew his arm, and she stepped into the gloomy smoke-filled interior.

His face became jovial again, that same shit-eating grin plastered across it. 'Go have some fun on me, amigo!' He tossed the small bag to the detective.

Armando caught it.

'But you can't disturb the *jefe* tonight. We didn't expect you until *manana*. It's always on Friday *hombre*,' Filippo added.

Armando looked at the bouncer – the full layers of undulating chin, the small sleazy eyes set into what was a massive pancake of a face. A wave of loathing rippled through him, so much so that Armando had to catch his breath as he pressed closer to him.

The bouncer was a good deal bigger and wider, but Armando was also stocky and solid. He felt the low-level current of rage, which seemed to flow through him all the time nowadays. He felt the sour taste of whisky in the back of his throat, metallic and slightly salty, almost like blood.

He spoke in a low voice, 'Listen to me, you fat piece of shit. You are going to take me upstairs. Otherwise, she ain't gonna be the only one on her knees!'

The fat man's face crinkled, his small dark eyes reflecting resentment.

'Why do you have to be such a *cabrón*, eh?'

Armando felt tired again and sighed with impatience. 'Just … move.'

He followed in the footsteps of the surly bouncer whose huge frame seemed to blot out the small staircase that led upwards. They arrived at a slim corridor, which overlooked the club floor below through a tinted glass divider. He could see the stage, the bar at the back, and the seats in the corners. But he knew that anyone on the floor looking up would have only seen a dark window.

He continued following Filippo to an office at the far end of the hall.

The big man *knocked* on the door, pushed his head inside, uttered a few words, and then ushered Armando in.

The detective entered, Filippo glaring at him before turning on his heels.

Juan Carlos III was sitting in the far corner of the office, one leg resting on a large desk. He was a man in his mid-twenties; good looking with slick black hair, white-pearly skin – despite his Mexican heritage – and an elegantly shaped moustache and goatee. Armando knew the kid's background. Juan's father, Juan Carlos II, was the criminal power in the local district, a shrewd, grey ruthless man, who had started out as a slum landlord, and eventually bought into a dozen strip clubs and brothels across the city.

The father was rarely seen, but the son was another story. He was visible in every respect, especially in the more salubrious places – the swagger in his step, the girls on his arm, the golden crucifix that lay heavy on his chest. Armando knew that little Juan had attended university to study business and economics but was then thrown out after his father's money couldn't smooth over the latest date rape allegation. The victim, apparently, had not only been sexually assaulted but also badly beaten. Naturally, her outraged parents had pushed her to press charges.

In the gloom of the smoke-clogged office, the gold crucifix shone. The young man narrowed his eyes, looking at the detective intensely for a few seconds. Eventually, he beckoned Armando to take a seat. The older man accepted the invitation as his gaze flickered around, taking in the table, the tracks of cocaine running across it, and a series of notes fanning out to the side.

'Armando, Armando, Armando! *Que paso, chico*? What has happened, son?' the younger man asked, his tone laced with smugness.

'I've come to pick up my payment,' he replied tonelessly.

'You people want everything at once, as soon as you want it. But we are running a business here. Do you know what that means?'

The detective's eyebrows rose slightly, his lips tight.

Juan Carlos ran a finger across the top of his moustache as though he were wondering how to make things clear.

'You, my friend, are an emissary of the state. You're good at your job, and I respect that. But you take orders, go to work, and deal with this or that issue. And then you go on to the next one. But my job is very different.'

Armando threw him a thin smile.

Juan Carlos raised his right arm up, a silver watch glinting on his wrist.

'Let me tell you something, *amigo*. Rolex makes the best watches in the world. People think it's about the name or the quality of the material, but it's none of those things. The real reason why Rolex is as bad as fuck is because of their technique. Other watch companies make their watches in combination – they make this part and then that part. Eventually, they stick them all together on the production line. But Rolex, every watch they make, they cut it from the block – they make the guts and soul of the watch by chipping away at a single mass. And that is why they're so precise, so indestructible!

'And that's what I do here. Unlike you, Armando, I don't focus on the single part, the single task. I oversee a series of operations, and I have to make sure they all work in tandem, like one perfect clockwork machine. That is my business. So, when you come here, threatening my staff with that plastic badge of yours and asking for your envelope one day early, well, that upsets me. It disrupts my otherwise perfect machine – my business!'

Armando nodded as if he understood.

'But it's your father's business, right?'

The young man's expression paled in the way cream curdles and grows sour. Those full dark pupils seemed to narrow into dots, and Armando could see the flecks of white powder, which lightly dusted the rims of his nostrils.

They peered at each other for a moment longer before Juan Carlos stood and moved towards the far wall. He looked back at Armando, his face displaying a manic grin, girded with drugs and booze.

He wagged his finger paternally. 'You are something of a card, *chico!*'

He turned to the wall again and opened up a panel, revealing a metallic safe. Armando watched as he tapped his finger against the small silver buttons four times and twisted the handle, pulling the door open. He thrust his hand inside, and Armando suddenly felt the absence of his firearm. He had left it back at the apartment. Juan was a dipshit, for sure, but there was something manic in those eyes. The little *jefe* was capable of doing anything out of sheer reck-lessness.

But would he draw down on a cop?

Armando tried to clear the whisky from his mind, so he could act if the kid did indeed do something stupid.

Juan Carlos turned sharply. He sent something flying towards Armando, who flinched but caught it. It was an envelope bulging with cash.

Juan Carlos laughed. 'Nice catch, *chico*. See this as me still hav-ing your back. After all, my *father* and I always want to maintain good relations with the *policía*.'

Armando got to his feet, his heart pounding. 'Good to hear.'

He went to leave, but Juan Carlos stayed him.

The other man's expression changed; the pale youthful mask now shimmered with childlike uncertainty. Almost involuntary, he pressed a finger into a line of coke and tasted the tip.

'Hey now, what's the hurry? I got some good European brandy – it's probably as old as you.' The younger man chuckled. 'Please, stay, as my ... guest. I can organise a couple of *chicas* for company, eh?'

'No thanks.' Armando raised the envelope. 'Until next time, *eh?*'

Outside, the air was still warm, yet Armando felt a coolness teth-ered to it. If that had been a gun in the safe, rather than the envelope, he might still be in there, blood pooling from a hole in his skull.

He cursed under his breath. He badly needed a drink.

Two

The petrol fumes rose from the city's concrete in plumes of shimmering heat. The sun had become swollen; a bloated ball of bloody red and deep orange, which seemed to throb in the murky grey sky. The metallic tops of the houses in the shanty towns glinted, bright and remorseless, while their dark purple-hued windows imprisoned the glow of strange, otherworldly light. The shadows seemed to lengthen. Armando felt the heat tingle against the back of his neck and head. He opened the door to his old Chevy Sedan, the tired, rusted hinges *wincing* mutinously as he *creaked* the metal frame back. He sank into the soft, weathered fabric of the driver's seat with a groan, his robust frame filling out the space, protruding and pressing into the edges.

'My woman says there are three sure-fire ways of knowing when you are old,' José Luis said, perking up from the passenger seat. 'One, every time you sit down, you make a noise like you are taking a shit. Two, at least one time in the night you need to get up to take a piss. And three, you start thinking that everything was better in the old days, and you have the overwhelming need to tell everyone else about it.'

Armando grunted and handed him a hot empanada wrapped in paper, having just brought two from the stall outside. He put his – already half-eaten – on the dashboard.

'Everything *was* better in the old days. In the old days, a patrol car was a place of peace and quiet and solemn reflection where nobody said much, and you just got to driving!' He stuck the key in the ignition, *revved* the throttle, and pulled away.

They got caught in traffic on the junction of Boulevard 18 Sur and Avenue San Manuel. Armando contemplated putting the siren on, but then rested back in his seat. He took another bite out of the now lukewarm empanada. It was spicy beef melded with hot melted cheese, and even though the provenance of the ingredients was not something one could always trust, they were dirt cheap – less than half a peso each. Nevertheless, they tasted delicious; they tasted of the sun and the land.

José Luis was right, though; with spicy beef, Armando would pay the price these days more and more – a handful of late-night trips to the bathroom.

He cranked open the window, but it gave little respite from the heat.

A man in sandals, with a poncho draped around an otherwise bare chest, was walking in between the aisles of the traffic. He was white, but his baked skin had a brown hue, and dirty locks of reddish hair tumbled from the sides of his face. He held a sign; black felt streaked across wrinkled, dirty cardboard.

El Fin del Mundo está Cerca! **The End of the World is Near** it read.

Impatient motors *revved* throatily. A few horns blasted. A pneumonic drill gnawed the concrete.

'The time is nigh!'

Armando jolted, the homeless man had his head in the window, a shadow against the brightness. He had barked the words into Armando's ear.

On reflex, Armando grabbed the man, flexing one arm while using the other to pull so that the man's head was pressed against the edge of the window.

The vagrant squinted, face contorted with pain, and yet his lips formed a rictus smile. His eyes flared. One of them was entirely black, like a fruit that had petrified and turned. His lips parted slightly, revealing the smouldering, blackened stumps of teeth in a mouth that looked as though it had been gutted by fire.

But his voice, when the words came, was soft and smooth and seemed to *hum* with gentle pathos: 'It's okay. You are in pain. Everyone … is in pain. But that doesn't matter anymore. For *He* is coming. The Tall Man walks in the night.'

Armando shoved him back towards another car. The man tripped and fell onto the concrete. The poncho came away, revealing a scrawny torso, the brown wrinkled skin hanging in thin flaky strips over the emaciated outline of protruding ribs. Beyond that, a dense spidery set of black symbols covered the wilting flesh.

Armando suddenly realised that these images were not tattoos, in the traditional sense; the lines were swollen and black, as though they had been carved into the man's body with a knife. He saw the images of monstrous faces, bulging eyes, lolling tongues, and in the centre, there was a figure – a shadowy figure with two dark holes for eyes. It was surrounded by several, smaller and starkly drawn animals – a spider, owl, dog, and bat.

As the drill *thrummed*, as the cars *revved* and *honked*, as the heat baked the dirt and petrol fumes into Armando's skin, the black sockets of that figure's eyes seemed to swirl and swirl. The sights and sounds around Armando seemed to recede into the background, displaced by their strange darkness—

Slap!

33

Armando whipped his head around and glared at José Luis.

The other man had just hit him on the knee, tears of laughter in his eyes. '*Hombre*, that loony toon scared the shit out of you. You nearly jumped out of your skin!'

Armando grunted. His head was throbbing. He needed a drink.

The lights changed. He forced the accelerator down, and the old car jolted forward. Once it picked up some speed, the wind rippled along its sides, and the two men were able to breathe again.

Armando went to take another bite of the empanada, but the radio *crackled* into life.

'Calling 44. Dispatch. We are getting reports of large numbers gathering at Diagonal Defensores de la República by the canal. Can you attend for crowd control?'

Armando took the receiver. 'Yes, Dispatch. 44 attending.'

'Report back from scene, over and out.'

Armando spun the car around.

'Another day, another dollar, another fucking problem!' he muttered under his breath.

When they reached the scene, they saw a crowd of civilians. The majority were indigenous. Colours of tattered bright clothes clashed musically as wide-brimmed straw hats budded like flowers. Workers in overalls were taking an extended lunch break, and old women with lined fissured faces were craning their necks forward, peering out like turtles through dark timeless eyes.

The crowd was overlooking the canal where Armando saw a group of workers in fluorescent jackets standing around a mechanized digger. One motioned upwards at the crowd, clearly trying to shoo them away.

Armando couldn't make sense of any of it at first. However, as he got closer, he started to understand. The workers had drained the water from the canal, revealing a slick black sludge that shone in the light. On the surface, perfect lines of oily sediment had formed, and the broken bumper of a car stuck out like a jagged skeletal arm.

Then he saw another object. A human shape. It seemed to be curled and kneeling, the texture of its skin the same slick black, like some organic protrusion that had grown out of the oily ground.

But as Armando and José Luis made their way down the incline, Armando could just about make out the straggly strands of remaining hair, peeling from what was left of a hollowed-out face.

As they went further, he saw more strange alien forms, these outcrops that seemed to flow forth from the black. He was able to discern from their shape that he was looking at the bodies of several females. With the sun winking high in the sky, he could already scent the decay, the pallid, slightly sour smell of meat on the turn.

He swatted a mosquito, using his fingers to smear its faint stick-like figure into his arm, leaving a blotch of red in its wake.

He turned away, only to be confronted by another body, perhaps only ten feet from him. But this woman was more recent. The oily blackness had not yet percolated over her skin, its whiteness patterned with a series of red streaks – abrasions of some sort, almost like carpet burns. He could see the fabric of her panties and bikini top and the curl of her lips, set in a downward slant. But her head, from the nose up, had been cleaved away, a dark trail of matter flowing out a little way from it.

Even as a seasoned detective, Armando felt the bile rise in his throat, the taste of last night's alcohol, the stale mouldering whisky that was putrefying in his belly. Suddenly, the heat was more unbearable, and the stench of the bodies grew stronger; he was viscerally aware that the choked, clogged air he was breathing was also heavy with the particles of these decimated things strewn all around him. He fought to prevent himself from vomiting.

José Luis put an arm on his shoulder, and he shoved the younger man away violently. His head was throbbing. All at once, a pristine image came to his mind: a wall of rushing water, which would wash away all the rot, all the decay; whose *roaring* sound would blot out the noise of the city, whose cool waters would quench the heat and the stench covering those bodies and everything else.

José Luis was looking at him mournfully. 'What the hell is up with you?'

Armando felt the moment of abject nausea pass. 'I dunno. This shit, I guess. It's bad. We need to get it sewn up before any reporters come sniffing around.'

José Luis was mollified, much as Armando knew he would be. Those young puppy dog eyes lit up when Armando threw him so much as a scrap of attention.

'Can you go up there and see if you can get them to move off? My head is killing me.'

'I'm on it, *compadre!*' José Luis almost bounced away.

Armando unhooked his walkie-talkie. '44 to base, do you receive?'

'Go ahead 44.'

'Situation reads, we have multiple bodies down at the canal.'

'What the hell has happened down there?'

'Nothing at present. I've got a maintenance crew down here who have drained the canal, that's how the corpses have come to light. They've been here for a while. Cause of death, unknown. But we need to get buses down here ASAP. I'm looking at maybe twenty to thirty cadavers in various states of decay. I need those buses quickly before the press gets a heads-up.'

'Roger that, hold tight 44.'

Armando went over to the workers and told them to down tools and go home, that the area needed to be cleared. They protested, of course – the loss of time, money – yet the men's voices were soft, muted almost; they didn't meet his eyes or say anything about the bodies. No questions, nothing. Not even a glance in the direction of the canal bed.

One man, though, made the sign of the cross.

Sometime later, the ambulances were pulling away with their macabre contents. Armando and José Luis sat in the car, watching them go. Armando could still smell that lingering, curdling scent, but he wasn't sure whether it was actually there anymore or just his imagination. He caught sight of the remains of his empanada – brown, fleshy innards pressing out against grease-soaked paper. A fly alighted on it, stepping delicately across it with darting struts.

Armando felt the gorge begin to rise in his belly.

José Luis was unusually silent. Eventually, he turned to Armando and spoke with concentration, 'You know, as sick as that was … you know they were probably only *putas*, right?'

The word 'puta' had a double meaning; 'bitch' or 'prostitute'.

But Armando knew José Luis meant both.

'Yeah,' he finally said. 'You're probably right.'

***

It was evening when he left his apartment. The darkness had gradually seeped into the sky, the last residues of light forming a halo of pale blue over a melancholy horizon. Above Armando, the black vault of night began to spiral, flattening the faint forms of buildings and trees in a soft shadow. He made his way down an alley and then turned down another narrow incline. There was an explosion of light – a vendor on a candlelit stall with a *hornado* turning on a spit. The pig was thick and golden, its luminous skin flecked with charcoal. Armando felt his hunger stir, and yet the pungency of the meat – its blackened hide – called forth the images of the carcasses on the canal bed, their ravaged shapes, the putrefied flesh.

He bypassed the stall, his breathing constricted, as he clutched the bottle in his hand tighter, peeled off the metallic top, and poured the liquid into his mouth.

The alcohol was cheap. It was a 35cl bottle, just small enough to press into the side pocket of his jacket. Tropicool – an Ecuadorian brand – was a reeking, poisonous liquid made up of some unholy combination of aniseed and rum, powerful in its toxic, alcoholic bite. He felt the sourness, the corruption of the liquor coating his throat, and felt a hard ache in his abdomen. But the pain was relieving because its sharpness offset the nausea. It made him feel distant, abstracted from the things that rose from the depths of his mind, like miasma from a black sludge.

He took another long swig and spat on the ground.

He felt revived as he made his way towards a set of old rickety apartments. He went into the entrance of the first building; its heavy concrete walls were formed around a stark opening, wires snarling upwards. Deeper in, he found a buzzer and pressed it.

'Armando,' he said.

The reply was a *buzz*. The metal gate unlatched.

He walked into a small hallway – peeling wallpaper, warm stale air, damp flecks of old mouldy carpet. He walked up a flight of stairs in the gloom and heard music – salsa rhythms – and the sound of shouts and laughter.

On the first floor, he approached a timeworn, wooden door and *knocked* once.

A woman answered. She was in her late twenties perhaps, though Armando had never bothered to ask. She had long, lustrous dark hair that cascaded around her shoulders, and full dark-golden eyes that were hazy and unfocussed. In the soft light, her olive-hued skin was flushed with a tinge of pink, her lips breathless in the night-time heat, her nostrils ever so slightly flared. She was neither tall nor short, but curvaceous. She was wearing a silk chemise, a diaphanous whispery veil that outlined the flowing curves of her body – the full heavy breasts, the large dark circles of her areola, and then, further down, the black shadow of her pubic hair.

Armando felt a shudder of desire: the blood rushing to his thickening penis, the weight of his swelling testicles, the thickness of his lips, and the throatiness of his voice.

'Hello, Esmeralda.'

Her face was heart-shaped, and despite her sweltering body, there was something guileless and girlish in her expression.

'Hello, Armandito.' She slurred her words, trying to sound erotic.

He pushed into the apartment, taking her face in his hands, kissing her lips hungrily, before forcing her into the small bedroom. Though the window was ajar, the air was thick and stagnant. He scented the saccharine odour of perfume, and behind it, the more musty and kippery scent of bodily fluid, of sex.

He shoved her down onto the cheap double bed, onto its heart-shaped pillows and flowery red-and-purple sheets. His fingers found the fabric of her chemise and pulled it off urgently.

She giggled and then moaned theatrically as his mouth found her breasts. He kissed them and started to suck on the hardened nubs. He closed his eyes, relishing the pillowy softness of her tits. As he moved his mouth from one breast to the other, in the blackness, he saw again the strange shapes and forms; the corpses growing out of slick, oily sediment like burgeoning otherworldly plants.

He heard her voice – that giggle again – gleeful and artificial.

'Hey, baby, not so hard. Besides, you know the rule: Cash *comes* before you do.'

He pulled away, breathing hard, and took out some notes from his jacket. He tossed them onto the bed. Then, he shucked off his jacket and pants, grabbed the condom packet in his pocket, and tore it open. His penis, rigid and erect, was throbbing, desire resonating within every molecule in his body. He hadn't been this hard for weeks.

He slipped the condom on. Again came the images of those figures, distended, curling, reaching out for him from the oily black. Only now, the dead women were writhing, bodies undulating, dark arms caressing dead breasts, brittle fingers slipping into the space between rotting legs. Sex and death.

Sex ... and death.

'Get on your hands and knees,' he whispered, his tone husky and imperative.

Esmeralda obeyed, sticking her bum in the air almost playfully.

He grabbed the globes of her buttocks hard, pulling them towards him. He thrust all the way into her, a single driving penetration.

She gasped, but there was no pleasure in the sound.

He moved his hips mechanically, pumping into her.

'Oh yeah, just like that baby,' she said, but her voice was toneless and automatic.

'Oh baby, that cock is so big and so hard. Fuck me with that cock.' The same anodyne voice.

He felt a shudder of disaffection. How many men in the last few days had she delivered those same lines to? He wondered momentarily if she even washed between cocks.

He felt his penis start to wilt inside of her, even though she was still gamely pushing her buttocks against him.

'Fuck that pussy, baby!' she cried out.

Armando tried to concentrate but still felt himself flagging. Then came the stabbing resentment. How many men had she fucked in the last several hours?

He focused on her peach-like buttocks, willing himself not to lose his erection. He slapped them hard, the sound reverberating across the room.

'Ugh.' She yelped – it was the most human sound she had made.

He started to thrust faster and slapped her again. Harder.

'Ugh! You know I like it kinky, baby. But not so hard, yeah?'

He raised both hands, higher this time, and brought the palms back down on her soft wobbling flesh. Now his erection was throbbing and pulsing once more.

Smack.

'Owww! *Puta madre.* That hurts.' Her whole body was trembling, breasts bouncing.

His hands came down harder.

'Ahh, please!'

He raised his hands yet again, propelled by some deep-seated instinct, some compulsion – he couldn't stop himself.

He brought his hands down once more, a violent *twanging-slapping* sound on soft weltering skin.

This time, Esmeralda screamed.

41

As she jerked and convulsed in pain, he felt her undulating body moving against his penis. All at once, he let out a single guttural groan and spilled the contents of his testicles into her, his teeth pressing against the nape of her neck.

Her knees buckled as he collapsed on top of her.

They lay there, panting.

Finally, he withdrew, rolled onto his side, and got to his feet. He took the bottle from his jacket and swigged.

Esmeralda moved on the bed, pulling those gaudy, tasteless covers around her as if they might provide some kind of defence against … something. Anything.

Armando peeled the condom off, tied it in a knot, and threw it on the dresser, alongside the shitty set of perfumes and paraphernalia.

He thought about the dead women again. He felt dead inside too.

He turned to her.

She was looking at him with resentment. 'I thought you were one of the nicer ones.'

'One of the nicer ones?'

'Yeah.'

He grinned. 'You should know better.'

'Why are you acting like such an asshole?'

'Am I?'

'Yes.'

He shrugged and went to knock back another mouthful of Tropicool. 'Shit.'

The bottle was empty.

He remembered the coke Filippo had given him and fished about in his jacket pockets. When he found the small plastic bag of shimmering white, he tossed it to her.

'An asshole with high-quality cocaine, though.'

Esmeralda squealed with excitement, opened the bag, and dipped her finger inside.

'You got any liquor?'

She sniffed the powder. 'What?'

'Alcohol?'

She nodded and ran her finger across her gums, eyes fluttering. 'In the dresser.'

In seconds, Armando found several bottles. He picked up the first one, a dust-coated bottle of brandy. A present from a gringo client, he assumed. Brandy was rare and expensive.

He took a couple of sips. The liquid was coarse and bitter. He drank a little more and put it down on the dresser, next to some pony figurines. He had the sudden impulse to smash them.

'Oh, I'm really starting to feel it now. Hmmm …' Esmeralda pushed her chest out slightly. She wasn't trying to entice him; it wouldn't have mattered if he was there or not.

Her legs were parted. Her labia was swollen – a result of his violent penetration – and he looked at it with strange incredulity. The reddish-purple of those puckered lips seemed less human and more like the glistening slick texture of some aquatic entity, a slimy mollusc or whelp. Only a few minutes ago, this thing between her legs had claimed him entirely; he had been unable to think about anything else.

But now, deflated and drained, he saw her for what she truly was. The sex was over – all her mystique, all her allure, was gone.

43

He felt a wave of hate flow through him as she dabbed her finger into the bag once more. He gazed at her, thoroughly repulsed. What kind of human would do that? Would open their legs to be mounted and beasted by an endless series of strangers?

He glimpsed her cunt again and was sickened by how such a thing could compel him, enslave him almost.

He turned away in disgust, but she didn't notice.

When her voice came again, it was hesitant. 'Hey, uh, Armando? Guess what? My dad was around your age when he passed. God rest his soul. What a fucking cliché, right?'

Armando grunted.

'He was a big bull of a man, too. Strong like you.' She tried to flutter her eyes, but the coke kicked in again. Her face twitched.

As he watched her, he wondered if the coke was bad. Looking at her – those pleading, pathetic eyes, that well-fucked cunt – he found that he couldn't make himself care all that much. He just wanted to go.

He took another swig of the brandy.

'You can stay a while if you want. It'd be nice … I mean I'd like to talk to someone for a while, if you want. You were my last one for the night.'

'*You were my last one.*' She had said it almost like she was proud. Like she had finished a good, hard, honest day's labour. At that point, Armando had the urge to ball up his fist and swing it at her. Obliterate that lazy drugged-out expression.

Cynthia would have said something else, of course. She would have told him that Esmeralda had never been given a chance, was most likely abused as a child, had little other choice. But Armando knew better. Many kids that had been abused didn't turn out this way. Lots of people came from poverty. They didn't all end up turning into sluts.

He swallowed the bile rising in his throat, grimaced, and walked out of the room.

He heard Esmeralda mumble something more, but he moved further into the corridor.

Just as he took another step, he sensed movement.

There was one other room to his right, its door slightly ajar. In the gap was standing a little girl. She was wearing a tattered top, which had clearly once belonged to an adult as it hung down to her knees. She had dark hair like Esmeralda's, but it was cropped short, with a cowlick stuck out at an awkward angle.

The girl watched him in the gloom, big eyes glistening with both fascination and wariness.

He saw some words on her battered T-shirt: *'No soy tímida. Solo no me gustas! I am not shy; I just don't like you!'*

He smiled and pointed at the words. 'But you don't know me. So, how do you know you don't like me?'

She giggled and disappeared into the room.

Armando blinked. Waited.

A few moments later, her head peeked out again, those huge eyes looking up at him incredulously. 'What do you do?'

'I'm a policeman.'

She seemed to process the information. 'Do you hit people with a stick?'

'Not usually.'

Her button nose wrinkled, lips curled in a contemptuous smile. Then, those eyes flashed, impish and cruel. 'That means you are a shit policeman. When I grow up, I'm going to be a great policeman and hit all the bad guys with my stick!'

Her eyes shone at the impossibly daring statement before she disappeared again.

Armando stood there, baffled.

But sure enough, she reappeared once more. Only this time, her expression was hesitant, vulnerable.

She spoke in little more than a whisper, 'Are you one of Mama's friends?'

He went to respond, but his voice was caught in his throat. He thought about the woman back in the bedroom.

'Yes, I am,' he whispered.

'What's your name?'

'Armando.'

'Do you ...' Her eyes were turned down, lips puckered, her expression set in a slight frown as though she were trying to pick her words carefully. 'Do you want to know my name?'

'Okay.'

'My name is Salome.'

Three

Like most other people, cops looked forwards to the weekends. On Fridays, José Luis would often regale Armando with stories of dinner with the in-laws, and how José Luis would chew in silence because his mother-in-law was a bitch. But even though he was ostensibly complaining, Armando heard a note of pleasure and satisfaction in the young man's voice. Cops were meant to be family men, proud of their families and their country. It was one of those unwritten rules. Just before the weekend, the other men in the precinct would be similarly animated; the talk would be of hunting or fishing trips, bar crawls, church events – a relative's baptism or a daughter's *quinceañera* – or just a football game with the kids. Armando would nod along, sometimes even interjecting a plan or two of his own. However, more often than not, he would lie. He didn't want them to know the truth: how the weekends were the low point of his whole week.

Cynthia had left some years back. When they were still living together, he'd often drunk too much on a Friday evening, and yet she'd end up coaxing him out late Saturday morning like a bad-tempered bear from his cave. He'd protested, of course, and groaned in resignation at the latest art exhibition or history museum she would make them visit. He would inevitably get into it, though, because she just had a way of making things interesting when she talked about them.

Even more than that, he knew that their weekend routine was important. That it was the closest thing to a family life he had. That it kept him tied to the world in some fundamental way. In the last few years of their relationship, she had grown soft and wistful around children. More and more, she would tentatively broach the subject, saying in a shy, breathless way that she thought they might have beautiful children together, and how would that be? He would bat away her comments with a casual laugh – 'A kid, now, in this flat? Wouldn't be fair to bring the little sprog into such chaos!' – but he knew from the look in her eyes, the soft smiling sadness gathered at the corners, that the issue was gradually becoming a dealbreaker.

He had waited for that moment. The moment that many men assume will come at some point in their adult life, where the switch is flipped, and they suddenly realise that they want to have children, want to be a father, and embark on the next stage naturally and at the right time.

But for Armando, that moment never arrived.

When he'd watch Cynthia *coo* and *aww* over her two-year-old nephew, he had felt nothing except the vague surprise that something so small could make so much noise. He had smiled and nodded when she'd talked about how wonderful the little boy was, how miraculous his small life was, and how special. But Armando had remained unmoved as if there was a tiny stone lodged at the very centre of his being, something hard, inanimate and unmovable.

They'd argued about other things, of course, but those other arguments – about his drinking, about her unbearably prissy friends – flowed around a fundamental and deeper silence; the unspoken subject: she wasn't getting any younger. Towards the end of their relationship, his taste for liquor had only gotten worse. One morning, after a particularly heavy night of drinking, she came into their bedroom where he'd been sleeping it off. He remembered that she wasn't wearing any makeup, and he could see the crinkles around her eyes. He thought she looked beautiful and serene as the late morning sunlight filtered through the room, making the motes of dust in the air dance and wink. She had told him in a soft voice that she loved him very much, but it was time to move on, and that she would be leaving for Mexico City later that week.

Through the angry fug of his hangover, Armando had decided that she was being manipulative, using this as a threat to control his drinking.

'Why do women always do that?' he'd asked her savagely. 'Commit to a man and then spend the best part of the relationship trying to manipulate and change him?'

He'd grinned sarcastically, tried to bait her, but she'd only looked sad. Somehow, that made him angrier. All at once, he was right up close, his large, robust body throwing her petite frame into cowering relief.

He snarled the words in her face: 'Well, fuck off then! You think I give a shit? But remember, it's probably too late for you anyway. You're probably all rotten and dried up in here.'

Grinning obscenely, he patted her belly, the gesture a grotesque parody of their everyday intimacy.

She had blinked a couple of times, taken a breath, and then left the room.

In the days that had followed, he'd tried to make amends. He had also gotten drunk and harangued her. Told her he knew she was leaving him for one of her 'fancy educated' friends and that he would pound his 'fancy educated' face in. Again, she'd endured these convulsions stoically. Perhaps, he later thought, they'd merely made it easier for her, shored up her commitment to leave.

On that last day, he had felt sick to his stomach, but he had seen her to the bus station with her suitcases. Her eyes had been wet, but she didn't cry.

Instead, she said to him – trying for light humour as she smiled bravely – 'Well, like old Confucius always said, "All good things must come to an end."'

The bus *hissed* into life.

She had kissed his cheek, her eyes impossibly wide, with that same tentative smile, desperate for some kind of recognition.

'*Do you love me, Armando?*'

As he had gazed at her open, beautiful face, he'd realised that he'd never loved anyone more. It rose in his throat, that feeling, that certainty. But somehow, he couldn't form the words.

Instead, he made his voice as even and emotionless as possible. 'Well, good luck with your new life. Hope it all works out.'

He'd smiled winningly, turned around, and walked away without looking back; one final act of senseless cruelty.

Back at his apartment, he had sat there, watching as the light faded and the shadows lengthened across the wall, the late afternoon gradually melting into evening. He'd stared into space and then gotten drunk long into the night.

A couple of weeks later, she had rung him. For a while, they'd kept up a series of telephone conversations. Yet they felt false and awkward; Armando often hadn't known what to say. After a time, he felt sure she had found someone else. He would ring her at all hours, drunk. Launching tirades. Unearthing every inadequacy buried inside him. Giving vent to it in bitter rants.

'You think you are better than me. And you always have,' he would say.

The last time he had called, he'd ended up with a dull tone. Her number was no longer in service.

A long time back, he'd seen a film. It was set on a space station, and in one scene, an astronaut had to go and repair a fault on the outside. But then something went wrong, and the chord attaching him to the station snapped. Gradually the astronaut floated out into space.

Armando remembered the man had enough oxygen inside his spacesuit to last a few hours. He was – for all intents and purposes – dead. Still, he was forced to watch on, helplessly, within the strange eerie silence, as the space station got smaller and smaller, and the last remaining contact with other people and the life he had known faded away. Until all that waited was the yawning blackness of infinite space.

In the time after she had left, Armando had felt like that. As though he were floating away from his own life unable to do anything but watch as it grew more and more distant.

Eighteen months later was when he'd gotten the call. Apparently, Cynthia had first started to get ill in the weeks following her relocation to Mexico City. It was a malignant tumour in her stomach. She'd fought for the best part of a year before she succumbed. She died back in her home town of Cuantinchán, less than an hour's drive from Ciudad Puebla. The woman who informed him was Cynthia's close friend, Felisa, who didn't hide the bitterness in her tone. All he could think about at that moment were some of his last words to Cynthia.

'It's probably too late for you anyway. You're probably all rotten and dried up in here!' he had said, touching his fingers to her belly.

51

But the truth was that he knew he had been wrong all along. It wasn't her who was rotten inside; it was him.

He hoped … that she hadn't thought about those words when the cancer took hold. He hoped that she hadn't been in pain.

That day, for the first time in a long while, he sobbed – dry, violent convulsions that choked him.

Even now, years later, he still thought about Cynthia on most days. No, every day. The hard thing about it was that he hadn't had a chance to see her again. Not even at her funeral. Felisa had told him that Cynthia was already buried and he knew Cynthia's family would have wanted it that way – with him out of the picture.

The person he was angry at, however, was Cynthia herself. Though it was hard to stay angry at someone who had died from cancer, he couldn't help it. He thought about how ill she must have become, how she'd turned to everyone else in her life except him, how she'd robbed him of the chance to say goodbye.

Armando was furious because he felt so utterly worthless, so negligible. So yes, sometimes he did hate her, even though he knew he would never see her again. However, most of the time, he settled for hating himself. So, the weekends were tough. Sometimes he'd catch an afternoon matinee or go rowing on the lake at the nearby *Parque Ecológico,* or visit an art exhibition. He would imagine Cynthia standing alongside him, her smile wry and amused, as he'd once again *guffaw* at some strange 'modernist' installation that didn't make any sense.

But those scenarios were no more real than the lines he would feed his workmates about weekends spent visiting family members or the girl he'd just started dating. It was as though his existence had a texture of unreality, as though he were gradually moving away from everything and everyone around him.

Now, it was Sunday, two days after the council had drained the canal. He'd woken up bleary, still drunk, and knocked back some Valium to take him past the throbbing ache of the hangover, along with a couple of whiskies. By the time he had left his building in the mid-afternoon, he'd felt almost human again.

He went the large thoroughfare, closest to his neighbourhood *Chulavista la Puebla*. A wide strip ran through the centre of the road, a place where people could sit and eat and drink under the large trees with their generous plumes of green leaves, through which the light from the sun glinted and flickered. There was a section with stone chairs and stone tables where old men would play chess in the afternoons.

Some of the men were homeless, ran stalls in the night, or worked the '*granjas*' – the backroom bars, which served illegal alcohol. But no matter their background, they were serious about the game and knew their way around the board. They would drink beer and peer out through red-rimmed eyes. They didn't tend to have all that much to say, though if an opponent made a good move, it would be respectfully greeted by the grunted word 'played!'

For Armando, the quiet contemplation, the anonymity, was relieving. And the game itself was satisfying. The formation of strategies, the ebb and flow of any individual game, the need to second guess your opponent, to outflank them; these elements appealed to his logical nature. They abstracted him from his memories. He was one of the better players, though he didn't have the chance to practise as much as the 'old boys' who spent every day there. But today, he was up by nine games and down by one.

He left around eight in the evening, the baking heat of the day having dwindled, and bottles and bottles of that cheap watery beer weighing down his bladder.

He made his way back to the apartment. As he opened the door into the lobby, he met Celia locking her postal box.

'Expecting good news?' he asked.

She turned to him, her face catching the dying light. He noticed how her lank dark hair was streaked with red stripes.

'You know what?' She looked at him as though she were seeing him for the first time. 'I think I am. I come down here at exactly the same time every Sunday evening after taking the trash out. And I check my mail because despite all the years I have spent on this earth and all my experience to the contrary, yeah, I am actually expecting something good! The fucked up thing is that I don't even play the lottery anymore, so I can't even imagine what I'm expecting to receive!'

She looked at him and crossed her eyes in a loopy, fruity way as if to emphasise her own insanity. One strand of hair fell over her forehead, and Armando noticed the slight vein that showed up when she smiled like that. She was one of those women who looked good as they got older. Her face had, in his opinion, 'character'. Her eyes were dark with a tinge of reddish-brown and seemed to sparkle with dry, rebellious humour.

She was studying him with them, open and amused.

He shifted slightly, the need to take a piss was increasingly paramount.

'So then, you notice anything different about me?'

He motioned to her hair and grunted.

She copied his gesture, cracking out a dazzling smile. 'And … what do you think, Armandito? What's the verdict?'

He found himself smiling too. 'You look … good,' he said with conviction.

She nodded slightly and smiled all the more.

He smiled back, the pressure on his bladder getting worse.

'You need to piss, don't you?'

He blinked. 'How do you know that?'

Her smile contracted somewhat. 'I've been around. I know men!'

She said it matter-of-factly, no flirt in her tone.

'Well I guess …'

She looked past his shoulder. 'Anyhow, before you go, I think we finally need to get this down … What do you say to *enchiladas con mole* next Thursday evening? Can you make it for dinner? After all, my son shouldn't be the only one to suffer my cooking.'

Armando felt a strange tingle of panic mixed with pleasure. The image of Cynthia flashed momentarily in his head. He blinked her away. Celia had mentioned having him over for dinner several times in the year since she and Cristóbal had moved in. But she'd never really firmed up the invitation until now. This moment, this conversation, seemed significant somehow.

He smiled again, trying to make his face kind. 'That would be good.'

'Okay then. Next Thursday at eight?'

He nodded, trying to make himself look casual and unconcerned.

She raised one eyebrow. 'Good. Now, go piss!'

***

The light fell in shards, which slipped into his eyes, momentarily rendering the other people in the room into dark shadows. Armando put his fingers to his eyes and rubbed. The rickety air-conditioning *whirred* and *buzzed*, and his skin felt aggravated by the hot air. When he opened his eyes again, the short, rotund man had finished smearing a handkerchief over the top of his glistening bald dome. He dabbed the fabric against his forehead several times before he started to speak. All the police in Armando's building were gathered there for – despite his diminutive appearance – this man was important: Samuel Agosto Flores, the mayor of the whole Puebla region.

He was flanked by several uniformed men. The Mexican police force was run along two separate lines: the *municipals* – the people whom, like Armando, operated within the jurisdiction of a particular state like Puebla – and the *federales* – the police who operated across regional borders in the name of the central state. The latter were paid more and generally ex-military. The men surrounding the mayor wore thick, blue uniforms replete with an exoskeleton of black body armour, a heavy-duty garb, especially in this stifling heat. They gazed out through implacable dark visors and from their sides hung thick automated weapons.

The mayor slotted his handkerchief into the front pocket of his perfectly tailored white jacket.

'I've come here today to congratulate you on the superb job that you're doing in our region's capital. I can't claim that I could do your job and survive for a day, but I do know about our city. I was born and raised in Puebla City. I have some idea of the challenges the city faces. We live in an ever-changing world, but at the same time, we Mexicans are stubborn and proud people, and we find it difficult to relinquish what has gone before. We have …'

He glanced at one of the *federales* to his side, at the jutting mechanised black of his automated rifle.

'… the very latest technology, and yet our streets are filled with faith healers and snake-oil salesmen, mystics, and miracle workers.

The Mexican mindset is hard to change. But change is coming, believe me. The election of Carlos Salinas de Gortari is a case in point. I don't exaggerate when I say our mayor is a new breed of politician. An idealist, yes, but also an incorruptible moderniser.'

A couple of the men sighed through their teeth.

The mayor continued.

'He is going to help transform this country from a Third World backwater into a fully modernised and vibrant nation ready and primed to step into the twenty-first century. We will show the world that our cities are rich in art, architecture, and cuisine. We will show that our people have a history and culture, which equals London or Paris. Above everything, we will refute once and for all the gringo stereotype of a Mexico that is only conducive to drug dealers, thieves, and murderers …' He paused.

'And corrupt politicians,' someone added quietly.

A couple of people tittered.

One of the dark-suited visitors turned his visor-clad head slowly in their direction.

The mayor went on.

'Recently our sister city, Juarez, garnered press for the activity of its dealers and, in particular, the slaying of large numbers of females. Naturally, there is no smoke without fire. Some of these crimes have occurred and continue to occur. But they are vastly exaggerated by a press fuelled by sales and sensationalism. Indeed, even a couple of international papers have already picked up the Juarez events and quite shamefully insisted that great and historic city is unsafe for women. I understand that journalists have to make a buck – just like all of us – but much of what passes for news is rank opportunism. And it works against *El Presidente's* crusade to help show Mexico in a better light – in a truer light.'

The small man panted as he spoke.

The heat made Armando's skin crawl, with beads of sweat clinging to the nape of his neck. He wished the little fucker would put a sock in it.

What I would give for a cold beer...

'So ...' the droning voice continued, 'that brings me to my next point.'

Here it comes, thought Armando.

'I know that last week, a couple of your detectives came across a very distressing scene at the Cuauhtémoc canal. The canal had been drained, and some bodies were recovered. The superficial reports from the scene suggest that most of the bodies were female. I must advise you against this type of assumption, however. The condition of the bodies was such that a definitive assessment cannot be made until further forensic investigation is carried out. Also, I must tell you that our preliminary enquiries suggest that the Cuauhtémoc canal has been, for a number of years, a prime spot for suicides. We believe it is highly likely that the majority of these deaths were suicides, not murders.'

A couple more of the *locales* whistled in disbelief.

The department's boss, Ximena Ponce, glared at her subordinates.

The mayor glanced at her briefly before returning to his speech.

'Really, sincerely. I'd like to congratulate the men who discovered the bodies on the exemplary and professional way they handled a difficult situation and isolated the crowd from the scene. It will make the process of discovery and identification much easier. But the case has a broader significance. The press will try to turn it into another Cuidad Juarez. That city became anathema overnight. The tourists don't visit there anymore. All because of speculation, of rumour. But we must base ourselves in fact. We cannot let a sad, tragic situation become twisted and distorted into another horror story about Mexican, Third World primitives!'

He looked out at them with heightened eagerness.

'Because this is a case which could affect all of Mexico, I must naturally turn it over to the Federal Police.'

At this, there was a unified murmur of protest.

The mayor's small, grey eyes glinted, mole-like in the afternoon light flooding the room. He took out his handkerchief and mopped his head again. He looked towards the police chief and issued a curt nod.

She smiled.

The mayor turned and left the room. In a single motion, the *federales* flowed after him, their bodies burgeoning with bulletproof vests and titanium metal, uninterrupted by the snarled whispers from the men left behind: '*Hijos de puta!*'

At once, the room became a hubbub of activity, of quick babbled sentences, indignant refrains, curse words, and lurid speculation.

The rich, shredding voice of the boss, short and stocky Ximena Ponce, cut across the cacophony.

'Okay, boys, I really feel your pain. Your dicks were hard, you were ready to fuck, but now some annoying politician has gone and stolen the llamas from the field. Unfortunately, you are just gonna have to suck it up, put it back in your pants, and get on with doing some actual police work.'

She strode back into her office and slammed the door.

The men lowered their voices.

Armando and José Luis were the centre of attention.

'What was that shit about?'

59

'How many bodies were there?'

'Could you tell if they were women?'

José Luis began to chatter happily, projecting the image of a gnarled, worldly-wise detective whose eyes had seen everything.

'One of them was missing half a head. Another missing a leg. I've seen a lot of things, but I haven't seen any suicides cut off their leg before they throw themselves over a bridge. And they were women alright. I tell you something, I know women ...'

Armando had to stop himself from groaning out loud. His head was pulsing.

'I know their shape, and even death can't take that away. Not completely. They were mangled, yeah, but they were definitely women. Or once upon a time at least!' José Luis gave a soft, knowing laugh. 'It was sure something!'

Eduardo Munro, a lanky detective about Armando's age with rat-like, yellow eyes, piped up. 'But they were bitches, right?'

José Luis smirked. 'Yeah, that was my impression. One of them had thin panties on, like a thong. I guess she was touting before she got tossed over.'

The other detective's voice was quieter, but with an undercurrent of excitement in it. 'Well, if you play with fire, you eventually get burnt.'

Some of the others agreed; some demurred.

'Even so ...' another detective said, with a sceptical voice, which trailed away.

Munro raised his hands. 'Hey. I'm not saying that they deserved ... *all of that*. I'm only saying that if you're *a certain type* of woman, and you go into *a certain type* of job ... sometimes there's *a certain type* of consequence.'

Nobody said anything.

His smile smouldered. Gained confidence. He added illicitly, 'A cunt always ends up getting fucked. One way or another – that's a fact of life.'

José Luis looked at Armando with wide eyes. 'What do you think, pal?'

Armando winced. 'I think you talk too much.'

José Luis looked stung. That was the thing about the young man; what he felt inside flowed across his face.

At that moment, Armando realised he didn't like his younger partner very much.

Munro put his hand on José Luis's shoulder. 'Don't worry about your partner there. He doesn't say so much.'

Munro looked at Armando with a wry grin before throwing up his hands again in mock apology.

'Hey, Armandito, I reckon you're a solid detective. But let's face it, conversation is not your strong suit, eh? I mean, you don't have a family or kids, right? So, you probably don't have all that much of a chance to get talking when you get home. Unless you got yourself a couple of cats, that is. I reckon you could have a good natter with them!'

Some of the others laughed heartily.

Munro's expression was mischievous, and it seemed to break the tension and resentment that had been left in the wake of the *federales*.

On seeing the others laugh, Armando chuckled along, too. He gave Munro the kind of defeated, humorous look that said the other man had got the better of him this time – but he would get him back on another occasion.

Munro's eyes narrowed. 'It's all good, Armandito. I guess since your woman left – Cynthia, was it? – probably practising with cats is the closest you have gotten to any real pussy!'

The others laughed even harder.

Armando's eyes crinkled, his grin widening as he laughed along with the rest, nodding, turning his body somewhat – and then bringing the back of his hand across the side of Munro's face. *Smack.*

The other man staggered back from the force of the backhand but recovered in seconds. He lunged at Armando. 'You mother-fucker!'

The other men pulled him back.

Armando's lips curled into a deeper leer.

A voice cut across the kafuffle.

Ximena Ponce stared at Armando with cold appraisal. 'My office, detective. Now!'

Armando turned away from the commotion and headed in her direction.

Her office smelt of stale coffee as he sat down in front of her desk.

Ponce opened her glasses case, took out a pair of thin black specs, and set them on the bridge of her nose. She adjusted them twice and peered at him inquisitorially, lips pursed.

'Rough night, detective?'

He coughed into his hands. 'They're all rough.'

Her lips thinned. 'Detective, I don't know what's going on with you, and to be frank, I don't care. I don't even want to know what happened out there just now. What I do want to know – no, what I need to make clear – is simple: what I just saw won't be repeated.'

Armando gave a solitary nod. 'Won't happen again, boss.'

She looked at him for a few seconds longer. 'Everything is changing, Armando. The mayor was right. The buzzword is modernisation. Everything is to be streamlined, audited, and accounted for. Our police force, one of the oldest institutions in the country, won't be an exception. We have to work as though we are being watched, assessed – we must be professional at all times.'

'We want to impress the mayor and his federal friends,' Armando murmured.

Ponce raised her hand to her glasses once more and adjusted them slightly.

Armando caught a glimpse of the small dark eyes behind the lenses, flashing momentarily.

When she finally responded, she spoke in a hissing whisper, 'Fucking … macho … arrogance. There isn't a day when I don't enter this building and this place doesn't *reek* of it.'

Her lips were thin, a sour line set into her face. Her voice became temperate.

'There I am, some office-bound bureaucrat kissing the ass of her superiors, and then there are men like you. Men who work on the ground and who get the job done without fear or favour, and who are not bothered about climbing the ladder, right?'

Her lips relaxed, and she chuckled, but the sound held no warmth.

'I've heard that narrative before, Armando. So many times. But like most ill-thought-out, macho stupidity, it's not nuanced, and it's not clever, and it certainly doesn't take into account what goes on behind the scenes. Do you know how many times this year I've had to make concessions to "modernisation" so I don't have to make "concessions" to your salary? Still, why worry about any of that. Why worry about thinking. It's much more satisfying to just lash out, right?'

She paused briefly.

'Like I said: Fucking … macho … arrogance.'

Armando didn't say anything; he just watched her.

She spoke again, but her voice sounded tired now. 'You're not indispensable, Armando. No one here is. If you do anything like that again on my watch, I'll hoist you out of this department so fucking fast your feet won't even touch the ground. Do I make myself clear, detective?'

Armando nodded.

'Good. Now get out.'

He left the office – some of his colleagues were back sitting at their desks and raised their heads, watching him pass. When he got to the stairwell, he exhaled and punched the wall. Immediately, pain forked through his knuckles. He thought about Ponce: overweight, middle-aged, and saggy. She probably hadn't been fucked in a *real* long time – which was why she behaved like such a prissy cunt.

He felt another wave of simmering anger, which for a few moments, left him dizzy. Outside the building, he sucked in a breath and stepped out into the glittering sunlight. He fumbled around in his pockets, his hand still aching, and took out a cigarette. He lit it. After a few puffs, he felt the rage start to seep out of his body, and in its wake, a heavy-headed sense of exhaustion.

The previous night he had drunk some whisky and watched a documentary on some Roman playwright and philosopher called Seneca. He had been fascinated – one quote, in particular, was stuck in his mind. Seneca had said that 'anger was a form of temporary madness'. Armando agreed. It passed over you so suddenly and so completely in a black wave, swallowing you whole. It was like being in thrall to an alien power. He got angry more and more these days.

He sucked harder on the cigarette – breathing the air out in smoky plumes. They floated upwards in reams, which gradually faded into a diaphanous vapour before disappearing entirely into the blank blueness of an infinite sky.

Four

Some days later the call came through. The sun was beating down. Another woman. Another body. As a cop, he was used to receiving these types of notifications, making these types of trips. A corpse here, a corpse there. A body nestled between the black bags of overflowing rubbish in a back alley, or dumped on the side of a busy freeway like a feral animal that had fallen foul of the rushing cars. Sometimes the victim was a gang member or a prostitute. Sometimes they were just a citizen in the wrong place at the wrong time. The majority were women, dirt poor. Armando was required to 'close' the scene – cordon it off with yellow tape, phone for the 'bus', and make a preliminary report based on his immediate observations – a few lines scrawled in a notebook.

But the bodies were so commonplace that – beyond noting the crime and signing them off, the briefest nod to bureaucratic procedure – no investigation would ever be opened up. A given body would be removed and then cremated. Most of the time, they didn't even make the morgue. The exception occurred when the woman had been murdered within the confines of a specific location, and the body had remained there. So, if a woman had been murdered in a flat or a house by her husband or an intruder, a case would be opened and an investigation would ensue. Unless, the suspected killer was a man of high standing and the woman's absence wouldn't matter to society as a whole.

The call, which came through to Armando, was ambiguous. The man who had called it in had been babbling. Armando was told to head to avenue 30 Pte (west) and the Parish of Our Lady of Refuge. He arrived at a non-descript place. The buildings on either side were austere concrete structures; unadorned, with bars on the windows – the majority were commercial rather than residential, the occasional 'vende' sign hung hopefully in large white letters over a drab, vacant façade. A couple of trucks had pulled up outside, but there was little traffic. A large white wall separated one side of the church from the street, and across its decaying paint were scrawled a few harsh black words of graffiti – no art, no images, only a few skeletal swearwords, the products of frustration, aimlessness, and a lack of hope.

A strange epithet for a holy building, Armando reflected, but then again, perhaps not that strange after all.

He still went to church now and then, cleaving to the childhood routine of his past, but when he found himself in God's house, emptiness was what he felt. It was not that he rejected any belief in God; he just felt so listless sometimes that the question of whether He did or did not exist felt like a question that Armando was too tired to grapple with. Most cops were religious, of course – it was tied up with the whole family thing. Marriage, baptism, first communion, the last rites. Such rituals were centred on the family and revered. They were the point of wages and kept the people 'decent'.

Of course, many of those same cops kept a mistress on the side. Most of them, including Armando, took bribes to supplement a meagre state salary. But the really important thing was not to do such things openly and to keep banging on about family and church events so that the whole system could keep ticking over.

Armando was as corrupt as the average Puebla police, but he didn't have a family. And maybe that was why he didn't give a shit about the church and its legions of holy men.

He walked around the wall at the front of the building. The late afternoon was just curdling into the evening, the light blue-hued sky gradually giving way before deeper, thicker strips of purple. The church was an older building but substantial. It had been painted white, its different sections delineated by elegant, simple red lines. Its belfry had been painted in the same terracotta red and it had two towers, which were also white, capped off with red-ridged roofs. Its main building was large, two storeys high. It was not gaudy, because of the simplicity of the colours and the basic nature of its design, but it was nevertheless grand, especially given the dull nature of the buildings in its vicinity. The walls around it met in a large red arch at its front, and Armando now went through it. He walked across the concrete patio and into the church itself.

The inside was less well-kempt. It was cool compared to the heat outside, and it reeked of mouldering damp, a wet sulphur smell. The benches were solid black, but the paint was peeling away, and the altar at the front displayed a rather wretched approximation of the Guadalupe Mary. The details of her face and body had softened and lost definition over time so that she looked more like an amorphous figure, without any real features. Armando's eyes were adjusting to the gloom – the thick high walls cast shadows everywhere – when he was startled by a sudden rapid muttering. He saw another human-shaped figure bent over one of the pews, muttering into his hands.

'Our Father who art in heaven, hallowed be thy name ...'
Armando coughed.

The priest turned with panicked eyes towards the detective, and then got to his feet. He must have been around sixty years old, but he was sprightly.

In the gloom, Armando noticed the other man's features; his miniature manicured hands, the grey hair that was delicately arrayed around the smooth bald pate of his head, the small, glistening dark eyes, and the thin tendered beard that formed a perfect V underneath the man's bottom lip. Mexican men tended to have thick beards or were cleanly shaven. Nothing in between.

The priest's beard reminded Armando of the faggots who hung out at the edges of the business district, touting for business from the rich perverts who cruised by in their sleek black Mercedes. Perhaps the priest was a *maricon*, too – Armando knew a lot of them liked to interfere with small boys when given the chance.

The smaller man shuffled towards him, his expression an odd combination of horror and relief. He must have had some twenty years on Armando, yet he gripped the detective's arm like a child clutching a security blanket.

'Please. I've never seen anything like this before. I don't know what to do.'

Armando moved his arm away, yet the priest didn't seem to notice. He just continued to look at Armando with those wide helpless eyes.

Armando felt his skin crawl but concentrated, making his voice toneless. 'Calm yourself, Father. From you, I need to know two things. First, where is the body? Second, if you were the one who hurt her, I need you to tell me now. It will be better for you.'

The priest looked at him uncomprehendingly and then spoke in a smaller voice, as though he were dazed, 'No, I've never hurt anybody. I didn't do ... *that*. I don't ... even understand what *that* means.'

Armando noted the strange turn of phrase, the 'I don't even understand what that means'. He believed the other man was genuinely in shock, but at the same time, the language was all wrong. People never described a body in such terms, even if they were religious nuts.

He softened his voice, making his next sentence a question rather than a demand. 'Would you be kind enough to tell me your name, Father?'

The priest blinked and then exhaled, as though he had finally been presented by something that made sense.

'My name is Father Diego Ramirez. I have been a priest for the majority of my adult life. I took the vows on September 7, 1950. I have—'

'Okay, Father, that's okay.'

Armando knew that guilty people would often start blathering inanely, talking about everything in a panicked deluge of fear and misdirection. Yet the feeling he got from the priest was not so much of someone who had committed a crime but rather someone who had been traumatised by one. Nine times out of ten, crimes where the criminal remained on the spot were remarkably easy to figure out. Someone who was spinning every story under the sun still couldn't hide the truth written in the blood spatter at the back of their trousers or the dark matter lodged under their fingernails. But Armando had noticed straight away how impeccable the priest's appearance was. Not a hair out of place. This, of course, could be a very perfectly contrived piece of theatre acted out for the detective's benefit, but the priest's strange and erratic manner made this seem unlikely. Though, Armando couldn't afford to dismiss the possibility.

'Take me to *her*, Father.'

'To her?' For the first time, the priest's tone was vacant of emotion.

Again, the detective felt that sense of dislocation; he knew what murder was and how people responded to it, but this was something else.

'Take me to her, *Padre*,' he repeated softly.

The priest's mouth opened ever so slightly, the lips full and wet with saliva. But he said not a word; he simply turned and walked away.

Armando followed him.

They walked from the main chamber of the church into an outhouse – a kitchen where a series of sinks were filled with pots soaking in tepid water. The priest went out through a back door, leading to a vivid green yard with trees. The sunlight flickered downward, making the leaves shimmer.

The priest stopped and turned to the detective. 'You didn't cross yourself when you entered our church, sir.'

'Father, I really have to be—'

'Will you please make the sign?' The small man was trembling, his eyes wide and expression aghast.

'Do that … Do that for *her*.'

'Sure thing, Father.' Armando crossed himself.

The priest wandered into the trees, and at once, the light died. The canopy above made the man Armando was following a shadow, and for a moment, Armando felt strangely spooked, as though the priest was an otherworldly figure leading him into some netherworld. Armando gripped the hard material on the handle of his gun, snug behind his jacket, and its coolness was relieving. He didn't believe for a second that the priest was capable of hurting him, but it was the situation itself that was other to him, unnerving in a way he could not yet describe.

Then the light broke forth again. They came to a square amid the trees, and a single stone table with a figure laid out on top of it. It was a woman. Armando could see the smoothness of her back, the crack of her buttocks. She was 'sitting' upright. He wandered around the table to see her from the front. When he did, everything else seemed to fade away – the rapid breathing of the priest to his side, and Armando's own throbbing heartbeat.

The woman was naked. Posed. This was unlike the bodies at the canal. Unlike the women he had seen, who had been raped and then shot or strangled. It was more like … one of those strange modernist exhibits Cynthia used to take him to. The body did not smell – or at least it didn't smell of decay. There was a scent of lemon and oil, which flowed from it, and as he got closer, he saw her skin was slick and hard like it had been laminated. These details he took in almost unconsciously, at the back of his mind. His conscious mind was still struggling to understand what exactly he was seeing.

Her face was set in a leer – the jawbone had been ripped downwards, and her cheeks torn apart so that her mouth was a vast gaping chasm, the remnants of her lips pressed upwards at the edges. Her eyes had been removed, and some type of black lining had been placed into them so that they looked like the dark pockets of a pool table. Small dashes had been carved into the flesh around one nipple, but they had been filled in with a black gel so that they resembled markings rather than wounds. There was a gaping black hole on the other side of her chest where her heart should have been. It, too, had been filled with the same black substance. Across her belly had been drawn out a series of symbols. They looked like some form of hieroglyphics. Her legs were parted somewhat, the knees pressing out at angles. Her vagina had that same black thickening gel spread across it.

Armando understood that this had once been a person – a person made into something else. He knew death; he understood it. He understood the poor fucking bitch who had been battered to death because she had giggled involuntarily at the small size of a client's penis. He knew about the bitches who had stolen a client's wallet and got caught in the act. He knew about the gang-banger's girlfriend who had too much of a mouth – had told her pimp and his friends to suck their own dicks, and ended up in the back of a dumpster. He was familiar with female corpses that had been battered every shade of black and blue. But this …

He heard a *rasping* sound. It took him a few moments to realise the noise was coming from himself.

The *Padre* was tugging on his arm again. He shook him off, hard.

'Christ, won't you give me a fucking moment!'

Armando didn't feel sick – at least not in the way he had when he'd seen those slick black bodies at the bottom of the canal. He felt something different now. Like his brain was trying to process something that didn't make sense, to figure out some kind of trick of the light … That jaw positioned down, almost to her chest … Those wide black eye-sockets, which seemed to bore into him … There was a level of unreality to this, and he'd had enough.

He moved away.

'Are you okay?'

The strange little priest was asking him if he was all right.

Armando felt a rush of sympathy for the other man. 'I'm okay, Father.'

He glanced at the small man. The priest looked utterly bereft, exhausted.

'You did good,' Armando said. 'You did good to call this in, to deal with this.'

Armando turned towards the dead woman again, his eyes acting of their own volition. He noticed something he hadn't seen before. Beside her body was a carving, a small wooden figurine with a broad smiling face. It had no eyes and only a hole where the nose should have been. It was folding its bony arms, with a torso made of bones and a mouth bared in a toothy skeletal grin.

'I felt it, you know?' the priest said in a small voice. 'I came in late today. I'd been out speaking with parishioners, and when I came here, even though it was a sunny afternoon, when I stepped back here, I had this feeling. There was this stillness in the air. I felt it even before I saw ... you know?'

'I know, Father.' Armando put his arm on the priest's shoulder and gently angled the man in a direction facing away from the body.

They walked through the small glade, under the trees.

Eventually, the priest spoke again. 'Why would someone ... do that?'

It was something Armando, too, had been thinking over ever since he had arrived on the scene.

They walked back into the main church building. Everything was so quiet. Through the gloom of the main chamber, Armando imagined the images of all the people who had passed through it: wedding processions, funeral speeches, rows and rows of people across time, crying softly or smiling brightly; the same rituals acted out over generations.

He returned to the here and now. He looked at the priest, but it was as if he wasn't really seeing him at all.

'You have your ceremonies, Father,' he murmured.

'What do you mean?'

'The ... taking of the wafer, the conversion of Christ's body into bread, his blood into wine, the Eucharist. The posing of Christ on a cross – his death, the key to our lives, our fullness, our redemption. A ceremony performed to achieve a certain result ... a religious ritual. I think that whoever did this is doing the same thing. With her. *He* is using *her* body as a way of performing his own type of ritual.'

The priest's expression darkened. 'Detective, I find such a comparison shocking. To utter such a sentiment in this place is nothing short of obscene. Christ chose to die for our sins. He chose to die for us *out of love*. I don't think that poor creature out there had any kind of choice. There was nothing of ... love in what I saw out there.'

The sudden flash of bridling anger on the priest's part dulled into great sadness. The man's eyes filled with tears.

Armando blinked as though seeing him for the first time. 'You are right, of course, Father.'

He cleared his throat and took out his notebook.

'What time did you arrive today?'

'About an hour and a half ago,' the priest replied.

'Did you see anybody else? In or around the church?'

'Not really. The place was locked up for the morning. There were no services, you see.'

'And were you here last night?'

75

'Yes, I stayed until late.'

'Did you notice anything out of the ordinary?'

'No, it was very quiet. It is … the church is quieter these days.'

A silence stretched before them.

The other man looked at him, his eyes wide.

'Many people believe priests are sheltered, that they are cossetted by their robes and churches, and don't really encounter the realities of the outside world. But I have seen a lot, detective. A lot of poverty and pain. But … never anything like this. Have you ever seen anything like this?'

'No, Father, nothing quite like this.'

Armando realised that the priest wanted to keep talking and didn't want to be left alone. He suddenly seemed childlike.

'Can I give you a piece of advice, Father?'

The priest nodded.

'Leave this place and don't come back today. Go and visit with your parishioners some more. Take a walk in the sun. Find a place with a lot of people, an afternoon park maybe.'

The priest nodded again. 'Will you make sure … *she* is properly looked after?'

'I'm gonna go back to her right now, Father. I'll make sure she's taken care of. But until we know what this is about, I'm going to ask you to keep what you have seen to yourself. Can you do that, Father?'

'Yes, I can do that.'

Armando watched the priest shuffle away and then went back to the space between the trees. He could hear the sound of his own breathing shredding the empty air. He gazed at her, trying to look past the mutilations and the strange sheen of her lacquered skin.

He stayed there for a few moments like someone attempting to adjust their eyes in a different type of light.

Finally, he called it in. He took out his notebook and wrote a brief description of the body, the way it was positioned. He drew a quick sketch, which loosely corresponded to the body's size and the objects around it – the trees and the table.

Finally, he scrawled the words 'ritual', 'religion', and 'purpose' along with three jutting question marks. In work, in thought, he was gradually abstracted from the terrible details of the scene. So, it came as something of a surprise when he looked up from his notebook again to find *her* staring straight into him, those unseeing black cavities suddenly prescient.

Armando turned away as though he had stumbled across some private, intimate moment. He thought about it a little.

Perhaps someone's death is the most intimate thing of all.

That final moment before the all-encompassing dark. What could be more intimate than that? With a weary sigh, he reached into his jacket, took out the yellow tape, and began to cordon off the scene.

***

Armando had put on an old suit, which was now a little ruffled and small for his full frame. He stood outside the door for a few moments, holding the yellow daffodils and bottle of wine, his brow beaded with sweat due to the heat of the day, which had carried over into the evening. From within, he could hear music.

He rapped on the door twice.

Celia opened it, and he could tell she had been cooking. Her hair had been strafed by the heat, with a thin film of condensation on her fine white skin. Her expression was flushed and exultant as her eyes twinkled with mischievous humour.

'Ah, Armando, you've arrived in time for the tenth round. *Mujer contra Enchilada – Woman Vs Enchilada!*'

He followed her in. Her apartment was similar to his but nicer. She had thrown the windows open, and a breeze seeped in, tickling his hot face. Music drifted out from a record player, the disc soft and scratchy but beautiful, too; a single guitar – rich, delicate notes rising and falling in a yearning cascade. Celia had a rug of llama wool, which spread across the weary wooden planks of the floor. There was a couch and a couple of chairs, their polished mahogany frames glinting, partly in shadow.

At the far end of the room was a typical Mexican dining table covered with a white lace tablecloth. The table had been set elegantly. Even though she didn't have all that many things in her apartment, he felt the place was kind of classy.

He followed her into the little kitchen at the side. She began to pound a pan theatrically with a spatula, and then turned to him, her bottom lip protruding.

She blew away a lock of hair that had fallen across her forehead and grinned wickedly. 'Here. Taste this.' She brought the spatula to his mouth.

He took a little, as delicately as he could manage, which wasn't all that delicate. He felt the flavour infuse his mouth. It was good, and he was suddenly reminded of his hunger.

She put the spatula back in the pan and tasted a little herself. 'Mmmm.'

Armando noticed that she had used the same spoon, and this gesture – this small, shared intimacy – made him feel less like a lug in a badly fitting suit, standing in a stranger's apartment, fiddling with his hands.

He took out the daffodils. They had been crushed against his side, the flowers drooping down at an angle, their heads hanging slack and inconsolable. He blinked at them in surprise. Then, he looked at her.

She glanced back at him, her lips locked, thin and tight when suddenly they started to crinkle around the edges.

She burst into helpless laughter. 'Oh, my God, that's the saddest thing I have ever seen!'

Armando laid the flowers on the side with all the dignity he could muster. 'I haven't done this type of thing for a while.'

She became serious again. 'Oh. Well, it was a very thoughtful gesture. It was very – what is the word? – *chivalrous* of you. It was …'

The rest of the sentence fell away, melting into more hysterical giggles. When she laughed, her eyebrows arched elegantly, and her eyes shone. Armando found himself smiling right along with her.

With his other hand, he put down the bottle of red next to the defeated flowers. 'Perhaps we will have more luck with this?'

'Now that, *hombre*, is something this woman can work with.'

She popped the cork and dribbled the wine into two glasses.

He took a large gulp before remembering himself and starting to sip tentatively.

She served the food. 'Cristóbal!'

The young man came sauntering into the room, dressed in a pair of dark leather trousers and sunglasses lodged behind his ear. His hair was slick-backed, and there was the faint outline of a thin moustache just above his top lip. For Armando, the strangest thing was his eyes. They had been emphasised by what looked like eyeliner, dark lines running underneath and trailing from the edges – something a woman would wear. His lips were also tinged with purple.

'Cristóbal, you remember Armando?'

The boy's gaze flickered across Armando.

'Yeah, sure, how are you?' he murmured before loading food from the pan onto his plate.

At once, he started to eat.

His mother watched on with soft, bashful eyes and an amused smile. It was as if the process of him shovelling food into his mouth was something miraculous to behold.

'Aren't you forgetting something? Don't we say grace before we eat?' she said.

The muffled snuffling of his eating was aborted as the young man looked up from his plate. He had an acid smile on his face, his eyes gleaming with contempt.

'When did we last say grace before we eat? You're only saying that because *he* is here.' He nodded in Armando's direction.

'Why don't we say it anyway?' his mother replied, her tone clipped.

Cristóbal sat back in his seat and stretched out his arms.

Armando wondered how they could do that – how surly teenagers could manage to convey disdain for the world without even saying a word, merely by their physical arrangement. He had the urge to slap the boy hard.

Cristóbal's sardonic smile wavered. He put his hands together. 'Bless this delicious meal and my loving mother, who has worked over a hot stove all evening to make it. And thank you God for our health and the fact that we have each other …'

Celia was looking at her son again with a kind of soft wonder.

'And bless this apartment, even though it's a cheap tiny shithole, and even though you can hear the rats running around at night. And bless my dear mother, who can't keep a man but is trying to find love once again tonight. Amen!'

Armando saw it; the nakedness of her face – how that moment of gentle, open happiness had been so easily obliterated by the sharp words of the young man. Armando looked at Cristóbal, taking in the violent, black streaks of his greasy hair and eyes that had narrowed into malicious slits of mirth. He was a good-looking young man, but there was something rodent-like about him. Armando felt the blood pounding in his temples. He lowered his gaze to the table and saw that he had balled his right hand into a clenched fist. He relaxed his fingers and took his wine glass, sipping it steadily until it was empty.

'Why do you have to be so fucking cruel?' Celia asked her son softly.

'What kind of language is that for a lady, Mum?'

Cristóbal looked at them both, still grinning.

He finally raised his hands in mock surrender. 'Hey, I was only joking. Can't you take a joke, Mum?'

She gave a thin smile. 'Eat your food.'

They commenced eating, the masticating sounds of food being consumed uncomfortably loud in the quiet that followed.

Cristóbal stole glances at Armando as the conversation was resurrected:

'So, you're a cop, right? What's that like?'

'Okay, I guess.'

'Do you have a gun?'

'Yeah.'

'Did you ever shoot anyone?'

81

'It's more of a deterrent. You rarely have to draw your weapon.'

'You didn't answer my question.'

'That's right, I didn't.'

'Cristóbal,' his mother chided. 'Enough.'

The silence resumed.

Armando noticed how Celia's eyes focused on her son, wary one moment, enraptured the next.

'You know, Armando.' She looked at him and smiled. '*My Cristosito* has an artistic streak. At the school's parents' evening, the art teacher told me that she thought Cristóbal showed "genuine promise".' Celia smiled, delighted by the memory.

Cristóbal tucked his head down and played with his food.

But Celia seemed rejuvenated. 'And why not tell Armando about the stuff you do with your friends? The … *anime* stuff.'

She looked at Armando, her eyes shining.

'Do you know what *anime* is, Armando?'

'No.'

'It's art they do in Japan, like cartoons and stuff. Cristóbal has a group of friends, and they make anime comics. Some of the stuff he draws, you should see it. It's pretty cool, isn't it, Cristóbal?'

'Whatever,' the teenager muttered.

He wouldn't look at them.

Suddenly, he slid his plate out across the table. 'Finished. Going out.'

Celia blinked. 'But you haven't had your dessert. I made a *flan de tres leches*, your favourite!'

'Gotta go.' He sauntered into the hallway without out a backwards glance.

The door slammed.

Celia flinched.

82

Armando took the wine bottle and topped up her glass.

She nodded and gave a weak smile. 'He marches to the beat of his own drum, that's what you have to understand. He's very … independent minded.'

Armando could think of some other words to describe him.

'But hey, I guess we all want to go our own way as teenagers. *Jesús Cristo* – some of the stuff I put my parents through. I bet you were the same. I bet you were something of a hellraiser as a teenager, right?'

There was a pleading look in her eyes.

Armando nodded. 'Sure.'

At that moment, there was a *cracking* sound from outside, and the soft electric lights of the room dimmed into nothing. They were shrouded in gloom.

'It's the electrical box,' Celia said in a flat voice. 'It's gone again.'

He could see her looking at him, her eyes shadowed.

'It wasn't… I mean this evening … wasn't supposed to be like this.' Her voice caught in a sob.

He stood up, walked over to her, and put his hand under her chin, gently turning her face up towards him. Her eyes seemed impossibly wide.

'It's not the end of the world, Celia. You got candles? And another bottle?'

She nodded.

'Okay, you sort out the candles and wine. I'll pop back home and get my tools.'

Minutes later he was on his back, underneath one of the kitchen cupboards, gazing up at the tangle of wires and circuits of the electric box. It was an old device, most likely late seventies; the bulky transformer was probably overheating because of an overloaded circuit board. Several circuit breakers had been fried to a black crisp, and a couple of the fuses had gone. Armando turned off the power and did basic emergency rewiring. The work was physically hard because of the odd position of the box; he had to raise his hands up and make fine adjustments with more delicate tools. But within a minute, he was absorbed.

As a kid, he and his friends had scoured the local rubbish dump for 'parts' – their big childhood dream was to build a motorbike from scratch and use it to get to Mexico City. It never occurred to them that a motorbike could not transport all seven of them. Still, such stubborn facts couldn't trump their sense of childhood exhilaration, the shared dream of building something themselves. Of course, they never managed it, but Armando never lost his fascination with mechanics. Over the years he had fixed cars, bikes, telephones, fridges, TVs, installed two kitchens, built cupboards and tables, fitted new windows, rewired whole apartments, and tons of other things.

He supposed that since Cynthia had left, he hadn't been as 'handy'; there didn't seem much point. But he found working, here and now, immensely satisfying. Whereas before, sitting at the table, he had felt rusty and awkward, not sure of what to say, now, the rhythm of the labour had somewhat steadied him.

He slid out from underneath the skink and pushed himself up, panting a little.

Celia was sitting with her back against the wall, half in shadow.

'Almost done,' Armando said.

Celia raised her glass.

Armando took his and drank.

She was smiling, amused, intrigued, and he thought she looked beautiful in the soft gloom. It suddenly felt comfortable, and nice, like they were a couple; the familiar intimacy of just being in the same space and not saying all that much. He had missed that.

A slight frown crossed his face. He spoke quietly, 'Why do you let him do that?'

She looked back at him quizzically.

'Why do you let him talk to you like that?'

Her face changed. 'Tell me something, Armando.'

'Sure.'

'Do you have any children?'

'No.'

'None? None whatsoever?'

'No.'

'Then what the fuck do you know?' She'd said it softly, but her eyes flashed with determination.

Armando smiled involuntarily and raised his hands. 'Alright. Maybe I better get back under here for my own safety!'

She looked away and patted his leg. 'I'm sorry. This is probably not what you expected. Not the kind of fun evening for a first date. Or … whatever this is.'

He caught her gaze again.

'This is okay,' he said sincerely. 'This is good.'

Five

It was late morning as Armando drove through the city centre. His head was a little clearer. He'd had a couple of whiskies the night before, after he'd returned to his flat. Then, the heat had abated, and he'd fallen asleep. Looking back on it, Armando thought the 'date' had gone well. He'd got the power on. There hadn't been any sex. They'd kissed, briefly. Nothing more. And that was okay. What had made him feel good was the sense of normality, the feeling of talking to someone in the late evening, of hearing someone's voice while he worked indoors. He felt a sense of warmth rise in his belly.

But then it was gone. Replaced by the image of Cynthia – her body withered, head bald, eyes large and reddened – staring out from the formless white of a hospital bed. Such images came to him at the strangest times. It was all in his mind, of course – he hadn't even known she was ill at the time. And yet those images would come, and he would turn them over and over in his head.

He felt his breathing become laboured. His heart rate climbed. Ribbons of bright shimmered across his vision.

The car swerved, and he was revived by a *blasting* cacophony of beeps. His heart still *thudding*, he managed to pull over.

He got out and took a few faltering steps forward. He walked half a block and stepped into one of the new commercial centres, which had opened up in the last few years. As his feet *clapped* against the pristine marble-coloured floor of the mall, he caught sight of the bright green neon lettering of 'Comercial Mexicana'. Two private security men were at the door, machine guns draped at their sides. They regarded him balefully, but he paid them no mind, keeping his gaze towards the ground.

He found the drinks aisle and took a small bottle of cheap whisky. He cashed it out, left the store, and stepped onto the street.

His breathing relaxed. Just feeling the bottle, the hard-rimmed plastic, was enough to do that. He unscrewed the top and brought it to his mouth. He smelt the dusky odour of the rich dark liquid. He closed his eyes and inhaled. Paused momentarily. Then put the cap back on.

Back at the car, he slipped the bottle into the glove compartment and started the engine.

A few minutes later, he pulled up outside the building where he signed in before going downstairs and stepping into the mortuary.

Arturo Herrera, the chief mortician, was mulling about on the 'shop floor'. Herrera was held in light contempt by Armando's colleagues. They called him 'the penguin' because he was short, tubby, middle-aged, and balding. He waddled around the lower echelons of the building in conditions of refrigerator-like cold. Yet, Armando found him to be useful and effective; he was clear, logical, and didn't waste much time on small talk.

'Ah, detective,' he said when Armando entered. 'It's been a while. I trust that you are keeping well?'

The mortician's tone was as placid as ever, but his face crinkled in what might have been construed as an attempt at a smile. It was the most emotional Armando had ever seen him.

'I take it you are here for your girl. I noted your badge number on the notes when she came in. A strange case, to say the least.'

The phrasing 'your girl' offset Armando. He thought about Cynthia again, saw the brightness of her smile in his mind's eye, and then imagined her in a place like this.

'Well, this way …'

Armando followed the mortician deeper into the chamber, the whole room cast in an austere silvery grey. He barely glanced at the cold naked bodies that had been laid out on the large metal tables, whose texture and hue seemed to meld with the clinical paleness of the chilled room.

'*Voila*,' the mortician said with a brief flourish of a pudgy arm.

When Armando had first visited the morgue, some twenty years ago, nothing more than a beat cop, he'd vomited into a bag. Growing up, he'd known violence, but never dismemberment. But there had been lots of bodies since, so, gradually, his sensitivity and shock had become something else. Numbness perhaps. Now he was standing in front of the corpse he had come across at the church several days earlier. Despite everything he had seen, Armando knew the image of what had been done to her in that church would be with him for the rest of his life.

Now, though, she looked different. Herrera had laid her out carefully and put a solvent in her eyes and across her labia. It had dissolved the hardened black material, which had been pasted across those openings. He'd also closed the gaping cavity in her chest. The wound, which ran across her belly and torso, had now been stitched up. Her hair had been clipped, combed, and pulled back. Her mouth had been closed, and the gashes that had been opened up from its corners, towards her ear on either side, had been wired and stuffed with cotton buds.

Her face looked almost human again. Her skin had been washed. Her fingernails and her toenails had been cleanly cleaved away, and a soft, blue gel squeezed evenly into the rims. The mortician had attended to her meticulously. Armando even felt that there was something somehow gentle in his efforts. How strange that would be: a life which had probably known so little gentleness, to find something of it, at last, in death.

'Well, as you can see, your girl has been through the wars. Murdered? Almost certainly.'

'Almost?'

'I'm covering my bases, detective. Her neck was crushed, but there were no fingerprints on it, nor the impression of someone's knuckles or shoeprint. Therefore, it's likely her windpipe was crushed by the ridge of someone's arm, or the blow from an iron bar, or something similar. Though less likely, it is conceivable that her neck was crushed in some kind of accident. In such a scenario, her body was then … altered by whoever discovered her.'

Armando scribbled down notes as the mortician went on.

'It's also possible that she was murdered by one person and then a second party mutilated the corpse. This, however, I find unlikely. In any event, a precise time of death is difficult to establish because of how the body has been treated. Her stomach was empty of food, and the level of acidity indicates she hadn't eaten in some time. Along with the level of rigor mortis, and the relatively well-preserved state of the body, I'd say the likelihood is that your "VIC" was killed by someone four to five days ago, who kept the body for a while – in a cool place, preparing it – and then deposited it where you had the – *ahem* – misfortune of discovery.'

'Is there evidence of sexual assault, secretion?'

'No. This is difficult to establish definitively. But there were no traces of fluids in the places where you would expect to find them. There was no tearing or internal bleeding. It is quite possible that she was raped, but the specific nature of her injuries don't attest to that. I found no biological trace of her assailant on her body: no hairs, no flesh under her fingernails, which might have indicated a struggle.

'The black material – which had been smeared into her eye sockets, over her genitals, and into the chest cavity after her heart was removed – I dissolved and cleaned away, but took a sample. A cursory examination of the material revealed it to be some kind of mortar. I'd hazard the type of thing used on building sites and industrial equipment. I can investigate its origins more extensively if you wish, but only if the department signs off on it, detective.'

Armando gave a brief nod.

'If we knew who she was, if we had the context in which she was killed and a feasible suspect, then a more detailed examination might be justified. It might go some way to securing a conviction in court. But do you have any idea how many unidentified dead women are processed in any given month? Ninety per cent of them will never be identified, let alone have their assailants brought to justice. There simply isn't the manpower. I have to log my hours, detective, and I have already spent more time on her than any other "Jane Doe" who has come through these doors for some time.'

'There is something different about her, though,' Armando cut in. 'She's not just another "Jane Doe", is she?'

'No... no, she isn't.'

'Why do you think someone would have done something like this?

The mortician looked up at Armando, his grey eyes glinting in the dull light, his lips set in a small, rueful smile. 'Come now, detective. You know better than that. My realm begins and ends with physical matter, that which can be tapped and drawn and observed under a microscope. Of the dark night of the soul, I know very little, and wouldn't care to speculate. There's also this …'

The mortician walked away from the table and opened a metal cupboard. He took out the now-bagged wooden figurine that Armando had found placed by the corpse and handed it to the detective. Armando took it. He looked at the mortician, looked at 'the penguin'. The small rotund man might have been a figure of fun among Armando's colleagues, but the clarity of the way he saw things, and the scrupulous and logical nature of the way he worked, greatly appealed to Armando.

'Can you tell me something? Anything? Even if it is not based on … complete concrete facts.'

The other man stared back at him, and in as much as those grey eyes reflected anything, they seemed to hint at a gentle sorrow.

'Only this, perhaps: I have seen women's bodies come through those doors, bodies broken and damaged and destroyed in every way you might imagine. There is, I sometimes think, no limits to the variety and creativity of death. But I have never seen anything quite like this.'

Armando left the morgue and stepped out into the warm evening.

He sat in the car but didn't turn the key in the ignition. Behind the sleek high buildings of the business district, he could see the waning sun – a shimmering haze of bloody red bleeding into the horizon, leaving in its wake a landscape of cloud fissured with deep purple and orange. From the east, he could see the vast climbing shadow of the Popocatépetl volcano in the distance, and beyond, the darkness of the oncoming night.

He grabbed the whisky bottle from the glove compartment and took a long lingering drink, feeling the alcohol burn and sizzle in his throat, and then flow into his belly, provoking that sharp, acrid feeling before it melted into his blood. He felt his eyelids flutter – he hadn't understood just how badly he had needed this drink until now. He breathed out, and all the tension and creakiness of his body seemed to seep away. He took another, smaller sip. He was off duty now, so this was okay. He deserved this.

He thought it might be nice to knock on Celia's door. Just turn up out of the blue, bottle of wine in hand. Hell, perhaps he might even make some headway with that brat of hers – the kid was clearly some kind of asocial freak. Perhaps Armando could set him straight, make some bawdy jokes, cuff his head – but in a friendly way. He imagined Celia's eyes lighting up, delighted by the fact that Armando was showing an interest in her boy. Surely she would show him how grateful she was, later …

But Armando knew that just knocking on the door wouldn't work. They didn't have that kind of relationship yet, and he sensed that Celia wouldn't be rude exactly if he did something like that, but she wouldn't appreciate it, either.

She'd said of her son that 'he marches to the beat of his own drum', but Armando thought that was truer of Celia herself. She was a sexy independent woman. She had experienced life. That's why sex with her would be so good. Armando pictured her on her hands and knees, her panties down, him entering her from behind, the sound of her sonorous moans. Making her his. Making her know it. After that, they would lie together, her head nestling against his chest, and he'd run a finger through her hair. Maybe he'd take Cristóbal out the next day. Watch a baseball game with him or something.

That's what people did, right?

He blinked. The sun had almost set, the last residues of light fading behind the vast shape of the volcanic belt. The loneliness beckoned; soon he would return to his apartment, drink more whisky, and watch some documentaries, maybe.

But it was a Friday, and every second Friday, he would go and make the collection. If he arrived early, he might have a better chance of missing Juan Carlos. He loathed the young man, but Armando knew he had to be careful because of Juan Carlos's father and the money their organisation provided him with.

Virtually every cop in Puebla City was on the take; however, this was not corruption, not in the truest sense of the word – at least not to Armando. For him, it was simply an issue of survival. The average beat cop made around 3,000 pesos a month, roughly the same salary as an unskilled labourer. As a detective, Armando made more, but the amount was still negligible. Cops in Puebla took money from certain criminal organisations that had been vetted; organisations that would, in return, comply with the police on certain issues and ensure that the violence on the street remained within 'manageable' levels. Many people complained about the connection between the police and criminal organisations, but they had no idea of the realities of crime in Mexico's bigger cities.

Armando knew a place where they could stick their opinions.

He started the engine and pulled away, hard.

Some twenty minutes later, he was at *Septimecielo*.

He rapped on the door.

The fat bouncer opened it.

'*Hola*, Filippo. Do us both a favour. Move that fat ass, get me my money, and we can avoid bothering "the boss"!'

'You know something, Armando? You always make nasty cracks about my weight. That's actually a little ignorant. My doctor says

93

that some bodies convert food into fat at a greater capacity. He says you can't help being fat. That's just genetics. Ain't you ever heard of genetics, motherfucker?'

Armando gave a thin smile. 'I'm tired, Filippo. It's been a long day. So please, waddle up those stairs and get me my money. Before I put my foot up your fat "genetic" ass!'

The bouncer's face crinkled and his small, porcine eyes smouldered. Finally, he turned and went up the stairs.

Armando heard him panting and grinned.

When the bouncer returned, he was stone-faced. 'He wants you to come up. He wants to give it to you himself.'

'Alright,' Armando muttered.

He made his way up the dark corridor, across the hall, and into the backroom.

Juan Carlos was sitting on the couch, a glass of whisky loose in one hand. In front of him was a small black table with several tracks of cocaine. A few feet beyond it, two women, wearing only thongs, were swaying and gyrating, while in the background, Leonard Cohen crooned out his gravelly voice in a soft, lugubrious lament. Both women had their eyes half-closed as their bodies undulated.

Armando felt a strange combination of depression and desire, his head throbbing, his eyes tingling in the smoky gloom.

Juan Carlos was watching the women, his handsome, smooth features fixed but expressionless. Armando had the disquieting sensation that the young man was wearing some kind of mask. The corner of one lip twitched upward, and Armando realised Juan Carlos was smiling. But those eyes remained bereft, a strange dull blackness within them. His skin was also unusually pallid – Armando wondered if he wasn't close to some kind of overdose.

94

'Would you like to sit down, detective?' Juan Carlos said in a toneless voice, his gaze still on the women.

'No, I'm fine. I just came to collect—'

'I know why you came, detective.'

Armando felt his head throb.

The large bouncer standing by the door shifted his feet.

'Would you like a drink, detective? You do like a drink, don't you?'

Armando shook his head.

'You know, when I was a kid …' Juan Carlos was speaking in the same neutral voice. '… I used to think about what it would be like to be with a woman. I'd talk about it with my friends. Most of us would make up stories even though we'd never had a girlfriend. And then, when it eventually happened, it was the most amazing drug.

'But like any drug, the first time is always the best. Once you know what to expect, it's never quite as good again. So, I wanted to do it in different ways, in different positions. But soon that became routine too.'

Those dark eyes never left the writhing bodies before him.

'So, after that, I didn't just want normal sex. I needed to do different things. I'd want to do it on speed or coke. Then, after that, I'd want to tie her up. Or I'd want more than one girl at the same time. And I'd want to tie them both up. When that, too, got dull, I'd start to do … other things.'

He turned to Armando for the first time, his face pallid and ghastly, and behind it, a dark shadow. His eyes were still like small black stones, devoid of life.

'Then I realised that there comes a point where you can't feel anything anymore. Because … there's nothing left to do. And it's then when you feel … nothing. Nothingness everywhere.'

He leaned over and snorted a line of coke, his face contorted in a twisted grimace. 'Patty.'

One of the women turned to him, her eyes glassy, her smile lurid.

'Put your tongue in her ass.'

The woman hesitated for a fraction of a second. Then she walked around the other woman and knelt down behind her. She pulled the fabric of her panties aside and deftly pressed her face against the other woman's buttocks.

Despite himself, Armando watched, unwilling to draw his eyes away.

The other woman started to moan softly. And then a little louder.

Juan Carlos turned his face to Armando, a sickly smile playing across his face. He regarded the women for a few moments longer before speaking in an incredulous whisper, as though he had just learnt something for the first time.

'That's something inhuman, that right there. I mean, you and I might get angry, we might even be violent, right? As men, we lash out. That's what we do. But we'd never, ever do this type of shit. I mean seriously. All the money in the world couldn't persuade me to stick my tongue in your hairy asshole, Armando. I really, sincerely mean that. But that's how they are. These bitches will do anything for money.'

He took the crystal tumbler of whisky, knocked it back, and stood. He made his voice louder, brighter, as he removed his Rolex. The platinum glinted, partly shadowed.

'Hey, Lupita!'

The other woman stopped moaning. She opened her eyes and fixed him with a smile, artificially bright.

'You know how much this costs, baby?' He held up his watch.

She shook her head demurely.

'Thirty thousand pesos. You'd have to suck a lot of cock to make that kind of money, right?'

She giggled, but the sound was automated, empty.

Juan Carlos put the watch on the table and eyed her seriously. 'You can have it.'

Armando saw something shimmer almost imperceptibly in the young woman's eyes. She looked at the watch and then back at her boss, studying him cautiously.

'All you have to do,' Juan Carlos continued, 'is take this glass and balance it on your head for two minutes, while she continues to eat your asshole. If you manage that, the watch is yours.'

Juan Carlos gave a simple shrug.

The woman glanced at Armando as though looking for some kind of reassurance. She looked back at Juan Carlos wordlessly before allowing him to place the cup carefully on her head.

'I don't have time for this', Armando muttered. 'Give me the money, and I'll get going.'

Juan Carlos looked at him. His expression was serious. 'Why, of course.'

He walked to the desk and bent underneath it. When he came back, it took Armando a couple of seconds to process what he was cradling in his arms. The skeletal metal, the wide arches, the chamber, the bolt, and the wooden underlay. The crossbow was covered in dust and cobwebs, but it was a heavy, powerful contraption – Armando could see that at a glance.

The woman, Lupita, was faced away from Juan Carlos. He moved around her, murmuring, 'You're doing excellently, just thirty more seconds, just keep as still as possible.'

He stepped out, some few feet away, and raised the weapon.

'Stay still now, don't move, keep as still as possible. I only want to hit the glass!'

Armando caught the moment when the woman made sense of what was happening; her whole face froze. In the same instant, Armando had unclasped his pistol, flicked off the safety, and raised it.

He snarled the words in a hissing rasp. 'Lower your weapon. You lower it now.'

Juan Carlos looked at him as a smile crept across his face. 'Hey, relax, *companero*! I was just having a little fun with Lupita here.'

He lowered the bow.

Lupita had her arms wrapped across her chest, trembling violently.

At that moment, the cup fell. The sound *tinkled* in the darkness.

Juan Carlos looked from the shattered vessel to Lupita. Still smiling, he raised the bow a fraction and shot a bolt into her leg.

The woman screamed in agony.

Armando lunged forwards and kicked the bow from Juan Carlos's grasp, sending it *clanging* to the ground. He pulled the other man around, wrenching him from his feet, and forcing him back onto the couch.

He put one hand around his throat. 'You sick piece of shit!'

Armando felt the anger course through his body, the white-hot brightness of it, as he tightened his grip on the pale, slim neck of the younger man, feeling the filigree of tendon and bone compressing against his fingers, seeing Juan Carlos's eyes roll back in his head.

Filippo grunted and waddled forward, but Armando's other hand was already on his pistol, and he aimed it smoothly, training it on the large bouncer.

'Get back in your corner, you fat fuck!' Armando snarled.

The bouncer stopped and stepped back – deflated and panting from the sudden burst of adrenaline and energy his movement had required.

Armando turned back to Juan Carlos. Flecks of white spittle had gathered on the other man's grinning lips. His expression was lurid, almost orgasmic.

'Yes, that's right. Just like that. Make me … *feel*,' he said.

Armando released his hand from Juan Carlos's throat in disgust. All the anger drained out of him. In the background, the raw shrieks of pain from the wounded woman shredded the air. Armando's head felt like it might crack open. He got up, though he was unsteady.

Juan Carlos was still grinning and wheezing.

Armando holstered his weapon. The bouncer was looking down at the injured stripper. The bolt was hanging from her leg like an appendage. Armando caught sight of a piece of bone peeking out from a thick ruby-red pocket of blood.

'Shall I pull it out?' the bouncer asked dumbfounded.

'No, you idiot. Not unless you want her to bleed to death,' Armando snapped.

Juan Carlos was on his feet, shakily. 'It's okay. Filippo, Patty, help her out of here – take her to the Betania Hospital. I have an account there. They will patch you up real good, sweetie.' He eyed Armando. 'You wanna go with them?'

Armando looked at him in disbelief. 'I can't be here. I can't be connected to … this.'

Juan Carlos rubbed his neck. 'Oh, yes, I almost forgot – your money. You still want it, right?'

Armando didn't say anything; he just took the packet that the younger man handed him and left.

As he was exiting the building, he heard the girl's agonized scream and prayed that they were only moving her out.

Six

He was lying by her side, staring up into the darkness. After the sex, she had turned around, nuzzled her face into her pillow, and fallen fast asleep. There was, Armando thought, a rather ugly sensuality to her. Esmeralda was utterly at home in her body. Her generous breasts, her voluptuous form – being fucked, having a stranger in her bed, to her, was no different than drinking a glass of water. She was snoring softly, her nostrils flaring. He thought about slapping her, shocking her out of her complacency.

He wondered why he kept coming back to her, kept paying to do this to her, for as soon as the coupling was over, he was filled with a feeling of listlessness and loathing. Lying on the bed, whose sheets were no doubt glazed with the substance and follicles of other men, gazing into the shadows in the early hours, he felt, along with his ejaculation, everything human in him leave his body. It was as though all the colour of the world had been drained away, as though everything had turned grey in the blink of an eye.

Involuntarily he thought about that sick shit Juan Carlos and the words he had uttered: '*There comes a point where you can't feel anything anymore. Because ... there is nothing left to do. And it's then when you feel ... nothing.*'

Lying there, Armando felt that nothing. He heard the scream of the hooker in his head, like an animal in pain. Had they really taken her to the hospital? Or out into the *tierra*, the harsh, rugged terrain beyond the city's periphery? It would have cost a lot to treat that

101

particular injury, so perhaps Juan Carlos had simply snuffed her out and left her body to the lizards and coyotes.

Armando could have gone with her. He should have gone with her. He knew that.

Yet, he also understood that he did not care. Not in the slightest. Some part of him wanted to. Some part wanted to feel for the brutalised stripper. But he simply … didn't feel a thing.

He needed to get up, to be on his way. Only he felt so sluggish. He couldn't face the journey, couldn't face the darkness of his apartment in the early hours.

He looked at her again. She seemed so beautiful in that sick carnal way. Her eyes fluttered as she shifted her body, lost in the throes of some fever dream. An odour emanated from her hot skin, hair, and mouth; a strange sweetness. He knew the smell; this room was often heavy with it. Heroin. Her drug of choice. There were never any tracks on her arms, so he presumed she inhaled it.

He got up, lethargic, and put his trousers on. He went into the corridor, feeling his way through the dark hallway and into the pokey kitchen. He opened the small squat fridge, and a blue-grey light flooded out. Inside there was a pizza box, several large peppers, carrots, potatoes, and three generic brands of beer. He took one of the cans with relief, plucking it open with his thumb, the released gas creating a satisfying *hiss*.

He drained half of it in one gulp, closed his eyes, and turned.

'Motherfucker!' He violently reeled back, his full body causing the fridge and the wall behind it to shudder. The small shape illuminated in the blue light was wearing a shimmering white dress and looked like a figure from a horror movie.

Armando snarled, his heart beating furiously, trying to catch his breath.

102

The small figure giggled melodically. 'You just said a bad word. A *really* bad word,' she said triumphantly.

He felt his body calm, his pulse slow. 'Yeah,' he whispered with some hostility. 'You're lucky that's all I did, kid. I could have crushed you like a grape. You ever think about that?'

She looked at him with wide dark eyes. She was not in the slightest bit frightened.

He rubbed his eyes. 'What the hell are you doing up at this time anyway?'

'It's the witching hour!'

Armando killed the rest of his beer. 'What the hell is that?'

Salome's wide eyes narrowed into slits of contemptuous amusement. 'I thought you were a policeman. Policemen are meant to know things. But you don't know anything at all, do you?'

Armando took the empty can of beer in one meaty fist and crushed it, the *tinny* sound rippling across the late-night quiet.

'I know I could take your little head and do this with it,' he said with a good degree of feeling.

Salome's expression didn't change. Instead, she put her hands on her hips and exhaled with theatrical exasperation. 'The witching hour is a time at night when the spirits come to life. It's like *el Día de los Muertos*, only it doesn't last as long, and it happens every night. That's why I wake up late at night. Because I want to see the spirits and the fairies, and the ghosts and the vampires.' She blinked at him.

Armando took another beer from the fridge. Popped the cap. Took a swig. 'How do you know any of that is true?'

The small girl screwed up her face defiantly. 'Because my mama told me.'

'Okay then. So, let me ask you this … Fairies live in gardens, vampires live in castles, ghosts live in graveyards, and spirits live in mirrors. Why do you think they would all be together in one place at this particular time?'

For the first time, the child's eyes shimmered with uncertainty, her whole expression retreating into a tentative frown. Then, her face fissured into a sharp sneer.

'What the hell do you know? You're just some silly fat man. Why don't you go back into Mama's room and continue to make your silly, stupid noises!' Her dark eyes glowered at him. 'Oh, ohhh, ohhhh yeaahhh. Ohhhh emm, ohhhh.'

Armando raised one eyebrow, somewhere between amused and disturbed by her parroting of sex noises. He spoke a little softer, 'Have you ever seen any of these spirits and things?'

Her voice was a resentful whisper. 'No, not yet.'

'Okay, that's alright. Let me ask you something else … Why do you wanna do it? Why would you want to see them?'

She hesitated and again came that same frown – the small puckered lips, her eyes shining faintly with the weight of the world. She clasped her hands together in a cradle and stared at her feet. Armando could see she still hadn't decided whether he was a friend or foe.

Yet, she chose to answer honestly. 'Sometimes … I do naughty things. Sometimes I go into Mama's room when she's working … and I'm not supposed to do that. And sometimes I do other naughty things. I take things when I'm not supposed to.'

The little girl nodded ruefully towards the fridge.

'Sometimes I take stuff from there, *especially* chocolate. But … but even though Mama gets very angry with me sometimes, and even though she sometimes shouts, she told me that whatever

104

happens, people still love me. She says that Grandpa loves me. But … Grandpa is dead.'

Salome made this statement to Armando with great solemnity but without great emotion, and yet her eyes were so wide. It felt to him as though they might contain the world.

'He's dead,' the girl continued. 'But dead means leaving the house and leaving people, and leaving Mexico and leaving the world, but still being with me.'

The girl touched a finger to her chest, to her heart.

'Here,' she said to emphasise – to explain to this strange, lumbering adult what he clearly had not grasped.

Armando felt something in him move. The thought of Cynthia came to him violently, and all at once, ridiculously, his eyes welled with tears.

The girl looked up at him, seeming to pick up on his sadness. '*Mi abuelo* is with me all the time. That's what Mama says. When Mama is too tired to play or has to work, he stays with me. But … I can't see him. No one can. So sometimes …'

'Sometimes?' Armando asked in a husky whisper.

She looked away, shy again.

'Sometimes I wake up, to look for ghosts. Because I want to find him. To say … thank you.'

Salome turned and gazed up at Armando again, those wide eyes filled with both hesitancy and hope. '*Entiendes?*'

'*Entiendo*,' Armando said in a low voice. 'I understand.'

He returned to the bedroom.

Esmeralda was propped up on a pillow resting against the bed's backboard. She had switched the radio on.

She peered at him, her stare unfocused. 'You're still here,' she mumbled.

'Yeah, looks that way,' he muttered.

She smiled dreamily.

The radio *crackled*.

'This is the most amazing thing – this programme,' she went on. 'You should listen. It's talking about telescopes. The gringos have a giant telescope, which is called the Hubble telescope. They can look through it and see all the stars in the universe. Can you imagine that? So … beautiful!'

She'd breathed the last word fragrantly, her eyes fluttering. She focussed again, and her gaze glowed in wonderment.

She spoke in a small voice, 'Perhaps … perhaps they might even see God. Do you think they will see God?'

Her eyes were beseeching; she was looking at him like she didn't quite know who he was.

Armando felt a ripple of bitter contempt. 'Oh sure, Esmeralda. They'll definitely see God alright.'

The young woman smiled.

Armando continued, 'The other thing is that God is gonna be looking back at the world through the other end of that Yankee telescope, seeing all the happy things that are happening down here.'

Esmeralda blinked; she'd registered the edge in his voice but couldn't quite understand it.

'Things like you taking all that heroin and getting fucked every night by a load of strangers. God is gonna be watching that happen through that shitty fucking telescope. He's gonna be your ultimate client, beating off while you go at it!'

'No,' the young woman mumbled piteously. 'No. You just … you just go away.'

Armando felt the sarcasm and the anger drain out of him.

Esmeralda rubbed her eyes, trying to focus.

The radio *buzzed*.

'Why do you do it?' he murmured.

'What … w-what do you mean?' she slurred.

'Why do you do what you do … with your kid around?'

She faltered, trying to assimilate the question, and then lifted her eyes to meet his. She was drugged out, but when she spoke, her words were uttered with a halting, dry determination, which for a moment took him aback.

'You listen to what I say. Everything. Every … fucking … thing … I do … with men … like you … I do it for her. So my daughter can have some kind of life. You understand?'

'Yeah, whatever you say,' Armando mumbled.

Esmeralda's eyes narrowed, and her nose crinkled. At that moment, she looked like her daughter – small, furious, scowling out at the world.

'I pay for this *apartamiento*. This is my home. I pay the rent. And I don't want you here!' Her face crumpled with emotion. 'I want you to go, Armando. I want you to get the fuck out!'

He nodded, gave a cold smile, and put on his jacket. Just before he left, he reached inside it, with ceremony, and took out a couple of notes. He made a point of putting them on the bed and patting them. He had already paid her – earlier – but he was making a different kind of point here. He was casually dehumanising her, making her aware of his contempt, showing her that she was a thing to be bought rather than a person to be engaged with.

Esmeralda kept looking at him, tears in her eyes. But she said nothing more.

He left the small squat apartment without looking back, his face locked in a rictus grin of disdain. As he stepped out into the night, he felt his anger return – she was, quite literally, a *bitch*. She depended on him for her livelihood, and he was certain he paid her more and treated her better than many of the dirtbags who got off on her. But in the sudden fuzz of his ire, he also felt a pang of regret. There was a moment back then when Esmeralda had looked so much like her strange, goofy little kid.

The coolness of the air hit him. He gazed up into the firmament. The night was cloudy, but he could see the silver of the stars shimmering behind the dark mist of sky. The rag-tag gipsies who hawked their cheap cards on the buses claimed to see people's future in the stars. To him, the glinting balls of gas seemed beautiful but futile. They held no mystical properties, and he knew that many of them had long since died out, and yet their light had continued to travel for many thousands, if not millions, of years before it reached his eyes. A luminescence that flickered with the ghostly glow of the past, a cold and lonely perishing as fire eventually cooled into black. And yet, Esmeralda saw hope in the stars. To her, they seemed heavenly. They occupied the same beautiful and mysterious place of God himself.

As Armando continued to gaze up, he heard a distant voice from his childhood; his mother. She had sung to him about the stars … It came to him now, even if he couldn't remember the exact words. At that moment, the memory seemed precious, and he tried to cling to it. Only, in the same moment, he shook it away, for he was an adult, a man. The idea of taking solace in the sound of a woman's voice flowing across him and making him feel safe and loved made him shiver with repulsion. It made him feel vulnerable, almost like a woman himself.

He made his way towards the main street.

Soon enough, in the darkness, a different set of lights gleamed; a golden glow of bottles arrayed behind the window of a late-night liquor store.

***

Armando awoke early. His sleep had been fragmented, full of strange, broken dreams that he didn't quite remember. When he hauled himself out of bed, he brushed his teeth, gargled, and spat into the sink, leaving a bloody residue in the swirling water. He groaned, got into last night's shirt and trousers, and left the house.

He arrived at the grandiose building, his head still thrumming from the hangover. The *Biblioteca Palafoxiana*, the Palafoxiana Library, was established in 1646 and home to one of Mexico's largest collections of books. Some considered it the oldest library in all of the Americas. Cynthia had been here many times, as part of her research, but this was Armando's first visit.

He approached the front desk tentatively. Behind it was a large door embellished by lavish gold totems running upwards on either side and a series of crests and sigils along the top. The images were of shrieking eagles and swords wrapped in snakes, images that spoke of ancient aristocratic blood lineages. Armando was aware of his large shambling frame and crimped clothes – and part of him was aware that he was not an educated man, that he didn't belong in a place like this. Part of him also suspected that the old librarian at the front desk was certain to agree.

She looked up at him with watery blue eyes and grey flaking hair. Her voice was laced with disdain. 'Yes?'

He glanced down at his feet. 'I need to look at some books.'

'But you're not a member.'

He felt himself begin to get angry, his body expanding. 'How do you know that?'

'Because.' Her voice was shrill.

'Because what?'

'Because… there is nothing here to interest you. The books on these shelves are all written in Spanish. There's nothing to interest someone of your … *kind*. Do you even know how to read?'

The corner of Armando's lips twitched. He raised his hand and looked at the tan skin, which had darkened further after years of working in the sun and heat. It wasn't the first time someone had mistaken him for being indigenous.

'Oh, I see.' He offered her a rueful smile. 'I must apologise. I'm going to go about this a different way. I can see you're someone of … *breeding*, someone respectable. So, I hope you'll be kind enough to help me.'

Her lips thinned in a weak smile, but her eyes grew defined and strong again. He saw it happen; she was certain of herself now, certain of his deference. She was preparing herself to reject him again, looking forwards to it, in fact.

He spoke evenly, 'Actually, I'm not indigenous at all. What I am …' He reached into his jacket and produced his ID. '… is a member of a different kind of tribe. I'm a detective for the Puebla City *Policia*. Can you read that? It means you need to do what I say right fucking now, *entiendes?*'

The smile died on her face. She started to tremble.

Armando softened his tone. 'So, be a dear, eh? Help me out. I'm looking for … a specific type of book.'

The lady behind the desk nodded rapidly. 'Well, I do hope I can help you, detective. Would you kindly give me more details?'

She stared at him, her eyes wide and serious, fully focussed. She was no longer looking through him. She saw him now. The power of a badge could do that. But he felt offset by the strangeness of his request.

The blood rushed to his face. 'I need you to provide me with any books on *serial killers.*'

She appeared baffled by the statement. 'Serial? I don't know what that means in such a context. I can check our files.'

She pulled out one of her drawers and started flipping through the papers.

'No.' She finally frowned. 'There's nothing under that heading.'

He nodded thoughtfully. 'Okay. Can you refer me to any books which provide some kind of dictionary of crime in general?'

Her fingers flitted through the papers again and stopped. 'We have a few books that might help you there, detective. Shall I take you to them?'

Armando nodded his assent.

He followed the woman through the door and into a great chamber. On either side, storeys of books rose higher and higher, giving way before a great domed ceiling. The high shelves, packed with thick, leather-bound volumes, cast shadows across the surrounding desks and mahogany floor, giving the interior a sense of preternatural gloom. At the far end of the library was a large rectangular window. It shone with an effervescent white, casting reams of light downward, illuminating the dust in the air that flitted and danced.

Armando felt a sense of helplessness.

Could anyone ever really read all these books?

He followed the librarian, the sound of his shoes on the floor echoing through the quiet. Except for them, the vast hall was

111

empty. From somewhere above, he heard the sound of an aeroplane.

The librarian motioned towards a single shelf. 'These might provide something concerning what you're looking for.'

'Thank you.'

He watched her walk away and ran a finger across the spines of the books, his fingertip smeared with dust. He picked up the first tome. It was weighty, leather-bound, and burnished with gold leaf:

The Detection of Criminal Deviance and Unnatural Lusts and Adultery in the Epoch of Godlessness and Democracy – written in the good year of 1841

Armando chuckled before gently sliding the book back into place.

The next one was more promising. Written in 1980, it provided a rather dry but systematic compendium of some of the more prolific examples of crime committed in Mexico going back to the nineteenth century. More importantly, it had a sub-section devoted to the category of 'Serial Murder'.

Armando took it and went and sat at one of the long tables, which ran in a line across the centre of the chamber. He began to read.

There were only seven entries in total. Despite the high murder rate in many Mexican cities, it seemed that 'serial murder' was a *very* rare crime.

Or perhaps, Armando thought, *one which is very rarely detected.*

The entries were written in a factual, dispassionate fashion, and next to each was a black-and-white image of the 'serial murderer' in question. Three entries caught Armando's attention. The oldest case was Francisco Guerrero Pérez, a man born in 1840. The picture of his face was small, a heavily pixelated black-and-white image that had about as much clarity and definition as a stamp. Armando viewed what seemed to be a rather well-dressed individual in a black jacket and white shirt. His dark hair was combed to one side. He had an even brow, a straight nose, and a long tidy beard. He looked like a European gentleman. His eyes … Armando couldn't really make them out. The man had killed several prostitutes, crimes which involved sexual mutilation. When he had eventually been captured, he had testified that prostitutes were 'by their very nature adulterous, and female adultery should be punished with the death penalty.'

He thought about the previous book's title: *The Detection of Criminal Deviance and Unnatural Lusts and Adultery*. It occurred to him that both the killer and the justice system thought the essential problem stemmed from the same thing: women fucking around.

The next individual Armando focused on was Macario Alcala Canchola, dubbed 'Mexican Jack'. This man looked diminutive and harmless despite the rather sinister *nom de plume*. His picture – also black and white but much clearer – showed a small, fastidious man, relatively young, with hair receding from the top of a high-domed forehead. His mild dark eyes gazed out from behind tidy, thin-framed black glasses. All in all, he had a smooth face except for a well-tendered triangular patch of hair just above his upper lip.

Canchola looked like one of the legal bureaucrats that Armando had to deal with when he was sent to one of the judiciaries to re-quest a warrant – the same smug blandness, the same slight whiff of disdainful superiority. He, too, had targeted prostitutes, murder-ing them in motel rooms in the Mexico City of the 1960s. He was suspected of killing at least twelve women, though he was only con-victed for one. This was because the police had not managed to connect the crimes, and early crime scene evidence had been discarded. Murders like this were so common yet so random that it was hard for any investigation to discern a pattern.

However, it was the last case that really caught Armando's attention. Alexandro Juarez de la Benedición had been arrested in the late 1970s. His picture had been snapped in prison, the bars behind him long snaking lines of black. He had a large head, a broad, thick neck, and tiny black pinpricks for eyes. One side of his face was slack, the corner of his left lip turned violently downwards, as though he'd had a stroke. His whole face was immobile, bereft of emotion before the flash of the police officer's lens. He was physically more powerful than the other men Armando had read about and had not operated in the big cities but in smaller rural towns. He had spent time working as a tree-cutter and a land labourer. He, too, had targeted prostitutes – raping and then killing them by strangulation.

Later, he had driven them out in his truck to local forests and plastered their naked bodies in a chemical varnish designed to preserve the flesh rather than dissolve it. There was a small picture of one of the bodies. It had been placed on its back but in an arc. The feet and ankles had been planted deep into the soil, the legs flowing up and across into the torso at the top, before the back turned downward once more towards the neck and head, which were buried in the earth again. The cadaver made an 'n' shape over the soil, almost like a gymnast, her belly pushed up, her hands behind her head and legs arced down. He had posed all of his victims in the same fashion in different forests. According to the article, when the authorities spoke to the killer, the large man slurred his words like a drunk or young child. When Juarez de la Benedición was asked why he had posed the women in this way, the thick-set farm worker

114

said that what he had done was sacred – that all pleasure and pain, all of life, arose from the soil and disappeared back into it.

When pressed on this, he said nothing more.

A wrinkle of cloud passed over the high window of the library, and the shadow at once thickened and fell, rippling across the floor and the desks in a single wave turning away the light. All that was visible on the page for a few moments were the small dark eyes of Alexandro Juarez de la Benedición gazing out at Armando, flickering in the gloom before the light cast its shine across the chamber again.

Armando sat almost rigid in the chair. A feeling akin to excitement pulsed through him. He thought about the body of the woman de la Benedición had posed and positioned in the soil. Then he thought about the body that the priest had discovered in the Parish of Our Lady of Refuge… The way it had been altered and posed…

His hunch was a certainty now.

He was dealing with a serial killer.

Seven

Armando and José Luis were driving back to the station in the early evening. Armando took a right and then pushed on the pedal. The car choked before roaring forwards, propelled with a sudden burst of speed upwards over the wide flyover, which rose up out of the concrete warehouses and petrol stations dotted along the edges of the city. As the car reached the top of the flyover, Armando took his foot off the gas and let the car glide into the shoulder of the road. He stopped the car, his big frame pressing back in the seat, the air seeping from him in a soft sigh.

'Why have we stopped?' José Luis asked.

Armando looked at him and then glanced at the skyline.

They could see across the city. The lights of all the buildings had just come on as the dusk was setting in, a canopy of glittering jewels coming to life against the thinning gloom of the gathering shadows. They saw the big wheel of a fairground, its spokes streaked with silvery light, rotating gently as though it was measuring the time out for the denizens of the city as they went about their lives; the retailers and store owners bringing their shutters down after a day of work, the bar owners and their staff stepping out, preparing to open up, ready for the night-time flow of customers from the streets. And behind that shining, shimmering wheel of silver was the large swelling shadow of the mountain, coughing up a ream of smoke, which had been rendered in a dusky red by the dying light of the falling sun.

The flyover was positioned on the edge of the city, and the air seemed cooler here, perhaps because it was away from the force and brightness of the city centre. More than that, it was as though one were watching all human life from a distance. Armando had come to this place first many years ago when he was still in Vice. The whores used to linger on the side of the road, puffing out their tits – visible in the gloom in their sparkling ruby and emerald bras and bottoms, like a set of strutting, exotic birds seeking to attract mates. The men would pull over for either sex or drugs. It was a useful place for police, not just for arrests but also for leverage. Occasionally, one of the johns would be some big city guy, a politician or a high-up businessman, and while these types of individuals would seldom see the inside of a jail cell, they could be bartered with and provide a useful source of information or support in future times, provided they were treated with 'discretion'.

The whores and the johns had long since abandoned this place; the whores had gradually filtered away after the steel and petroleum factories either closed down or relocated. Armando had always remembered the view, however. Maybe because when he first saw it, as a young, green cop, the city seemed like some glittering playground replete with lurid dangers and otherworldly experiences. He'd felt as though all those possibilities were laid out before him as he stood in this place, gazing out from the dark across a panorama of flickering dwindling lights.

Many years later, as an older man, he had bought Cynthia here; he hadn't really quite known why it was important to him that she saw this place, why it meant something to him that she liked it. He felt it nevertheless. And she had liked it. She had told him that it was beautiful, that she had never seen Puebla City in this way before. And behind it all, he had sensed something more elemental;

she was thrilled by the beauty of the city, but at the same time, this place was dilapidated and dangerous. It stank of poverty and urban decay. Despite her left-wing politics – or perhaps because of her views – he knew she liked to get close to the flame, that there was something in deprivation, in hardship, that she found authentic and compelling. It was probably why she taught in a community college, whose roof was leaking and whose students had such a high mortality rate. It was why, he sometimes thought, someone like her had fallen for someone like him.

'What the fuck are we doing here, man?'

Armando snapped out of his reverie.

Do you like the view?' he asked José Luis.

'Yeah, it's great. Houses, lights, mountain. Pretty much like anywhere else in this shithole.'

Armando looked away, his expression tentative.

'This place,' he said in a soft voice, 'has memories for me.'

'Really? Did you have your first fuck here?' José Luis's face was lurid and enthusiastic.

Armando realised that the young man was repeating what so many cops did. To have a conversation about something other than the job, something personal, cops would often retreat into a dialogue about fucking or drinking, for there were things and feelings that lay behind those kinds of subjects, which you just didn't talk about.

Armando looked at the young man. 'Hey, I'm being serious. I'm trying to talk to you here.'

His partner looked baffled, hesitant.

Armando turned away. 'I used to bring Cynthia up here.'

'Yeah?'

'Yeah. Not anymore, of course.'

118

The other policeman shifted in his seat.

Armando gave a rueful smile. José Luis looked at him, the younger man's face almost naked in its expression of wide-eyed concern.

'I mean, I knew you split up with her and stuff. Everyone knew,' José Luis said.

A car flashed by them. The night was falling now.

'Well, whatever. In any case, we came up here, Cynthia and me, and not just to fuck. We'd look out over the city, and it was always beautiful to her. In fact, I actually planned to ask her to marry me here, can you believe that?'

'Why didn't you, *hombre*? Why didn't you?' The young man's voice was animated.

Armando looked out across the skyline again. He spoke in almost a whisper, 'Sometimes life just doesn't go your way. You don't get round to doing the things you should do. And eventually … it's just too late.'

The younger man went to speak but then closed his mouth again.

'You're … not always the easiest person to talk to, you know?' he finally said. 'Sometimes I think you think I'm just some stupid idiot. That you don't take me seriously. That—' José Luis frowned as though his words had taken him far too far.

Armando looked at him. 'I know I can be a little short at times, but I know you have my back. And that's the important thing, right?'

'Yeah, for sure, *hombre*. You can count on me. We're partners.'
Armando smiled.

José Luis continued, a little more hesitant this time. 'So … Cynthia? Where is she now?'

119

Armando's smile thinned ever so slightly. 'Last I heard, she was living somewhere out in Mexico City.'

The lie had come easily, automatically.

'But don't you think—'

Armando raised his hand. 'That's an issue for another time, *chico*.'

José Luis's face fell. Even though Armando had spoken softly, the young man felt as though he had been cut off again.

Armando looked at him. The whole conversation had come surprisingly easy to him; the false intimacy he was creating, the trust which José Luis craved, the lies about Cynthia which had slipped so naturally from his lips. He looked at his partner, noting his imploring eyes. Finally, he came to the subject that he had been leading up to all along.

'I wanted to talk to you about something else as well, José. Only it's a bit …' Armando searched for the word, '… unconventional. It's something I need you to keep between us two. At least for the time being. Can you do that?'

José Luis nodded.

Armando looked at him for a few moments longer, hesitant and appraising.

'I came upon a case a couple of days ago while you were busy with the Lopez robbery. A murdered woman, young. Her body was found in the grounds of a church.'

'Okay. So, what?'

'Well, I took some pictures of the cadaver.'

Armando took out some Polaroids that he'd had developed. Some he'd taken at the scene, and others were from the autopsy.

The younger man flicked through them. 'What … the … fuck?'

'Exactly.'

120

'What the fuck?' José Luis repeated.

Armando chose his words carefully. 'The way the body has been positioned, the way it has been … attended to. It's out of the ordinary. And I've been doing some research.'

'Research?' José Luis was blank-faced.

'Yes. In my view, there's something ceremonial about this killing. It's not about a client murdering a whore. It's not about some random *mujer* raped and strangled. It's about …'

Armando struggled to form his thoughts. He thought about all those museums that Cynthia had dragged him to, all the strange and monstrous displays.

'… art,' he finished.

José Luis bore an expression that bordered on horrified incomprehension.

Armando realised he was in danger of losing his mark. He frowned as he sought to explain himself.

'Cynthia used to drag me to these art exhibitions. Some of the stuff, *hombre*, you wouldn't believe. They'd make statues out of street trash, and one of these crazy guys made a picture of a volcano using his own blood. The pics often sold for big bucks, so to me, it was just another example of rich people with more money than sense. I never thought about it again until I saw that body in that church courtyard. As soon as I saw that, I thought about those exhibitions. I think this guy is doing something similar, something like that. This isn't about an everyday rape-murder, a simple run of the mill *fuck-and-shut*. It's something ceremonial. It's …'

He paused.

'… the work of a serial killer.'

José Luis's eyebrows rose. 'Like in Hollywood movies?'

'Yeah, I guess so. This type of thing hasn't been recorded all that much. But we've had several in Mexican history – several real-life murderers who kill on that basis.'

'Have you told this to the captain?'

'Nope. Just you.'

'But you got this body autopsied, right? You signed off on that. That right there … that's gotta be hundreds of pesos, an expensive procedure. It would've had to have gone through command.'

Armando's eyes narrowed. 'Normally, yes. But with everything that's going on – with the *federales* and the bodies that were discovered in the canal and the mayor and the issue of publicity – I thought maybe now isn't the best time to add another issue into the mix.'

José Luis cocked an eyebrow sceptically. 'What is it that you're asking me to do, Armando?'

'Nothing. I'm only after your opinion.'

José Luis flicked through the photos again. 'It's fucked up,' he muttered. 'But serial killing – that means a pattern, multiple bodies. I don't see how you can establish any pattern from just the one.'

Armando allowed an element of irritation to creep into his voice for the first time. 'Someone who does something like this? So grotesque, and yet so specific, so planned out … You think that's the first time they've done it? This had vision, scope. There are more bodies out there. We only have to find them.'

José Luis frowned thoughtfully. 'I don't know. The stuff this guy has done with her eyes and her … you know what. It's bizarre, for sure. It's shit house crazy, in fact. But maybe it's just a way of covering up actual evidence of what's just a regular fuck-and-shut after all. Maybe whoever did this … Maybe it's just a fucked up strategy of misdirection. Or maybe the perp was high on drugs. People do fucked up things when they're high.'

Armando turned away in frustration. He had prepped the young man, offered José Luis up certain intimacies from his own life to gain his full confidence, to at least have someone else onside. But now, the young man was showing independence of mind, which Armando hadn't anticipated.

'Do you have anything else?' José Luis murmured.

Armando felt his certainty and confidence wane. Then he remembered the evidence he had in the plastic bag in the back seat. He reached back and took it out: the figurine made of strands of wood, its black eyes and open engorged mouth.

'This was found next to the body.'

José blinked in surprise.

'What is it?' the older detective asked.

'My wife has got something like that. Cristina has the same thing. The same type of design, the same wood, everything. It's just like that!'

Armando nodded. Now he was getting somewhere.

***

They headed out the next afternoon, driving through the suburbs. José Luis was strangely quiet.

Armando took one hand from the wheel and *snapped* his fingers. '*Companero! Estas alli?* Are you with me?'

José Luis had the window peeled down, his arm outstretched across it.

'I dunno, man. What are we doing here? Chasing our tails? I haven't even logged out on this.'

'That's okay, pal. I've chalked this down as a routine follow up to a 647, lewd conduct – specifically, flasher in the park. No need to take a witness statement if they don't remember details and don't wish to pursue it. For the next few hours, we'll be *incognito*.'

'Yeah, okay, but I was supposed to be helping Munro with an actual crime, a series of burglaries.'

Armando threw him a wry grin. 'Yeah, but you and I both know Eduardo Munro is a grade "A" asshole!'

José Luis gave an involuntary smile. 'Yeah, okay, Arman. But this … this is something else again. I tell you that Cristina has something similar to what you found in the church, and you think that might be the link to a serial murderer? It's a little far-fetched, don't you think?'

Armando looked out the window at the blue sky. It was warm, coming close to sundown. He felt the breeze tickle the underarms of his shirt as the car glided towards the edges of the city. Pursuing the case on his own terms made him feel, in some way, free. He thought about those days he would drive out with Cynthia to the Pacific Ocean in the late summer.

He glanced at José Luis and smiled. 'Far-fetched? Maybe. But don't forget what Confucius used to say: "From small acorn grow big tree!"'

'Confushee who? What the fuck, man?'

That momentarily buoyant sense of freedom and optimism suddenly seemed absurd, and Armando felt embarrassed by his attempt at humour.

'What do you want me to say? We've got to start somewhere, don't we?'

'Yeah,' José Luis said in a voice that Armando found incredibly whiny. 'But there must be thousands of these weird doll-figures out there. What's the chance of this actually leading to anything?'

'Right or left, right or left?' Armando snapped.

'Right, second right!'

He pulled the car into a side street. They were driving through Barrio de Analco, one of Puebla's oldest and poorest neighbourhoods. The population was largely indigenous, full of street vendors and alcoholics. Armando did not hate these people – like some did – but he didn't understand why they couldn't shape up and pull themselves together. You could only blame Christopher Columbus and *conquista* brutality for so long. After several centuries, it was time to get over it and turn the page.

They pulled up in a side street, which looked as though it had succumbed to some kind of disease, swollen eruptions of upturned concrete fissuring across it like lesions. Municipal dustman, cleaners, and street maintenance people rarely made it this far afield. With his car windows cracked open, Armando couldn't blame them – there was a stench in the air, a sweet mouldering heavy decay.

Armando glanced at José Luis. 'Cristina does her shopping *here*?'

José Luis shifted in his seat. 'Yeah, well, my wife – she gets these hippy notions. She doesn't come here a lot, mind you. But … she feels these people have a real spiritual side.'

Armando didn't need to ask which 'people' José Luis was referring to.

They got out of the car and made their way through the gap and into the market. A makeshift banner fluttered in the air. It read: 'Tianguis de Analco'. The smell still lingered before they stepped from the road into a raffish but pretty place. Various market stalls were topped by frilled roofs of purple and red fabrics. The contents underneath flowed forth in a deluge of colour: the blue and white of porcelain plates, the blood-orange and cream of various shawls and scarves, the sparkling silver of hundreds of trinkets set against a dull, dark backboard – a myriad of bright that reared up in a profusion of blushing, colourful flowers.

As the two men made their way deeper into the market's central aisle, Armando found himself aware of a different type of smell – the rich, charcoal aroma of succulent sizzling meat. He broke off and went to the stall that was selling it.

'How much?' he said, pointing at a twist of brown, sinuous meat, his belly aching.

The old indigenous man behind the grill gazed at him, his eyes set into a burnished brown face wrinkled with the lines of time. 'That there is the best meat. Two pesos – a bargain. You won't get it any cheaper.'

Armando turned to José Luis.

'You see that?' he said as though the vendor was not there. 'He says it's the best meat, but he doesn't say what type of meat it is.'

The old man gave a wry smile. 'Well, my friend, it's *carne*, the typical beef. Only, it's the part that's cheap, but also the best, that part of the gut, and the best is on the inside. You … you do like this …'

The old man threw his head back, opened his mouth, and made a delighted *slurping* sound for several seconds. He looked at the men as if to confirm his delight.

José Luis whispered to Armando, 'I think that's how he eats pussy.'

Armando chuckled.

For the first time, the vendor's face fell. 'Hey, I say two pesos, but I also say you try some for free. If you don't like, you don't pay.'

The old man's face had lost its bright humour. He was earnest now, resentful even. He took a slice of the meat, pressed it into paper, and pushed it at Armando.

The bulky detective, somewhat taken aback, took the offering and popped it into his mouth.

Armando chewed on the rubbery oily meat, and as he bit down, it released a colder, more gelatinous substance from itself, an ooze that trickled into the back of his throat.

The old indigenous man was smiling, nodding, as though this was confirmation of something he had always thought.

Armando's eyes widened in horror and disgust. He spat out the broken-up food. 'Is that what you people call fucking food?'

The old man at once became conciliatory. 'It's free. No charge, okay? No charge!'

Armando opened his wallet, dug out some coins, and flung them at the vendor.

'Take those. I'm not a freeloader, unlike some,' he said with disdain.

His throat contracted as his stomach lurched; he barely managed to stop himself from vomiting. His eyes were burning.

To his side, José Luis was bent over, heaving with repressed laughter.

Armando snarled at the younger man. 'I can't believe you let your wife shop in this shithole!'

José Luis laughed all the more.

Armando managed to recover his dignity somewhat and added, 'Just tell me where exactly Cristina bought the damn thing.'

'I don't know, *hombre*.' José Luis shrugged, still smiling. 'She only told me it was somewhere in the *Tianguis de Analco* market.'

The two men moved on and looked around. There were all sorts of stalls with decorations and figurines, but none of them had what Armando was looking for. Eventually, the market stalls came to an end, and they found themselves in another street. The light was fading now. Armando noticed a liquor store – and just past it, in another store, he caught a glimpse of the types of figurines that resembled the one he was looking for.

He strode inside. The woman behind the counter looked about fifty, but she could have been thirty.

You can never tell with these people, Armando thought.

He took the figurine out of the bag he'd brought with him and raised the wooden effigy to her. '*Tienes algo así? Do you have anything like this?*'

The woman looked at what he was holding up. Something in her eyes changed, shimmered. Without a word, she reached up and pulled down the metallic shutters. The *clicking* sound of a turning key seemed amplified in its finality.

Armando blinked; he couldn't quite believe what had just happened. He felt the anger build, that same anger, which came so quickly. He shuddered and moved forward. His hands were shaking; he felt as though he was about to rip the metal panel from the side of the shop and slap that bitch so hard that her dull-eyed complacency would be wiped away. Then she would understand that some *fucking indigenous bitch* didn't get to dictate terms, especially when she was dealing with the *bona fide* representatives of the Mexican state.

As if detecting his anger, José Luis placed his hand on Armando's arm. 'Let's keep going, eh?'

They went further down the street and came to another indigenous shop filled with trinkets, pipes, and alcohol. Again, they recognised the same style of effigies.

Armando showed his to the proprietor and once more caught the change in the other man's eyes – but this time, it was one of abject fear.

Once again, the guy turned away from them, preparing to shut up shop, but Armando grabbed his arm.

'Not so fast, little indio man. You're going to talk to me!'

The man, small and elderly, was trembling furiously.

Armando relaxed his grip. 'You're not in trouble. I just want you to tell me about this.' He put the effigy on the counter. 'Tell me what you know about it.'

The man shook his head. A shadow had fallen across his face. Armando couldn't understand why the vendor was so afraid.

He looked at the other man and tried to calm him down. 'Hey, listen, this is no different to the stuff you have up there.' Armando motioned to the various wooden figures on sale in the shop.

'No,' the vendor's husky voice finally arrived. 'Not the same. This …' The man indicated Armando's effigy. 'This … It's … *him! Mictlāntēcutli.*'

'*Mictlāntēcutli*? What does that mean?'

The man behind the counter crinkled his face in a look of cowering fear.

Armando felt another rush of anger. He took hold of the old man, raised him off his feet, and pulled him over the counter.

Armando mouthed the words deliberately. 'We can do this the easy way or the hard way.'

The man's body went limp as he began to wheeze.

Armando did not loosen his grip. 'Do you stock these?'

129

The vendor looked at him with dead black eyes. 'No, *nunca* – *never!*'

'Do you know who does?'

'I don't know anything.'

Armando *slapped* him across the face. 'Do better.'

A woman stepped out from the shadows behind them. As she caught sight of Armando, her eyes widened.

'You … you just let him go,' she said in a trembling voice. 'You let go of him right now.'

As her eyes found the figurine, her gaze was transfixed, as though beholding something serpentine, something that held poison.

'If you don't stock this, you need to tell me who does.' Armando snarled.

The woman was large, but she moved swiftly. She took a pen, tore a strip of paper from a newspaper, and scribbled on it. She flung the paper towards the figurine, her eyes never leaving it.

'There, that is the address. It's the only place that would ever stock such an … abhorrent thing. Now, you let him go. He has a weak heart!'

Armando relinquished his grip, and the old man fell to his knees, panting.

The woman was looking at him now, those small shrewd black eyes gazing right at him. The hatred coming off her was palpable. The *rasping* sound of the old man's belaboured breathing seemed to scrape through Armando's head. He took the scrap of paper and held up the manikin one more time.

'Why are you people so frightened?' he asked contemptuously. 'It's only a few bits of wood. What does it mean, to make you so afraid?'

The old man's lips were flecked with saliva. He was still trying to catch his breath, but this time, his lips curled into a malevolent smile. In the shadows, his eyes appeared utterly black.

His voice arrived in a rustling whisper: 'It means that you're already dead. You just don't know it.'

Eight

In the background, the TV *crackled* – the image was particularly bad tonight, a *buzzing* static from which shadows of distant images and shapes emerged but nothing cohered. Armando could hear the rain *pattering* against the roof's corrugated iron. The effigy was on his table, and in the evening gloom, it shone with a dull ghostly light. Even though there were two hollow circles where the eyes should be, the wide skeletal grin and deep sunken cheekbones gave the mannequin a strange sense of expressiveness. Its bone arms were crossed, shielding the skeletal torso underneath; it seemed at one with the blackness of the room, the gathering gloom, as though it were calling these things to itself as it grinned from the shadows.

Armando shivered and took a slug of whisky. The effigy should have gone back to the station basement floor to be marked and packed with all the other items of evidence, but something had held him back. That same something had stopped him from putting the church Jane Doe autopsy through the normal channels.

It was what police called 'a gut feeling'. Along with thinking things out rationally, he also had to listen to his gut once in a while. Sometimes, one's life depends on it. That … intuition, that sixth sense, was something every cop worthy of the name relied on.

Armando thought about the indigenous people he had encountered at the market and their fear of a simple wooden doll. He felt great contempt for them, for such ridiculous superstition. But perhaps that 'gut feeling', which he made use of, was not all that different. It represented the point where the boundaries of the rational world began to fade before more nebulous and mysterious instincts and forces.

He looked at the effigy as it smiled out from the dark. *Mictlāntēcutli* – the old man had called it. Armando had noted that down as soon as they'd left. He wondered what the word meant.

He thought about that old man – his small, dark beady eyes gazing up, glistening with fear and loathing. That was another thing about being a cop. The hate. He felt it from everyone all the time. It was rarely about screaming violence. It wasn't often in your face. But that hate … it was in people's eyes, it was in the curl of their lips, the way they stood. It came off them as something palpable, a dark heat. It worked its way into you.

Armando took another hit of whisky and rubbed his eyes. As the alcohol melted into him, he felt a gentle numbing, the kind of feeling he had more and more these days. The shadows crept across the walls with a floating inevitability. The flickering, familiar light from the TV threw into relief the gloomy solitude of a living space, which was both familiar and lonely. Loneliness had crept across him now, almost like a second skin, so gradually that there were times when he wasn't even aware it was there.

He was closer to fifty than forty; he felt as though he were entering into the twilight of his life. He could see the figure of his future self, shuffling through the apartment – an old man, sinking into the couch, holding up a glass of whisky in one trembling hand, drifting off to sleep with the TV still on. He would never have relatives surrounding him again. Cynthia was long gone. The few friends from his youth had fallen by the wayside, and he had the soft certainty that it was in this place where his existence would finally trail away, peter into the darkness with a gentle lack of ceremony, the TV still flickering in the background. Sometimes in the night, that moment seemed close, seemed to press against him, in the loneliness, in the solitude, and his big barrel-like chest heaved and contracted, struggling for breath in the dark.

He took yet another drag of whisky. The bottle was empty now. From outside, he heard a commotion, the opening and *slamming* of a door. Footsteps. Raised voices.

With a sigh, head thrumming, he got to his feet, a heavy, boozy movement carrying him to the door before he stepped out onto the landing. He saw Celia standing by her doorway in the dull fluorescent light, her eyes wide, her face streaked with tears. She was usually so ironic, so composed. Now she looked dishevelled and exhausted.

He walked over to her. 'What's wrong, Celia?'

She looked up at him with shimmering eyes. 'I had a fight with Cristóbal. I gave him money for schoolbooks. But he spent it on music tapes instead. I know it's hard for him sometimes. We don't have a lot of money. He doesn't have what some of the other kids his age have. He was always such a sweet boy, but these days … he's just so angry all the time.'

Armando took her in his arms and was suddenly aware of how slight she seemed, how fragile women could be, even the strong ones.

They stayed there like that for a few moments before moving apart.

He touched her face, raising it to his. The left side was flushed in a pink hue, the skin swollen. 'He hit you?'

She flinched and looked away. 'It's not his fault. Like I said, it hasn't been easy for him.'

Armando brushed a lock of hair away from her forehead. 'Feel better, Celia,' he murmured.

He turned and went back down the corridor, down the stairs, and stepped out into the night. His destination was already set; the local late-night liquor store. He bought a bottle of whisky and a pack of cigars.

Back at his apartment building, he sat down on an old chair in the lobby. The air was cool and mouldering, always thick with damp. Outside, the rain resumed its *patter*. He took out a cigar and lit it, puffing in the gloom.

By the time Cristóbal returned, Armando was on his seventh cigar. He inhaled smoothly, causing the tip of the cigar to flare, a smouldering red glow in a sea of soupy grey smoke. The eyes of the young man caught the light from the cigar. He was startled when he saw the outline of Armando sitting squat in the chair, watching him through the fog of smoke.

The words tripped from Cristóbal's lips, high-pitched and on edge: '*Mierda*! You made me jump!'

At once, the young man tried to recover himself; his voice assumed its practised tone of sardonic awareness.

'What are you doing, Armando? You meditating or something? Thinking about the meaning of life? Funny, you don't really strike me as much of a thinker.'

Armando didn't move. He just watched the young man.

Cristóbal's voice rose again, the words were shrill: 'Is this what it looks like to have a night out at your age, Armando? A trip to the lobby with a bottle of booze and a cheap cigar. I mean, if that's the case, you might as well kill me now, eh?'

A short giggle hiccupped from his lips, a jumpy, hysterical sound.

135

Armando got up slowly, exhaling with a heavy sigh. 'I was waiting for you. I thought you might like to have a talk.'

Cristóbal's eyes narrowed. 'Yeah? You wanna talk to me, man to man? Give me some good ol' fatherly advice. "You gotta buck up, son. Take life more seriously. Be a man!" That kind of thing?' He gave a mirthless laugh. 'Well, that's one way into my mother's panties, I guess.'

'Now that right there,' Armando said, sounding thoughtful. 'That's not a nice way to talk to me. And it's definitely not a nice way to talk *about* your mother. When you talk like that, you don't make a good impression at all.'

Cristóbal's grin widened, his dark eyes shimmering with malicious glee, and he went to say something else.

But Armando punched him before he could get the words out. It was a quick, glancing blow to the side of the young man's jaw, with hardly any power behind it. But it was enough.

The young man jerked and danced backwards before he folded and landed on the floor hard. Cristóbal's eyes were wide, whites of shock and disbelief. His nostrils flared as his flimsy chest expanded and contracted furiously as he fought to take in a breath. He made a sound; it was as if he were trying to say something, but instead came a single, unarticulated noise, an animal-like grunt: 'Ughh'.

Armando looked at him in the same way he might a long, segmented worm unearthed and exposed under the midday sun. He noted with distaste that Cristóbal's nose had started to bleed, long reams of lucid slithery red liquid.

How did that even happen?

Armando had caught him a glancing blow to the side of the face purposely to avoid that.

He looked at the young man, his fine features, his pale white skin, the dark dye on his eyes and lips; he looked more like a slip of a girl than a man.

Armando was seized by the certainty that Cristóbal was indeed a faggot, a *maricón*. A new wave of anger and hatred washed over him as the boy squirmed on the floor, his face slick with mucus, blood, and hot tears. Faggots were always 'bleeders', the slightest touch, and they would start bleeding their faggoty blood everywhere.

Armando moved forwards and took hold of the boy's legs, so Cristóbal was flat on his back. He dragged him to the centre of the floor and forced the boy's legs apart.

'No, please, no ughhhh.' Cristóbal was trembling.

Armando spoke softly, deliberately. 'I'm gonna give you some good ol' fatherly advice. You gotta buck up, son. Take life more seriously. Be a man!'

Armando pressed the bottom of his foot into the young man's testicles.

Cristóbal screamed.

Armando took his foot away. 'I need to know you're going to do better by your mother, Cristóbal.' He pressed his foot down again.

The teenager screamed again.

'You know. Give her a compliment now and then. Perhaps even buy her a present on the odd occasion. Do you get what I mean?'

He put his foot down once more. Again, that ragged scream.

He raised his foot one final time.

The young man's voice came out in a broken gasp. 'Y-yeeesss! P-pleeease.'

Armando was about to say more when he felt something smack against his arm. The impact was almost insignificant; it barely moved him, for Celia's body was slight in comparison with his, but she shrieked with a violence that rent the air.

'You bastard. Get the hell away from him. Get the hell away from my son.'

Armando stepped back, surprised. He hadn't heard her approach.

She fell to her knees beside the prostrate form of her son and pulled Cristóbal to her, rocking him in her arms.

She spoke through choked sobs, 'It's okay. Oh, my baby. Oh, my poor baby. It's going to be okay. I'm here. I love you so much.'

Armando looked at them, and for a moment, both mother and son had the same face – the same large, anguished eyes, the same weeping femininity, slick and visceral, spilling out in a deluge of liquid and self-pity.

He looked at Celia. Looked at how her makeup had run. Caught the crags of skin that fissured from her eyes. Her lips pursed and sour. Glimpsed the whites of her breasts already sagging like deflated balloons. He saw all of this, and it seemed impossible that he could have ever wanted her. Her son could beat her black and blue for all he cared; what business was it of his?

'Don't. You. Ever. Come. Near. Us. Again!' Celia said in a bitter, violent whisper.

Armando looked at her for a few moments longer. Slowly, his lips curled into a lurid grin. Then, he picked up his whisky bottle, took another pull, and walked back up the stairs, whistling as he went.

He opened the door to his flat and stepped into the darkness. The TV was still on; its flickering glow cast across the shadows. He sank into the couch and poured the rest of the whisky into a glass. But when he raised the glass to drink, he noticed his hand had a slight tremble.

He drank some more.

As he gradually slipped into unconsciousness, as the shapes and definition of the room around him faded into black, the last waking feeling he had was the sense of the effigy on the table. The feeling that it was watching him from within the dark.

***

Armando went to Septimecielo in the late afternoon. He walked through the doors of the club and into the main hall. Although shutters had been drawn down over the windows, light filtered through the gaps in wide slats of bright, which revealed the torn, worn-out leather of the black seats that ran along the wall. The floor was coated with cheap alcohol and cigarette ash, along with the occasional splash of vomit or a stain of black blood, which had dried out in the afternoon air. In the light of day, it seemed a crust had grown across the place – a lacquering of all the rotten effusions of the previous night, and the flat air was pervaded by a putrid sweetness and the sour tang of mouldering damp. The whole place reeked of despair.

Filippo, the bouncer, was leaning over a table in one corner, wiping it with a squeaking wet rag. His whole flaccid frame was wobbling with the effort; even from a distance, Armando caught the thick rustling sound of his breaths, like the rumblings of a choked, overheated boiler.

Armando slapped him hard on the back, causing him to groan and fall forwards across the table. Panting with anger, the fat bouncer forced his hefty body around to confront the author of the surprise attack.

He gasped. 'Motherfucker.'

Armando stepped back, raising his hands, his face breaking into a helpless grin.

'My bad. I didn't know you'd go over like that. You usually seem so …' He looked meaningfully at the bouncer's bulk '… robust!'

Filippo glowered at him.

Still smiling, Armando said, 'So, the little shit has got you cleaning the furniture like a maid, eh?'

The bouncer's eyes were dark beads of resentment set into a pudgy, angry face. 'You shouldn't talk about him like that!'

Armando mock-frowned. 'I'm surprised he didn't give you a sexy little maid's outfit to slip that fat ass of yours into while you go about dusting and cleaning and stuff!'

The larger man's bottom lip trembled, and his expression became peevish and malicious.

'You, what would you know? The only respect you get, Armando, is because you carry around a shiny plastic badge. Without that, you're nothing. But the boss … he has faith in me. He can see my potential. He thinks I'm management material, and that's why he made me head of security.'

Armando looked at the bouncer, his pancake face flushed with the effort of delivering this particular revelation. Despite himself, Armando felt something like pity for the other man – perhaps because Filippo was so stubborn, so deluded.

'That's good, Filippo. I'm sure that title is gonna work wonders on your CV. Oh, and by the way … where is your boss?'

The bouncer nodded towards the left, his small porcine eyes still shining with resentment.

Armando wandered over to the other end of the club floor, passing the podium where the strippers would dance and around towards the bar at the back.

Juan Carlos was sitting on a stool with a drink and a bottle propped up on the bar. He didn't register Armando's presence at first. Finally, he spoke in a soft but definitive way.

'Ahhh, Armando. I thought you might have come to see me before now. The way we left things last time … it never sat well with me. But the point is, you are here now.'

'The way we left things?'

'Yes, precisely that. You seemed to react … emotionally the last time we interacted. Indeed, I would go as far as to say you got rather neurotic.'

Armando threw him a grim smile. 'You mean when you shot that woman in the leg with a crossbow?'

Juan Carlos's eyes flared into life, and the sculptured whiteness of his youthful features contracted into the sharp lines of bitter fury.

'No,' he snapped, 'not a "woman". Only a "whore". I shot a whore with my crossbow, and you know what? Despite her gimpy leg, she still shakes her titties most nights on that podium over there.'

Those patrician features relaxed into the type of smooth placid beauty, which was vampire-like in its bloodlessness.

The young man looked at Armando with a voluptuous smile. He spoke lightly this time.

'And it's the oddest thing … After the cripple has done her broken, jerking dance, there are more men lining up to take her into the backroom and fuck her than before she was injured. Before she was a gimp. What do you make of that, eh?'

Armando said nothing.

Juan Carlos gave a shrill giggle. He raised his glass; the thick, lucid liquid inside shimmered white in the gloom.

'Well, let me ask you something else. Do you know what this is?'

Armando sighed. 'It looks like a glass of rum.'

'You're right. It is indeed a glass of rum. But it is more than that. In fact, it is a glass of Rhum Clément. Do you know what that is, Armando?'

'No.'

'It is the most expensive brand of rum in the world. It's bottled at Habitation Clément in Le Francois, Martinique. It's the Mecca of rums. The bottle I'm drinking now is a 1952 – worth about twenty thousand pesos, which makes each glass around one thousand pesos a pop ... Would you care for one, detective?'

Armando felt the overwhelming need for the drink, not because the rum was luxurious but because he needed the sting of alcohol more and more these days. But he would not be beholden to the bratty lunatic any more than he already was.

'I'll pass,' he replied.

'Hmm. It must seem obscene to you – a single glass of this must represent some months' work in your department. I guess you drink something more down to earth ... Cheap whisky from a late-night liquor store, right?'

'Whatever you say,' Armando muttered.

Juan Carlos downed his rum, got up, and walked to Armando, looking up into the older man's face.

He spoke cloyingly sweet. 'That's okay, Armando. You drink your drink, and I'll drink mine. It denotes the people we are. The truth is: there will always be a world of difference between a Rhum Clément and the cheap stuff you drink. That's why ...'

Juan Carlos raised a hand and brushed his fingers across Armando's shoulder as though he were scattering away dandruff.

The young man's voice continued in a sibilant whisper. '... you should never have put your hands on me. You should never have even presumed to touch me. Do you understand this, Armando?'

Juan Carlos was so close that Armando felt the warmth of his breath against his chin. He bristled; he felt his own physical strength, the potential to simply reach out and smash both his hands across the temples of this repellent, pristine, pampered little creature.

Instead, Armando said casually, 'Knock the whole Godfather performance on the head, will you? I've seen that film too. You don't worry me too much. You're a jumped up little prince strutting in Daddy's shadow. But as big as Daddy's gang is, don't forget: my gang is bigger. We have twenty-six state police forces alongside over a thousand municipal forces. That equates to some three hundred thousand men. That's a whole army of cheap whisky drinkers right there.'

Juan Carlos stepped back, his face creased with humour. 'For a big man, you take everything so personally, don't you, *hombre*? I was only busting your balls. I love cops. They form a vital part of my company!'

The sound of a toilet flushed in the background.

Juan Carlos's face lit up. 'What perfect timing. This is exactly what I mean. Meet a friend of mine ...'

A tall, thin older man emerged from the bathroom.

On instinct, Armando's right hand moved underneath his jacket.

'Armando, may I present Hernando Martin. Hernando is my man. He works for me full time – gets to enjoy the best of life in his retirement. He drinks the best rum any time he wants. You could take a leaf out of his book,' Juan Carlos said.

Martin nodded at Armando.

'And on that note, gentlemen, I need to use the little boy's room myself,' Juan Carlos added.

He left the two cops alone.

Armando looked at the other man.

Martin gazed back, his grey eyes flickering and appraising.

'I knew you when I was coming up,' Armando murmured. 'You caught the Actinver Cholula Bank case in the early eighties. I remember that because it was big at the time, and those guys had worn clown masks. They shot everyone nevertheless. But you got to them. What you did was in all the papers. You were ... a real somebody. How does someone like that end up working for this guy?'

The older man's eyes never faltered. His voice was gravelly. 'Before you get all misty-eyed about the past, rookie, remind me why you're here again?'

The toilet flushed again.

Juan Carlos emerged from the bathroom.

He handed Armando a large paper envelope, enacting the gesture theatrically as though for Martin's benefit.

Armando winced.

'Hey, what's the problem?' Juan Carlos asked with mock playfulness. 'Take the cash, Armando. Maybe buy yourself a better brand of whisky, eh?'

144

Armando took the envelope from the young man's hand, avoiding the eyes of the older ex-cop. He heard Juan Carlos chuckle but didn't turn around. His head was throbbing with violence.

As Armando exited the club, Filippo waddled up to him, a wide grin plastered across his fat face.

'Hey, Armando,' he said with a guffaw. 'Perhaps you should be the one wearing a maid's uniform. Perhaps you should be—

Armando turned towards the fat bouncer, his face expressionless. Without preamble, he punched Filippo in the face hard. He had not pulled the punch in the same way he had when he'd hit Cristóbal. He hit Filippo full-on, putting his solid bulk into the blow, and the twenty-stone bouncer fell back onto a table, which buckled and collapsed under his weight.

Stepping out from the club and into the light, Armando felt as though he could breathe again.

Nine

He picked José Luis up in the early evening, and they drove to the Santa Clara District, out to the west. The place where the outskirts of the city met with the dark brushlands of the *tierra* – the scarred, barren terrain marked by the purples and greys of a strange, alien soil, and the skeletal cacti, which protruded from the ground in ragged fingers of brittle green. Desolate and lonely, the deep hues of the craggy landscape seemed somehow not of this world as they stretched into the distance only to fade before the dark silhouette of the great mountains. Santa Clara was on the very edge of the *tierra*, the point at which the thin winking lights of civilisation gave out before the timeless dark beyond. Armando had been directed to this place by the old indigenous lady in the market. Places like this were strange, more like village outposts than city boroughs. Often, their local magnates, big men, or religious institutions created a culture of informal laws and networks, which meant their communities remained in some sense independent from the life of the city as a whole.

A bloody sunset was melting over the plain of clouds as they stepped out from the car, the chill in the air palpable. The shadows were starting to move – sleeking from the edges of the streets, creeping from the corners, gradually swallowing the pools of evening light.

Eventually, they entered the main thoroughfare, where the pale blues of the evening threw into sharp relief the dark elegant shapes of palm trees. Bright neon signs on old, dilapidated buildings advertised the various bars and strip joints. The reds, blues, and yellows of these lights fused with the smoke that belched from cars crawling their way across the strip, such that the vapour was tinted with a deep, otherworldly glow. Young women flitted out from the steam seamlessly. Their lithe bodies swayed like spectres, floating towards the two men, their haunted faces illuminated by the strange light, their blood-red lipstick grins overwritten by dead stares.

Armando flashed his badge a couple of times, and the women edged away, watching the policemen warily with strange, spiteful gazes.

'And the angels told Lot the time of judgment was nearing and hastened him to get out lest he be a victim of the evil of that place,' José Luis murmured.

'What?' Armando asked.

'Something I had to memorise as a boy. It's from the Bible. Genesis. The story of Sodom and Gomorrah. How God destroyed that city.'

Armando glanced at his partner. 'You really believe any of those stories are credible?'

José Luis smiled, but it never reached his eyes. He whistled through his lips.

'Not until now,' he said in little more than a whisper.

Without ceremony, he crossed himself.

Armando looked at the young man with a trace of bitter amusement.

'What?' José Luis asked.

'A true little Catholic. After some of the things we've seen, it's a few teenage whores in scanty clothes that get you reaching for your Bible and screaming damnation.'

'You don't believe in God? Are you some kind of atheist?'

Armando pursed his lips.

'What I believe—' He peered into the murky gloom. '— is that we have just found our street. This is it. Calle Fuencarral.'

It began to rain, a cold hard rain.

They turned away from the main promenade, heading down a sloping cobbled street where the darkness was punctuated every so often by the weak flickering of a gas lamp. The buildings here were even more broken, even more derelict, but there was no gaudy brightness or neon signs to paper over the decaying concrete and old black windows, which formed gaping cavities of shadow within the gloom. A single rusty metal sign hung from one of the crooked buildings. It read: 'Nevermore'.

'This is the place,' Armando murmured.

They pushed through the door, which caused a bell to *tinkle* in the wet air. Inside, the interior was a little brighter, and at first, Armando thought it was just some kind of pokey furniture and decoration shop that sold various knick-knacks. The kind of place which, in another lifetime, Cynthia might have taken him to. But once the room's details became clearer, the hairs on the back of Armando's neck prickled. A large glass cabinet, which might normally be reserved for watches and jewellery, instead displayed the jagged greying silver of jutting swastikas and Nazi military medals.

He moved deeper into the store and found machetes and swords, their thick and serrated blades shining dully in the dim light. Further on was a video section. Armando perused the titles – most had cheap, improvised, low-quality covers. Armando recognised some from the Faces of Death series, which recorded fatal accidents, shootings, and executions. He knew the brand because a good few of its scenes had come from Mexico. Next to these were films with pictures of naked big-breasted women and various farm animals.

Armando's head began to ache.

He walked up to the counter. A large Confederate flag hung on the wall behind it, the hard outlines of its garish red, blue, and white drawing his gaze. He recognised the flag from a documentary on the American Civil War that he'd watched a few months ago.

In the backroom, he heard someone shuffling about.

He rapped on the counter. 'Hey!'

A large, thick-bearded man wearing Ray-Bans wandered out of the backroom. His faded orange T-shirt, which barely covered a hairy belly, read 'Beer Season' and had a picture of a beer can sporting antlers. Armando was surprised; the man was a Yankee, a gringo, and though Mexico had its fair share of those, he wouldn't have expected to find one in a place so far off the beaten track.

'Don't nobody in this godforsaken hell hole of a country know no manners? Why don't you try an "Excuse me, sir" like educated folk?' The proprietor's Spanish was fluent, but his thick Texan drawl clogged up the words.

'Because we are the authorities here. And you don't look like "educated folk" to us,' Armando replied.

The proprietor lowered his sunglasses, peering at the two policemen through watery blue eyes. The pupils were tiny dots, barely visible against the strange ghostly *azul* of the corneal rings. The proprietor seemed to stare right through them.

He's completely blind, Armando noted, catching sight of the black cane by the man's side.

'I always have time for law enforcement. In a country with a large population of savages, the rule of law and order is essential.'

Armando caught a sudden scent, a mouldering odour, the warm, fetid smell of bruised seeping fruit, and then a kippery tang like rotten fish. He heard a low penetrating *buzz* from the backroom – the sound of swarming flies. He saw the images of those women on the covers of the videos in the barnyards with the animals – their lurid grins, their dead-eyes – and he saw the hard, violent edges of the swastikas. All at once, other images intruded … A cascade of pain and death … He saw the blackened corpses in the drained canal … The inhuman, shrieking expression of the woman from the churchyard, whose jaws had been wrenched apart.

He looked into the pale eyes of the proprietor of the shop, saw the nothingness behind them, and noticed the gringo's beard. It was flecked with tiny reams of white gelatinous fat, the residues of food that hadn't made the journey to the mouth successfully and looked for all the world like shimmering pallid maggots clinging to the spaces between the thick bristling hairs.

Armando blinked.

The blind man's wet lips unfurled, sluglike, in a ghastly smile. 'How can ahhh help you, officers? Ask me your questions and ahhh give you my answers.'

José Luis stepped forward, cringing with disgust. 'Why don't you start by telling us exactly what the fuck this place is, you sick—'

Armando shot José Luis a violent look, but the blind man didn't seem offended one bit. In fact, his lips curled all the more sensually, as if pleased by the question.

'This right here, this place right here, my hot-blooded young friend is history.'

He reached out his arm, groping, and found the fabric of the flag, running his fingers along it reverently.

'This is the problem, with your country and mine. People forget their history. We forget the things which make us who we are. And when you forget who you are, you lose your identity. Your bloodline gets polluted. You're overwhelmed by lesser races, and you don't even know it's happening. But the place you are standing now, yes sir, this here is a temple to memory. To all the people who refused to relinquish their roots, their originations.'

Those translucent blue eyes flickered. The Yankee's blind gaze was focussed intensely on something in the middle distance, something neither of the policemen could see. His lips were slightly parted in an expression of eerie wonder.

José Luis had moved to the other side of the store, and now he waved his hands up and down.

Armando turned.

Despite his blindness, the proprietor, too, cocked his head like a bird responding to movement.

José Luis nodded towards a selection of old wooden dolls.

Armando instantly recognised one: it was a larger version of the effigy from the church – skeletal chest, swollen holes for eyes, the gaping grin demented and macabre.

Armando spoke carefully. 'You talk about memory. Well, that's why we are here. We're investigating an item, which you might have sold. I need to know if you remember. It's an effigy made from coral tree wood.'

Armando took out his notebook, flicked to a later page, and peered at the word. 'The name of the figurine is Mict ... lāntē … cutli.'

151

The blind man's lips widened in a reptilian smile, his crystal-blue eyes glowing in the gloom.

'Ah yes,' he said, as though savouring something fragrant, '*Mictlāntēcutli* – the Aztec god of the dead.'

'Aztec?' Armando let out a small breath. 'I'm surprised you stock Aztec icons as part of your … memories. The Aztecs were indigenous people. A "lower race", no?'

'I guess it all depends on your system of classification, *chico*! Me, myself, I am a traditionalist, a man of classical tastes. So, I generally rely on *El Maestro*.'

'*El Maestro?*' Armando queried.

'The man himself – Adolf Hitler. He used a five-fold raceology. The Arians at the top, the Slavs or Baltics at the bottom. The Führer never talked about Indian type savages in the continental Americas, hey-hey, but by my reckoning, he would've put them all pretty much down at the bottom.'

'So again … why the Aztec memorabilia?'

'The Aztecs were a lower race. There's no doubting that. They were tainted by negritude. But they were impressive nevertheless because they made themselves more than their biology. While the other tribesmen were swinging from the trees with their monkey brethren, the Aztecs were the only savages to develop writing. They were warriors, overmen, and they subjugated all others. They believed …'

Those pale blue eyes grew wistful.

'… they believed in blood sacrifice. They thought that bloodletting released a mystical energy, which kept the universe moving, the planets out yonder turning, the suns a' burning. And in their way, they were right. Our world is run on bloody violence, detectives. The great men of history have always known this and did not shy away from the consequences. One time, those Aztecs, they killed damn near a hundred thousand in a single day.'

The proprietor whistled under his breath.

'That there shows some kind of vision. Some kind of imagination. As a man, you gotta admire that!'

Armando asked the next question casually, as though the two men were just shooting the breeze. 'And what kind of customers do you get? What kind of people seek out your "memories"?'

'All shapes and sizes, detective, all shapes and sizes.'

'Do you remember anyone in particular? Do you remember someone who showed a particular interest in the Aztec stuff, in Mictlāntēcutli?'

The proprietor squinted shrewdly.

'It's hard to remember who comes through that door on a dark night, detective. I've been down here for years now. The people who come through that door ...' He pointed a finger towards his unseeing eyes. 'The people who come through that door ... To me, they are just shadows. Shadows in time. They could be angels. Or they could be monsters. But tell me, detective, which one are you looking for?'

The blind man grinned from the shadows.

'Thank you for your help,' Armando said curtly. 'We'll be in touch.'

The blind man cocked his head. 'Anytime, detective. Anytime. I'm always here.'

When Armando and José Luis stepped outside, the rain had gotten stronger. It fell in hard sleek lines, forming rivulets of water that rushed across the rickety cobbling of the winding alleyway, creating a black stream.

From somewhere deep inside Armando's head, the sound of the water was amplified until it became a distant roar – water so powerful that it might wash away the dirt, smoke, houses, people, and the city itself in the onrush of one vast, surging wave. His head was aching. He needed a drink.

They moved deeper into the alleyway's murky darkness until the slope plateaued out, and they arrived at a wide black strip of derelict land. Some of the working girls were huddled near a couple of men, haggling over prices for drugs, while elsewhere, the homeless gathered around metal barrels filled with debris, from which flickered the mournful light of weak fires.

Eventually, the rain abated, but it was cold this close to the *tierra*. The icy winds were carried across the flatlands from the mountains in the distance before finding this scattering of individuals huddled in the night with their cold, frosty breaths.

Armando found a vendor roasting some kind of dark meat on spits, with an accompanying selection of beers. He bought three cans, cracking open the first and knocking most of it back in a single gulp.

The two detectives moved away from the people and to the edge, where the concrete platform gave way before a sleek, silent river. The water was thick, black, and still, but in its darkness were reflected thin threads of blurry orange, the refractions of the winking lights from the city's edge.

Armando closed his eyes.

He felt José Luis tug on his sleeve. 'What the hell are we doing out here? And that creepy old gringo – why didn't you brace him? He had more to tell!'

Armando took a deep swig from the second can. 'He didn't know anything.'

'How do you know?'

He looked at José Luis and furrowed his brow as he gazed out across the black water.

'First of all, the blindness. The chances of him providing any kind of witness description are low, to say the least. But more than that … Despite all his talk about the master race, I think that was one frightened old man. He may have lived here for years, but you can be sure he has never felt at home here. I doubt there's anywhere he calls home anymore. But did you notice how keen he was to talk to us, about his stock, about his beliefs?'

José Luis nodded thoughtfully.

'I don't think he has a chance to talk to people all that much,' Armando continued. 'He would have told us about our man if he knew anything about him. He needed to talk. I bet my left nut that he has some pokey little room above his pokey little shop. He stays open as long as he can, putting off that moment when he has to feel his way upstairs, to sit alone in the gloom. He's got no one else. His life is pretty much fading away in the dark.'

José Luis looked at him. 'But all that is just speculation, not police work. I mean, how could you know something like that?'

Armando's lips tightened ever so slightly. Something changed in his eyes. He continued gazing into the velveteen blackness of the night river.

'Armando, I … I didn't mean to—'

'This is my fucking case, junior. You're just here for the ride. Don't forget that,' Armando snapped.

José Luis made to say something more but thought better of it.

The silence stretched between the two men, palpable and numbing, like the cold air.

Armando turned a little but didn't meet his partner's eyes. 'You know, José, what we do, it's chess, not chequers. We play the long game, and we look for small details. You think we didn't get anywhere tonight, but we know a little more.' He handed the other man a beer. 'We know that the effigy is most likely Aztec in origin, so that opens up another branch of possibilities. And that store, so small, out here in the sticks – who's going to know about a place like that? Most likely a local. I bet my other nut that our man lives around here, or if he doesn't now, he has at some point in the past.'

Armando looked past the river and out to the flatlands and the strange silhouettes of the plants, their skeletal-like fingers pushing out of the hard, bleak earth. He looked beyond the barren flickering shadows of the steppe and towards the forms of great mountains, which arose in the night, welding the heavens to the earth.

When he spoke again, his voice was more conciliatory. 'You can be sure that the body at the church was not his first. He's been out here, doing what he does, for a while now. He has been with us for some time.'

Ten

It was early afternoon when Armando walked up the steps of the police station. He furrowed his brow, raising a hand before the glare of the light. He squinted and blinked, at which point the height of the building cancelled out the sun, and then he moved into its shade. As the brightness dissipated, the figures of a dozen uniformed men materialised, and he took in the group of *federales* who were positioned at the station's entrance, their motorbikes angled against the concrete. They watched him approach, their machine guns protruding from one side like mechanical outcrops, which flowed from the thick black metallic body armour they sported.

Their heads rotated, following him, with eyes unseen from behind dark visors. Armando knew this was part of their gig. They were more than men – they were the forces of fate, nemesis, figures raised above local populations and cities, the determined ruthless servants of a higher federated power, and so on. But Armando also knew that behind the uniforms and armour, they were just men – as he himself was a man, despite the power he had when he flashed his badge. Just like him, these men shat, drank, ate, and wanked in their spare time, so he found the whole cold, dispassionate ruthless charade to be annoying. As he moved towards the front doors of the building, he unfurled his arm in their direction before extending his middle finger.

Inside, those milling about on the office floor seemed muted. Distracted.

His captain, however, registered his presence immediately, sticking her head out of her office door. 'Detective, a word. Now.'

He wondered if she was going to bust his balls. It was a Monday, and he had missed her little pep talk – the small speech she gave each week designed to 'gee' the forces up, to remind the men that she was one of their number, the great general who shared in their battles, even though she rarely removed her fat ass from her chair. He hoped that was what he was about to be subjected to – for he could just mumble his apologies and tune her squeaky voice out. Only, he felt sure it wasn't going to be that easy. That she had something else in mind.

'Take a seat, detective.'

He sat in the flimsy plastic chair in front of her desk. Neither Armando nor his boss was particularly slight, but whereas she reclined in a broad black leather chair, his bulky frame was squashed between the hard back and the short plastic handles of this little seat. They did the same type of thing to criminals in the interview rooms – they put them in short, low, ill-fitting chairs because it diminished them physically, and that often carried over into a suspect's psychological state, even if they weren't aware of it. Armando felt angry inwardly because the management used the same frame of reference for its subordinates.

'Do you know why I asked to see you, Armando?'

Here we go.

Armando knew what she was doing. Two things: First, ask an open-ended question, which suggests to the person being interrogated that the interviewer has information about them that they are not aware of. Thus, putting them off balance and coaxing them into talking more freely.

Second: Go from using a generic name or title – 'Detective' – to a more familiar or personal assignation – 'Armando'.

He observed such tactics with deep contempt but crinkled his face into a good-humoured smile.

'Well, yeah. Yeah actually. I got an idea why you wanna see me. I think it's got something to do with the word –"commendation".'

Ximena Ponce gave a wintery smile.

'That's very amusing, detective. But no, that's not why you're here. Take a look at this.' She took out a folded newspaper and opened it.

Armando saw the blurred black-and-white image of a canal and the shapes and hunks of the human forms, which had been exposed after the water had been drained. The headline read: 'The Ladies of the Lake'.

'Those are the buzz words, detective. "The Ladies of the Lake". That's what they have dubbed it. The photograph was taken, the press has caught it, and all hell has broken loose. Exactly what the mayor wanted to avoid! And you were the one who was entrusted with closing down the scene, making sure that this couldn't graduate into some kind of public panic.'

'Hey,' Armando said, speaking for the first time with genuine feeling, 'we did exactly what we could. We closed down the scene as quickly and efficiently as possible. It's not our fault if some sneak took a quick flash!'

He paused for a moment before adding, 'Anyway, I wouldn't worry too much, ma'am. Stick to the mayoral line. Just keep telling everyone that those dead women all ended up in the river because they all got really sad and decided to do themselves in. They were, each and every one of them, suicides. People would probably buy that coming from you. What with you being a woman too.'

159

Ponce paused. She went to say something but then blinked and adjusted her glasses.

'What with me being a woman too,' she echoed. 'I guess that's why you think I am in the position I'm in, using my feminine guile, manipulating people, never doing any real work, of course.'

Armando's smile was frozen on his face, his eyes unmoving.

You got that right.

But he didn't say a word.

She tittered; it was a cold laugh. 'Well, I shall take that silence as agreement, detective. And that makes me sad in a way. Do you know why? No, let me tell you why … In some ways, we're not so different. I am a woman, yes – as you have managed to notice. But that also makes me an outsider in the job. I'm no María Félix, and I'm no Marilyn Monroe. I didn't get to this position by giving out furtive blowjobs. I had to use my guile. I had to think outside the box. I had to come to solutions that macho men like you would never have conceived.' Her voice had risen.

'But at the same time, you are an outsider too. In one way, at least.' Her tone lowered. More controlled. 'People always think that the boss, locked up in her office, doesn't see into the life of her employees. Doesn't really know what's going on. But I do notice the way people are with you. The other guys, they talk to you, they tolerate you, but they don't like you. I think that's perhaps because you're on the outside.'

She turned a photo frame on her desk towards him. It showed two smiling teenage girls.

'Even though men hate taking orders from me, I don't mind all that much because, despite the resentment and hatred I experience in this place, every night I go home to these two miracles of creation. Most of the men who I direct enjoy that same privilege. But you don't, do you, detective? I mean, for a while, there was a woman in your life – Cynthia, right? – but you never managed to make that stick, did you? You're all on your own in the world. After a certain age, a man without family, without kids … Now, that's the type of man I would start to question, detective. The type of man we haul into our interrogation rooms every day of the week, no?'

Sick fucking cunt.

Armando felt hatred rattle across his brain, *clickety-clack*, like a steam engine. His fists were white balls on his thighs. He wanted to reach across the desk and dig his fingers deep into her eyes. He wanted to make her scream. He wanted to pull her ugly, pudgy face off. He had to take an even breath.

'I get the feeling you want to say something to me, detective. Please do feel free.'

He raised his eyes; they were white with loathing. His heart was pounding, but he didn't say a word.

'Okay then. If you don't want to say anything else, let me add one more thing.' She looked at him, her expression sour. Her voice reduced to a harsh whisper, 'Tell me why I have been footed for a bill for an autopsy I didn't sign off on?'

All the rage drained out of him then. He realised that his boss had always been moving him towards this point. The conversation, the meeting – it had all been about this. And he knew, if he said the wrong thing, he could be out of a job.

'What autopsy?' he asked.

'You know very well. The body that was discovered at the Lady of Refuge Parish. I understand that you did this – that you had it autopsied without going through official channels – but I need to know why.'

'Boss,' he said, taking a much more deferential tone, 'I had no idea that I hadn't run that body through the books. I visited the penguin – I mean Arturo Herrera – and in my mind, I had already run the body through the official channels. I guess the trauma of seeing something like that, something so awful, made me sloppy. Boss ... I am so sorry.'

Ponce gave a tight smile. 'Okay, detective. I guess I'll have to take you at your word. But you still need to explain why you sent the body for autopsy in the first place. Given the lack of witnesses to the incident, given that the body has almost zero chance of being identified – why did you push this Jane Doe through processing, and at such cost to the state? What was going through your head?'

Armando's mind raced. He thought of several, fleeting explanations, but they were all too weak, and he was suddenly aware of the sharpness of the other's technique.

He stuttered momentarily. 'I think ... I think this one's different.'

'Different? How so, detective?'

'I ...' He felt his voice decompress. 'I think that this Jane Doe ... is the victim of a serial murderer.'

Ponce reclined in her seat. 'Really, detective?'

'Yes,' Armando said, beginning to speak more quickly. 'The body was marked in ways that suggest something ritualistic, something religious almost. To support this, over and above the specific mutilations, a wooden doll – relating to certain pagan rituals of blood sacrifice – was also placed next to the corpse—'

'Dear God, man! Mexico has a high murder rate. Nobody is denying that. When violent men are high on meth, coke, and whatever else, they tend to decorate their horrors in any number of weird and baffling ways. However, the notion of a serial killer is one that belongs to gringo movies rather than actual historical fact. At least here in Mexico. And certainly in Puebla.'

'What about Francisco Pérez? What about Macario Canchola? What about Juarez de la Benedición?'

The captain blinked. 'Pérez? Some "puro chaleco" who raped poor women and then had to shut them up? Someone who was arrested in what … the late nineteenth century? The most surprising thing was that he got caught. Hundreds, maybe thousands, of men indulged in that self-same activity. And nobody even noticed them. Macario Canchola? Oh, you mean "Mexican Jack"? Some retard who tried to pretend he was Jack the Ripper, another gringo inspiration, to get some attention for his pathetic, miserable life.

'As for Juarez de la Benedición, as far as I can remember, he was keener on fucking farm animals – only a couple of women happened to get in the way. In any event, those are three names over a century and a half, over a whole country. And you … you have just this one single body in Puebla City. That's some leap, detective. That's a fairy story you got right there.

'Don't get me wrong, everyone likes a good fairy story, but you don't bring them into the office. And you certainly don't consider spending the resources of a state, which has to deal with real social problems on such things. You understand now, don't you, detective?'

Armando – staggered by the way she had so easily marshalled information he had presumed would be unknown to her – nodded dumbly.

'You will drop this independent investigation right now, you hear me?'

Armando bowed his head.

'Right. Now, I need to ask you one more thing, detective.'

Armando raised his head.

'Would you please get the fuck out of my office?'

Armando walked by the desks and the chairs of the main corridor of the first floor of the police station in something of a daze. He saw José Luis with Eduardo Munro and some of the other men hunched over, chuckling by the water cooler. When he passed them, they went silent.

Armando looked at José Luis and nodded.

The smile on José Luis's face died. He looked at his feet. 'Hey, Armando.'

Armando turned away and went through the exit, stepping out into the stairwell and down several steps before a feeling of dizziness overcame him. He had to lean against the stair rail. Armando tried to blink away the feeling, but now he felt something else; a thickness pressing against his chest. He started to breathe harder, to pull the oxygen in, only the weight became more oppressive. His heart thrummed, and the blood surged to his head. Panting, he fumbled his way down the staircase, staggered out through the door of the building, and moved unevenly towards his car.

His fingers trembling, he managed to slip the key into the lock and gain access to the vehicle. He was sweating, a cold sweat; he thought perhaps he was having a stroke. From the glove compartment, he took out the bottle of whisky and took a long glugging swig. At once, his heart rate began to slow, and his breathing evened out while the ache in his head rescinded into a faraway throb.

Armando closed his eyes to the pink light.

He sat in his car for a few moments longer, allowing his body to slump, allowing his mind to calm and adrenaline to abate. Just as he went to take another hit of the amber liquid, someone rapped on the window. He flinched, the hard glass of the whisky bottle pranging his teeth, its contents spilling down his face and onto his shirt. José Luis's face peered in at him from the other side of the window.

Mierda.

Armando tried to slip the whisky into the space between the seats, but he knew his partner had already seen it.

He got out of the car and got right in his partner's face. 'What the hell do you want?'

José Luis raised his hands. 'Hey, I just wanted to check in, partner.'

'Really, partner? So, you could report back to that asshole, Munro? You two looked as thick as thieves back there!'

José Luis looked stung. 'What the hell is going on with you? You come in halfway through the day looking like shit. Straight to the boss's office, and then back out here, hitting the bottle in your car in the early afternoon. I'm only tryin' to make sure you're okay here.'

Anger perfumed across Armando's brain in a red-hot mist. His eyes narrowed, his lips curled in a predatory grin.

His voice arrived in a savage whisper. 'Is that where we're at now, José? You're gonna judge me? Read me the riot act? Tell me how to do my fuckin' job?'

The other man was taller and younger but seemed to shrink before Armando, taking an involuntary step back.

'Fuck you, Armando. I was only trying to help,' José Luis muttered.

Armando's grin distorted into a vicious leer. 'Fuck me?'

He grabbed José Luis by his lapels. Twisting the bulk of his own body, Armando lifted the young man off his feet and up into the air before throwing him onto the bonnet of the car. Armando was on top of him, pushing his hands into José Luis's chest, while the other man wheezed, fighting for breath.

'You listen to me, you miserable little pissant. I don't need your help!'

José Luis's arms flapped weakly against Armando's, and Armando caught a glimpse of the whites of his eyes as they rolled back. The rage drained out of him. He relinquished his grip.

Still panting, José Luis raised himself up and pushed Armando hard. 'You motherfucker. The boss had me in her office for an hour today, trying to dig up dirt on you, on what you're doing. I told her nothing, and do you know why, *cabron*? Because I am the one … the only one … in that whole fucking building, who looks out for you. And this latest thing of yours. Not so much a case, by the way. More of an obsession. You got tunnel vision, detective. You can't even see what you're headed towards. So yeah, fuck you. You're on your own!'

José Luis spat on the ground and walked back into the building.

After that, Armando drove for a while. Eventually, he pulled over hard onto a curb, stopping outside a bar. He walked into the darkly lit interior, pulled up a stool, and downed a couple of doubles before the tempo of his drinking started to even out. Gradually, the throb in his head quietened.

The barman said something, but it was like hearing words from underwater.

Armando laid a few notes down on the bar and turned to his side. An old man raised his glass, cracking a smile full of broken, blackened teeth.

He lingered for a while, drinking. The sounds of the room seemed to blur and merge. To his left, there was a small plastic tray laid out on the bar, with several plates of food on offer. One had scrambled eggs that had been whisked with what looked like a greasy mayonnaise, flecked with slivers of avocado and red pepper, but a shade of yellow had started to seep into the frothy white – perhaps because the food had been in the open air for some time. A large fly was moving across the gelatinous surface of the eggy mixture, its strutting black form stopping every so often to feed.

As Armando watched it, everything else seemed to fade away until his whole vision had narrowed to the single point of that fly. He saw the lucid tendrils that spread across its dirt-flecked, diaphanous wings. He saw the thick black jutting hairs that sprouted from its segmented legs. He saw the vast orbs of its dirty orange eyes lit with blind instinctive greed as it hoovered into its mouth more of the mouldering liquidity from the pools of fat it had wandered into.

And now, he could hear it, too – the thick rustling of its brittle wings, the clicking of its cocked head, the sharp scraping of its forelegs being rubbed together almost gleefully.

The sounds raked through his brain. He felt a sickness in his belly, and his temples were pounding again.

He knocked back the drink in his glass and stood up shakily, leaning on the bar.

'Are you alright?' he heard someone ask.

But Armando ignored them. He moved away and stepped out onto the street. The daylight had transformed into a thick, murky grey, and all around, the rain pattered.

He got back in his car, the windscreen drizzled with water, turned the ignition, and pushed down the accelerator. As the car passed from junction to junction, he felt disembodied, like he was floating. The sound of the pattering water, rhythmic and relentless, merged with the dull pall of the sky, and the ethereal forms of cars shimmered momentarily into view before melting away in the rain.

Suddenly, the whole car was illuminated in a stark, peeling yellow light. Seconds later, he heard the *screeching* of brakes before the impact, which sent his head into the steering wheel as the car span and span before rolling to a stop. From within a momentary blackness, he heard beeping and the revving of another car pulling away.

Armando raised his head groggily, bringing a hand to his throbbing face, feeling the sticky skein of blood there.

Outside of the car, the driver who had hit him had already fled the scene. Armando was trembling but alert now. The right side of the car bonnet had a craterous dent, which was still smoking, the arch of one, front wheel warped and twisted out of shape. He got back into the car and started it. It choked momentarily and then spluttered into life.

He drove slowly, the car pulling hard to the right, but he got back home.

As he climbed the steps to his apartment, his legs felt wooden and heavy. Along the corridor, Celia's door opened, and she stepped out. She saw him, stopped, and folded her arms. She stood watching him, immobile but grim.

He blinked at her. 'Yeah?' What do you want?'

She didn't respond, just continued to watch him with hateful eyes.

He could taste the blood in his mouth. He was close to vomiting.

Still, Celia didn't move. Still, those eyes burned into him, her lips set tight, as though she were looking at something not quite human, something animal-like.

'You fucking cunt,' he muttered.

He leered at her defiantly but already felt that sense of constriction in his chest, the same building tightness, the feeling of his ribs pressing down, crushing the organs underneath. The struggle for breath made his vision shimmer, and he turned away, fumbling his keys in desperation, before opening the door and staggering inside. He was panting now, rasping for air, groping his way about in the dark of the apartment. His fingers found a bottle of whisky at the side of the sink. He drank about a quarter of it in one motion before finding his way to the couch and sinking into it. He closed his eyes; his heart was slowing, his breathing abating, so now he could feel the swelling pain in his face, the angry throb. The panic attack had passed, but a darker and equally perturbing sensation had taken its place.

Armando stared into the gloom and realised that he could feel … nothing.

That strange numbness seemed to spread through every part of him. Eventually, he stood up, the movement heavy and mechanical, and walked out of the apartment once more. He wandered through the streets in the rain. The brutalised, bruised skin of his face – the dried crust of blood which overlaid it – felt like a mask that had been grafted onto him from the outside, a barrier against all feeling.

He walked on. Heard the beeps of cars swerving to avoid him. Waited for the impact. Waited for the darkness to fall. But it never came. So, he walked some more. He walked until the rain had soaked through his clothes. Until he found himself outside her building. Her door. He knocked on it softly.

The door opened a crack.

Esmeralda peered at him through the gap. 'What do you want, Armando? You said some horrible things. I don't want to see you. This is my night off, and you're not supposed to be here.'

Her eyes widened as she took in his face. Then, she unlatched her door and stepped out, reaching for his face without touching it.

'What happened to you?'

He went to say something, to explain why he was here, but his voice came out in a croak. 'I-I ...'

He looked at the ground.

Esmeralda gently took him by the arm, leading him into the dull hallway, past the squat little kitchen, on towards the back of the apartment, and into a room he had never before been. It was warm inside and lighted by a soft orange glow. There was a shelf above a petite electric fire, and on it was arrayed a series of Russian dolls, growing in size from the smaller to the larger. Each one had the same face – the flushed spots of pink on the cheeks, the wide circles of unblinking black eyes. An old pirate's map of the Caribbean hung on one wall, replete with sea monsters and a skull and cross-bones. On the other side was a thick netting, and caught inside it were various furry, cuddly toys – giant starfish and miniature whales with large benevolent eyes, grinning out from their watery world.

The eyes were cheap stick-ons, the Russian dolls were plastic replicas – which you could buy at many cheap stores – and the map was a poor-quality photocopy. Yet, despite all this, the room had an air of child-like magic to it, full of colour, both tacky and enchanting. It surprised Armando, for he had never thought of Esmeralda's living space beyond the blushing pinks and reds of her boudoir. In some way, he felt he was seeing something more personal, more intimate here.

Salome was sitting on a small plastic chair in the middle of the room, watching Armando with lively interest. In front of her was a Monopoly board laid out on a little wooden table. Her fingers were curled around a bundle of fake banknotes.

Esmeralda helped Armando into a weather-beaten, woolly chair. He sank into it and groaned.

Salome watched him, unblinking, fully enthralled by the performance.

Esmeralda asked if he wanted something to drink.

He said a beer would be good, and she disappeared to get it.

The wide eyes of Salome never left him.

He looked at her, glanced away, and then looked at her again. 'Ain't nobody ever told you it's rude to stare, kid?'

She was not in the slightest bit chastised. Instead, she seemed delighted that his attention was on her because it opened up the situation to a question.

'What happened to your face? Did someone do that to you?'

He rubbed his temples gingerly. 'I pretty much did this to myself, I guess.'

'That is very strange,' she said matter-of-factly.

'It feels very strange.'

'Does it hurt?'

'Not anymore.'

Salome's large eyes widened with devilish glee. She spoke in an excited gabble: 'One time! There was this one time when I ran away from Mummy because I wanted to go exploring, and I went into the bushes, only the plants were sharp, their leaves were sharp because they were jungle plants, and I ran through them waving my arms …'

She made the gesture, waving her arms furiously and grinning manically as if to register the veracity of her account.

'… and my arms got all cut up by the sharp jungle leaves, and when I came out again, there was blood everywhere. Lots of blood. From my arms, from my body, and it was hot and sticky and wet!' Her eyes shone, delighted at the sheer gruesomeness of the recollection.

Despite himself, Armando let slip a wry smile.

But then, Salome frowned. 'But when I came out, Mummy shouted at me very loudly. But then she told me that the reason why she shouted like that was because she was very frightened very much and that she loved me, but I had scared her because she thought I was hurt.'

The young girl frowned harder in concentration as she tried to process the contradiction inherent to all this, to life itself. 'Do you shout at the people you love?'

Armando thought about the question. 'I shout at everybody.'

She giggled.

Esmeralda returned with a white china cup, which rattled on its matching white saucer. 'No beer. I bought you coffee instead – with a little whisky.'

She handed it to Armando, and he winced as he took it, feeling pain run up his arm. But once he sipped the rich dusky liquid, he felt a warm shiver run through him, and the tension in his body began to subside.

He glanced up at her and nodded a thank you.

Esmeralda gave a shy smile and began to busy herself with Salome's hair.

Armando noticed how alike they looked, not just their faces but their poses, the way they moved. He looked at them in this soft room and then down at the delicate saucer in his hands. He felt overlarge, clumsy, and awkward, an ogre who had suddenly stumbled into a fairy tale scene. He thought about Esmeralda's kindness and remembered what he had said to her that last time, and something caught in his throat.

He coughed and looked away.

Esmeralda spoke to Salome. 'Armando is going to take my place, *princesa*. He's going to be the car.'

Esmeralda looked at Armando.

'I am going to prepare something for your face.'

Salome watched as he picked up the dice and rolled a one.

She laughed.

He moved the car one space.

She took her turn and rolled a three.

He took another sip of coffee.

They played for a few minutes in silence. He lost 6,000 pesos; she made 9,000.

Salome suddenly straightened in her chair as though she had received an electric shock. 'When I am older, I'm going to have more money than you. I'm going to have more money than me!'

She held up her Monopoly money in one bunched fist.

'I am going to have more money than all of the Monopoly game. And I'm going to be able to buy all the toys I want!'

Armando fought back a grin. 'You think cops make that much?'

'I'm not going to be a cop.'

'When I spoke to you before, you said you were.'

'Well, I'm not now.'

They stared at each other from across the Monopoly board.

173

Finally, Salome spoke again. This time, with great dignity. 'I am going to be an explorer. I am going to discover the lost city of El Dorado and all its gold. And after that, I'm going to find all the silver of the secret Potosí mountain, and finally ...'

Her eyes glinted with wonderment.

'Finally, I'm going to find the secret tunnels that run under Puebla City. And then I'll be famous.'

Armando chuckled. 'You got one problem, kid – El Dorado doesn't exist. Potosí isn't so much of a secret, and its silver got used up years ago. And those secret tunnels running under this city ... That's just a fairy story.'

'No. No, it's not,' Salome challenged. 'My friend Jorge told me all about it at school. He even said that he's seen the tunnels. So there!'

Armando regarded her seriously. The kid's voice had risen in a high-pitched tremble, so he made his as soft as he could.

'Look, kid, I heard those same stories when I was your age. But nobody has ever seen them. And do you know why? Because they don't exist.'

'Yeah? *Yeah?* Well ... well maybe YOU don't exist!'

Armando looked at her with great gravitas. 'Well, if I don't exist, I probably couldn't do this.' He reached over to her side of the board and filched one of her notes.

Salome watched him, her eyes growing progressively wider, not quite sure of what he was going to do, and then shocked by the sheer audacity of what he actually did do.

She looked at him open-mouthed. 'You ... you just ...'

She burst into scandalised laughter.

Esmeralda came back with some cloths and ointment.

'Mummy, Mummy,' Salome trilled delightedly. 'He just cheated. Armando actually cheated. He stole my money. I just saw him do it.'

'Okay, baby,' Esmeralda murmured. 'Roll your dice and win it back.'

Esmeralda looked at Armando. 'Stay still. This is going to hurt.'

She began to clean the blood from his face, gently daubing it with antiseptic. He hardly noticed the stinging feeling. He was overwhelmed by something else. It had been so long since someone had touched him like that. He wished it would never stop.

When Esmeralda had finished, Salome looked at him, a strange half-smile on her face.

'I can see you now,' she murmured.

Armando felt something inside him move.

Eleven

His eyes fluttered open, tickled by the morning light. He felt the throbbing of his bruised face, but the pain was clean, the feeling of tingling damaged skin repairing itself, the feeling of cells regenerating, life returning.

Armando got up.

After breakfast, he found his toolbox and spent some time working on the battered car. With the equipment he had, there was only so much he could do, but he was able to straighten the warped metal of the chassis somewhat, which then allowed him to change the wheel. He pushed out most of the dent on the bonnet too. His body was humming with the effort of the work.

He drank a glass of cold milk, hit the shower, got dressed, and jumped in the car. He wouldn't go to the station, but he didn't want to waste the day.

He drove to the Palafoxiana Library. The same librarian regarded him with lined, doleful eyes, but he barely registered her presence.

He stepped into the main reading room and selected several books, his notebook and a small bottle of whisky accompanying them on the mahogany desk. He took the first book and began to flick through it, taking small sips from the bottle as time unfurled against the aged, dusky aroma of rich mouldering leather and the brittle crispness of antique parchment. There were a couple of other people in the library; a taller figure in the far corner whom

176

Armando couldn't quite make out, and a twitchy young man with glasses who took furtive glances at him every so often. At first, he thought the young man was looking at his whisky with disapproval. But then Armando realised it was probably because he – Armando – was speaking the words he was reading under his breath in a continuous mutter. It was a habit he had picked up at school and never quite lost.

Armando stared back, glowering ferociously.

The young man turned away and didn't look up again.

Armando frowned and returned to his reading. He looked at chapters in several books. Most were interesting but irrelevant to the present investigation. He read how Mexico had been shaped by indigenous peoples before the Spanish and their ships ever arrived: the Olmecs and the Zapotecs, the Purépecha, the Totonac, the Toltec and the Mayans – peoples who had thrived for thousands of years before the Columbine era. He saw images of the colossal stone heads the Olmecs had constructed. He saw Teotihuacan, the ancient city that existed at the time of Christ and whose vast stretching Avenue of the Dead culminated in the great Pyramid of the Sun. He saw the remnants of civilisations that had risen and fallen across the epochs and whose great buildings provided a mausoleum-like reminder of what was but is no longer – colossal husks gradually sinking into the sands of time.

When he looked up from the page, the light had changed; the bright rays of the morning had given way before the gentle blur of a blue afternoon.

He stepped out to buy some tacos from a vendor. The elements of the outside world seemed luminescent and vivid, and his eyes sharpened and adjusted, as he took in the wideness of the square and the large numbers of people gathered in it: the colourful rush of traffic and a bright red-and-blue striped tour bus from whose open-topped roof a handful of tourists leaned out, snapping with their big black cameras. He saw the modern buildings several stories high, with their peaking concrete arches and smooth Perspex windows whose dark-pearly sheen glinted in the afternoon light.

And then the view started to unravel. The cars grew fainter, the tops of the buildings lost their outline. The definition of the roads began to fade, and the sound of the traffic was muffled and softened. Now, new images emerged, clarified, and achieved definition.

Armando watched as a solemn set of figures moved in procession across the main square: men with torsos wrapped in animal hides and dark wooden masks plumed with rich, colourful feathers. They progressed in sombre fashion towards a building that was rising out of the ground. Armando saw the shape of the great, grey temple attain body and definition. The high stone steps led up to a cavernous, black entrance with flaming lanterns on either side. The lanterns cast great shadows, flickering from themselves. Thick trees everywhere erupted from the ground, and the strange otherworldly pink and blues of the horizon were dotted by the flitting black shapes of great birds. The warm breeze carried the sweet smell of burning flesh …

He blinked. He was standing in front of the taco vendor again.

Armando paid for the food, took the taco, and bit into the hot meat, the crispy shell. The sights and sounds of the city were normal again; the rhythms of the traffic, the beeping horns, the well-ordered forms of the tightly compressed buildings, the trim concrete mosaic of the city square. Everything seemed to resonate with solidity and permanence, so it was difficult to imagine a time before or a time after. Only an eternal present in which people went to work, came home, did their shopping and lived out their lives as the city ticked over.

But Armando now had a new idea for his research.

He finished off the rest of his taco, letting the greasy paper flutter to the ground, and stepped back underneath the canopy of the large library building. He found his way into a narrow, rickety aisle between two high, crooked shelves that blocked out the light. He fumbled in the gloom, peering at the titles of old books until he found what he was looking for.

A History of Puebla City.

He took it back to his seat. The young man with glasses had long since departed, but the figure in the corner, its face wreathed in shadow, was motionless. Yet, Armando sensed the stranger was watching him. He looked for a few moments before taking a sip from his bottle and returning to his reading.

The city had been officially founded in 1531 within a great valley, on the recommendation of one Julián Garcés, a Catholic bishop who was liaising with the Spanish Queen and had recognised the need for a settlement somewhere between Mexico City and the port of Veracruz. However, the first attempt at settlement failed – wiped out by one of the great floods the valley area had been vulnerable to for time immemorial. Eventually, the settlement managed to get a foothold, becoming a centre of agricultural and textile production, supplying Mexico City to the west.

Armando further discovered that Puebla City had been built on a site that had been a hub of pre-Columbian activity; specifically, the valley on which the city was constructed had been a battleground for the wars of the great city-states of the period. 'The Flower Wars', as they were known, were a response to the great floods, when the Aztec priesthood had declared that the gods were

179

angry, and to propitiate them, vast armies were sent into terrible collision. The aim was to batter the enemy into submission and then take as many prisoners of war as possible. These prisoners would, in turn, be used for the great blood sacrifices in the hope that the gods would be appeased and the floods would come to an end.

Armando turned the page to find an image from an Aztec codex, which depicted one such sacrifice. A basic drawing of a stone temple on top of a series of steps realised in black and white. On the highest step, a cartoon-like figure with an open mouth was thrusting what could have been a knife into the chest of another figure slumped over a plinth. The standing figure was in black and white, except for one arm that had been drawn almost felt-tip red, and the hand at the end of that arm was clasping a bloody heart.

Armando stared at it. Suddenly, he was back in that church's courtyard, the body of the Jane Doe posed on the table, her eyes plucked out, her heart … missing. He felt his own heart quicken.

He turned the page. There was some information about how the Codex, known as the 'Codex Magliabechiano' had been discovered, and some more on the legal battles between various interests, which had sought possession of the ancient document.

He read quickly and flicked over to the next page.

This time he was confronted by another image. A drawing of a dark figure, shrouded in shadow, squatting over a series of bloodied bones. This depiction was more modern. The figure's face was spectral, indistinct, except for the two black holes of its eyes, but its body was marked with hieroglyphics. A grey muscular arm stretched out, on top of which was perched a tawny owl with glowing red eyes. Behind the figure was the shadow of a giant spider, and above it, the shape of a bat. To one side was a large black dog.

Each animal had those eyes of dull red fire. But the figure itself – as large as it appeared – was little more than a great shadow. And yet, at once, Armando was certain he knew exactly who it was. He looked at the caption underneath the image. It read:

Mictlāntēcutli, the Aztec god of death, pictured with his familiars, bat, spider, dog and owl.

Armando glanced at the next page. There was mention of Aztec blood sacrifices and a discussion about whether the practice of capturing people as prisoners of war and then sacrificing them was any more barbaric or primitive than the millions of men who had been mowed down in the mud by the machine guns that rattled throughout World War 1. But the issue of Mictlāntēcutli trailed away; there was no more information, and the god himself seemed to retreat back into the past.

Armando was flicking his way through the last few pages, trying to catch that name again, when he felt something touch his shoulder. He looked up. The light had changed again. The library was shrouded in shadow.

The old lady was peering at him meekly. 'I don't mean to interrupt you, detective, but we're about to close.'

'Yes, yes, of course. Thanks.'

Armando gathered his things up and left.

He drove home, keeping his foot light on the accelerator, not pushing the vehicle too hard. The sun was descending in the sky. He thought the light might hold out, that he might have time to do a bit more work on the car once he had got back. On reflex, he switched on the police radio. The chatter at this point was the regular stuff – stabbings, robberies, the report of gunshots – when abruptly through the static, a new priority and code came across the airwaves. Armando didn't recognise the number – and therefore the

181

crime it referred to – but he did catch the location. Cuexcomate. On the outskirts of the city. He knew that the codified message was probably something picked up from one of the *federale* broadcasts.

Without a second's thought, he spun the battered car around and headed in the direction of Cuexcomate. He drove until the buildings began to flatten and give way before the grasslands and urged the car upwards, across a rickety muddy road, hoping that the violence of the terrain wouldn't cause the vehicle to conk out. The car protested, spluttered, but struggled on.

Armando smiled wryly. The vehicle wasn't so different from its owner.

He brought the car to a stop before a cone of white that had grown out of the ground, forming a hill. It was a place that the tourists visited, a landmass pushed up from an active volcano underneath many aeons ago. But now, there were few people, and those that lingered were all in uniform. A long yellow strip had been wrapped along a line barring entry to the landmark. Past that, he saw several sleek black and silver bikes arced on their sides.

The *federales*.

Armando made to duck under the yellow-striped barrier but was interrupted by a young, fresh-faced officer that he half-recognised from the precinct.

'I'm sorry, sir, but I'm under orders not to let anyone pass.'

Armando looked at him, his expression calm.

'I realise that, officer, but I'm also under orders – having been instructed to liaise with the *federales* as part of a twin operation,' he said, ducking under the tape.

The lanky junior officer put his hand on Armando's shoulder.

The older cop looked back at him in disbelief. 'Son, I understand. Orders are orders. But use a little common sense. I am not a criminal. I'm here because I'm also under orders. I have been told to talk to those men up there and record their findings. You didn't get the memo. Sorry about that. But sometimes you have to think on your feet. So, step back. Let me do my job. Oh, and … don't put your fucking hand on me ever again.'

This time, Armando didn't give a backwards glance. He made his way up the slope, the light from the falling sun flaring across the horizon. He caught sight of the things below, the trees leading up towards this pinnacle, and beyond them, some way out, the coppery and craterous landscape of an old mine, which had eventually caved in. Now, it was little more than a red-tinted ragged desert crater, with only a few wooden shacks perched precariously on its edges.

He swung his head around and upward, up towards the top of this strange ivory hill, and beyond to the blue-black of the sky, through which the first winking silver of the stars had perforated. He got to the top of the hill and was panting.

They were standing around the edges of the wide dark hole, which descended deep into the earth. He moved forwards in the gathering gloom, close enough to see the shape of the body in the black leather bag just as they were zipping it up. Just as the shadows thickened, he caught a glimpse of the cadaver's face before the material covered it. That was also when the first of the men saw him. What happened next was almost instantaneous.

Armando raised his hand, flashing his badge. 'Hey, fellas, I don't mean to rain on your parade. I got called up here, something on the intercom …'

The *federales*, in their dark uniforms and with visored eyes, fanned out. He tried to keep his eyes on a couple of them, but they moved so fluidly, so quickly – almost like shadows – and when

Armando turned again, another was flanking him, his pistol already drawn. Armando's voice trailed away.

Two of the men turned to one another. A rapid whispered exchange took place.

Armando felt his stomach sink, and the tips of his fingers turn cold. Fear gripped him like ice. For at that moment, even though he couldn't catch any of the words, he knew, without a doubt, these men were debating whether or not to shoot him dead.

He turned to them, raising his hands slowly in supplication but speaking loudly and warmly.

'Hey, guys,' he said, grinning. 'My bad. This is clearly your op, though why the fuck I was called out here is anyone's guess. I'll relinquish the glory … and the paperwork … to you!'

As he began to back away, his fear heightening, the image of Cynthia came to him: an emaciated, pale Cynthia in a hospital bed about to be put under, a frightened Cynthia, her eyes gazing at him from a place that could no longer see.

One of the men made a sudden movement, and Armando flinched, waiting for the sound of a bullet. But it never came. Instead, the *federale* extended one arm before opening his hand and raising his middle finger.

Armando nodded, his lips clenched in a rictus smile before he turned away and began moving down the steps again. His foot touched the ground beneath the white hill, and he felt giddy with relief. The younger cop from before came up to him again, muttering some type of apology, but Armando couldn't hear the words because he was shaking so hard. He got back into his car and opened the glove compartment, but the whisky was gone. There was just an old bottle of tequila. He took it, popped the cap off, and drank as though he were taking in life at his mother's teat.

The liquid was rancid. He spluttered some of it out, his belly heaving. But the alcohol was potent. He braced himself, held his nose, and knocked more back. This time, he kept it down.

Another feeling began to creep over him. Once his heartbeat had relaxed, he felt … rage. Those men, those *federale* assholes, had humiliated him so easily. They had made him raise his hands, gibber haplessly, and then retreat. And he hadn't challenged them in the slightest. But in his heart of hearts, the worst thing, the thing he didn't even want to admit to himself, was that those men had really scared him. They had made him feel deeply afraid.

Armando drank more of the tequila. Even though he was getting drunk, his thought attained the clarity of rage. They had their weapons. He had his. It wasn't a contest he would win. Any one of them was army trained and could shoot. He wouldn't stand a chance. But … they were on bikes. He had a car. As they pulled away, he could come out of the shadows, lights off, and ram them so hard that they wouldn't even know what had hit them. Then he could get close with his weapon.

He sat back, imagining how he could hurt them, imagining how they would scream.

Eventually, though, he realised this was pure fantasy. He wouldn't do a thing. And they could do whatever they wanted. Because they were the *federales*.

Armando had his gun resting on his lap. He touched its hard metal, metallic dust transferring to his fingers. He smelt them, the cold, sharp tang. His head throbbed again. He rubbed his eyes, took another swig of that putrid tequila, and chuckled momentarily, the sound erupting from nowhere. He thought about Salome, that strange, goofy, beautiful kid. She wasn't afraid of anything.

Wouldn't that be nice?

The anger melted into a less emotional and deeper sense of determination.

He pulled the car back, over the rugged dirt track road, and into a space between the bushes, which sprouted from the undergrowth. From there, Armando watched and waited. Sipped on the tequila. Finally, the men in dark uniforms glided by in their sleek purring bikes. A short time afterwards, a couple of local police cars followed. Now the night had claimed the hill.

Armando got out of the car, opened his boot, and took out a torch but did not turn it on. He still wasn't certain that he was completely alone.

He made his way to the shadowy outline of the hill and crept up the stone steps, which curled upwards around it. It was dark, but he could just make out the shape of his feet through the black. Above, an efflorescence of stars twinkled in the firmament, and from the valley below, the lights from buildings glowed dully like ships in a rolling, night-time fog.

He reached the top of the hill. This was where the *federales* had drawn their weapons on him, but now it was as still as the grave. He turned away from the panorama of the city and looked over the small barrier into the gaping interior of the hill. The path formed a cusp around hollowed-out depths that seemed bottomless in the pitch-black.

Armando edged his way along the path until he found the opening, which led onto a rickety steel staircase that snaked and furled its way further down into the insides of the cavernous rock formation. As he stepped onto the metal stairs, the structure trembled, and whereas before he had felt the violent fear from the physical threat of the uniformed *federales*, now something else had taken its place; a rolling elemental dread that prickled in the depths of his very being. As he went deeper into the maw, the darkness flowed over him like a black tide, absolute and implacable.

From the depths below, he heard a yawning, creaking groan; the echoing sound of the rocks, the sound of the ancient hill itself sensing something entering into its blackness. He felt the chill on the back of his neck and fumbled for his torch, sending a beam of light across the far wall of the cave, illuminating tendrils of creeping twisting plants in its ghostly light. He walked down the narrow metallic staircase, which melded into a rocky ledge before continuing its journey deeper into the hill's interior.

He was certain this was the place where the body had been discovered.

He heard the sound of something nearby, a rustle – a movement from further down – and fought to control that prickling sense of fear. He shone the torch against the wall, and with his other hand, he pulled the creeping vines away from the harsh façade of rock. He parted the thick, sinewy stalks here and there, looking for blood spatter, looking for … anything. He had almost given up hope, too, when he caught a glimpse of something.

There.

Underneath a vine, faint in the gloom, was white lettering; a series of jagged hieroglyphics set against the dark grey of the stone. At the far corner of his vision, he caught the image of something else. He shone the light in the darkness. The large black eye sockets, the skeletal grin – the effigy leered right back at him, eerily animated in the flickering shadow. He took a step backwards in surprise, dropping the torch, careening dangerously close to the metal barrier. As he got a glimpse into the darkness below, something came rushing at him; the sharp shadows of black objects hurtling upward, one of them brushing his cheek. He yelled and fell to his knees, scrabbling for the torch. He managed to find it and shine it upwards just in time to see the bats flapping through the thin halo of dark blue above.

With a weary trudge, he began to make his way back up the steps.

***

It was the strangest thing. Walking through the main floor of the police offices. Men whose barbeques he had attended on sweltering Sunday afternoons, whose promotions he had celebrated on boozy Friday nights in the cop bar 'Diego's' just a few blocks down – these same colleagues now found his eyes with cold, impassive stares, or turned away, avoiding his gaze altogether. Since Cynthia had left, he had been less involved, less attentive to his colleagues, but this was something different. It was as though he were now standing outside the herd, as though the others sensed in him some invisible blemish, the presence of some undisclosed, burrowing disease. When he was at his desk, it was like people's eyes were on him. When he walked out of a room, he had a sinking feeling they were discussing him in low, furtive whispers. A place that had once promised a sense of security and safety in numbers now seemed to be a world inhabited by alien characters, people he no longer knew.

Armando felt the need for a drink – just a quick shot of whisky – something to take the edge off, to help him think more clearly. However, he put that sense of need out of his mind and tried to concentrate on the issue before him. Currently, he needed to cook the books. He recorded entries and appointments for the next few days on his own log – a couple of robberies and an arson. Placing

188

these things on the books would buy him some time and space, the opportunity to investigate the case he was truly involved in.

He took the elevator up two floors to human resources. He would retrieve any files related to robberies, arsons, and homicides in the Santa Clara District but just concentrate on the latter. Besides, only he and José Luis would be able to connect the serial killings with Santa Clara, so anyone seeing the files he was taking out would have no reason to suspect what he was actually investigating. Despite his row with José Luis, Armando judged that the young man would keep quiet. Even for someone who talked that much, José Luis knew to keep his mouth shut when it counted.

The human resources department was airy and run with brisk professionalism, which was out of sync with the nod-nod, wink-wink mentality of other police operations – the system of patronage and favour whereby you did menial things for people in high places, made connections on the sly, and scratched the back of others so that – when the time arrived – yours would not go unscratched. But the human resources department was run on a more modern basis: you signed out the files you needed for a given number of hours and the person behind the desk took your badge number and recorded exactly what material you had requested.

When Armando arrived at the counter, he recognised the chubby figure on duty.

'Paula,' he greeted her and began to rattle out the list of things he was after, placing his badge and number on the counter.

However, he did not fail to note the lines of tension that stretched from the sides of her thin mouth, and her wary eyes.

'I'm sorry, Armando. I can't take those things out for you. You don't have clearance.'

'What do you mean? I've been coming in here for the last five years.'

He pushed his card across the surface of the counter. He was smiling, but inside, he felt a lick of desperation. He was gradually being shut out of everything, and he needed this information.

'Just record my number and put me down like usual,' he said, trying to sound normal.

'I can't.' Paula was looking at her hands. Her long nose wobbled, her red hair curled around the flabbiness of an ageing face; she wouldn't even look at him.

'Can't or won't?' he asked in a soft voice.

Her eyes found his again momentarily. She spoke more sternly, irritation creeping into her voice, as though he had put her in an intolerable position, as though it was she who was being treated shabbily in this exchange.

'Look, Armando, rules are rules!'

His heart rate had increased, so he made a physical effort to slow his breathing down, to allow his logic to intrude. 'Tell me something, Paulita ... Do you remember a couple of years back, when we were on the Christmas shift?'

She looked at him as if he were really trying her patience. 'Your point, detective?'

'We had a skeleton staff. Only a few of us. But it was the early morning. Everything had died down. You asked me if you could knock off early, see your ... boy, right?'

She wouldn't look at him. 'I don't see what that has to do with this.'

'Well, I gave you the okay. To leave early. But that was in defiance of protocol. Rules weren't rules then, were they?'

He smiled, trying to keep his voice friendly.

She pursed her lips and looked straight at him. 'Perhaps I should call the captain up here. That seems to be the only way this thing is going to be resolved.'

He moved back from the counter, arms raised. 'Hey, hey. Okay, I get it. Never let it be said that Armando doesn't know how to take a hint. It's not the end of the world. I'll see if I can get it sorted out officially downstairs and come back to you. By the way, though, how is your boy? Rodrigo, right?'

'Roberto. He's fine. Thank you, detective.'

'Roberto, right, right. Listen, I'm sorry for any awkwardness. I don't want us to have any problems in the future. I didn't mean to put you in a bad position, and I just wanted to say ...'

He beckoned her forward, and she leaned in hesitantly.

He allowed his face to form a big, beaming grin as he spoke in a genial whisper, 'I wanted to tell you that I have always considered you to be the useless fat bitch you are. I wouldn't touch you with a bargepole.'

He hawked the saliva that had built up in his mouth and throat and spat it into her face in a splashing wad of warm, sour liquid.

She made a sound, the type of noise an animal might make, a low, incoherent, unlettered sound: 'Ughhh.' Armando found that satisfying.

He walked away and took the elevator to the ground floor. His whole body was tight with fury, and behind it, the building sense of claustrophobia. The feeling that everything was closing in.

He got straight into his car and took out the whisky he had bought the night before. Took a long lingering drink of the burning liquid. He put his hand on the steering wheel and felt his breathing begin to slow. He forced himself to think. He couldn't retrieve any information here, but that information would have been, by

191

definition, second hand anyway. So, instead, he could go straight to the source. He could travel to the local police headquarters of Santa Clara and check their homicide records directly. It was what he should have done in the first place.

Armando drove carefully – his beleaguered vehicle would not survive another collision – and stopped at a store. He brought a bottle of the most expensive whisky they had and then headed off to Santa Clara again.

When he got there, he stopped in a residential neighbourhood. On a corner, he found the local police station. It had a couple of old black-and-white cruisers, along with one rusty unmarked vehicle sitting in the concrete lot. The building itself was nothing like the large complex of the central police station. It was little more than a two-storey house; a pale grey-blue building whose peeling front was painted in black lettering: 'Caseta de Vigilancia'.

He pushed through the front doors into a small, squat waiting room where the dust had gathered in thick sloughs across the hard, tiled floor. When he went to the front desk, the shoddy counter was lacquered with dirt and the scattered corpses of a hundred black flies. Despite the fact that the only light in the room was busted, and everything was shaded and shadowed by thick windowless walls, there was a dry heat that never let up, parching and oppressive. The air carried a sour scent, too; the bitter pungency of rat poison overlaid by the sickly sweet of cheap air fresheners. It took him back to his early childhood in the village – days passed in rooms like this, adults deliberate and watchful, children silent and subdued; all of life slowing to a single crawl measured out by the interminable rhythms of the beating sun and the slow, inevitable graduation of day into night over and over, unchanging, eternal.

The quiet was interrupted by the crisp rustle of the large man behind the front desk flexing his newspaper and turning the page.

Armando coughed.

With a sigh, the man got to his feet and looked at Armando with greying lugubrious eyes, underneath which hung drooping pockets of jowly flesh.

'Yes?' he asked.

Armando took out his badge. 'I'm a detective with the First Precinct. I've come to ask for some help, some information. I want access to your records if possible.'

He stared at Armando without blinking, rubbed his eyes, and looked at him some more. 'What do you want to look up?'

Armando thought about lying, trying to cover his tracks. But although these people went at their own pace, they were far from stupid. They had a good detection system for bullshit. So, he went with the truth. Or at least a part of it.

'I've been investigating a homicide. I found something near the body, which might mean the perp is from here. It's not much, but it's all I have at the moment. I thought your records might show me something more.'

Armando took the bottle of expensive whisky out of the bag and held it out.

The other man took it, examined the label, nodded, and put it under the counter.

'I can take you down if you want. But it might turn out to be a big ol' waste of time. We've been flooded out several times – the last time a few years back. The records ain't up to much, but you can take a gander if you like.'

'Appreciate it.'

The large shabby police officer came around and opened a door to the side. He ushered Armando through and took him down a narrow set of wooden steps leading into a basement. The atmosphere was cooler down there but mouldering; the acrid dank of dirty water, which had seeped into the walls and the floor, clung to the heavy air.

The officer kicked a small seat towards him before regarding him with those droll, melancholy eyes. 'Well, detective. *Mi casa es tu casa*. Good luck!'

Armando nodded. He waited until he heard the footsteps of the other man peter away. Then he took his notebook out from his jacket and a small flask of his own, cheaper whisky. He set them down and got to work.

He went through the homicide files spanning the last ten years. The policeman had been correct; they were in a sorry state. Some of the pages had been drenched with water, and the ink had run, leaving them illegible. But even the pages that had not been ruined were difficult to decipher.

The notes that the police had made were threadbare, bereft of detail. The descriptions of the crimes were haphazard, and the technical information was sparse. He sipped on the whisky as the same words tripped rhythmically through his head:

Elva Abril Santos – rape, strangulation.

Alonsa Jimenez de Fe – rape, stabbed through heart.

Generosa Ariela – rape, strangulation.

Brigada Hermosa del Lourdes – decapitation.

Emilia Margarita de la Cruz – rape, strangulation.

Sometimes the perfunctory reports were accompanied by a faded black-and-white image of a young woman, her skin pallid in death, with unseeing dark eyes.

He knocked back more whisky and read on.

From the corner of his eye, he caught a slight movement. A small shadow moved out from a grate near the floor. It scuttled forwards and stopped. Then moved again. Armando followed its journey. Then another movement. The first spider had been succeeded by a second. Its legs flickered – it skimmed across the ground like a small black ball rolling in a perfect curve. From the other side, he caught another movement. Another spider, only this one was scaling the wall upwards to the ceiling. It was at that point he felt something brush against his hand.

He looked down just in time to see the small black form scurry over the edge of his hand, and he jumped up, flapping his hand, brushing it smartly against the fabric of his trousers. He saw more of the black shapes scampering across the ground, and now they were flowing towards his feet in a single wave.

He stepped back, but as he did so, he saw another stream of black rushing at him from the other direction, and he felt a choking sense of trapped panic. He tried to raise one leg and then the next, but it was no use as they flowed upward across his body, blanketing him in a heaving mass of scuttling darkness. His mouth went to form a single scream, but the sound was plugged by the hundreds of spiders tumbling into it.

He jolted up from the desk with a violent start, his heart thudding. The room was empty. He'd fallen asleep. He touched his fingers to his face where he had felt the spiders so vividly, but, of course, there was nothing there.

He took a long drink of the whisky and forced his eyes across the devastated pages, the same relentless rhythm of the words, rape, murder, rape, murder, pattering out across his brain. All at once, the task felt utterly hopeless. Most of the words had washed out, and the remaining information was of no use.

But then he saw it. A single entry.

Mercia Laurita Sanchez.

Early '84. Some seven years ago. Sanchez's entry was different. Alongside the recognition of the homicide, a couple of other details had been added. Just two rapidly jotted, truncated sentences, yet they were unlike anything else he had come across:

'Split mandible.'

'Cavity in chest.'

He felt that tingling deep inside. A strange, perverse excitement in the face of abbreviated, unadorned death. 'Split mandible' – nothing else he'd come across had referenced such a bodily injury. In this case, the jaw. The image peeled through his mind; the Jane Doe in the church, her jaw ripped open, set in that demented, eternal scream. And 'Cavity in chest' – wasn't it possible that such a cavity was what had been left once the heart had been removed? Five words, written out in fading black pencil years ago, and yet they somehow linked Armando to the figure who was, as yet, only a shadow to him, the figure of the man he was seeking out.

He turned over the page hoping for a picture of the body, an image of the corpse – which would confirm his conjecture – and was delighted when his fingers discovered a thin square photo. However, it was not of Mercia Laurita Sanchez dead but Mercia Laurita Sanchez alive. A dark-haired girl with slightly bulbous crossed-eyes and a dull expression was looking at the camera – it was a mug shot, and next to the photo was recorded both the date and the charge: 'May 1982, soliciting'. Taken two years before Sanchez' murder, the fact that the girl had been arrested for prostitution meant everything for Armando's investigation because the

196

report had also recorded details of the next of kin, the young woman's parents, Placida and Miguel, and a contact address.

Armando noted the details down and drew a large box around them on the page. He breathed out slowly, a tension that he hadn't even known was there seeping from his body.

He packed up and left.

He stopped at a bar. Had a few drinks. Got a battered copy of Puebla City White Pages from the barman and flicked through it. Found the name he was looking for: Sanchez, Placida. In the background, an old Mexican ranchero singer's throaty voice crooned about love and suffering, but as Armando stepped into the darkness of the backroom to use the phone, the dramatic guitars and violins of the romantic ballad faded before the soft crackling behind the receiver. It was an old phone. He dialled the number, rotating the circle dial for every digit before allowing it to spin back into place.

Eventually, the ring tone *burred*, and a woman with a tired voice picked up. Mercia's mother. Armando confirmed her identity before providing his. He told her straight out that he was a cop and had questions about her deceased daughter. He asked if he could pay a visit to the house.

The voice on the other end fell silent. And then said, 'Okay.'

He could come in two days. At eight in the evening. Then the phone went dead.

Armando stepped back into the greater bar. He thought about the young woman, Mercia Laurita Sanchez, and her grainy black-and-white image, her dull, faraway eyes.

By the time he got back to his apartment, the sun had set. He felt ragged with tiredness. As he moved through the gloom, he saw a flashing red light coming from his phone. As someone who liked to tinker with technology, Armando had recently installed a new-fangled device. It was a tape recorder attached to the phone; when you weren't in the house, but someone phoned you, that person heard an automated voice inviting them to leave a message. They could then speak into the phone, and when Armando came home, he could listen to that message. Of course, these days, he didn't get that many calls. Yet, he still felt proud of his 'answering machine'. It had been finicky to set up and pricey, but it seemed to him as though, in buying it, he had purchased his own little slice of the future.

And so, when he caught sight of the answering machine and its winking red light, he felt the type of satisfaction a fisherman might feel on nabbing a large, glistening fish. He took a sip of a drink and pressed the button.

At once, he went cold.

'Well, aren't you a dark horse? I'd always pegged you for an old-fashioned kinda guy, but look at you with this swanky techno-gadget!'

Armando had recognised the soft, mocking sidle of Juan Carlos.

'I'm going to need you to come to the club a little early tomorrow. Noon. We have … things to discuss.' The voice gave a little laugh. 'See you later, alligator!'

Armando pressed the whisky glass against his forehead. In itself, the message was disturbing; the young man was volatile and unpredictable at the best of times, but mostly, Armando felt in control of the situation. He felt like he had Juan Carlos's number. The irony, therefore, was simply this: now it was the other way around. Armando had never given Juan Carlos his home address, and his phone number was unlisted.

But Juan Carlos clearly knew both.

Twelve

He got to Septimecielo just before midday. He looked at the place, the shabby exterior, the dark door leading into the shadowy interior. Everything about it was wrong. There was no one on the door. He pushed it open and stepped inside.

As he walked onto the main floor, he heard a sound in the gloom. It was music but unlike any of the pop songs that the club played while the girls danced. It was classical, the signature theme from Tchaikovsky's Swan Lake. The soft, haunting tones of a melancholy clarinet seemed almost ghostly in this place, and when he looked up, he saw a silvery-blue light rippling across the podium like the glistening shine of water in an underground grotto. A figure, a woman, was on the podium, turning gracefully to the strange, sad riffs. Only, again, she was different; she wasn't dressed in the typical thong and bra, which the dancing girls nearly always wore. Instead, she had a diaphanous white dress that shimmered in the ethereal blue light. She was swaying with her back to him. As the music got louder, he moved closer and closer, hypnotised almost by the sinuousness of her movements.

The music was building towards a crescendo, and just as the whole of the orchestra thundered into life, reaching a crashing climax, she turned to him, the blue light flickering and playing across her face. Her face had been plastered with thick white makeup, and around her eyes were large dark circles of black mascara. But what caused Armando to take a step back, to take in a breath, was the stark bloody lines running from the corners of her mouth up to her ears. The gashes of red streaked across her cheeks made it look as though she were grinning a demented, bloody smile. The image of the body in the church came to him. He felt his chest constrict, that familiar feeling of losing control of his own body, the sense of struggling for breath. But then he caught sight of her eyes. They were very much alive, glistening dark pools of desperation screaming silently from within the confines of her head. She stood looking out across the shadows, and now he was close enough to see she was shaking.

From the other side, a figure materialised.

'*Ven aqui, mi amor.* Come to me, my love,' Juan Carlos commanded.

The dancer moved towards him, and he reached out his arm. She took it, and he twirled her around him, floating her, and then he brought her down the steps before releasing her hand. All at once, the ethereal blue glow faded, and the main lights came on again.

Armando saw the young woman's face; the gashes at the side were nothing more than scarlet lipstick. But she was still shaking.

Juan Carlos kissed her cheek, and she flinched.

'See you later, alligator,' he said.

The young woman immediately retreated.

Armando looked at the young man. 'You're not well, are you? Why did you do that? Why would you paint her up like that?'

Juan Carlos raised his hands. 'What can I tell you? You see, my friend, you only know Juan Carlos, the working man. The Juan Carlos who stands at the head of a business empire, who has to coordinate the lives of his troops and send them into battle daily. The Juan Carlos who has to be cruel to be kind. However, this, my friend, is not the only Juan Carlos to know! There is another Juan Carlos entirely.'

Armando groaned, but the young man didn't seem in the least bit perturbed.

'There is the Juan Carlos most people never see. The poet, the thinker. *Si*, dare I say it … the romantic!' Juan Carlos smirked. 'That is why I like to decorate my girls sometimes. To give their lives, which otherwise lack shine, a little bit of sparkle. Between you and me, my friend, I am a romantic at heart.'

'I'm not your friend. In fact, I think you're a sick fuck,' Armando said, his tone level.

The young man blinked at him, his lips trembling ever so slightly. Then, he laughed.

'Well, that's okay. I don't blame you. After all, I'm not really all there, eh?' He pointed to his head in amusement. 'Now, walk with me. I need a drink.'

Armando felt the solid weight of his pistol underneath his jacket. Everything about this felt off, but he followed the young man anyway.

Juan Carlos poured himself a drink at the bar. He offered Armando one. Armando refused.

'Some company, perhaps?'

'I'm not interested in your girls.'

'Oh.' Juan Carlos frowned. 'No, I'm sorry. You misunderstand. That's not the company I was talking about.'

He clapped his hands, and five men stepped out of various doors of the building. They were dressed in suits, all of them carrying firearms. Private security, Armando could tell. The fifth man was Hernando Martin, the decorated detective, now retired. Martin was watching Armando with an appraising gaze.

201

Armando turned to Juan Carlos. 'What the hell is this?'

'This? This is contemplation. Reflection. Consideration. You see, I thought about what you told me the last time we met. About how your gang was the biggest. Three hundred thousand men, correct? I took your point. It was a good one. But Mr Martin here tells me that you've ruffled some feathers in your group. That you're on your way out, and they don't care all that much what happens to you anymore, Armando. I guess nobody does. However, then I got to contemplating, reflecting, and considering. It's my conclusion that your gang is no longer the biggest. You have lost some 299,999 men. You're now a gang of …'

Juan Carlos frowned in concentration as he did the sum.

His face lit up. 'You are a gang of precisely one.'

Armando felt the back of his neck prickle, a sinking feeling in his belly. He tensed, allowing the anger to return.

He moved towards the largest of the security men and raised his fists, scowling ferociously. 'Right then. Let's get on with it. Let's have you.'

His expression of bravado was, in reality, a last-ditch survival strategy. If he could incite one of these men to strike him, he was certain they would all pile in, and he would take a vicious and bloody beating. Nevertheless, in using their fists and boots, they would be less inclined to use their guns. Being carried out in a battered mess, dumped on the pavement but alive, was better than the alternative. He closed in on the biggest of their number.

Juan Carlos clapped his hands again. 'Armando, before you do anything to get yourself hurt, there is an alternative.'

Armando looked at him, his heart pounding.

'I just need you to do me a favour, that's all. Nothing much really.'

Armando waited for him to continue.

'A week from now, I need you to pick up some cash for me. Bring it back here, and then take a bag to some friends of ours in another part of town. Round trip – a one-hour drive tops. Simple. We'll even provide the car. Then, afterwards, you'll be back in that nice little apartment of yours in the lovely Chulavista la Puebla.'

Juan Carlos threw him a winning smile. Armando glimpsed the whites of his teeth. He knew he had been boxed into a corner. He had no protection now, and they all knew it.

In a last attempt to muster some kind of objection, he muttered: 'If it's so simple, why can't you get one of your men to do it?'

'Because despite your recent problems with your brothers in blue, you're still an active officer. If anybody pulls you over, that is an asset to us. People will be less likely to nose around. And the things you'll be carrying are not for prying eyes.'

Armando could find no excuses. He had no more words.

'So, I will see you next Thursday. Shall we say at eight o'clock in the evening?'

Armando nodded. He had that sense of something pressing against his chest. That need for a drink. He backed away from the men.

Juan Carlos smiled at him, a crocodile's smile. 'Don't forget this, Armandito!' Juan Carlos handed Armando a yellow envelope filled with notes. 'See you later, alligator. And never forget … you are in my gang now.'

Outside the club, the glare of the midday light hit Armando full-on, and dizziness fluttered like butterflies in his head. The faintness and the heat overcame him, and he sank hard onto one knee, scraping the concrete. The sensation of his burning skin cleared his mind.

Eventually, he staggered back onto his feet. He didn't have the appointment with Placida Sanchez until the following evening, and he knew that was a shot in the dark, so long after the crime had occurred. Now, however, the day stretched. He could not go back to the station. He couldn't face the people there.

He has me.

Juan Carlos had played his cards perfectly. Short of fleeing the city, there was nothing Armando could do but acquiesce to the young man's demands. It seemed as though his life was a single concrete room. He was standing in its centre, and from every side, the walls were drawing in, coming closer, on the verge of crushing him.

He looked at the envelope in his hand. It was thicker than normal. The light winked in the blue sky, and he saw the way it made the hard concrete shine with a brief, golden lustre. He saw a mother pushing a pram and an old lady in one of the flats across the street. She was watering purple plants that billowed out from her balcony – a streak of bright colour against the tawny brown of the building's concrete. The unexpected beauty of these ordinary details calmed him.

He took a cab back to his neighbourhood. From there, he walked to a restaurant on the nearby thoroughfare, where the chess games were played on the stone tables outside. Most of the places on this side of the street were cafes and bars, but there was one more expensive restaurant that Armando hadn't been to in years. He stepped into its dark insides, inhaling the aroma of coriander, onion, and garlic. In the corner, strings of smoked meats were suspended above a series of old barrels. The solid tables were fine-quality oak, the table cloths clean and white, and the silverware pristine.

As soon as he sat down, a waiter approached him and floated a napkin down onto his lap.

Armando gave a wry smile, for such a ritual seemed a little odd somehow, but despite himself, he felt grand.

Instead of his normal whisky, he ordered a bottle of red wine. He swirled it around in the large glass they brought him and sipped it. For his meal, he ordered a grilled bavette steak, guacamole, grilled spring onions, pickled onions, salsa ranchera, blue corn tortillas, and a side dish of grilled sweetcorn stripped from the cob, with guajillo chilli powder, epazote mayo, lime, and cow's milk cheese. He ate until he felt a satisfying warmth in his belly.

He saw Cynthia sitting in the seat opposite him, that mysterious, slightly ironic smile playing on her lips.

'I could get used to this,' she murmured happily, using the same phrase she always did whenever he'd taken her out for a special meal.

He offered a regretful smile. 'So could I, kiddo. So could I.'

When he left the restaurant, the afternoon was blooming. People basked in the light. There were some artists at work – by their feet a selection of colourful images: tropical jungles and snow-swept mountains yawning out from the hot flat pavement. He bought a pack of beers and walked lazily in the sun. He came to an empty chair by a stone table, with the black-and-white board etched onto its top, and sat down.

The man in front of him, an old black man, nodded. 'Hey there, Armando.'

'Hey there, Cheese and Bread! You gonna let me take white today?'

The old man chuckled, a rich, throaty sound. 'You know the rules, baby. Winner always takes white. And you just now done come to the table.'

Armando pulled two beers from the pack and handed Cheese and Bread one.

The old man took it, nodding his thanks, popped it open, and took a swig with a sigh. 'I'm sat here thinking life don't get much better than this. You got the sun shining. You got cold beer. And you got chess.' He pronounced the last word almost reverently, a thick Oaxacan accent shaping a voice that sounded like whisky filtered through peat. 'Dat there seem like the perfect day to me.'

He reached down to the board and made his opening, sliding a white pawn two spaces forward. He looked at Armando, his blue eyes shining.

Armando looked back at the other man. He took in the shabby grey shirt, the patchwork jeans that were riddled with holes, the dark scar that ran across the top and side of Cheese and Bread's bald head, and the tired white curls of hair that bloomed from the tops of his ears. Armando reckoned Cheese and Bread was old, eighty at least, and he probably didn't have all that much time left on the clock. Yet, although he was a homeless old man, he seemed genuinely happy. Happy to just shoot the breeze. Happy to play chess. Those blue eyes twinkled with the mischievous enthusiasm of a child.

Armando made his move.

For a while, they played and sipped their beers.

Cheese and Bread took out a couple of cheap cigars. He handed Armando one, and they puffed on them amiably.

Armando used his bishop early. Freed up his castle. Took on a more aggressive strategy. He played his chess at a quicker rhythm.

Cheese and Bread, on the other hand, had all the time in the world. He would look at the board with a slight smile, raise his hand slightly as if he was going to make a move, and then lean back in his chair, stretching his wizened body in the sleek sunlight.

'Why they call you Cheese and Bread, Cheese?'

The old man looked at him with quizzical amusement. They didn't usually talk all that much when they played.

'Well, dat there be a relic from my days on the inside. The menu den weren't up to all dat much, so most of what I ate was cheese and bread.'

'You did time?'

Cheese nodded philosophically. 'Some thirty years of it.'

'How come?'

'I was a hot-headed kid. One day, I got into a knife fight. I got lucky. The other kid didn't.'

Armando nodded, handed Cheese and Bread another beer, and cracked open his own. He had tried to open up the other man's defence with pushy and punchy attacks, but it was like trying to write the Good Book out across the crest of a wave. Cheese didn't play defensively exactly, but elusively, and over time, the more Armando punched, harried, and jabbed, the more he found his own pieces scattered and disorganised across the larger terrain of the board.

Gradually, Cheese began to pick him off. He felt the momentum of the game turn against him.

Finally, he flicked his king down with a smile. 'I don't know how you did it, but I gotta give in, Cheese.'

The other man grinned like a delighted kid and reached over, using one thin, rickety limb to give Armando a pat on the shoulder.

Then he creaked back in his chair and handed Armando another cigar.

The two of them puffed in silence for a while.

'You play clever, Armando,' Cheese said, breaking the quiet. 'You tink quick in the moment. But you don't have all dat much patience. You don't play a long game. In prison, the one thing you have is time. And from dat, you take patience. A day can feel like a month sometimes. So, you have to learn to wait. And watch. Let life do its ting. Roll with dat. Then you make your move. You feel me?'

Armando turned it over in his head. There was wisdom in what the other man said. He felt sure of it. He thought about Juan Carlos. How the young man had manoeuvred him into a corner. He'd underestimated the young man's savvy, that was certain. But now, Armando didn't feel panicked. He would acquiesce. He would give in and do what was asked of him. Only, along the way, he would also watch. And wait. And learn.

Thirteen

He arrived at the Sanchez house at 8.00 pm on the dot. It was a single floor building with a small garden that was trim but featureless. The end of the road trailed away into a steep muddy incline covered with weeds and rubbish, plastic bags billowing and flapping, coke cans of bright, battered blue-and-red tin pushing out from the ground. The incline led down into a wasteland, and beyond it, the tierra and mountains.

Armando felt the chill in the air as he rapped on the dusty metal doorknocker. A thin, angular woman with dark greying hair answered the door. Her voice was soft and grave as she beckoned him inside.

The interior was as unremarkable as the outside. Dull browns and greys. A large cabinet contained a series of decorative silver cups and plates and some photos above them. A table with a netted mauve cloth and metal candle holder with three candles forming in a trident. They were lit, their flames flickering softly. But there was a stillness to the rest of the room that was almost palpable. An old grandfather clock sat in the corner, its intricate face forged by gold and copper clockwork set into a rich wood-wormed mahogany stand. Armando found himself almost creeping through the room, anxious not to make any noise, though unsure why. The clock's time was wrong; the hands pointed to the numbers two and five, and they weren't moving at all. It was as though time itself had stopped.

The woman gestured to a chair by a coffee table. The chair and a nearby sofa were still in their see-through plastic wrapping from the shop. She left him for a few moments, and when she returned, she was carrying a tray of biscuits and two cups of hot tea.

He took one cup and supped tentatively, watching her discreetly. Then he took a bite of the biscuit. It was infused with cinnamon and a hint of chilli. It tasted good, home-baked, and he told her so.

She smiled. 'I try to keep busy.'

Armando noted how her clothes were as pristine and tidy as everything else in the house. But her fingernails, those had been gnawed away, the tops obliterated into crusty stumps.

He spoke gently. 'Placida, my name is Armando, and I am a detective out in the First Precinct. I work robberies, domestics, carjackings, and other things. But I also work homicides. I want to talk to you about your daughter. If possible, I'd like you to tell me a little bit about her. We have some new information pertaining to her case. I have to tell you that this information, at this stage, is thin, but I think … it's worth running with. Are you up to talking?'

'Yes, yes, I am,' Placida said, her voice suddenly husky. 'Where should I start?'

'Wherever you want. Whatever you feel comfortable with. And as you go, I might have a few questions, if that's okay?'

She took a breath, and then she began in a measured voice.

'It is hard to try and … sum up a life – her life – like this. I should begin at the beginning, perhaps. She …'

The old lady took another breath.

'Mercia … she was born prematurely. She was very underweight, 1.5 kilograms, which is low, even for around here.' Her eyes were focused on a point he couldn't see, with a slight smile on her face, a flickering recollection. 'Mercia was born a weak child. My husband used to call her "the runt". But she made up for that because she clung to her life from the start. She had a huge personality. And she was very beautiful, to me.

'When she was at school, some of the other kids used to laugh at her a bit because her eyes were a little crossed. And she was always wearing this big goofy grin. We used to worry about her because she would run barrelling up to people, people she didn't know. Anyone who caught her interest. One time she saw a guy in the street who was missing a leg, and she was intrigued by that, so she ran up to him and tapped him on the arm and forced the poor guy to listen to her gabbling.

'She'd run up to older kids all the time. One time, there were three older kids, I mean much older and bigger. And they were doing … these dance steps. This was in a park, see. She went right up behind them and started copying their moves, even though she couldn't have been more than five or six. But that man with the peg leg, and those teenagers – they didn't get upset or angry. Once they saw her, they started smiling, too, because … she was that type of kid, see? The type who makes you smile, even if you don't want to. Even if you've had a shitty day.'

Placida's eyes were wet with tears.

Armando shuffled in his seat. He wanted to grab another biscuit but felt like it wasn't the right time.

Instead, he coughed and mumbled into his sleeve, 'I'm sorry to dredge all this stuff up.'

The older woman's voice was thick and husky again. 'No. Don't be sorry. I want to talk about this. It's been so long since I have talked about her … to anyone.'

A silence opened up.

211

Armando was wondering how he could lead into the questions he wanted to ask. He wanted to keep Placida talking, but he didn't want to ask the type of direct or indiscreet question that would cause her to shut down. At the same time, there were certain themes he had to pursue. In all his work as a detective, it was in this kind of situation that Armando felt most inept.

Finally, he managed, 'It sounds like Mercia had a very happy childhood.'

'I think so. I really do.' Placida nodded. 'But we were worried the whole time. As a parent, as a mother, you have the evilest premonitions. Mercia was so open, so … filled with joy. Such a sweet, sweet child. In my heart of hearts, I thought it was only a matter of time before the world brought her down. I used to fret so much. I think, when you have an only child, you can't help it. But I also think she was happy. That she had a lovely childhood. I really do believe that.

'It began to change when she was a teenager, though. She stopped talking to me, stopped telling me her dreams. Puberty was cruel to her. The kids in her high school, too. She kind of retreated into herself. The other kids, they bullied her. We got the gist of that from the school. They called her names about her eyes, the way they went together, and their size – that kind of thing. It always baffled me because she was beautiful – in a funny, wonderful, lovely way.

'Every now and then, I'd see a glimpse of the joyful girl underneath, but that school, those kids, beat that out of her. Not with their fists, perhaps, but with their vile words. People say, "Sticks and stones will hurt my bones, but names will never hurt me," but I think that's one of the most ridiculous mottos anyone has ever come out with, don't you, detective?'

Armando was taken aback by the sudden directness of the question. He nodded and mumbled his agreement.

'I'd see glimpses of the open, happy child she was, but it was rare. She wasn't angry or hateful – she didn't seem to have that in her. She was just subdued and uncommunicative. One time I caught her crying quietly in her room. She tried to duck her head under the covers, but I pulled her to me. She was fifteen. My girl was fifteen years old. When I didn't give her anywhere else to go, she just looked up at me and said, "I am disgusting, Mum. I'm so fucking ugly." I told her it wasn't true, that she was the most beautiful girl in the world, and I held her close to me, but even then, I had that cold feeling … The feeling that she was already too far away.'

'You mentioned your husband, Mercia's father, briefly. What did he think?'

'Oh, at first, he said it was just a stage, an adolescent thing. Even when she started spending more and more time away from home, staying with "friends" overnight, he told me I shouldn't pay too much mind to it. He said that she was acting out because I was smothering her. That I should give her space. It was unnatural for a mother to be too involved when a kid was more or less an adult, that's what he said.'

Armando asked the next question with great care. 'And what happened when the police contacted you? After they had … brought Mercia to the police station in 1984?'

'Miguel hardened after that. Before that, he could believe that Mercia was wayward, and out late, and doing her own thing, but in his heart of hearts, she was still his little girl. Once he found out that she had been doing that …'

Placida took a quick breath.

213

'Once he found out she had been … selling her body, he got almost vicious. He called her a no-good slut, but was also angry at me. Most of all at me. He said that it was my fault. That I hadn't provided the type of discipline she needed. That I'd let her down. By that point, I was so exhausted that I believed him. He told me we had to be stronger, to not enable her. And it wasn't just the prostitution – she had a drug problem, too. I mostly agreed with him. I was too exhausted to think for myself. Or maybe that's just an excuse.'

'And the last time you saw her?'

'She came back to us for a few weeks, near to the end. She looked so different, of course. Emaciated. Her lips were pierced, and she had a piercing on her left eyebrow. She had a lot of makeup. Her lips and eyebrows were painted black. She looked gaunt. She looked … Oh God, she was so thin!'

The old lady started to shake. She closed her eyes. Composed herself.

Armando thought she was strong enough in her own way.

'But in some strange sense, that was actually a good time. I was frightened, yes – sometimes in the night, I heard her retching into the toilet. But Mercia was with me. I felt the same closeness to her as I did in the hospital when they first put her into my arms, and I looked into her eyes. In some way, my connection to my daughter was even stronger.'

Two lines of tears slipped down her face.

'I think that's what I'd like to tell you most about my child, detective. I let her down, I know this, but she never really changed, not really. Even in those darkest moments – the drugs, the prostitution – I think my daughter hated herself, detective. But she never hated anyone else. That wasn't in her. There were times when she stole money from us, when she broke promises, when she out and out lied. We had arguments, but she was never cruel. She would always look away, retreat into herself. There was a kindness there. I never knew the like of it before. And ... I won't ever again.'

The old lady rubbed her eyes.

'So, that's Mercia's story, detective. That's the story of my daughter.'

Armando looked away and then back at her. The old woman's face was fissured by time and pain; ravines wrinkled her skin, her eyes almost dried out.

Armando felt something in him change; the thought came to him of Salome and the delight that had flared in her eyes some evenings ago when she had relieved him of some money on the Monopoly board.

Armando looked around him. The room was tended to, pristine, but it didn't look like anyone actually lived in it. Certainly, there was no messy masculine presence.

'And your husband?'

'We stayed together for a while, detective, after she had gone. But a living daughter helps cement a marriage. A dead daughter rips it apart. At first, we were united in our anger. Nobody would tell us anything. We went to the police station here in Santa Clara daily. But we're not important people. And we didn't have money. At first, they brushed us off politely. Then, eventually, they got irritated.

'One of the sergeants barked at us – told us that Mercia had run away to Mexico City with her boyfriend and that everyone knew it, but no one wanted to tell us. I knew that wasn't true. But I didn't care that he had said such a thing. The only thing I could think about was my daughter. But Miguel … The way those people treated us … it fed his rage. He was so angry all the time.

'And behind it, that feeling of powerlessness. He talked about the people he was going to hurt, the people he wanted to kill – the police who had covered up the truth, and the magistrates who knew what had really happened. And, of course, he was angry with me most of all. And I … I with him. I had believed what he had told me – that I was coddling her, spoiling her, and that I should leave her alone, not give her the attention she was looking for. I had believed him because it was easier for me to do that than imagine the type of pain my child was really going through. And …' Her voice trailed away.

She raised her trembling hands up a little way, a gesture of utter helplessness.

'And Mercia's body?'

Placida looked at him, her expression now composed and directed again. 'Well, we never actually saw that. I am told that some parents want to, but part of me is relieved we never had the option. I kept going to the police station day after day. Eventually, I was told that her body had been discovered. Perhaps they found it before, perhaps after. Perhaps they only told me because I was so persistent.

'I knew it was true because they gave me the silver locket, which I had given her for her first communion. I broke down then and there, of course. I cried my eyes out while they waited for me to leave. But I was in some way also … relieved. Because it meant that Mercia had something of me to hold onto in those … last moments.'

Placida stood up and turned away.

She spoke in a clipped tone, 'I am sure you have other questions.'

'Yes,' Armando acknowledged, 'I want to know if you have any contact details of any friends or contacts of Mercia in the two years leading up to her – to 1986?'

'Yes, but only the one name. I gave it to the police at the time. It was a number Mercia left on her desk the last time – during those last few weeks before she left here again.'

'Can you give it to me now?'

'*Si.*'

Placida left the room.

Armando took another biscuit, but this time he bit into it without thinking about it, without tasting it.

He stood up and walked around the room. He looked at the old grandfather clock and the pictures in the wooden cabinet. Two pictures: the family out camping, their images not quite in focus, jumping up and down in front of a tent in the forest, and from the same setting, Mercia looking up towards the sky with a huge grin, her big beautiful eyes slightly crossed as the rain pattered and splashed over her upturned face. She couldn't have been more than thirteen.

Armando had a flash of the black-and-white image of the prostitute in the mug shot, the same large eyes, slightly crossed. The realisation that these two totally different images were of one and the same person seemed to jar.

He jolted when he heard the old lady's voice again. Placida probably couldn't have been more than fifty, but she looked so terribly old.

'Here it is, Veronica T – 0147-297-214. I saw her once, waiting for Mercia outside the house. She was doing … what Mercia was doing. Both of them … on the streets.'

Placida spoke without even looking at the wrinkled slip of paper she handed Armando.

'And did you ever try to get in contact with this person?'

'Oh yes, many times over the years. But nobody who answered the phone had ever heard of this "Veronica". And each time, a different person picked up. After a while, they just stopped answering.'

'Okay … You also told me that she, Mercia, came to stay with you for a few weeks before she disappeared. Do you think it would be possible for me to see her room?'

Placida looked baffled by the question before she nodded. 'Yes, of course. This way.'

She took Armando into a corridor and then into a far room. She opened the door.

He turned back to her. 'I realise you have already been incredibly kind, but could I ask you for one more cup of tea?'

Again, she looked baffled, but her sense of decorum, of politeness, overrode everything else. Armando knew men and women like this. People from the lower classes.

They might not have much, but they would never refuse a guest a cup of tea.

She retreated back down the corridor.

He closed the door behind her. He didn't have much time. If this had been a typical investigation, he could have ripped the room apart, looking for leads. But it wasn't.

Armando took in his surroundings. A freshly made bed covered in sheets with black-and-white cartoon pandas against a pink linen haze. Walls with glimmering posters of 70's glamour boy groups

218

with large bouffant hairstyles and glitter makeup. A small desk with a mirror. On the mirror were pictures of Mercia as a kid and then a young teen, huddling together with her friends in a photo booth, all of them giggling.

None of this came as a surprise to him; like the rest of the house, this room was preserved by the past. He swiftly took in the images, flexed his muscles, and pushed up the mattress, looking underneath towards the bottom of the wall, behind the bed.

Nothing.

He moved across the rest of the space and then returned to the small white desk with the mirror. He felt behind the mirror. He looked through the drawers. He tapped the top of the desk and then the sides. The sides were hollow – two thin balsa wood slats on either side.

He heard the footsteps of Placida, bringing the tea, and took a gamble. He pressed his fingers under one of the sets of slats.

Nothing.

He tried the other. A rustle. He forced it open. Something dropped to the ground. He managed to pick it up – a book – and slide it underneath his shirt just as the door opened and Placida entered with the tea.

Moments later, he made his excuses and stepped out into the night. He turned briefly, nodding at the silhouette of the old lady standing at the door, raising her hand. He had just stolen some-thing from her. Something precious. Something that had belonged to her daughter.

Armando got into his car, took out the book, and placed it on the passenger seat. The interview had been worthwhile, but as he went to start the car, he felt a shudder.

Something rose from deep inside him, culminating in a violent sob. He tried to take control of himself, but he couldn't. Instead, he let out a strangulated gasp.

He pushed his face into the steering wheel, the tears warm on his cheeks.

Then, he turned the key.

***

Armando drove the short distance to the Santa Clara red light district again. He parked his car in a quiet street, a block before the main boulevard, and put Mercia's diary into the glove compartment before locking it. It was lightly raining, and from the mountains on the horizon came the distant rumble of thunder. He entered the main thoroughfare, where thick night-time darkness was interrupted by the glowing neon lights of the bars and clubs. The prostitutes on the street watched him with chary eyes.

He wandered into a place called the Taj Mahal. It had a weary interior; women gyrating mechanically on the podium, while others floated towards the shadowy figures of men sitting at tables watching with dulled desire. It was like every other place of its kind. It endeavoured to cover up the peeling paint of its walls, the damp mouldering wood, and the leaky, overburdened toilets with a lacquering of exotica. Behind the main podium was a plastic water feature – a large rocky mound over which the water flowed – and the water had been lit underneath by green lights, casting an emerald glow. On both sides were miniature plastic palm trees.

The women mingling with the punters at the tables were dressed in Middle-Eastern garb – sparkly, bejewelled bras and panties – while the faces of the dancers on the stage were veiled in the oriental style, even though they were wearing nothing else. Despite the gaudy props, lights, and glitter, nothing could disguise the unsmiling eyes of the dancers, the fumbling fingers of the clients, bodies in motion, bodies in repose. Behind it all, the prosaic and mechanical exchange of cash for the type of relentless pneumatic grinding that promises a strange, elusive relief from within the great gulf of solitude that opens up between human being and human being in the dark.

Armando ordered a double whisky at the bar and pursed his lips when the barman told him the price. Nevertheless, he paid and went to find a place to sit.

He sat for a while, keeping his eyes on the stage as he sipped the whisky. He saw the security cameras and noticed which ones were recording. He took in the door to the dressing room of the girls and the shimmering one-way mirror on the far wall that allowed the management to keep an eye on the floor. He watched the girls, the ones who led customers into booths in the back of the club, and the others coming out of the toilets sniffing furtively.

He observed one girl dancing on the lap of a large and inebriated middle-aged man whose eyes were rolling. She switched off her lurid sensuous grin to give a quick curt nod to another, who moved behind the man, ostensibly to take one of the empty glasses from the table, but slipping her hand into his jacket, deftly relieving him of his wallet.

A couple of girls came up to Armando, stroked his shoulder, and shimmied in front of him. Yet even in the dark, he could tell they were not what he was after.

Too young. Too fresh.

He got up and bought another whisky, returning to his spot in the gloom to nurse it. In the background, the opening strings to "Hotel California" started to play.

Another stripper came over. She looked older, rougher. Her face was plastered with heavy makeup, but it wasn't enough to hide the lines that sprung from her eyes and the corners of her mouth; years of hard living etched into the skin like rings in a tree trunk, denoting the indelible and irreversible passage of time. He glanced at her slender forearms; she was brittle, stick-insect thin, except for the bulging balloons of her fake boobs whose scarred shiny skin was barely contained by the thin fabric of lace just about covering them. She was exactly the person he had been looking for.

She moved her body in front of him, her sallow eyes glinting at him from the dark. She reminded him of a sharp, feral cat. He took out a note and slid it into the hem of her panties. She trailed her fingers up his thigh and then across the fabric of his crotch, tracing the outline of his penis. He felt utterly flat.

He took her hand and moved it away. 'Not yet. I want to talk a bit first.'

He saw contempt flash in her eyes momentarily before the default expression of lewd artificial desire was reapplied.

He gestured for her to sit. 'So, what's it like working here?'

'Oh, baby, I love my job.' Her voice was monotone with just a hint of a foreign accent. She looked out at him from hard green eyes beneath a fringe of peroxide-blonde hair. 'Because I love life, you know? I love to drink. I love to dance. I love to . . . fuck!'

'You been here long? In this place?'

'A few years on and off, baby. Don't worry – you're in good hands.'

Armando took another note and slid it into the space between her breasts.

She giggled tonelessly.

'Is the turnover rate high here?' he asked.

For the first time, she looked slightly uneasy. 'New girls come in all the time. Some of the old ones come back again.'

'Like you?'

'Yeah, like me,' she said sullenly, perhaps detecting something disparaging in his remark.

'And what about the ones that don't come back?'

There was a tenseness to her now. He could see it in the way her lips curled back.

'I've heard stories,' he went on. 'About girls who have worked in and around the area. Have worked for months, maybe even years, like you. And then one day, they just disappear. Maybe they just up and leave – make some money, start a new life. Or maybe they meet their Prince Charming, who whisks them away to a fairy tale land of happily ever after! Or maybe they meet a different type of man, and he takes them to a different kind of place altogether.'

'I don't know about that. I come in, do my shift, while a group of raincoat types stick their hands in their pants, and then I go home. What do you want from me?'

'I want you to take a look at this picture.'

Armando took out the faded black-and-white image of Mercia Sanchez and slid it across the table.

'Don't know that person. Never seen her before.'

Armando put his hand on the stripper's arm. 'Look again, and look properly this time.' There was an edge to his voice now.

The woman took the picture tentatively. 'No, I don't know. She could be one of a thousand. All with that same look.'

'Same look?'

'Like they've been walking down a long dark path, and it's too late in the day to find their way back.'

She looked at him for a bit longer and then snatched her hand away. 'Why don't you go somewhere else? This place isn't twenty questions. It's a dance club.'

'Is that what it is?'

He watched her stride away to the little door next to the large walled mirror. The door opened, and she slipped inside.

He waited for a few moments and then raised his hand and gave a cheerful wave in the direction of the one-way mirror. He took another sip of the whisky.

In the background, the song continued, the words in English, melodic and wistful:

'And she said, we are all just prisoners here, of our own device

And in the master's chambers

They gathered for the feast

They stab it with their steely knives

But they just can't kill the beast ...'

About a minute later, the door opened again. This time a short, stumpy middle-aged woman came out flanked by two large men dressed in cheap black suits.

Ah, here we are, Armando thought.

The woman stood near to him with a grim smile. 'Hey, fella, this ain't the place for you. This is a legitimate place of business. You're making the girls uncomfortable. So, you can walk out of your own volition, or you can get carried out.'

Armando smiled. 'Well now, you got the first thing right. This isn't the place for me. But after that, you kinda went off the boil. Because I am not going anywhere, not for the moment anyway.

You think these two paid chimps give you authority and power, but they don't. You're on your own – you just don't know it yet. And the last thing this shithole is, by the way, is a legitimate place of business.'

He spoke softly and still with that amiable smile, but there was something in his calmness that deflated them, even before he had flashed his badge. The two brawny men at her side had fleshy young faces, tinged pink, but there was a slight flinch in their postures now, a hesitation, as though the menace had been sucked out of them.

Just like that, Armando had control.

'I've seen multiple violations in the short time I've been sitting here. The coke, the pickpocketing, the little deals carried through in the backrooms. I've already got enough to burn you to the ground. I only need to make one phone call, and we'll be all over this place like a rash. Do you understand?'

'What do you want?' the squat woman asked in a cold voice.

Armando looked at the two men. 'You two, fuck off!'

The security men looked at the woman.

She nodded.

Armando watched them walk away.

'What do you want?' she asked again.

Armando looked at her. 'I bet you've seen thousands of "dancers" come and go. You've been doing this for a while – measuring them up, letting them burn themselves out in this dump, all the time lining your pockets.'

The madam regarded him, her lips tight, measuring him with her gaze.

'Her,' he said, snapping his fingers in front of the woman's face. 'I want to know about her.' He slid the picture of Mercia towards her.

The madam's eyes narrowed. She didn't even glance at the photo.

She hissed. 'I know men like you. You and your friends in Vice. You're okay with your wife performing for you in the bedroom, so she can get a little hand out from you to feed the kids that week. Or the mistress you keep, buying her cheap little trinkets so that she does the stuff your nice Catholic wife is too disgusted to do. But when a woman brings it to a place like this, when she stands up on that stage and struts her stuff, when she makes those men below her cash out, night after night ... that's what you can't fucking abide. 'Cause it's no longer yours. That woman owns it now.'

Armando motioned towards the photo of Mercia Sanchez again, gazing out from her subterranean world of black and white. 'Look at her. She's little more than a girl. She's not a woman – and she's never going to be one. The only thing she owns is a cold hard hole in the ground, so look at the fucking picture!'

The madam reached out, her eyes never leaving Armando, and brought the picture close.

'I don't know her. Never seen her,' she said eventually.

'You need to do better,' Armando whispered with a ghastly smile. 'You won't get another chance.'

The madam's face soured all the more. 'I really don't know her. From what you just said, I'm guessing ... she was one of *las desaparecidas*, the disappeared.'

'The disappeared?'

'Some years back. After Las Asturias closed.'

'Las Asturias? What is that?'

The madam produced a silver case and opened it on the table. She took a cigarette and lit it.

'The old copper mine. Not too far away from here, a little out into the *tierra*. It wound down in the early eighties. Closed permanently in late 1983 – and that changed the whole area. Many men lost their jobs. It had a knock-on effect. Lots of other businesses closed down. The money drained away.'

'But not around here,' Armando murmured. 'All that poverty. All those families – and all those daughters. Places like yours must have been overflowing with new "dancers".'

'Yes.' The madam's voice was toneless. 'There were lots of girls after that, for a couple of years after. This whole street was built up during that time. And that was the time when it started happening. Sometimes a girl wouldn't turn up for work. Not out of the ordinary, you might think, but this was different. Even if she was owed money. One day, she just wouldn't come in, though her locker was still full. It happened every so often, just like that, in all the clubs. Some of the girls talked. Some of them mentioned the same man – a stranger. "Someone passing through," they said. Someone of the night. Someone who wasn't really a man at all.'

'And what do you say?'

She looked at him, her mouth set into a bitter downward curl, those hard, grey eyes glowing dully in the gloom.

'I say young women who get frightened easily, get stupid easily. There were more girls around at that time, less money, more desperation, more violence. Working conditions were … hard. A few got sucked under. Maybe they were all disappeared by one lone stranger. Or maybe they were lost to the usual suspects: drunken boyfriends, jealous husbands, possessive fathers. Who knows? But the girls got frightened, and the girls talked 'cause that's what girls do. At some point along the line, they decided to give that fear a name. To make it into a person. You see, detective, people never want to believe that the people closest to them will be the ones to really hurt them, the ones who will always let them down. So, it's easier to invent some monster waiting in the shadows, something which comes for you in the dead of night. Easier than seeing the monsters you share your life with every day of the week.'

Those grey eyes flickered as the smoke uncurled in drifting reams of grey-green light. The women had departed the stage in between shows.

Armando heard the clear trickle of the water feature at the back of the podium. Behind it, just for a moment, he heard the sound of louder water, a gradually building sound from far away. Then the lights flashed, and the next song kicked in, and the women sidled onto the stage again.

He rubbed his eyes wearily and went to take another sip of whisky, but the glass was empty.

The madam's eyes watched him, cold and amused.

He looked around him with derision. 'I guess you see this place as … some kind of refuge. Someplace away from the dangerous boyfriends and angry husbands.'

'I don't know if I'd go that far, detective. But after what went down in eighty-four and eighty-five, we changed things up. All … "private dances" were kept on the premises. We installed security cameras, and if any of the girls did meet punters for "activities" outside working hours, they started giving each other the names of those men and the places. Most of the clubs on the strip did something similar. And we ain't had a girl out and out vanish for years.'

'I am sure your ethical standards are flawless,' Armando said grimly. 'But I'm thinking to myself, despite all your talk, all this advertising, I don't know a whole lot more now than I did when I stepped into this shithole. And I still got an urge to make that phone call.'

The madam looked at him, pursed her lips, and then put the cigarette to her mouth and pulled on it before exhaling slowly.

'I don't know your girl, whoever she was, detective. I really don't. But she might not have worked in a club at all. She might have been a streetwalker. They don't have the same protections. They're invisible. Nobody sees them.'

'Your point?'

'Maybe you should move on from here, talk to some of them.'

'That would be convenient for you now, wouldn't it?'

'Yes, but for you, too, perhaps. I can give you something more … There is a woman, a fixture of this area. She's been around longer than most. In her day, they said she was the most beautiful whore ever to walk the promenade and that the most powerful men of the time would pay thousands for a night with her.'

She gave a morbid grin.

'That must have been a while ago, though, because she's not so pretty now.'

'Why are you telling me this?'

'If anyone might know a girl from back then, it would be her.'

'Name?'

'I only know her as Kassandra. But she ain't so difficult to find. Go down to the embankment by the river. Walk east half a mile. There's an old tunnel. Some of the homeless sleep down there. You'll find her there.'

Armando left the club and walked down the same path towards the river, passing the store 'Nevermore', which was now shrouded in dark. When he reached the river, he headed east. It was still

229

raining a little, only now he heard the rumble of thunder, and in the gloom, he felt a shadow fall across his face.

He looked up into the night to see a vast column of black cloud rotating slowly on its axis, while behind it, a sash of silver stars was spread out across the sky. He blinked and took out the whisky bottle from inside his jacket. He took a long swig.

A peel of light rippled from within the cloud, illuminating it; a vast tubular mass of seething black that moved smoothly and steadily, like a cog rotating in the sky. It seemed neither random nor spontaneous but as though some presence had set it into motion with great and terrible purpose.

He saw the outline of the tunnel now, and as he got closer, he made out several figures stood before the gaping maw of its entrance.

He got closer still and saw they were standing over another person – a bunch of rags, cowering on the floor. At first, he couldn't make sense of the scene. Then, he saw how they had surrounded the person on the ground, and he saw the streams of liquid flowing from their waists, arcing downward. He heard the sound of their giddy, bleary laughter as they pissed on their victim.

Armando increased his pace, striding towards them.

The first, a man in filthy rags, turned, his mouth still curled in a leering grin. Armando pulled back his right hand, and with a building roar, hit him so hard that his head flapped at an angle all the way to his shoulder. His legs buckled, and he collapsed.

Another man, trying to pull up his pants, moved towards Armando. Armando stepped in with his left leg and then swung the right upward, kicking the man cleanly in the face.

The final man, his mouth open with slack-jawed astonishment, was backing away, so Armando gripped the side of his head and swung his other arm over the top, smashing it down as hard as he could. All of them were on the ground now. None were moving.

Armando looked up, panting, just in time to see the person who had been on the floor scamper into the maw of the tunnel. He followed them into the opening.

At once, he was swallowed by the darkness.

He moved deeper inside, hearing the sound of rustling up ahead. He was breathing hard as he fumbled in his jacket, found the lighter, took it out, and sparked it. He raised the small flickering flame in the dark, and it cast great shadows out from itself, rippling and expanding. The light revealed the wall on his left, and he saw the ghostly white lettering tripping across it – the alien hieroglyphics of some long-lost language.

Armando moved the flame to the other side and stepped back, taking in breath – for the flame had thrown into relief the lifelike image of a dark dog sketched out across the wall, its teeth bared, its red eyes glowing.

As he retreated further, he brushed up against something solid; he spun around, illuminating the hunched figure of the person behind him.

Her face was like nothing he had ever seen; in the soft light, the fissures of flesh, which ran tumorous over her cheeks and her forehead, made her look as though she had been filleted, as though he were looking at a piece of raw, marbled meat that happened to have a pair of eyes set into it. Those eyes were pale blue, almost milky white, and her face was still dripping with piss, yet her cracked, parched lips were curled in a deranged smile.

Armando made a gagging sound, not just because she looked so repulsive, but because the liniments and sinews of her insides showed through the thin film of withered skin of her face, and he couldn't comprehend how someone could live in a condition of such suffering.

But when her voice came, it was light, and the way she spoke was almost girlish. She blinked twice, lids of pale skin crossing those pallid eyes.

'Hello, mister. Would you … like a bit of fun? You can take me home …' The girlish voice faded in the shadows.

He could see she was reverting to the type of patois she might have used decades ago but was struggling to remember her words.

She found her pitch again. 'You could take me home, and I can make you feel good all night long!'

Forcing himself to look at her, Armando tried to soften his voice. 'Kassandra?'

'Kassandra, Kassandra,' she trilled back. 'That's my name, but it's not a battery, don't wear it out!'

'I'm looking for someone, Kassandra. Do you think you could help me?'

Armando reached into his pocket and took out the picture. He showed it to her under the glow of the flame.

She cocked her head, blinked a couple of times, and smiled again.

'Little Meercciaaa,' she said with a soft sigh. 'Mercia … the girl!'

'Did you know her?' Armando asked.

'Oh yes. But she's not here anymore.'

'Where is she? Where did she go?'

'Mercia the girl.'

'Yes, Mercia the girl. Where is she?'

Her eyes struggled to focus. 'She's in Mictlán. And she can't come back?'

'Mictlán? Is that a place? Can you tell me where it is?'

Those white eyes raised to look into his directly for the first time. She put her finger to her lips and then looked down at the ground.

She spoke in a whisper, her voice soft and inviting, as though she were revealing a secret. 'It's wet. And so very cold. You will know soon enough, though. You'll be there soon. I can see *his* shadow on your face. He is coming for you!'

'And Mercia. Did he come for her?'

'Mercia. Mercia the girl!'

'Yes, Mercia the girl.'

She looked at him again, and through her battered, shredded expression, he saw something underneath trying to achieve clarity.

'Mercia the girl,' she said again. She pointed to her face.

'He … did … this. He … helped me. He helped me take off my mask – in Mictlān. He helped me take off my mask in the wet and the cold, so I could see. He gave me true sight for the first time.'

Her lips had cracked open, her eyes blinking as though she was trying to understand.

'He took off my mask, so I could see. So I could see Mercia the girl …' All the girlish softness in her voice was gone now, and there was a rasping sound that came from deep within her throat. 'So I could see Mercia the girl. So I could see her. So I could see. I could see what he did to her. He made me watch. He made me watch as he …'

Her head was vibrating now, and she was drawing in breath faster and faster.

'He took off the mask, so I could see. Mercia the girl. And how he … how he …'

The rest of the sentence fell away in a wailing sound as her head jerked up and down, her eyes focussed on some horrific point that

Armando couldn't see. The sound graduated into a scream, and now she was taking in breath only to scream again with such violence and such agony, over and over.

Armando staggered away from her, away from that devastated face, that shrieking sound, and back out of the tunnel and into the night. Outside, he saw that same turning funnel of darkness in the sky, and as he looked at it, he thought he saw a galaxy of stars swirling on the inside. He knew he was hallucinating. From somewhere, thunder rumbled, and he stumbled onward into the night.

He returned to his apartment in the early hours of the morning and ran a basin of soapy water to soak his raw, bruised knuckles in. Afterwards, he applied some antiseptic and felt the tingle as though it came from far away. He was exhausted.

Armando kicked off his shoes, laid down on his bed, and tried for sleep. But the feeling of sickness was working deep inside his belly, and when he closed his eyes, a jumble of images flashed across his mind. Kassandra screaming in the tunnel. Cynthia's coffin being lowered into the ground. Mercia looking out from that photo with dark, haunted eyes. And finally, a legion of women rising up from the ground – black, crippled bodies the colour of the sludge they were mired in, only no longer at the bottom of a drained canal as he had seen them that day, but somewhere else. Somewhere infinitely dark, infinitely cold.

His eyes snapped open.

Whisky.

He stood up, turned on the light, and went and poured himself a glass of the amber liquor. Then, in the soft light, he made his way to the living room. On the walls were plastered all the information he had gathered up to this point – a map with marks indicating where bodies had been discovered, notes on the first body, information on the chemicals that had been found on it, sketches of the effigy. But Armando did not glance at these things. Instead, he took his whisky to the table, where her book was waiting for him. He opened the first page. It read:

'The Life and Times of Mercia Sanchez: One Girl's Super Struggle to Take Over the World!'

Next to the word 'World', she had drawn with coloured felts the image of a cartoon globe with a face and a big smile. Armando found himself smiling too. He turned the page. There were images of a younger Mercia, with a couple of friends squashed into a photo booth in a mall, sticking their tongues out and giggling insanely, and later, photos of the same girls splashing each other in a pool. Later still, the girls were snapped in a picture where they were each holding a piece of pizza to their mouths, grinning deliriously – only Mercia was taking a sudden, surreptitious bite out of her friend's piece, much to her friend's scandalised horror.

The photographer had captured this moment – Mercia's naughty sneakiness, the friend's delighted outrage, the laughter of the others.

Armando smiled all the more. He got the feeling that Mercia had been the 'funny' one of the group. They all looked so happy. They couldn't have been more than twelve years old. Mercia had written a title above this set of unfolding scenes: she had encapsulated it 'My Perfect Day', and each letter was written in a different bright colour. Around the pictures, she had drawn musical notes and cats.

The next pages were also colourful: images of friends, doodles, poems, and pictures of smiley cartoon-like figures – the soft, gentle and magical colours of the world a young teenage girl very much wants to see. Inevitably, however, the pictures of friends became fewer, the colours less bright. Mercia was older now.

Armando turned another page to a picture of her in her bra and panties on the bed in her room, trying to look alluring, but her babyish features and large eyes simply looked lonely.

As he turned more pages, it was as if her life turned with it, hurtling towards its denouement, for now, the poems had grown darker in tone; he recognised a growing preoccupation with loneliness, futility and death. Those brightly coloured musical notes and smiling cats were replaced with darker images of monstrous black creatures – bats, dogs, owls, and spiders running across the edges of the pages – while the writing became ever more disjointed.

Armando turned yet another page, and now the writing had morphed into strange hieroglyphics, lines and lines of them crunched together. There was a drawing of Mercia, a childlike representation of the young woman holding hands with another figure, a tall darker figure with claws for hands. Gathered around them were the bats, dogs, owls, and spiders.

Next to the image appeared the one word struck out in stabbing black letters:

'MICTLĀN'

He looked at the dark figure in the drawing, and he touched his finger to it in the gloom.

I'm getting closer.

He took another sip of the whisky, rested his head in his arms, and blinked. When he opened his eyes again, the light in the room had changed; the gathering darkness had thinned, the first hues of early morning sun infiltrating the shadowy gloom.

Armando moved stiffly, his eyes focused on the image of the page still open.

Then a loud *buzz* cut across the quiet – his phone.

He went over to it and answered it, but on the other end, there was only static. And then, another sound. Like someone breathing heavily or the sound of rushing water.

Armando hung up. Perhaps it was Juan Carlos's strange idea of a joke. But after a moment, he recalled Kassandra's words, her strange, muted prophecy: '*You'll be there soon. I can see his shadow on your face. He is coming for you!*'

He went to the small squat kitchen, opened the bottom kitchen cupboard, and flicked the electric switch to heat the water. As he did so, a spark leapt out and illuminated the scores of black beady bodies that were flat against the stone of the inside wall; the cockroaches nestled in the cupboard.

Armando went to the couch as he waited for the water to warm up. He poured a second glass of whisky and turned on the TV, hoping for a documentary, but this early in the morning, there was only a shipping forecast.

Eventually, he got in the shower, got dressed and wandered out of the flat.

Fourteen

At the housing office in the city centre – yet another modern building with a set of offices – it was enough for Armando to flash his badge to get the information he needed.

He gave the phone number of Mercia's friend Veronica, and the woman behind the desk confirmed that the number had been discontinued but provided Armando with Veronica's full name –Veronica Miranda Torrego – and her current whereabouts.

Armando was surprised to hear that 'Veronica' was no longer turning tricks on the streets but registered as living at the Universidad Iberoamericana Puebla campus, where she was enrolled as a mature student. He wrote down the address and headed to the city centre for an early lunch.

On the way, he hit traffic. As he waited for the lights to change, he heard a loud spluttering roar. On either side of him, several black motorcycles had pulled up. Their riders were kitted out in body armour, those black visors strapped across their faces. When the lights turned green, the group of *federales* screeched away, leaving a cloud of smoke in their wake.

Armando drove to the big commercial centre, the Angelópolis Mall. It was a massive shopping centre with several floors and various shops, restaurants, cinemas, and bars – somewhere he rarely visited. As he walked across its marble-coloured floors, Armando took in the large numbers of well-dressed, clean people, the pristine and organised window displays, the smooth, rolling escalators, and the clear crystal lights. He felt a sense of relief. Here, the dark underbelly of desperation and poverty – which he had walked through on the edges of the city the night before – seemed like little more than a dream.

He bought a cocktail and then went into a gadget shop. He found what he was looking for and shelled out more than three months' salary on it. But it was something he needed to do. It gave him the feeling his life was ordinary and stable again, a feeling he very much required – if only for a few moments.

Back at the car, he put the newly purchased item in the boot.

Armando drove to the university campus, which was close by. Like the modern mall, it, too, had a well-organised feeling; large breezy campus greens arrayed with trim trees and blocks and blocks of white concrete dorms laid out in a hexagonal formation.

He found the first floor and door he was looking for. He went to knock but saw the door was slightly open.

He pushed it and called out, 'Hello'.

A pretty woman in her mid-twenties, with strict dark eyes and a long ponytail, appeared. She was dressed in a black skirt and demure cream blouse. To Armando, she didn't look like a student at all.

More like a young teacher, perhaps.

'Veronica?' he asked.

Her expression flinched. Then, her composure and poise returned. Her eyes flickered over him, penetrating and clear. She'd figured him for a cop straight away.

'If this is about the marijuana, that was my room-mate's and her friends, and they've already been called to the Dean's office. All the first-year students smoke, but I'm not here to do that. It doesn't interest me.'

'It's not about the marijuana, Miss Torrego.'

He saw something in her dark eyes then, a shimmering helplessness, a fear. But she was in control of herself again, almost instantaneously.

'Well, if you want to talk to me, you had better walk with me. I'm late.'

She walked quickly, and Armando struggled to keep up.

'What do you study here?'

'I'm doing a PhD in cultural and gender studies.'

'What does that … What do you do for that?'

'You look at how the mistreatment and exploitation of women become normalised via certain cultural tropes and practices. Forms of cultural behaviour that render it invisible.'

Armando didn't understand some of those words, but he knew Cynthia would have loved this kid.

They stepped out into the central campus square and into a stream of people. Most of them were young women in bright, colourful clothes and holding placards. Many had their faces painted white with black eyeliner and black lipstick – in the fashion of 'La Catrina', the skeleton character females dressed up as during the Day of the Dead ceremony. But that was still a couple of months away. It was then that Armando noticed some were also holding photos – images of other women with blurred and hazy features.

'What are they doing?' he asked.

'They're protesting femicide.'

'Femicide?'

'Yes, the number of murders of women in Mexico has become a phenomenon in its own right. We describe it by this term.'

Armando thought about those broken, black bodies rising out of the canal bed, their limbs reaching out almost in supplication.

'We make noise, we shout, we march around,' Veronica went on. 'We dress provocatively. We do everything that, for years, Mexican women have been discouraged from doing. We will no longer be invisible.'

Veronica broke into a chant, her voice joining the others in a loud and chaotic formation.

'What do we want? Justice! When do we want it? Now!'

Armando put a hand on her arm gently.

She flinched ever so slightly.

'I'm here to talk about—'

'I know why you're here, detective. But that part of my life was a long time ago. I was a different person then. I have no desire to revisit it.'

'I understand. But it is important you answer my questions. They relate to the disappearance of someone you once knew.'

Veronica looked exhausted. She suddenly seemed much older than the other students marching.

She stepped away from the flow of marchers and led Armando down into a concrete corridor under the main dorms. The *chugging* of washing machines could be heard from the side as they turned their soapy contents.

She looked up at him from the shadows. 'What do you want?'

'I want to ask you about Mercia Sanchez. I'm investigating her disappearance and murder.'

'Why now?'

'It's possible that—' Armando tried to choose his words carefully. '—what happened to her is connected to a series of other incidents.'

'Incidents?' Veronica asked with a flat voice. 'Is that what the police are calling the murder of young women these days?'

241

Armando gave a light sigh. 'I'm trying to … do something. You could be more helpful. After all, you made it out of there. She never did. What are all your protests worth if you don't remember her?'

A look of anguish crossed the young woman's face, and she turned away, biting her lip.

'Ask your fucking questions,' she whispered.

'When did you see her last?'

'I don't remember exactly. We were both getting high on drugs, but the word "high" doesn't come close. More like "out of it". Something to numb life, to shut it out. I don't remember the last time I saw her.'

'You were her friend?'

'Yes, in as much as I was anyone's.'

'What was she like?'

Veronica hesitated. Her voice became small, the words laboured. 'She was … a sweet girl. I was a little older. I felt protective of her because she was so credulous, so kind. But I wasn't capable of protecting anyone. And those men … they just ate her up.'

Armando spoke softly. 'Was there anyone in particular? A regular client? A boyfriend? Someone who struck you as different? Someone who stood out from the rest?'

Veronica was trembling now. 'Yes.'

'Tell me about him.'

'I never met him in person. In fact, I don't even know if he was real. Towards the end, before she disappeared, Mercia was using a lot. Her behaviour was strange. One time, I came across her sitting outside on the pavement by the strip, her legs crossed, crying. I assumed the normal: she had been raped again, or a punter had gone off without paying, which amounts to the same thing. But it was a hot day. On the footpath, some cockroaches had got caught

242

in the sun. They were turned on their backs, legs kicking, but they couldn't escape, and every now and again, one of them would make this popping sound in the heat, and she was sitting there looking at them sobbing. Just … just sobbing her heart out.'

'And this man?' Armando queried gently.

'Well, that's the thing … Mercia had this thing for animals, and that's what reminded me of him. Towards the end, she said she had met a "magical man", "the tall man". Her voice would change when she spoke about him. Sometimes she spoke of him in a frightened voice like a little child, and sometimes she would speak … reverently almost, the way people do in cults. I was so fucked up back then. I don't think I heard much of what she said. But I remember this. The strangest thing … she said he could talk with animals. That he could make them do things.'

Veronica breathed out a sigh.

'As I say, I never saw the guy, and towards the end, Mercia … she would say stuff that made no sense at all, just rocking back and forth, talking to herself. The drugs, the life … it cannibalised her.'

She looked away.

Cannibalised.

An odd choice of words.

'Did she ever say anything about Mictlān? A place called Mictlān?' Armando asked.

'Not that I remember.' Veronica frowned. 'I don't remember anything like that. What is that?'

Armando ignored the question. 'And do you know where she might have met this guy? This "tall man"?'

'I don't know. There was this one time. There was this house. One of those old colonial places, which are dotted around the city. Relics of the conquistador period. It probably wasn't inhabited except by squatters and addicts, coming and going. She had me meet her there, this one time. And after that, she talked a bit about it, said it was his place, his realm – something along those lines. It was a creepy place, like something out of a film, and I didn't want to hang around, but at the same time, I didn't put much stock into what she said. Mercia … she was … like a kid in the first place. And by that point, the stuff she talked about – you got the feeling it was mostly in her own head.'

'Do you remember the number of the house? Do you remember the name of the street?'

She looked at Armando sceptically. 'No, of course not. I was on so much different crap back then, I couldn't even remember my own address half the time.'

'But you remember the neighbourhood, the rough location – where it was in relation to the main strip.'

Veronica hesitated again, thinking about it, and then her face was crossed by a shadow of real fear. 'No, no … I can't.'

'I need you to take me there. I need you to show me the place, nothing else. Just show me the place.'

'No, that's not possible.'

He raised his hands but didn't touch her. 'This is a police matter. You won't be in any danger. You will come with me, point the place out, and that's all. You will never hear from me again.'

'No.'

'You don't have a choice in this. Do you understand that?'

She didn't say anything.

'Will you take me there now?'

'I can't. I have a seminar in a couple of hours.'

'So, when?'

She sighed and touched her hand to her face.

She looked at him. 'Do you have a cigarette?'

He reached into his jacket and took out a packet.

She took one, and he lit it for her.

'How long have you been smoking?'

Her fingers were trembling, but their movement slowed as she inhaled luxuriously. 'I don't smoke. I quit four years back.'

'When, Veronica?'

She inhaled again. Blinked.

'Pick me up here, the evening after tomorrow, six p.m.'

Armando nodded. 'Okay. You're doing a good thing here. But I need you to know something else. If you decide it's too much for you to deal with, if you decide you're not going to turn up, I will be back. I'll drag you out of your class. I'll make sure that everyone knows why I'm talking to you.'

Those dark eyes flashed. She looked at him and spat in his face. 'You're just like all the others. You fucking disgust me!'

She stepped back, a flinch in her expression, but her eyes shining with bitter defiance.

Armando looked at her and had the same thought. Cynthia would have loved this kid.

He wiped her saliva from his face. 'That's okay,' he murmured. 'Just make sure you're here.'

He walked back to his car. On the way, he passed a student bar and went in. Ordered a double whisky. And then another.

The man behind the bar looked baby-faced, no doubt another student. He looked at Armando as if a grizzly bear had just wandered into the establishment.

From behind him, Armando heard a noise and the shattering of glass. It was a group of students, roaring and laughing – all young men, all very white, and all very rich based on their ridiculous black and white European suits.

He looked at them and knew exactly who they would grow up to be – politicians, bureaucrats, police administrators – and underneath it all, those people with their decorum and formality and etiquette were still these same rich brats having a party at everyone else's expense.

Armando didn't feel angry exactly; he knew that was just the way life worked. But he felt shitty because the one person in this whole place who'd had a rough time of it and somehow managed to drag herself up by her bootstraps – it was she who had been made to feel bad by Armando, had been forced into returning to an awful period of her life. She might have been a *puta* once, but she was worth more than any of these.

He heard the braying laughter of the rich young men as they belched and burped their way towards the success that was their birthright.

He threw back the remnants of his whisky and left.

He bought a bottle at a store on the way back. Sat in the car and took a long drink. Tried to put the day behind him. Because the evening might be positive at least. Might provide him with a chance to forget about the job, forget about the case. Forget about the point he had reached in his life. He even felt a little tingly. A little nervous.

He took a little more of the whisky. Then, he drove to Esmeralda's.

He retrieved the "surprise" from the boot and lugged it up the stairs. Knocked on her door.

She opened the door slightly, as was her custom, blinking out. She didn't look angry or resentful this time but surprised.

'Armando? Don't you remember? This is my night off,' she said, almost apologetically.

'I did … I do … remember,' he stuttered. His tongue felt thick in his mouth. 'But that's why I'm here. I wanted to say, uh, thanks … for what you … did a few weeks back. And also. I…'

His voice trailed off. He was struggling for words.

Her eyes widened with curiosity.

'Well, I also wanted to say that I … I don't really like children.'

She looked at him in surprise.

He realised he hadn't phrased that in the best of ways. 'What I mean to say is … I'm not very good with children. I don't really know what to say to them. But when I was here that last time, well, I got talking with the kid. And … it wasn't so bad.'

Esmeralda's eyes softened in wry amusement. 'The kid? You mean Salome?'

'Yeah, her,' Armando muttered. 'Anyway, I brought something by for her. She might not like it, maybe she is a bit young for it. I don't know. Anyway, I thought I'd drop it off. And be on my way.'

'Hold on.' Esmeralda seemed intrigued. She looked at the large box by Armando's side. 'What is it?'

'A telescope. You said something about a telescope a while back. I thought maybe that's something you and the kid could do together.'

Esmeralda gave a wide smile. 'You mean Salome?'

'Yeah, her.'

Esmeralda bent down and looked closely at the box. 'It looks big and complicated and … very scientific. Salome is better at building things than I am. She takes after her grandfather, I think.' She looked at him, her eyes lit with a knowing smile. 'Would you like to come in and help us put it together?'

'Yeah, okay. I guess I could stay for a bit, get you started.'

He followed Esmeralda through the corridor, past the bedroom and the kitchen, and into the room at the back of the flat. The room with the cuddly fishes and ancient photocopied map. He saw Salome at the same moment she saw him; her head snapped up, and her eyes widened theatrically.

She jumped out of her chair and trilled in a delighted sing-song voice, 'Armando, Armando, he went away! But he came back another day!'

She ran up to him, singing those words and beaming ridiculously, and that was when it happened. He felt something shift. The tension of everything that had been building inside him, the accumulated images of suffering and violence, and seeing that little girl come bounding up to him that way, displaced all that had hardened him, and he felt grateful, so absurdly grateful, that someone like that was happy to see someone like him.

He managed a low guttural whisper, 'Hey, kid.'

Esmeralda looked down at her daughter, her eyes twinkling. 'Looks like Uncle Armando has bought you a little gift. Not that you deserve it, you naughty little brat.' She tickled Salome under the arms.

Salome wriggled and laughed. 'What did he get me? What did he get me?'

'A telescope!'

Salome stopped wriggling for a few moments, the sheer awe of the concept striking her all at once, overriding the tormenting, tickling fingers of her mother. 'Wow. A tee… lee… scope? A real one? An actual one?'

'Yeah.'

'What's a telescope?'

Esmeralda chuckled. 'I think I'd better let Armando explain.'

Armando, put on the spot, stuttered, 'Well, it's-it's something which you look through ...'

'Like a window!' Salome interrupted, bursting with excitement.

'No, kid, it's not like a window.'

'It's kinda like a window,' Esmeralda said.

'Okay, it's sort of like a window, only when you look through it everything on the other side looks really huge and gigantic,' Armando added.

'Wow.' Salome breathed. 'Wow.'

Some minutes later, they had unpacked the telescope, and Salome and Armando were kneeling in the middle of the room. Armando was peering furiously at the joints that connected the metal panels of the mount. The mount was the large metal box on which the telescopic sight would rest. On taking the equipment out of the box, Armando was surprised by the sheer size of the mount. It was at least as big as a small chair, but its inside was completely hollow.

'Do you have one of the middle screws, kid?'

Salome riffled through an assortment of screws before producing one.

Armando lit up. 'Spot on, kid. You got that right – but let's see if you can screw it in this time, not so easy given the fact that Mummy only has the one screwdriver, and it's not all that good.' He shot Esmeralda a look of wry frustration.

'What do I know about screwdrivers? Esmeralda groaned. 'Except for the cocktail – those I can do. I wouldn't mind one now!'

'Go for it, kid.' Armando watched Salome pick up the screwdriver.

He held the screw over the hole. Her hands were clumsy, fumbling, but her face was puckered with determination. She pressed against the screw and began to turn; it wobbled for a few moments but then moved deeper into the groove.

Armando grinned. 'That's it. That's the ticket.'

The screw caught. He saw the moment she was about to press it hard, in a panic, but then she resisted the compulsion – stopped, thought about it – and began moving her hand at a gentler pace, so the screw found the contours of the groove again.

It was such a small thing, but in those moments, Armando realised he was holding his breath. When Salome began to turn the screw home, he finally exhaled.

He felt a rush of triumph. 'You fucking got it, kid. Just like that!'

Both Esmeralda and Salome looked at him with the same wide, shocked eyes.

Armando threw up his hands. 'I didn't say that word.' He looked at Salome seriously and put a finger to his lips. 'You just imagined it.'

The girl put her finger to her lips, nodded, too, and then smiled.

He glanced up at Esmeralda sheepishly.

'Well, it's about time I get myself that drink. Do you want one, Armando?'

'Sure,' he replied, though, in truth, he hadn't even thought about alcohol until she had mentioned it.

'Don't go, Mummy, not yet. We've almost finished!'

'It's okay, baby. You and Armando carry on.'

'But it's not so hard. I can show you. I can show you.'

'Show me when it's finished, darling. I don't know how to build it like you do, but I want to look through it when you have finished. Can I do that?'

'Me and Armando will let you take a look. Won't we, Armando?'

Salome smiled at him hesitantly, her eyes wide, her whole expression a single imploring question.

'I think that can be arranged, kid.'

An hour or so passed. Armando had knocked back several whiskies and Esmeralda a couple of tequilas, but the telescope was set up. Armando and Esmeralda wheeled it out to the balcony. Salome was jumping around them, impatient to see. Armando flicked the cover off the lens. The small girl looked through it.

'I can't see anything,' she said in a soft voice full of bitter disappointment.

'Let me have a go,' Armando said.

He adjusted the sight and angled the lens towards the moon, which he figured was possibly the best bet to see. He sharpened the image of the moon until it was crystal clear, a glowing ethereal circle, across which were dark shadows of craters and crevices. It was a little less spectacular than Armando had hoped for, but when he passed the telescope to Salome, and she looked through it, she gasped.

'I can see him!'

'Who can you see, my darling?' Esmeralda asked.

'The man in the moon. I can see his face. I thought you weren't telling the truth, Mummy. That there was no man up there. But now I can see him. Only … he doesn't look happy. You said he was happy.'

'Ah, yes. But are you always happy?'

'Most of the time, I think,' her daughter said.

'What about that time, last Tuesday – when *someone* told you to do your homework, and *someone* threw her book at me?'

Salome looked at Armando roguishly.

Armando winked at her.

Esmeralda pretended not to notice. 'So, you're not always happy, and nor is the man in the moon. But the next night that we look at him through the telescope, he will probably look different. For now, though, it's bedtime for you.'

'No, not yet!'

'Yes, now. We've talked about this.'

'Ohhh kaaayyy,' Salome said, drawing out the sound and lolling her head in exasperation. She looked up at Armando in a tired knowing way, as if one of the great pitfalls of experience was understanding over the years how people would send you to sleep before you were even all that tired.

'Are you going to say goodnight to Armando, who bought you such a lovely present?' Esmeralda reprimanded gently.

Armando went to say something but was cut off as the little girl went hurtling into him, gripping his leg. He patted her head awkwardly.

She looked up at him. 'Armando, Armando, go away, but come again another day,' she trilled.

Then she gifted him a huge beaming smile and scampered away to her room, her mother following in her wake.

Armando looked at the telescope on the balcony and then up at the sky, which now seemed so calm and pristine, the small, silver stars coddled by the navy blue and blacks of the dark.

Armando walked to the door.

Esmeralda came out of Salome's room, closing the door softly behind her. She met Armando as he was about to leave.

'Thank you. It was a lovely present. And you are good with … the kid.'

Armando looked down. 'Salome,' he said softly.

'Yeah, her,' Esmeralda said with mock playfulness.

Armando looked up again and rubbed his forehead. 'You can say no … but I was thinking maybe you and me might want to catch a film next week, at the cinema.'

Esmeralda's expression changed; she looked shocked.

Armando turned away. 'Sorry. That idea was stupid. I'm so much older than you. I shouldn't have …'

She touched his hand. 'No, it wasn't stupid … Isn't stupid. Just … unexpected. I'd like to go to the cinema with you. I haven't been in a while.'

Fifteen

They headed towards Santa Clara, with Armando driving and Veronica in the passenger seat. She hadn't said a word since she got into the car. Her face was still, immobile. A dullness set into eyes that stared out at the blazing evening sun as it travelled downwards across the horizon, over rusty copper clouds that fissured and gleamed with broken shards of light.

Finally, she spoke with a low imperative voice. 'Pull over.'

'What?'

'Pull over now!'

Armando slowed the car to the side of the road.

She opened the door.

He watched her carefully, wondering if she was going to make a run for it. If he was going to have to jump out and bring her back into the car. Instead, she just leant over the side and vomited onto the street.

Wordlessly, he handed her some tissue.

She wiped her mouth. 'Okay.'

Armando started the car again.

They drove through the strip with its lights and girls. Veronica had the same dead stare locked onto her face, but Armando could detect the tension just beneath the surface, the vein on the side of her neck throbbing violently. She directed him down a couple of cul-de-sacs, struggling to find the route, and he had to reverse the car, find a way back onto the bigger road again.

Soon the road itself got smaller, and they were crawling along the periphery of the *tierra*. Then, he saw it: A large estate, a hacienda in the old colonial fashion, three floors of crumbling dirty white brick, with a garden overrun by broiling purple bushes and sleek sheaths of stabbing yucca. A rusty gate hung limply from a tall and corroded concrete wall whose decaying centuries-old-gargoyles looked down on the garden with unseeing stone eyes.

Armando looked at Veronica. 'Go – walk back to the main road and then take a taxi back.' He handed her a handful of notes.

'I don't want your money.'

'Helping me to get here was brave. Mercia would have appreciated it.'

'Mercia's dead. And I never want to see you again.' She exited the car.

Armando watched Veronica go until she was just a small speck in the rear-view mirror. He took an evidence bag from the glove compartment, stuffed it into the inside pocket of his jacket, and then took a small torch and put it in the other pocket.

He took a deep breath before stepping out of the car.

As Armando walked through the gate and approached the main entrance, he un-holstered his firearm and flicked off the safety. To his right and from above, he caught a flicker of movement. His right hand found his weapon almost instantaneously. But when he looked up, all he saw was a bird sitting on an old metal perch – a large owl, its tawny feathers spiking out from its head like quills, its orange eyes watching him.

He felt a tingle.

This is the place.

He pressed his weight against the front door and pushed hard. It swung open. He slipped into the house, inching forwards, his right hand still resting on his gun. He stepped into a large foyer, a wide-open space, which led to a long stairway that rose upwards into the upper echelons of the old house. The walls were black and mouldering, and across them crept dense weeds. Thick reams of wispy white crisscrossed the floor on which Armando walked, and then he jolted, for behind those spider's webs, he saw a blackened, darkened image. A tall shadowy figure etched out against a gloomy background, and again those strange swirling hieroglyphics; dark marks set into a darker material still. From above, the dying light fissured through the cracks in the ruined ceiling as Armando made his way up the stairs and into a thinner, smaller corridor.

At once, the shadows fell. From within the dark, he felt the rubbish that blanketed the narrow hallway under his feet.

He came to a door to his right and pushed it open. Before moving into the small room, he took out his torch and shined the light around. It revealed a wooden surface attached to one wall; the room had been a secondary kitchen once upon a time, small and pokey. He shone the torch across the wooden counter. He could see the remnants of a fire, the crackled charred bits of debris, and some open, empty cans of food. He pressed his finger to the ash; it was recent.

He moved back into the corridor. This time, he opened a door to the left and stepped into an old-style bedchamber – the skeletal base of a double bed melding into the wall and floor, its rotting wood warped and eaten away. It was not as gloomy in here; the thin evening light flowed into the room from a window. There was an old set of drawers on the far side of the room and several withered objects and papers scattered across it.

From somewhere in the room came a low-level *buzzing*. The bedposts were draped with dusty mosquito nets. His nose twitched, an odour somewhere between the dry rancid decay of a rubbish tip and the heavy wet smell of the abattoir.

Preparing himself for the worst, using one hand to muffle his mouth and nose, Armando took hold of the thin dusty curtain with his fingers and pulled it aside. What he saw confounded any expectations he might have had.

On the weary, sunken, bloated remains of what was once a mattress lay the corpse of a cat, part of which had rotted away, revealing the skeletal rib cage and the grubs, which were curling around the last remaining strands of flesh, while flies *buzzed* intermittently above.

The cat's mouth had been pulled wide open, the shrieking bestial grimace, strangely human, in its aspect of demented terror. The very last instant of life. The horror of death. Captured, frozen in eternity. From somewhere outside the room, Armando heard a rustling sound. He endeavoured to blink away the image of the cat, to relegate the bodily stench from his nostrils as he drew his weapon, moving into the dark corridor again, trying to shut out the sound of his heart thumping in the black. There was just one more door on the other side. Reaching out his hand, he pushed it open as quietly as he could and stepped through.

A noise from inside and the door rebounded back at him with a force that sent him hurtling backwards. He crashed through the corridor and into the bedroom again. Armando was physically robust, strong, but the force of the impact had left him wheezing on the floor. Struggling for breath, he raised his weapon, staggered up, and lurched back out into the corridor just in time to see an almost impossibly tall, dark figure disappear at the far end. Wincing, he gave chase.

As he thudded down the hallway, his foot broke through the rotten wooden floor, and he pulled it out, grimacing in pain. He emerged at the top of the stairs, briefly catching sight of the figure he was pursuing as it disappeared around the bottom of the stairs.

He ran down and followed the suspect around before he hurtled down yet another set of stairs leading underneath into the lower reaches of the house. He pushed open a door and emptied the clip without hesitation, shooting six times into utter blackness.

He took out the torch once more and shone it across the shadows. He was panting hard. The basement was large, dank, but totally empty. No suspect, nobody.

He must've run straight along to the back of the house ... but how?

There had been no other route but down into here.

As he tried to make the calculation, he heard a heavy rumble from behind him, which grew louder until it sounded like thunder. He ran back up the stairs and to a front window, where he peered out through the murky glass.

They arrived in two lines, a smooth flow of glinting silver-and-black metal, those dark visors scanning the road, taking everything in. They pulled up outside the house, close to Armando's car. He was baffled – they couldn't have possibly have followed him because he would have seen and heard them much earlier. He didn't doubt they were here for him, though. How they had found him, he did not know.

He realised he was vulnerable. Even searching a house like this required a warrant – something Armando had failed to secure. At the same time, although he had lost the suspect, there was real evidence in this place – everything in the investigation had led here – and he couldn't bear to relinquish such evidence to them.

The *federales* were moving through the garden purposefully, their automatic weapons drawn and targeted. A cold creeping awareness crawled across the back of Armando's neck.

If I'm caught, I'll lose more than my badge.

For a few seconds, he was in the grip of paralysing indecision. Then, he broke away, running back up the stairs, across the rickety corridor, and into the room with the bed. He held his breath, took out his bag, and began sweeping all the items from the top of the drawers into it. He tore out each drawer and emptied as much of their contents into the bag as possible.

He ran back towards the corridor, a stitch-like pain twisting and snarling through his abdomen. He was already too late; he heard them coming up the stairs. Panting, he returned to that awful room, closing the door gently behind him.

He made his way to the window, a window which had stiffened and locked into place, but with a wrenching effort, he pulled, and the frame gave. He heard the *federales* clattering through the corridor.

He pushed out through the window and dropped the bag onto the ground underneath. Gripping some guttering and weed, he scrambled to ease himself down, but losing purchase, he slid lower, hard, his arms scraping against the brick.

He landed awkwardly, winded but not hurt. He snatched up the bag and forced himself to keep moving, to follow the perimeter of the wall around to the other side and back out into the front garden.

He pressed through the thick yucca, feeling the plants' blades cut the backs of his hands as he raised them up to protect his face. Gasping, he made it out through the gate, past the bikes, and into his car. Keeping his head down, he started the engine, and it sputtered into life before he turned the car and pulled away.

He drove through the darkness, the bag on the passenger seat. As he approached the centre of the city, the lights from the skyscrapers were reflected in the car's windscreen, forming ribbons of colour that rippled across the smooth blackness of the glass. Now the traffic was flowing smoothly across the sleek highways that cut through the business district. From the shadowy interior of the cut, Armando allowed himself to take a deep breath. He peeled down the window, the warm nighttime air tingling against the side of his face.

He turned on the radio. An emergency bulletin interrupted a traffic report – an old abandoned house on the edge of the city in the Santa Clara district had gone up in flames, and now the fire was spreading. It was thought squatters had been behind the arson.

Armando looked into his rear-view mirror and saw a distant finger of smoke climbing gradually upward into the night. He touched his finger to the evidence bag next to him. At least he had managed to salvage that.

When he arrived at his own neighbourhood and got out of the car, his shaking had subsided to a slight tremble. He stood by the kerb, looking at his battered vehicle. He tried to think more lucidly about the *federales*; he'd seen them earlier that week, but then nothing until they had surprised him outside the old hacienda.

How?

For the first time, the glimmering of an idea took shape.

He took out his torch again and knelt down, shining it underneath the car. It took him a few minutes, but eventually, he found what he was looking for: a receiver, its blinking red light denoting its activity, lodged underneath one wheel arch.

An actual tracker.

Armando had never seen one in real life but had read a little about the technology. He felt a strange thrill. This was how the *federales* had found him.

He went to remove the device but then stopped and frowned. He got up and went into his apartment building, taking the bag and torch with him.

Once he got inside, he poured himself a large whisky and turned on the TV. From the flickering screen came the image of a deputy from the Institutional Revolutionary Party – the party that had been in government for as long as Armando could remember. The man was telling reporters how Mexico was now more modern, more international, more outward-looking than ever.'

'Investment is up, capital is circulating and crime is down,' the deputy said. 'Mexicans have never had it so good.'

From across the gloom, Armando caught sight of Mercia's photo pinned to the wall, those dull, defeated eyes staring out from a sunken world of black and white, her lips pursed in silent, eternal recrimination.

He thought about the figure he had caught sight of at the end of the hallway, the shadow which slipped away. He wondered how many other Mercias were out there.

He finished the rest of his whisky and poured another. He tipped the evidence bag's contents onto the floor and rested a lamp on the table, shining its beam onto them.

What am I looking for?

What he wanted more than anything else was a photo or name. Failing that, any other biographical information about the person he was hunting – birthdate, blood type, star sign, anything. But what Armando had reaped was nothing whatsoever.

He looked through the clump of objects in desperation. There were a few tattered cards advertising sex services and strip clubs, some empty plastic containers streaked with dirt, and a cracked cup.

Then, he saw something else. An old poster: a black-and-white photocopy with a young woman's face staring out, her eyes subdued and melancholy, with a name at the top – Camila Valentina Alcon.

Below it was the one sentence:

'Do you know who killed me?'

And below that was a single phone number. There was also a date in the far corner: June 1987.

Later, Armando would try the number but find nothing but static at the other end of the line, hissing and crackling.

For now, however, something else caught his eye – a small fragment of eroded tea-coloured paper. He picked it up and peered at it. He saw a number – 445 61 – but it wasn't a phone number. It looked more like the kind of number that the police attached to a particular piece of evidence to log it. But it wasn't that either.

He also saw part of a word: 'Asturias … mi …'

Suddenly, he remembered what the madam had told him: 'Las Asturias', the mine that had closed in the early eighties. He would bet that partial word, the 'mi …' was originally 'mining'.

This is some kind of payslip.

He felt the excitement in his belly. Of course, it could be a dead end, but it could also be the next piece in the puzzle.

***

He arrived at the Colegio Comunitario del Juana Belén Gutiérrez de Mendoza in the early afternoon. He had not been here for years, but the college was much as he remembered. It was in a poor area, but an open and colourful one, with greens, parks, and playgrounds. The college building itself also acted as a community hall. It was a flat white structure with large, wooden-slatted windows that had seen better days. The paint was peeling away, and one of the windows was cracked, but upon pushing through the doors and into the main corridor – with its black-and-white chessboard tiling – the light streamed in. The walls were decorated with students' drawings, offering bright and vivid flavours of Mexican geography – from the mountains to the beaches to the jungles.

There were photos of the students, too – all teenagers, all grinning out from day trips to the mountains or lakes – and notices that gave news of clubs and community events.

Armando walked down the corridor and heard a scream of collective laughter from one of the classrooms. Something inside him shifted – the feeling of the past reaching out and touching the present, for this place had been Cynthia's whole world, her world of teaching underprivileged kids and putting everything she had into their messy, haphazard lives. He would come to pick her up from work, and they'd go for a drink at the Cubano salsa bar around the corner, a place whose floor had been put together from old wooden banana crates, but in the balmy night, when the cocktails were flowing, and everyone was dancing, it felt as though you could have been on a Caribbean beach underneath the stars.

A bell rang, interrupting the warm flow of memory. Kids piled into the corridors screeching and laughing, oblivious to him – oblivious to anything except the promised freedom of a sunny, late-summer afternoon. They flowed around him in a tumble of chaotic energy until gradually their loud noise waxed fainter, and only a ghostly echo lingered, reverberating off the walls, before petering away into nothingness.

He came to the room he was looking for, number 56, and knocked before entering. A young man in his late twenties was tidying up the classroom. He was dressed unusually well for this college, with a smart grey jacket with trim, tidy trousers. He was dark-skinned – indigenous – and well-groomed.

He looked at Armando, and even though his face was youthful, his dark eyes were penetrating. 'Hello. May I help you?'

Armando flashed his badge. 'My name is Armando. I am a detective with the First Precinct municipal police. I'm investigating a series of crimes that have … a certain religious aspect. I was told that you might be able to provide me with some useful information.'

The young man reached out and shook Armando's hand. 'I'm Jorge Taipan. I teach religious and social studies and history. But I'm at a loss to know how you came to me in this college, detective. Surely, it's a little out of the way?'

Armando hesitated. 'My ex, Cynthia, used to work here. So, it seemed … like a natural port of call.'

The young man's expression changed, his eyes narrowed slightly. He spoke in a soft, grave voice. Armando thought he could hear a hint of reprimand in the tone, but perhaps it was just his imagination:

'I remember Cynthia very well, detective. She was the life and soul of this place.'

They gazed at each other for a few moments.

'I've never had someone ask about my work in a police capacity, but please, go ahead.'

Armando nodded. 'Just a few questions.' He took out Mercia's diary from his folder and turned to the final pages where the symbols appeared. 'Can you tell me what these … hieroglyphics mean?'

The young teacher peered at them. 'They're not exactly hieroglyphics, detective, though the difference is not great.'

He trailed his finger across them.

'These words don't have a set reading order. You don't need to move across the page from one side to the other as you would with say … Maya hieroglyphs or even modern Spanish. This is much more fragmented. See that symbol there, that circle? It's actually a closed eye – that indicates night. The spiral here, wrapped around that straight stick figure with the two lines protruding – it's supposed to be a corpse wrapped up in a burial cloak … so that one symbolises death. Very dark, detective, but also rather incoherent. Meaningless. The script is Aztec. But the sentences themselves are just ramblings.'

'And you can read that? You can understand that … because your people taught you how to when you were young?'

The teacher wore a wan smile. 'My people, detective?'

Armando winced. 'Yeah, your people. Indigenous people. I don't know how else to say it. Christ, everyone is so sensitive these days. Everything is so damn politically correct!'

'As it happens, detective, both my parents are Catholics. More broadly, however, you won't find any indigenous populations nowadays worshipping Aztec gods or writing in the Aztec-Nahuatl script because theirs was a language and religion that died out long ago. Though the different indigenous groups in Mexico today have a shared heritage, it's Mayan. And if you want to know how I can make some sense of the words you have shown me, it's because I spent some years at Toronto University studying a masters in ancient cultures and pre-Columbian religions. However, personally speaking, I'm an atheist.'

Armando nodded and pointed towards the symbols he had copied in his notes. 'So, you're saying this writing probably wasn't written by an … indigenous person?'

'I don't know. It could well have been. But equally, it could have been someone of Iberian origins. Even at the peak of their power, the Aztecs didn't pass on much of a cultural legacy. They flowed down from the north. They were considered to be vicious, foreign conquerors. They were hated almost as much as the Spanish *conquistadores* who arrived in their stead. They subjected their victims to the most brutal repressions and rituals.'

'The cleaving out of the heart?'

'Yes, that was one element in their rituals of blood sacrifice. Such bloodletting was thought to keep the stars burning in the skies, the universe in motion.'

'I'd heard that. I tried to find out some stuff in the library. It's hard to imagine … people worshipping in those ways in this day and age,' Armando said thoughtfully.

'Indeed, detective. But remember, even today, the advocates of Christ make blood sacrifice the central premise of their religion. Christ on a cross, bleeding out. The consumption of his blood through communion wine. And, in terms of bloodshed, the Spanish Christian soldiers went on to teach even the Aztecs a thing or two.'

'Thank you, professor. What you said was … good. Just a couple of other things, if you would?'

The young man nodded.

'What do you understand by the name Mictlāntēcutli?'

'Another Aztec reference. This time, the Aztec god of the dead.'

'Yes, that's what I have read too. Can you tell me anything more?'

'The Aztecs believed that he had power over animals, dogs, spiders, and so on. It was said he could talk to them, make them do things.'

Armando remembered what Veronica had said. How Mercia had told her that 'the tall man' could speak to animals.

The young man continued, 'He governed over the souls of the dead. The Aztecs thought of the universe in terms of a series of cosmic ages. One of the ages was called the age of the sun. It was said to have lasted some two centuries. Then, it came to an end with a great flood. In a single day, death spread across the planet. Only two people survived. The rest belonged to him. To Mictlāntēcutli.'

'And what about … "Mictlān"? What does that word mean to you?'

'After the great flood, all the souls were sent there. Mictlān was the name of Mictlāntēcutli's domain. He was king of the dead, and Mictlān was his underworld.'

Armando bowed his head, fascinated. He scribbled a note: Mictlān = Underworld.

A shadow crossed the window; the light in the classroom had started to thin.

'I'd better get going. Thanks again for your help,' Armando said.

The young teacher nodded.

As Armando reached the door, the man's voice arrived again, soft and sad.

'I was very sorry to hear about her – about Cynthia's … illness, detective.'

267

'Yeah,' Armando said. 'So was I.'

***

When he came out of the shower that evening, Armando gazed at himself in the mirror, taking in the hard lines of his forehead, the shadows under his eyes, the receding hairline, the broad shoulders, and the bulging gut.

Time has its way with us all.

Armando picked up the device he had fashioned; a wire frame shaped in a harness, with some old magazines glued together on one side and some more on the other. He slipped it over his head and then took some thick masking tape and wrapped it several times around his body. He felt the tender bruises and scrapes on his torso shriek and flare when the makeshift body armour was pressed tight, but he had no idea what exactly he was getting into tonight, and some defence was better than none.

He had that same feeling, the building tightening pressure on his chest, that sense of powerlessness, as though forces outside himself were gradually crushing him. He popped open the cap of the nearest whisky bottle and took a long, deep drink. The whisky sizzled in his belly, and he felt a sharp serrating pain deep in his guts, but at the same time, something in him unclenched as the alcohol passed through the lining of his stomach and melded into his blood.

He got to Septimecielo a little later, as he had left his old battered Chevy outside his apartment building where it would sit untouched for some time. When he got to the club, it was already dark. The club itself was closed up, so he banged on the door.

Filippo finally appeared. He had a hospital brace on his nose from where Armando had caught him flush.

Armando couldn't help but smile.

'It suits you,' he said amiably to the big bouncer.

Filippo said nothing, just scowled.

Inside, Armando's heart started to beat faster.

Juan Carlos met him at the bar and handed him a piece of paper.

'Two addresses, Armando. You need to go to the first one and pick up a package. Needless to say, don't mention any names, especially not mine. Say to the guy behind the window one word: "Septi". He'll give you the package. Bring it back here to the office and give it to Filippo. He'll deposit it safely …'

'Where will you be?' Armando asked quietly.

'Not that it's any of your concern, but I won't be here. Not on these premises. In fact, that's the whole point of this exercise. You ever play chess, Armando?'

'Not really.'

'You should try it. It's an intellectual game, though. The point about it is that the king must always be protected, must always be above the fray. I can't have any contact with what happens next. If anyone wants to know where I am tonight, I'll be at "La Casa Blanca" – the single biggest casino in Puebla City – playing cards under state-of-the-art security cameras, surrounded by hundreds of witnesses. Whatever happens from this point on won't be traced back to me. The king must be protected at all costs, you see, for that is the key to victory.'

Armando nodded.

'When you get back here,' Juan Carlos continued, 'Filippo will give you another package. It needs to be taken to the second location straight away. You don't need to do anything, just hand it to the people there. And then you're done. Make sure you burn the addresses.'

Armando followed him through a side door into a back alley. Crouched in the shadows was a gleaming black BMW saloon.

'Like your new wheels?' Juan Carlos said with amusement, catching the surprise on Armando's face.

'Yes.'

'There's a map on the back seat. The car also comes with an in-built phone. If there are any problems, you can call me from it directly. You'll go straight through to this.'

Juan Carlos held up a large black mobile phone.

'Call only in the case of an emergency, understand?'

Armando nodded again.

'You're moving up in the world now, Armando. This is the big time.'

The detective looked at the young man, trying to suppress his loathing and make his voice neutral.

'Can I ... hold onto the car? After tonight. My car – it's broken down.'

Juan Carlos looked at him thoughtfully, as if he were coming to some critical conclusion.

Armando knew Juan Carlos was savouring his power.

'As long as you work for me, you can hold onto the car. And you work for me now, you understand that, too, right?'

For a third time, Armando nodded.

Juan Carlos may have been a prick, but that car was a dream to drive. A 7 series BMW sedan. The speedometer read a top speed of 250 km/h. The car didn't so much drive as glide.

The world of night rolled past the sleek shaded windows. But as smooth as the car was, it could not dispel the sickness in Armando's belly. He was a cop who had worked Vice for almost a decade, accrued hundreds of arrests, and, therefore, a legion of potential enemies. Only now, he was an ex-Vice cop who was presumably about to start transporting large contents of cash and drugs back and forth between the same set of people he had targeted in the past.

The situation was fraught with danger, and he felt himself yearning for another long pull of whisky, but at the same time, he knew he had to keep his mind clear.

The first address took him to a large gloomy housing estate with a forlorn courtyard littered with rubbish and a battered basketball hoop hanging at its far edge. The flats had dilapidated balconies covered with washing and the odd satellite aerial, while thick black bars crossed the windows.

Armando got out of the car, locked it, and put on a coat. He pulled the hood of the coat down over his face. It was the closest thing to a disguise he could manage.

He went to the front entrance and banged on the iron girded door. A man opened it up.

Armando said the word, 'Septi,' and was ushered in. The man patted down his legs and waist, finding and taking his firearm. He didn't catch the small, hooked dagger Armando had resting in his sock, though.

Inside, the air stank with marijuana, and the dull throb of rap music came to him from somewhere higher up in the building. He passed a few doors in the narrow corridor, following the man deeper in, and through the gaps, he saw tables stacked with plants and people with masks in the process of cutting them up.

He got to the end of the corridor. The man banged on a metal shutter, which rattled as it was slid up. Another man sat at a counter behind it, and beyond him were a series of desks with drawers on top. The makeshift office was illuminated by a dull green light.

In the corner, Armando could see a small security camera angled downwards. He turned his head away from its gaze.

Armando repeated the word, 'Septi.'

The man got up from his seat, opened a drawer, took out a parcel, and gave it to Armando. Then, the metal shutter came down again with a sudden rattle. Armando's companion motioned him back through the corridor, wordlessly handing him back his gun and then closing the door behind him.

Armando was relieved to see the BMW still in one piece. He got in and drove away. He realised that he was going too fast. His body was still flooded with adrenaline, and the car was so quiet, so he didn't realise right away, but he took a pause before easing his foot off the pedal and allowing himself to breathe.

Again came that aching need for a drink … but he only had one more trip to make – and this first couldn't have gone more easily.

He got back to the club and parked in the same alley before being buzzed in through the back door. He went to the office where Filippo was waiting and handed him the paper package, which Armando assumed was filled with cash. The bouncer, still smouldering, went over to the safe but then stopped mid-operation. He eyed Armando.

'Step away,' he said in a petulant voice, making sure there was no chance Armando could see the precious combination.

Armando put his hands up, turned around, and busied himself looking into the old gilt mirror on the opposite wall of the office.

When he turned back again, the safe had been locked, and Filippo handed him the next package – or rather, a set of brown paper parcels wrapped in a large see-through sack.

Armando took it.

Filippo glowered at him and pointed to the apparatus strapped to his nose. 'It cost me a thousand pesos to get this set, *cabron*. You think you're so much better than me. But now look at you, nothing but a low grade, burnt-out bag man.'

'Why do you keep doing this to yourself?' Armando asked mildly.

The bouncer blinked, trying to process the question.

Armando's right hand shot out and grabbed Filippo by the nose, squeezing hard, manoeuvring the large man down onto his knees.

The bouncer screamed in agony.

Armando hoisted the sack over his shoulder and walked back to the car. He put the bag in the boot, drove the car a few blocks, and pulled over. He removed something inside his jacket, a medical syringe still in its cellophane wrap. He tore it open, exited the car, and opened the boot again. He injected the needle through the sack's material, through the hard crisp paper of one of the packages, and pressed down on the syringe ever so slightly. He withdrew the needle. The mark from its point in the fabric of the sack was almost invisible. He felt certain that no casual observer would possibly notice the bag's contents had been penetrated.

He got back into the car and depressed the needle, shooting a fine white powder onto the top of the black dashboard.

Cocaine.

But he needed to be sure.

He smeared a little on his finger and hesitated; as vicious as Juan Carlos was, it occurred to Armando that he could be trafficking something worse, a chemical weapon of some sort.

Unlikely.

He smeared the powder against his gums, bracing himself. It was, as he'd thought, cocaine – and very high quality.

Absolutely pure.

Within moments, his heart had started to thrum.

He made a few quick mental calculations. Now he was almost certain of the pattern; he went to the first place to collect cash, and then the drugs would be dropped off at a second address. Juan Carlos was using him to distribute large amounts of cocaine in an unadulterated form, which meant that Juan Carlos's father was almost certainly receiving shipments by air from Colombia directly. This meant they had to be in league with the Sinaloa Cartel – the cartel that controlled the air routes from Colombia and the only people, therefore, who could supply such a high-quality product in such amounts. This, in turn, meant the power behind father and son was immense.

Armando's situation was more perilous than he had ever realised.

He rubbed his eyes. His head throbbed, and his hands were trembling, his whole body aching for alcohol. Finally, he gave in – pulled up outside a small store and got a bottle of whisky. He would have two swigs, no more.

He opened the bottle and drank. Studied the map. Drove to the destination – a gloomy backwater of industrial warehouses punctuated by jagged, skeletal pylons and factories belching out fire and smoke into the blackness of night. He drove through the grid-like complex of the various structures until he found the place he was looking for.

He got out and felt the tint of hot metal and ash carried by the balmy air, and from inside the warehouse, he heard the sounds of people.

There were two men at the door this time.

He said the same word, 'Septi,' and one of them slid back the large doors while the other motioned for him to enter.

Armando was not searched on this occasion, but he was told to take off his hood. He did so and followed one of the men deeper into the warehouse. It was dark and gloomy around the edges, the high roof cast almost entirely in shadow, but the floor of the warehouse was populated by different clumps of people, burning torches illuminating their doings. One group had made a circle, and as Armando got closer, he saw the forms of two cockerels, strutting and jerking, pecking at each other viciously, while the men cheered and shouted. Armando noticed the knives and guns protruding out from the hips of the various spectators.

He flinched, feeling the nakedness of his face, trying to keep his eyes to the ground.

The whole place was laid out in square grids – a massive underworld market. His eyes flickered to the right, to a group of large horizontal containers, pens almost. In one of them, he glimpsed a woman in her bra and panties, her smooth, *morena* skin smeared with grime, a rope tied around her ankle, tethering her. In the next, he saw another underdressed woman and another – they all had the same dull dark eyes, as though there was nothing else left in life except the need to endure it.

He knew that look. Trafficked women – brought up from Honduras, Guatemala, El Salvador and Panama – syphoned across the

Mexican border to be sold in the USA's big cities. They were all tethered like cattle, and the men were haggling animatedly over their prices.

Armando forced himself to look away, to keep concentrating on the ground. He was brought to the far end of the warehouse; a group of men with automatic weapons were lolling around the back end of a lorry. He was instructed to drop the bag on the ground and wait. The bag was taken away.

Moments later, he heard the men whispering to one another.

Then, the man who had brought him here told him he could go.

Armando nodded without raising his head and started to make his way back through the warehouse. He didn't look at the bound women as he passed. He kept his head down. He tried to keep his mind on what he would do. He thought about Esmeralda and how he had arranged to meet her at the cinema the following day, and how long it had been since he went to see a film. Suddenly that was everything he wanted, just to sit with her in the dark, in an ordinary public place, filled with regular people, whiling away the time in the way people do, far away from the stark contours of this midnight netherworld – the brutal excitement of the men, jostling like animals in packs; the slumped, exhausted forms of the women, dead on their feet, the dull inhuman eyes.

He willed himself to make it to the door, only to spot movement off to the side. A man with a pallid scar across his cheek turned, catching sight of him, and Armando caught the glimmer of recognition that flickered across the man's face.

'Hey, hey you! I know you!' He walked up to Armando.

Armando turned away. 'Don't think so.'

'Yeah, I know you!'

'I've never seen you before in my life.'

Another couple of men had broken away from the cockfight, walking up behind the first guy, watching Armando carefully.

'I really do know you.'

'So you said.'

He was through the doors now, the man on the front wall sliding them open for him.

Armando saw the moment in which the other guy's eyes lit up with excited hatred, the moment of realisation:

'This guy's a cop. He busted me a few years back. I fucking knew it.'

Armando was at the car now, the keys almost in the door. A couple of other men had come running from the building, but the first guy was nearly upon him, and now he changed tacks. He stepped back towards the first man, grinning, and pulled open the car door as he did so.

'Hey, listen to me, you piece of shit. It's one thing you walking me to the car, it's a whole other thing branding me a *puto policia!*'

He flexed his arms and spat on the ground. He caught the moment of hesitation in the other man's eyes and went to turn to get in the car, but at the last moment:

'He is a fucking *policia!*'

He felt the blow to his right side and crouched down before punching the first man in the gut and hearing the satisfying 'umphhh' as the wind was sucked out of him. In the same instant, he felt a violent shuddering blow to the top of his head. Someone else was holding onto him, so he shoved his shoulder upwards, hard, propelling the body away with some force. After turning once more, he made a beeline for the inside of the vehicle. He felt a hot trickle of blood from his forehead and briefly glimpsed a flash of metal in his peripheral vision as one of the other men swung an axe at him, the blade hitting his belly with a wallop and then sliding across, tearing and slashing.

Armando's hands were shaking, but he managed to clamber into the car and pull the door shut. At the same moment that he pushed the key into the ignition, the glass near his head exploded in a shattering wave, spreading across him and to the other side of the car.

He started the car and floored it, pushing away with a gliding whoosh, while the figures of the men giving chase grew rapidly smaller in his rear-view mirror. Seconds later, Armando heard a couple of small pops and realised they were shooting. He kept his head low, trying to stop himself from passing out.

The car turned the corner. He propped himself up and took the whisky bottle, opening the top and splashing liquid on the top of his head. At once, it felt like his skin was on fire. He gave a violent gasp because the pain was worse than he had anticipated, but he was revived; there was no longer any danger of losing consciousness.

He drank a third of the bottle in one go, feeling his gag reflex jerk into motion, yet keeping the whisky down. A trickle of blood found its way into his eye. He blinked it away.

By the time he got back to his apartment, he felt woozy. He got out of the Beamer and examined it. All in all, it had emerged unscathed, apart from the shattered side window. He stared at it for a few moments longer, parked at the side of the road in his raffish neighbourhood. Next to his battered old Chevy, the other car looked so incongruous, causing him to give a small involuntary hiccup from his throat. Then, he was laughing. Despite the pain, he laughed until his eyes shone with water.

When he got into his apartment, he took off his trousers and shirt. He lifted up the makeshift protector he had made for himself, the pain creaking through his arms, shoulders and belly. The axe had split the magazines almost through but not his skin. However, the force of the impact had left deep purple welts across his torso. There was a thick, throbbing swelling on the top of his head.

Tentatively, Armando removed glass fragments from his neck and the side of his face with a pair of tweezers. His fingers were still shaking, so he took another long drink of whisky.

Finally, he washed his face with soap and warm water and then dabbed it with antiseptic. He felt almost human again but so exhausted.

He put on his dressing gown and made his way down the hallway of his apartment, the whisky bottle in his hand. The light from the answering machine was flashing.

He played the tape. One message was from his captain, Ximena Ponce, her small tight voice 'requesting' a meeting at 2.00 pm the following day; the other was from Juan Carlos, a sardonic laugh congratulating him on a job well done and telling him that he would be making the same trip four weeks from now.

Armando wandered out onto the balcony. He didn't want to do anymore, to see anything else, yet it seemed as though he had been pulled into a sequence of events from which he couldn't escape. Images came to him; dead women, lifeless eyes, birds pecking at each other in that circle, his field of vision clouded with the red of his own blood.

Something caught in his throat. More water in his eyes. He gave a raw, husky cough. Blinked the visions away.

He gazed out into the night. He wanted to melt away into that darkness, but within the blackness lived another figure – a shadow at the edge of his periphery, a figure whose face was wreathed, a figure somewhere out there, moving through the black.

Hunting.

Sixteen

Armando knocked on the door of her office, his head still throbbing from the hangover and the bruises, the cuts from the glass tingling hotly on the side of his face.

Inside, he sat down, easing himself into the chair, a sharper, twisting pain convulsing his belly.

Ximena Ponce was peering down at some papers. In the background, he heard the men outside on the main floor going about their day – a sound so familiar to him and yet, at this moment, it felt strange. The squiggling rasp of Ponce's pencil against the paper seemed to cut across everything else. He knew she was purposely making him wait; that age-old ritual whereby the boss establishes that their time is worth something and yours is not.

Finally, she looked up.

'Detective,' she said thinly, 'I'll come straight to the point. In the past few weeks, I've barely seen you. The investigations you've recorded in your logbook don't tally with your hours. You don't seem to have closed any of what are relatively trivial cases – each is ongoing. All of which seems to suggest that you have been devoting your time to other activities.'

She didn't deliver this as a question, just a statement, an insinuation. She was trying to draw him out.

'My apologies – I got a bit behind on updating my casebook. It's been … hectic.'

'I'm sure, detective, I'm sure. But I have information that indicates you've been pursuing another inquiry. Would you like to tell me about that?'

'Would you like to tell me where this information came from? What exactly is the nature of the accusation?'

Ponce gave a grim smile.

They were fencing.

'Detective, you see me as the enemy, but you don't seem to see the leniency I've already extended you. Your casebook is incomplete. Your work attendance has been erratic. You've been involved in a violent altercation with another officer in this very office. You are consistently insubordinate, hostile and belligerent. And, on top of that, I can smell the booze coming off you from here. Can you give me any reason why I shouldn't just ask for your badge right now?'

'You know the Santa Clara district?' Armando said in a low voice.

'Of course I do.'

'I was doing some work there, looking through some files, because – and this is the strangest thing – my clearance at this station, my access to the information I need to follow cases, has been revoked. The files in their local precinct weren't in great condition, but they made for interesting reading nevertheless. For the last ten years, the murder rate of young women in that area has spiked. It's approximately three times higher than the average for Puebla City. Did you know that?'

'Not everything falls within the average, detective. In fact, that's the very meaning of the word "average". Some things fall above it, and some things fall below it. Santa Clara is one of the poorest areas, on the outskirts. A large red-light district—'

'We both know there are other poor areas, other sex districts, in Puebla City. None of that could explain a near triple rise in the murder rate. That kind of shift is an anomaly – and we both know why.'

Ximena Ponce leaned back in her seat, observing him with cold eyes. 'So, it's as I thought, detective – you're still chasing your phantom serial killer. After everything you were told. I really do believe your time here is at an end.'

Armando looked at her. His head was still throbbing, but his focus was crystal clear.

He spoke carefully, 'Phantom – an interesting choice of words. Because the person I'm looking for is almost invisible, something like a ghost. You can't see him because of your politics. Because protecting the public image the mayor wants to create is more important to you than solving crime. In Santa Clara, the police don't see him because the girls he hurts are poor and desperate. They don't matter. They, too, are invisible. But they're not invisible to the mothers who have lost them. I know that because I have spoken with such a person.'

He reached over, turned the picture on Ponce's desk towards him, and looked at it, at the image of her teenage daughters.

'Your kids look happy, healthy! That's good. As long as it's someone else's child who's missing, I guess it doesn't matter so much. Besides, the mayor always makes such pretty speeches – and we both know this is an election year.'

The captain's face had become ashen, her lips pale with tightness.

'Detective, I wish to inform you of the termination of your employment as of now. You'll receive a more detailed letter outlining the reasons for your termination, but in the meantime, I'll have to—'

Armando put his badge on the table. 'Take it. I have no more use for it anyway.'

He got up with a groan and left her office. He felt strangely calm.

He stepped out of the building and into the light, which poured from the afternoon sky rendering everything a blinding flickering white. It was only then that it hit him, the magnitude of what had just happened. He had worked as a cop for most of his adult life, some twenty years.

He turned to the wall and vomited. He had known this moment was coming for a while, had known it was only a matter of time, and now that it had happened, some part of him felt … strangely liberated, as though there was one less factor to deal with in the situation he was in.

When he got back to his apartment, he slept, and when he later opened his eyes, the light had changed. Night was descending. He peered through the gloom at the clock by his bed. In an hour, he was due to meet Esmeralda.

He showered. Spruced himself up. Used the aftershave he rarely wore. Ironed a shirt. Drank a quarter bottle of whisky. Shaved. Combed his hair.

In the shadow, the marks on his face were not so visible. He looked at himself and tried to smile. He didn't think he looked that bad.

They met in the city centre. Esmeralda was dressed in a short black dress and had combed the curls out of her hair so that it fell straight from the sides in a sleek willowy dark. Her olive skin shone in the night, and her full dark eyes seemed to glow, and yet her expression was uncertain, nervous almost. Armando was struck by how beautiful and youthful she appeared.

He felt large, awkward, cumbersome, as he gave her a hesitant kiss on either cheek – something which itself seemed odd, for he had laid on top of her so many times, spent hours in her bed, grinding over her body, but now, it was almost as if they were strangers meeting tentatively for the first time.

'Hey,' he said.

'Hey.'

They stood there, regarding each other for a few moments, and then her eyes grew wide as she stepped towards him, extending her hand but not quite touching him.

'Armando, what happened to your face?'

He blinked in surprise. His first thought was that his attempts to spruce himself up had proven so pitiful that another human being couldn't believe he'd done that to himself of his own accord. Then, he remembered the patter of red, which had been left by the exploding glass.

He touched the side of his face gingerly. 'Oh, this is nothing. Just …' He couldn't think of anything to say. '… work.'

She looked at him almost sadly, and again, he was caught by the beauty of her soulful eyes. He had the feeling that he was seeing her for the first time.

Esmeralda gave a slight smile and looked away.

Nobody said anything.

Finally, the detective broke the silence.

'Well, it's an hour until the film. Do you wanna get something to eat?'

She looked up at him. 'Yeah. Yeah … that would be nice.'

'Where do you wanna go?'

'I don't know.' She played with her hands.

He felt the first flush of irritation. 'Well, we could go that gringo restaurant over there, that McDonald's.'

Her face lit up. 'I've never been there. Are you sure? They say it's expensive.'

'It's okay. This is on me.'

He was rewarded with a delighted smile; she really was excited to be going to the gringo place.

He extended his arm. '*Señorita?*'

Esmeralda took it and giggled.

They walked across the square to the restaurant. She was right; it was pricey, especially for what you got – and you had to stand and queue like you would in any normal burger or taco joint. Nevertheless, it was kind of exotic, like being on a space station. Everything was perfectly clean – perfect plastic yellows and reds – while the tables seemed to flow out up from the floor, and the tidy young women and men behind the counter, also dressed in yellow and reds, gave the customers a crazed kind of smile as they ordered.

Armando was amused. He ordered something called a 'Big Mac' while Esmeralda ordered a cheeseburger and chips with a strawberry milkshake. They found a place at the back of the restaurant where it wasn't so bright.

Esmeralda nibbled her food but looked at him with enthusiasm. 'This is really good. I have never had a burger like this!'

'Yeah,' Armando said genially, having wolfed his down.

They looked at each other and smiled.

A group of rich teenagers were flicking fries at one another at an adjacent table and laughing.

Armando and Esmeralda looked at one another and smiled again, a knowing more adult look, which spoke to the follies of ridiculous teenagers acting out. But those boys and girls having so much fun, and so spontaneously, only a few feet away, seemed to throw into relief the awkward stretches of silence that had opened up between the couple.

Eventually, Esmeralda got up with a hesitant smile. 'I just need to use the little girl's room.'

'Okay. I'll be here when you get back,' Armando said with a big artificial grin.

She nodded slightly and walked away.

All of a sudden, the laughter of those teenagers seemed over-whelming, the glint of the plastic in this place far too bright. Armando felt the need for whisky – the need which was always there – open up into a desperate yearning. But they didn't sell alcohol in this shitty, sanitised gringo place.

He reclined against the hardness of his seat and felt dull despair; the events of the day came rushing back … He had lost his job … He had come to this place with a girl almost half his age … His life … it wasn't supposed to be like this at this point. He should have still been with Cynthia. He should have been married to her – having climbed high in his career, a detective inspector perhaps. But what was supposed to have happened hadn't. He felt bitter, as though life had refused to cash the cheque he'd been promised.

But promised by who?

He did not know.

Esmeralda arrived back at the table, sat down, and took a chip.

'Mmmm, this is amazing. This food, Armandito! I just think it's so amazing. You have the chips and the burger and the meat – it has a different flavour to the meat we have here. Maybe the cows in the USA have different lives.'

He blinked at her.

She elaborated: 'Mexican cows probably have harder lives. They only eat cactuses and things, and not much grass, but the cows from the US have lots of grass, and that's why they taste bett—'

The end of the sentence was interrupted by a burbling giggle.

Her face grew solemn. 'I am sorry. I'm talking too much.'

Armando took in the way she shivered momentarily, the way her eyelids had drooped.

'What's wrong with you?' he said in a harsh whisper. 'I fucking pay for a nice meal, and you go and start doing that shit in the toilets. What the fuck is wrong with you?'

He felt so angry. He was on the verge of swiping his hand across the table, knocking the meal away, and walking straight out of there.

'What? I don't know what you're talking about.' Esmeralda turned her eyes away.

'Esme, listen to me. I'm a fucking cop. That's what I do. So, I know when someone's on heroin.'

Her expression was befuddled. She flinched before his words as though she expected to be struck.

'Why are you being like this? Why does it ... I just ... Why does it matter?'

He stood up, reached out, and took hold of her face with his fingers. Not violently, softly. He turned her so that she was looking into his eyes and couldn't look away.

He spoke slow and deliberate: 'Because it makes you look like a fucking slut. Do you understand?'

She blinked a couple of times.

He felt like spitting on her face.

Her eyebrows narrowed, and he could see the cleft of flesh in between them. For some reason, that would stick in his mind during the weeks that followed.

Her eyes shimmered water, but she didn't cry. Instead, she spoke softly, 'I didn't ... I haven't been on a date for more than three years. So, I was ... I was very nervous about tonight. The last date I had, we went out a few times. And I was happy because ...'

She frowned, looking for the words, forcing her mind to concentrate – Armando had seen the same thing with both victims and suspects.

'Because I thought we were boyfriend and girlfriend. And that was something I wanted. Only, he found out about my job, and he ... he beat me very badly. I spent three weeks in the hospital. Salome ... she was young. I ... I can't think ... maybe around four at the time.'

Esmeralda seemed to lose her train of thought. She was shaking. She gazed at the red paper packet, which held the remaining fries. She was concentrating, but her eyes had lost their light.

Then she began again, her voice dull. 'He told me the same thing as you – before he kicked me in the face. He told me I was a slut. Many men have told me the same thing since. During ... what I do. Afterwards too. Some of them have hurt me, some of them, no. But they nearly always use that word.'

Her eyes closed momentarily.

'I just want to know one thing.'

Armando looked down, but she continued to speak.

'I ... in my job, I give men, men like you ... something. I give you pleasure, but maybe also some kind of escape – from your wives or your job, or those ... things. I try to make you relax, make you feel good. And you, all of you, are so quick to say this word to me,

289

to call me "slut". And when you say it, you're so angry. You say it with such hate. Can you tell me why that is, Armando? Can you explain to me why you all hate me so much? 'Cause, I think that's something I'd really like to know.'

She had a strange half-smile on her face, but it was a look of utter sadness, and then her body convulsed in a single sob. Yet, she held herself together. Just a single tear slipping down one cheek.

Armando sat down again. He spoke carefully but with feeling. 'Listen to me. I got this wrong.' He reached out across the table to her, but their fingers didn't touch. 'I've done a lot of that recently … But let me tell you something. Even though you're a cute princess and I'm a total bear, you and me have got something in common, big time. Do you wanna know what?'

She raised those large shining eyes to him.

He attempted a broken smile. 'What I told you about what happened to my face – that was bullshit. What actually happened was some guy put an axe through the window of my car, and another bonked me on the head so hard that I couldn't see straight for the next few hours.'

Armando gave her a goofy look.

Esmeralda didn't laugh, but she was looking at him now, openly, and that was enough.

His voice arrived in a soft whisper, 'I just wanted to say that people in my job – they're not so great to me either.'

Esmeralda's fingers reached over to clutch his.

He smiled at her, turned one arm, and checked the time on his watch.

'We've got about two minutes left before the film starts.'

She smiled, too.

***

They sat in the darkness of the cinema. Armando had got them a large popcorn and a couple of plastic cups of beer. The opening credits of the film began to roll. Fitting with the Yankee theme of the evening, it was a North American movie called *The Silence of the Lambs*. Armando was fascinated by it because it was about a serial killer, 'Hannibal the Cannibal'. Yet despite his own interest in the subject matter, what happened on screen seemed odd. The Yankees had the cannibal in custody, surrounded by *militares*, but he was still able to rip off one of their faces, use it to disguise his own, and then kill loads of other people in an ambulance.

Ridiculous.

Armando felt himself about to chuckle at one point, but what stopped him was Esmeralda's reaction. He saw that she was genuinely frightened. She would gasp with the audience and cover her eyes. Moments later, her hand curled around his, which felt like something good. When the end credits rolled, the audience whooped and cheered.

Afterwards, the foyer was packed with cinemagoers as the couple pushed their way through the crowds and into the balmy night. As they walked the streets, Esmeralda talked enthusiastically about the film.

'Did you see that Jodie Foster? Don't you think she's beautiful, Armando? Her skin was … flawless. And those cheekbones! She looked like she'd been carved from snow.'

Armando looked at Esmeralda. 'You don't look so bad yourself, you know? I think you put her in the shade.'

'Oh, in what universe? That's the silliest thing I've ever heard.'

But she was smiling.

Armando thought it was true too. Esmeralda was very beautiful – and that Jodie what's-her-face, well, she was pretty in a *gringa* type way, but she was paler and thinner than Esmeralda. Armando liked his women with a bit of meat on them.

'Do you …' she said in a soft voice, '… Do you think there are people like Hannibal Lecter in real life?'

She looked so impossibly ardent, so innocent and kind that Armando was struck by how much, at that moment, she resembled her daughter.

But then he blinked as the images of murdered women scrolled across his mind. He spoke softly, choosing his words as carefully as he could.

'Perhaps. I guess it's possible. But this guy … this Hannibal Lecter, he was very smart. He was a psychiatrist, and you saw in his cell – he was also this great artist who could do these incredible pictures. Some kind of mad genius, right?'

'Right.'

'Right,' Armando affirmed. 'I think, though, such a man – in reality – he ain't gonna be any kind of mad genius. Just someone who's mad. Maybe someone who …' Armando frowned as he tried to express what it was he wanted to say '… someone who doesn't work properly, someone who got broken inside.'

'What do you think could happen to someone to make them get broken like that?'

'I don't know.'

'Well,' Esmeralda said with finality. 'I hope I don't have any bad dreams tonight from that film. Do you get bad dreams, Armando?'

He thought about the question. 'I don't really remember my dreams all that much.'

They had arrived back at Esmeralda's building.

He went in with her.

An older lady came to greet her, kissing her on two cheeks. She looked at Armando appraisingly, like a market woman might look at a piece of fruit to measure its quality.

'So, this is your mysterious *hombre?*'

Esmeralda blushed. 'This is Armando. Armando, meet Lucillia, who has been very good to us and took on the task of watching over my crazy little one this evening.'

'Crazy? Whaddya mean, crazy? She is my *pequeña angelita,* my angel babe.'

'Did she behave herself?' Esmeralda asked with a wry smile.

'Oh yes, but she's not asleep yet. I think she's waiting for a visit from Mummy to tuck her in.'

Esmeralda hugged Lucillia again and walked her to the door. As she left, the old lady turned to Armando and gifted him with a saucy wink.

Armando didn't know how to respond to that.

They went into the *sala*, where Salome's toys were scattered over the floor with all the haphazard frenzy of a child at play. The light was soft, a single lamp in the corner; a children's lamp that threw the shadows of animal shapes onto the far wall.

Armando stepped on a rubber duck, and it quacked loudly.

'That wasn't me,' he mumbled apologetically.

Esmeralda giggled. 'Drink?'

'Whisky if you have it.'

She bought him a glass. 'I have to say goodnight to the little one. I won't be long.'

He sipped his whisky as he looked out onto the balcony and into the night. He saw the telescope, the lens angled in a different direction. He felt happy because he knew that Esmeralda and

Salome were getting some use out of it, and he liked to think about mother and daughter spending time together looking up at the stars.

Esmeralda came back into the room, regarding him with a strange smile. 'You might want another one of those!' She indicated his empty glass.

'Why?'

'The kid wants Armando to come and tell her a story. And she won't go to sleep until she has heard a story from Armando's lips!'

Armando must have looked frightened because Esmeralda smiled all the more.

'I've never had much of an imagination,' Armando said, looking at his large hands. 'I don't know what to say.'

She came over and squeezed his hands. 'I think you'll be just fine.'

He walked to Salome's room and softly knocked on the door before opening it. The little girl was sitting up in bed. By it, there was a small stand with a single flickering candle on top. She had a golden rabbit clutched in her arms. She didn't say anything, just watched him with those impossibly wide eyes.

He was too big for the doorway, and as he came through the opening, he caught the top of his head, the tender part. He winced. Salome's room was very small. He kind of managed to get himself into a sitting position, propping himself up against the small stand she had next to her bed. He groaned as his bruised body paid the price of the manoeuvre.

Salome giggled.

'Jeez, thanks, kid. You'd betta hope I don't sit on you by mistake when I get up again.'

She laughed all the more. Then, she became serious. 'Are you ready to read me my story or not?'

'You like to cut to the chase, don't you?'

He looked around the room desperately. She had some posters on her wall, but he couldn't make out their images in the dark. His eyes fell on the rather limp, worn figure of the rabbit Salome had clutched close to her.

'So, once upon a time, there was this rabbit, and this rabbit's name was …' Armando motioned towards the rabbit.

'Flossy. The rabbit's name was Flossy!'

Armando nodded. 'Yeah, exactly. The rabbit's name was Flossy. Anyway, Flossy was … a special rabbit because she was …'

He frowned.

'… a princess. And she lived in a magical princess castle which was … pretty and …and pink!'

Salome looked at him with haughty contempt.

'That's silly, Armando. In fact, that's the silliest thing I've ever heard. Flossy would never live in a castle, and she would *never ever* live in a pink castle. Flossy lives in the forest where she can run about, everywhere, free. What would she want with a castle?'

Salome's eyes were wide, her lips puckered in a ferocious frown as if daring Armando to contradict her.

Armando looked at her. 'Well, you definitely tell it as it is, kid. Truth be told, stories … they're not really my thing! I reckon that's more your mum's department.'

Salome's expression changed, just like that, abruptly and openly, like ripples travelling across water. She looked almost fearful.

'Please try,' she said in little more than a whisper.

Armando sighed and gave a gentle smile. He looked around the room again; it was so small, and Salome was so small. He felt like a giant.

He started to speak softly. 'Okay, so … once there was this bear, this giant bear. And he was a very bad-tempered bear.'

'Why was he such a bad-tempered bear?' Salome whispered.

Armando thought about it. 'Because he lived in a cave. But the thing was, the cave was very small.' He looked at her door. 'And every time he went in, he would bang his head and growl. But by the time he had sat down, he'd forgotten it happened. So, when he got up to go out of the cave, he banged his head again!'

Salome giggled with delight. 'And that's why he was so bad-tempered!'

'Well, that was definitely part of it,' Armando acknowledged. 'But it wasn't just that.'

'What else, what else?'

'Well, sometimes he would go out into the jungle and see the other animals. Some of them were scared of him, like the sloths and parrots. And some of them wanted to bite him, like the crocodiles and anacondas. So, he didn't spend much time with them. Instead, he would go to the river in the evenings, where the water tasted fresh and cool. He would have a long drink and then go back to his cave.'

'What would he do in his cave?'

'Not much, really. Sometimes, he would light a fire, so he could keep warm, and in the light from the fire, he would watch the shadows on the wall. He would watch their shapes, and they would become the shapes of other animals, only they weren't real. After a while, when he went to the jungle and saw the other animals, they started to look like shadows too. And the same thing with the trees,

296

the bushes, and the grass. They had no colour anymore. They were all just shadows. So, he spent more and more time in his cave.'

'He sounds like a lonely bear. The loneliest bear I've ever heard of,' Salome said with a small, grave voice.

Armando smiled. 'Maybe, yeah. But he didn't feel that way. He'd still go drink from the river, and his cave was still cosy and warm, especially when he'd made a nice fire.'

Perhaps it was the talk of the cosy and warm fire, but the young girl yawned and snuggled against her covers.

'What happened to that bear, Armando?'

'Well, that's the thing … One day, he was walking back from the river, only he took a wrong turn in the jungle. The next thing you know, he got lost. Bears can't hold maps because of their big paws. So, he walked and walked for a little while. Then, he came to a clearing, and from the top of the trees, he heard a sudden, really loud noise.'

'What was it?'

'It was this little monkey. She had soft dark hair and big dark eyes. He met her in that strange part of the jungle, and it was there where she and the bear decided to become friends. And even though she was small and very young, this monkey … she was so very brave.'

'Why was she so brave?'

'Because … because she would jump from tree to tree even though it was so high. And she would laugh at all the anacondas and crocodiles, but they could never reach her. The bear watched her because he'd never seen anyone like that. And that's when … the colour started to come back to the world. The bear could see the plants, trees, and other animals again. They weren't just shadows anymore. And then he realised …'

Armando felt something catch in his throat. He blinked.

His voice was almost a whisper: 'He realised how lonely he had been. And that, for all that time, he'd been waiting to meet the little monkey. And that everything before … had been about that. Only, he never knew …'

'But that's a happy ending. That's a happy story!' Salome said.

'Yeah, kid, it's a happy one.'

'So why are you crying?'

'Am I?' He touched his fingers to his face and then turned away. 'Well, will you look at the time. It's way past your bedtime. Your mum is going to kill me if I don't let you get to sleep.' He reached out his fingers and snuffed out the flame.

'Armando?'

'Yeah, kid?'

'Will you give me a hug goodnight?'

He leant into her, and she put her arms around him. She clutched him as hard as her arms permitted, as hard as she clutched Flossy the rabbit and the other things in her childhood world that meant everything to her. Salome gripped him hard, but to him, her body felt so small, so light. He had no idea that a human being could feel like that.

He eased her back down gently.

'Armando?'

'Yeah?

'That was the bestest story ever.'

'Night-night kid.'

'Night-night.'

Armando got up and left the room. As he went through the doorway, he caught the top of his head again and grunted. He heard the tinkle of the little girl's laugh in the darkness.

He stepped out into the hall, smiling to himself, and saw Esmeralda standing there.

'That was … beautiful, Armando. Would you like another drink? I think you've earned it.'

He nodded and walked into the *sala*, stopping by the balcony to look out into the night. He saw Esmeralda's reflection in the window. He turned and took the drink she handed him. He sat down, and the pain in his abdomen twisted with a sharpness that made him gasp. Esmeralda walked over to him. 'Look what they did to you.' She stroked the side of his face and touched her finger gently to his chest.

'It's okay, it's nothing.'

'It's not nothing,' she said, her voice quieter.

She kissed his forehead and then his lips.

He kissed her neck.

Very carefully, she eased herself on top of him. She undid his shirt and trousers while he peeled up her small black dress. When she pressed against him and enveloped him, he felt the warmness and softness of her against a backdrop of pain, the relentless throb of his bruises and cuts.

It was as if he could feel every molecule of himself.

He moved softly inside of her but gradually faster until she pressed his head to her chest, clutching the hair at the back of his head. They were quiet in the gloom, careful but tender. Only, as Esmeralda shifted position, one of Armando's legs moved a bit, his foot pressing down on the rubber duck, which generated another loud, ridiculous quack.

They giggled in the shadows and then hugged one another close.

He made his way back to his apartment in the early hours. In the dark sky, he saw the first traces of blue developing out of the black and the thin aura of light that ran across the far horizon.

He opened the door to his apartment and went straight to bed, his exhaustion settling on him like a soft, heavy blanket. His eyes closed, and just before he lost consciousness, he thought of Salome.

But in sleep, he dreamt of another child – a child who was stood on a desert plain alone. Armando couldn't see the child's face, wasn't even sure if it was a boy or a girl, but he could see the child looking into the distance, towards the horizon, from which came a low rumbling that grew louder like thunder. A shadow passed over the land, covering the small child in darkness, and then Armando saw the shape of a great wave, rushing towards the tiny figure—

He bolted upright in bed. It was lighter now but still early. The *buzzing* sound of the phone had cut across his sleep, and now the details of the dream were hazy. Yet, the feeling of dread still clung to him.

He forced himself out of bed and answered the phone.

'Hello?' he said, his tone groggy.

Across the static came the sound of someone breathing, a thick, belaboured rustle.

Then, the line went dead.

Seventeen

He was driving towards the city's periphery once again, towards the *tierra*. It was a warm evening, the sun forming a hazy glow against the deepening purples and blues of the changing sky. Armando had spent the day at the scrapyard, sizing up various cars before finding one that was roughly the dimensions he was looking for. He salvaged the left-hand passenger window from the old, burnt-out vehicle and then spent the next few hours seeing if he could install it in the BMW in the place where the first window had been smashed.

The window system of the Beamer was electronic, but Armando didn't have the soldering equipment required to connect the window with the circuit board. So, he removed the board altogether and fitted the window so that it worked manually. It was a finicky job, and he worked up a sweat, but it was satisfying all the same. He liked working with his hands, getting into the innards of the mechanism. When he was done, he tested the window. The glass windowpane slid down in shuddering jolts rather than peeling down in a smooth descent. But it didn't matter.

It doesn't have to be perfect.

Now, he was out in the evening, the window down, gazing out at the mountains. This was the first time he'd been able to enjoy driving the car, to ease the seat back, to press the accelerator and feel the smooth power when the vehicle pulled forwards.

He arrived at the Gracia neighbourhood, not all that far from the Santa Clara district, but this area was not poverty-stricken; the houses were single floor, more spacious and better maintained, with tidy gardens and wide streets.

He stopped outside one such house and exited the car. He knocked on the front door and was met by a man who looked to be in his late fifties. A trim, tidy man whose blanched grey suit and dishcloth features spoke of the trim, tidy order of this twilight neighbourhood, where the soft droning *buzz* of the last lawnmower gives way before the sedate quiet of the oncoming night.

The man introduced himself as Javier Betancourt and ushered Armando inside the house.

The interior was also tidy, sedate, but empty somehow, as though not really lived in. Armando noticed pictures of Javier as a younger man with his bride on their wedding day, gazing out with happy eyes – yet Armando had the feeling those days were long in the past. He recognised the type of man who lived here; someone who lived alone, who got back late from work, wanted to fix a quick snack in the kitchen but lacked the patience to cook dinner – someone who had long since lost the appetite for decoration or the creation of a homely space. It wasn't a bad house; it was well furnished, and everything was in good order.

But a stillness, a loneliness, tinted the air.

'Can I get you a drink, detective?'

'A beer would be good.'

'Fraid this is a beer-free zone, *hombre*. Kicked the habit some years back, after I got sick of the habit kicking me.'

Armando nodded. 'Water is fine.'

Javier Betancourt bought him a glass. He took a sip and then laid it carefully on the coaster on the coffee table.

'As I said on the phone, Mr Betancourt, I wanted to talk to you about your time in Las Asturias. More specifically, though, I'm here to ask about—'

'I know why you are here, detective. You're here to ask about … *him.*'

Armando might not have been a cop any longer, at least not in any official capacity, but he still had a cop's instincts. The other man had spoken softly, evenly, but that last word, that 'him', was pronounced in such a way that the hairs on Armando's neck prickled. He knew … He *knew* with that certainty cops sometimes have that they were talking about one and the same man.

'Can you tell me about him?' Armando took out his notebook. 'Can you tell me everything you know from the start?'

Betancourt got up and walked over to the window.

'It was back in the early eighties. As you already know, I worked as a foreman for Las Asturias. I'd had the job for some twenty years up to that point. And before that, I was five years in the pit. But in the eighties, everything changed. Before that, the mining industry as a whole was mostly nationalised. It was written into law that the state had to have, at the bare minimum, fifty-one per cent ownership of any mining corporation. Copper extraction was a booming, thriving industry. Our miners were skilled, and their wages reflected that. We had some benefits in terms of social care, too – health packages, insurance, what have you. But by the early eighties, things had started to change. The economy moved more in the direction of oil. It was a lot more profitable on the world market, you see. But there were political changes too. In eighty-two, Miguel de la Madrid came to power and, as I'm sure you remember, detective, there was an economic crisis in that same year. The new administration decided to tighten its belt. They cut state spending on industry and instead opened it up to private investment.'

Betancourt rubbed his eyes. In the last of the fading light, he looked exhausted. He made a small helpless gesture with his hands.

'Those private companies tore us to pieces like a coyote and then picked away what was left like vultures. The benefits were the first to go – they got rid of those at a stroke. Then wages were slashed. And after a while, they began to downsize technology – they stopped replacing much of the machinery. Where once men had used mechanical hand suctions and electronic tillers, now they more and more found themselves using shovels and forks. Towards the end, they even stopped supplying the men with masks. It was quite a sight, detective, seeing those men emerge from the pit in the evenings, their arms and faces covered with red dust, eyes streaming.'

His voice was sombre, but Armando noticed a slight tremor in one hand.

'Why didn't the men fight the changes?' Armando asked.

'Oh, we did, detective. We did. But the union leaders, who had fought for the mine in the sixties and seventies as poor radicals and young working men, were richer and older, some of them quite high up in the bureaucracy. They made rotten compromises, and then they betrayed. And when the workers created a fuss, they were replaced by unskilled labourers who were willing to work for a good deal less and could only use spades. These men, they had no background in mining. Many of them were thugs and criminals. They drank on the job, and there were fights and thefts almost all of the time. The private companies didn't look into their backgrounds, hell, detective, they didn't even ask for their names – they simply allocated each worker a number, and at the end of every month, they would get a slip and a few notes in an envelope, cash in hand. Naturally, production flagged. Eventually, they – the companies – closed down the mine, stripped what was left of any value, and sold it off. It all happened in under four years.'

Armando thought about the slip of paper with the number he had retrieved from the old mansion.

'And this man, the man you spoke about at the start, he was one of those – one of the casual, unskilled labourers they brought in?'

'Yes. I don't think I ever knew his name. But I remember him well. I still dream about him sometimes.'

'What can you tell me? Can you give me a physical description?' Armando asked with barely suppressed tension.

'I don't think I ever got that close to him. I don't think I ever wanted to.'

'Was he white? Indigenous? Black?'

'He was white, for sure. I can tell you that much. Dark hair, dark eyes. Also, powerfully built. But not … not like a weightlifter or anything like that. He was … tall, extremely so.'

'And what made him stay in your head for all these years?'

'The miners had their living quarters, temporary accommodations, close to the mine. At one point, these abodes had been reasonable. Small but clean and efficient. But by this time, they were little more than run-down shacks, sometimes housing whole families. He … he lived onsite, on his own. The other men were … wary of him. He kept strange hours. He would go walkabout in the night. Around the same time, pets started going missing. Some of the children on the camp had cats, rabbits, that kind of thing. The pets' bodies would turn up, and they'd have … things done to them.'

'Done to them?'

'Cut open. Insides removed. Things of that sort and then strung up.'

'Hearts?'

'Hearts?'

'Yes, do you remember if the hearts were taken out?'

'I think so, maybe, yes. But I … this is going back some time. I can't be sure.'

'Okay.'

'Okay. So, some of the men got to talking. They got real edgy about this guy – saying he was weird, up to no good – and decided he was the one behind the dead animals. There were loads of theories. You can imagine the kind of stuff. Gossip doesn't just go on between teenage girls, detective.'

'No, it doesn't,' Armando acknowledged.

'But I counselled against it.'

'Why'd you do that?'

'I don't know how much you know about mining, detective, but one of the most important things is trust. When you go down into the earth, there are so many factors, so many things that can go wrong. You have to be able to trust the man working next to you with your life. It was true that, by that time, much of the solidarity had drained away, but I didn't want to make things worse than they already were. I didn't want to set the men against each other if it could be avoided. And …' He frowned thoughtfully.

'And?' Armando prompted.

'And even though the guy made me as uncomfortable as anyone, I thought there was something a little off about it – deciding he was responsible just because he seemed weird, different. Only now, I realise I should have listened to my gut feeling.'

'What happened?'

'It was a Saturday night. I remember that. Me and some friends – some of the few remaining men from the old days who had stayed on after the new lot had been brought in – headed out into the *tierra* for a little camping. There was this hill we would climb a few miles from Las Asturias, and we'd pitch a tent at the top, get a fire going, cook some meat, and look out at the mountains. By that time, we were all struggling for money, and it was a cheap way of blowing off steam. We got there when evening was turning to night. As we climbed up the hill, we almost ran straight into him, coming down the other way, out of the trees. I can't remember if anything was said at that point, but after he had walked past us – once he had gone some distance in the other direction – my friend Guillermo cracked a joke, something along the lines of what a creepy guy he was. We turned round to watch him go … and when we did, he'd stopped. And he was watching us.'

The ex-foreman shuddered as though someone had walked over his grave.

'He must have been over a hundred yards away by that point. But I could have sworn he heard what Guillermo had said. He was looking back up at us with these eyes. They looked quite black. And he was smiling. He was very still. His mouth a little open. He looked …'

Betancourt fought to process the image.

'He looked something like … like a lizard does in the moments before it opens its mouth and swallows a fly.'

The older man massaged the sides of his temples gingerly.

'In any event, we just turned round and got on our way. Back up the hill. We started our fire, drank our beers, and pretty much forgot all about it.'

'Until?' Armando asked softly.

Betancourt looked at him with a haggard, helpless expression. 'Until … a couple of days later. Guillermo got back from work in the evening. He found his young wife, her name was Lupe, in the kitchen …'

Betancourt's voice trailed away. He looked down.

'In the kitchen?'

'Yes. I was one of the first people there. Guillermo was screaming, you see. At first, I thought it was an animal. That no human being could make that kind of sound. And then I saw what he saw.'

Armando waited.

'She'd been strung up. And … opened up. The same as with the animals.' He looked at Armando. 'I'm not a squeamish man, detective. I've seen many industrial accidents, limbs pulled off, eyes plucked out. I saw several fatalities in my time at Las Asturias. But I had never seen anything like that. She … she just wasn't … recognisable. Do you understand?'

'Yes, I do,' Armando replied.

The ex-foreman rubbed his eyes again and sat down. 'There was an uproar. Some of the men got together. They gathered up their picks and spades and went to his shack. They were incensed. But by then, he had already gone.'

'Why didn't you go to the police?'

'We did. We called them. They came to take away the body. But then we didn't hear from them. Sometime later, I went back to his shack. It was squalid and dank. Hard to believe anyone lived there. He'd left in a hurry, but a few things were lying around. I bagged them up. Guillermo was in no state to do anything. But I took those things to the police station. I told them at reception that they belonged to Guadalupe's – Lupe's – killer.

'I remember how the guy at the desk looked at me – with contempt. I think he thought I fancied myself as some kind of detective–hero solving a crime. He told me how everyone knew that the mine was a place of violence. He said they were always being called in to break up fights there or attend drunken domestics. He told me that Lupe had probably been beaten by her husband too violently and ended up just slipping away. I knew that was ridiculous. He hadn't heard the sound of Guillermo's screaming. And he hadn't seen what had been done to her body.'

Armando was hunched over in his chair, his body gripped by a sense of urgency. He looked at the other man closely and spoke very deliberately.

'Mr Betancourt, this is really important. Do you remember what happened to that bag with the things in it? Did you throw it away?'

The older man thought hard. 'No ... no, I don't think I did. I don't know why, but I'm almost certain I put it in storage, onsite.'

'Is it possible it might still be there?'

Betancourt looked at Armando. 'Possible? Perhaps. But likely? A week after I went to the police, Guillermo left. The mine, of course, but Puebla City too. A few months later, I got my marching orders, and they closed the mine for good. They stripped the remaining machinery. It's been abandoned for the best part of a decade, detective. I don't know if there's anything left.'

'I know that this is probably the last way you pictured spending your evening, but will you take me there? Show me what you remember? Show me where you left the bag?'

'Now?'

'Yes.'

***

The BMW cut a swathe of light through the darkness of the narrow dirt road, the black vehicle's long, sleek beams casting a ghostly glow before the forest of shadows and the vast darkness of the sky. It was a starless night, but in the distance, they could just make out the great silhouette of the mountains yonder, and in the small space of the car, they felt like little more than a speck set adrift on an ocean of black.

With one hand on the wheel, Armando reached down with the other to retrieve his whisky bottle. He removed the lid and went to take a swig but then hesitated.

'I'm sorry, I forgot. Do you mind?' he mumbled.

The man in the passenger seat shook his head and waved his hand dismissively. 'Don't worry, I haven't had a drink these past four years, detective. I'm not going to start now.'

Armando took an apologetic mouthful and then nestled the bottle back out of sight.

'What happened after you left the mine?'

'I went off the rails for a while. That's when the drinking got bad. By the time I'd got a hold of it, the wife had already jumped ship. I don't blame her. When you lose a job you've been doing for all those years, you lose your routine, and you lose something of yourself, too – your self-respect. And you're angry at the world. And the people closest to you. After my wife went, it got even worse. And then one day, I woke up in the middle of the street, the sun hot on my face, every part of my body aching, and no sense of how I had got there. Or what had happened to me. I made it back home, took a shower, felt the hot water on my face, and I thought, no more. I don't want to feel like this anymore. So, I stopped.'

'Just like that?'

'Just like that. It was like I'd been taking in poison for so long. Poison from the bottle, poison from the mine, poison from the memories I couldn't stop thinking about. I got to a point where I realised I couldn't take any more. I had to get the poison out of myself. It was time. I know for a lot of people it's a struggle, but for me, it was easy because it just felt like it was time.'

Armando thought about it. He had tried to knock the drink on the head several times over the years. Perhaps one day he would, but he could never imagine losing the urge, just like that.

What is it they say about alcoholics? Once an alcoholic, always an alcoholic.

'So, what do you do with your time now?' he asked.

'I have … I have a good life, detective.' Betancourt's voice was soft but with a slight defensive edge. 'I work. For a while, I worked as a surveyor. Then later, I worked as a gardener. Now I mostly do odd jobs. In my spare time, I'm learning to speak Danish.'

'Danish?'

'Yes. I have a pen friend in Denmark. I write to her regularly. We're planning to meet up one of these days.'

'That's … good. That's nice.'

'You need to turn soon, detective. A small slip road to your left, slow so we can see it.'

Armando turned the car down a thin dirt track; the Beamer was almost too wide for the path. They passed through rickety, net fencing and into the complex of what was the mine. Armando pulled over.

They got out of the car.

Armando could make out the shape of the mine's chimney. He took out his torch and shone it, revealing the skeletal architecture

311

of the main building and the huge wheels that sat motionless on great plinths. Beyond, he could see only darkness.

Betancourt took out his own torch. 'Go carefully, detective. The ground isn't stable.'

The torches cast cones of light over the abandoned buildings of the mine; in their spectral orange glow, the solitude of the jagged ruins felt almost like a ghost town. The ground was covered in a thin film of red dust. It was like they were explorers moving across the surface of an alien planet.

Armando shone his torch outwards to reveal the vast craterous gulf that had opened up in the ground, the rings and rings of layered earth forming great circles around the ravening maw. He moved away from the gap and followed Betancourt to a series of ruined huts, where he heard a soft whispering noise.

'Hold up,' he told Betancourt.

Armando pushed open one door and shone the beam inside. The sound was louder. He saw a ruined sofa and a cracked photo on one wall. It was then that he realised the black floor was moving. Instinctively, he turned the torch downward, and the snakes that blanketed the floor hissed and bridled.

Armando lurched back out of the hut. '*Puta madre!*'

Betancourt hardly heard him. The other man simply carried on walking – to Armando, it seemed as though he was in some kind of trance.

Finally, they came to a bigger building, a type of lodge.

'This is the place. This is where I used to have my office,' Betancourt said with a strange type of wonder in his voice.

Armando entered more cautiously this time. 'And the bag?'

Betancourt shone his torch through the devastated room – the broken desk, the fluorescence of mould that had developed across the damp walls, decomposing papers spread across the floor.

Armando followed him to the back of the room.

Betancourt opened an old cupboard and pulled out three bags. 'I think it's one of these. This was also the place we used for "lost" and "found". I don't know what made me keep the bag. Something, I guess.'

Armando took the bags from him and slung them over his shoulder.

They made their way out.

As they walked, Armando heard a strange gasping sound, almost like a yearning. The sound seemed to echo out from the bowels of the earth, eerily sentient in its tone, as though the earth itself was in pain – a prolonged ancient sigh.

The other man looked at him with dull still eyes. 'This is a "dead zone". They just sucked the life right out of it.'

Armando had never heard that phrase before, a 'dead zone', yet it was entirely fitting. They made their way back up in the direction of the car. Armando paused and then walked over to a couple of large barrels set against one of the walls. The top of one was open. It smelt acrid, pungent in the dry air. He shone his torch into it, ripped a bit of cardboard from a nearby carton, and dipped it inside the barrel. He brought the material out and turned the torch on it. The tip was blackened with a thick goop.

He looked at Betancourt. 'Any idea what this is?'

'It's a compound material. It's used round fuses. In certain temperatures, it hardens and creates a protective wedge. It means that fuses are better protected. That they're less likely to be sparked by accident.'

Armando nodded, but he was certain about something else too. He recognised the texture. Recognised the smell. This was the material found in the eyes, chest cavity, and vagina of the first Jane Doe he had caught – the woman whose body had been discovered at the church.

Lost in thought, it took Armando a few moments to feel the gaze of the other man on him. He looked at Betancourt and saw he was trembling.

'I need to go now, detective. Please.'

'Of course, yes. Before we go, Mr Betancourt, can I ask you one last thing? Very quickly. You spoke of a hill when you went camping. Can you point it out to me? The direction?'

The ex-foreman frowned in thought and then shone his torch back towards Puebla City, moving its direction little by little.

'Do you see it, the shape of it there?' he finally replied.

Armando felt himself tingle. He could see the outline of the hill in the distance. 'That's … Cuexcomate.'

'Yes, detective. Do you know it?'

'Yes.'

It was, of course, the very place where the *federales* had found the second body.

Armando loaded the bags into the boot, and they got back into the car. As he put the key into the ignition, the other man interrupted him in a gentle voice.

'Detective, I think I'd like a quick taste of that whisky bottle now if you don't mind.'

Armando looked at him. 'Hey, are you sure that's a good idea—'

'Just give me a fucking drink, detective!'

Armando was surprised by the sudden vehemence of his tone, but he took the whisky bottle out and handed it over anyway.

Betancourt took a long deep drink and closed his eyes. He kept them closed as he spoke calmly, 'Detective, I'm sorry for being ... abrupt. I know you're concerned, but I can tell you something. I won't want to drink again tomorrow, or the week after, or the year after that. I promise you that. But tonight, I do want to drink. Tonight, I'm going to get very drunk indeed.'

Armando nodded. Started the car. It was only a couple of miles across the brushlands and back to the city's edge.

He drove into Betancourt's street, easing the BMW to a stop outside the man's house.

The ex-foreman got out of the car and then looked back at Armando.

'Detective, do you think I could hold on to that bottle?' he asked, almost as a murmur.

Armando felt like shit, having put this man through such an experience. He wanted to say something ... anything. This guy hadn't needed to agree to do any of this. But the words Armando might have found never arrived.

'Sure, all yours,' he said instead and handed him the bottle.

Betancourt gave him a wintery smile, closed the door, and tapped the top of the roof twice with his hand.

Armando drove away, watching the figure of the ex-foreman grow smaller in the darkness, holding the half-full bottle of whisky in his hand. He felt curdling regret in the pit of his belly. He suspected that Betancourt was a better man than himself; Betancourt wasn't a violent man or corrupt. At the same time, Armando felt that they weren't altogether dissimilar. He and the ex-foreman were both practical men. They liked to work with their hands. Both had

problems with drinking. They were both living out the twilight of
their lives in empty rooms, in lonely spaces. Armando's investigation had collided with Betancourt's life – a quiet life, which was
soft, unobtrusive, and hurt nobody. For the first time in years,
Betancourt would spend the night drinking himself into oblivion,
which was Armando's fault. He hoped that what the other man said
was true, that he would be able to pick up where he had left off,
that he would wake up the worse for wear and never touch another
drop again. But Armando suspected that was not really how life
worked.

Once an alcoholic, always an alcoholic.

As soon as he entered his apartment, he grabbed the nearest bottle of whisky and glugged it into the glass. At once, the guilt, the
shame, began to wane. Betancourt would be alright. He was a sen-
sible, solid individual. There were people worse off than him. Now
Armando could put such thoughts out of his mind and concentrate
on the matter at hand.

He felt the same way he did when he made the first few moves
in a chess game. All at once, everything external faded away, and he
was absorbed in the rhythm, the flow, the logical sweep of the
game.

He emptied the contents of the bags onto the living room floor
and began to rifle through them. Much of it was crap, pungent,
and disgusting – he would have to bleach the floor after he was
done. Most of it was unrecognisable, congealed lumps of items that
had lost all form – just the odd glint of colour or lettering from an
otherwise thick, black hunk of matter. A drink can. A packet of
paracetamols. A tube of toothpaste. The ragged remains of a single
sandal.

But in the third bag, something caught his eye. A couple of blackened cards, which just about managed to reveal the faded image of some big-breasted women, and phone numbers scrawled below. Armando thought, though couldn't be sure, that these cards might be related to the services provided in the Santa Clara red light district, similar to the cards he had discovered in the old hacienda just before the *federales* had burned it to the ground. He thought that this bag's contents were likely what Betancourt had brought to the police some years before as evidence of a murderer.

Then, something else caught his eye. One-third of a ripped, faded black-and-white image. A photograph. He took it between his fingers, his heart thrumming with anticipation and a desperate sense of hope. He brought the fragment to the light. It showed a series of young children with severe scowling faces, and behind them was the darker image of part of a large building. However, what galvanized Armando – what put a fire in his belly – was the smaller sign that some of the children were leaning over, the letters on it just visible:

'St Cassian's Children's Home'

Armando took another deep swill of the whisky. He jotted the name down in his notebook – not that it was necessary, for the name was already imprinted in his mind.

He knew he was drawing closer.

Eighteen

Armando woke up early the next day, the light filtering through the window. He got up and took a swig of what was left from the whisky bottle by the side of his bed and then stepped out onto his balcony to smoke an early morning cigarette. Below him sat the sleek black shape of the Beamer next to his older battered vehicle. He gave a wry smile, for it was a miracle to him that the BMW hadn't been broken into yet or that its smooth dark-pearl paintwork hadn't been scratched up. But these thoughts were fleeting; what had really triggered Armando into wakefulness at such an early hour was a realisation, which had come percolating up from his dreams.

The body of the woman that the *federales* had snatched away, which Armando had only fleetingly glimpsed being zipped up in a black bag – that body had been left in that place for a purpose. Betancourt, the foreman, had described how they had seen the man Armando was looking for returning from the top of that hill, Cuexcomate. Then, some years later, a body had been displayed there. The man Armando was looking for, the so-called 'tall man', the man who 'talked' with animals and sacrificed them – he was no 'Hannibal the Cannibal', he didn't kill randomly like in some Hollywood picture. There was a logic, however twisted, to what he was doing, a ritual, a placing, which had a certain significance. This man had worked in the mine, in Las Asturias. The body that was left inside Cuexcomate was, therefore, bound up with the killer's past. And from that, Armando was able to make a further deduction: the corpse that the priest had discovered in the church all those months ago was a product of the same *modus operandi*. The location wasn't random – something about that church chimed with the killer's personal history. All Armando had to do was find out what.

Sometime later, he pulled up to avenue 30 Pte and the Parish of Our Lady of Refuge. He got out of the BMW and strode towards the church. The yellow tape had fallen to the ground. He walked into the church's main building. It was utterly abandoned. No parishioners, no priest. Inside it was dark, unkempt, and someone had sprayed graffiti across one of the walls. The angry black script read:

'The Christ Cunt is gone forever, but He waits in the down beneath.'

A single stream of liquid arrived from the roof in a *drip, drip, drip*.

But it wasn't raining.

Armando felt his head throb and pressed his fingers to his temples. In the back of his mind, he heard the sound of rushing water, a wave so strong that it would wipe away pain and struggle and indecision – and all life – in its wake.

He blinked.

Drip, drip, drip.

He left the church and went to the small residential building latched onto it. He knocked on the door.

An old woman answered. She had dark hair flecked with grey, and small eyes, not unkind.

'Hello. What can I do for you?'

'Is this the residence of Father Diego Ramirez?'

'Yes, but the Father isn't giving benedictions or confession at the current time. I'm so sorry.'

Armando smiled. 'No need to be. I'm here on other business.'

Her lips tightened a fraction. 'What business is that?'

'Police business.'

'May I see your badge?'

'No, you may not. I'm not here to arrest anyone. I have spoken to the Father before, some months ago, about a case I'm sure you're aware of. I was the first on the scene after he'd discovered the body. Tell him I'm here, and if he really doesn't want to speak to me, that is, of course, his choice. But I think he'll remember me.'

The woman frowned momentarily and disappeared.

A few moments later, she returned. 'Please come in … officer?'

'Detective, actually. But you can call me Armando.'

'I'm the housekeeper of *Padre* Ramirez. You can call me Isabel.'

'Thank you, Isabel.'

Armando was ushered into a small *sala*, a squat but cosy room completely out of keeping with the sheer size of the church attached to it. The priest was in his dressing gown and sitting in a green, furry chair. The Father looked as though he had aged years in the months since last Armando had seen him; his tidy goatee had been replaced by a sporadic unruly beard, grey and thickening, and there were dark circles under his eyes.

Armando sat down on a nearby chair. He smelt the reek of the alcohol that emanated from the priest.

Isabel, the housekeeper, stood by the side of the priest's chair.

Armando looked at the priest. 'Hello, Father. Do you remember me?'

The priest raised his head, those unseeing eyes focussing on Armando. His lips wobbled slightly, slick with drool – his was the slackness of skin and flesh that old age so easily provokes, allowing internal fluids to dribble out with strange and sudden abandon.

Armando found it difficult to believe that he was looking at the same person who had seemed so clear, so measured, only some months earlier.

'I'd tell you why I'm here, Father, but perhaps you already know.'

He let the statement hang in the air.

The priest's eyes lost their focus. They dulled like flames dwindling in the blackness of coals. At once, Isabel intervened. 'The Father has not been feeling well. Actually, detective, it might be better if you come back at another time.'

Armando looked at her. He spoke clearly and carefully. '*Señora*, a terrible crime has been committed. But it's not something I accuse the Father of. I only want to find out if he can help me shed light on a set of events that occurred a long time in the past.'

He turned to the priest once more.

'Father, you discovered a body some months ago. I spoke to you at the time. I think that the man who committed that crime was in some way related to this parish, your church. That he placed ... *her* here to make some kind of point. So, I need you to think about the past, to consider whether someone you once knew might have had some kind of connection with this crime. I need you to think carefully.'

The old man hiccupped and giggled. He blinked at Armando.

'Something amuses you, Father?' Armando asked.

The priest's voice arrived in a whisper. 'It just struck me.' He gave a lugubrious smile. 'You and I, we're in the same business, detective. We both offer purification. We ask the people we encounter to purge their souls, to confess their innermost secrets, to reveal their crimes. The only difference is that you ask on behalf of the state, and I ask on behalf of the Almighty. You demand confession, while I can only ever beg for it from my supplicants. I might only ever encourage it. And now it seems you are here seeking my own confession.'

Armando's brain was working rapidly; there was a hysterical edge to the priest's voice. He was clearly overwrought.

'Is there something you would like to confess, Father?'

Any humour drained out of the priest's face. He looked small, frail. 'Yes, detective. I'm so very tired.'

'Tired?'

The old man's eyes lost their focus again. Then he gathered himself. Forced himself to concentrate.

He spoke in a small wavering voice. 'For so long, I heard the same confessions. Day after day. From the petty to the terrible. Avarice, adultery, covetousness … all the way to rape and murder. They confess. And then they do the same things, over and over … and over. I am tired – not because of what they had done, but because of their … lack of faith. I started to wonder if they believed in Him at all. And I began to hate them for that. I started to hate …'

His eyes lost focus once more.

He resumed in that stuttering, halting voice. 'I started to hate the very people who were turning to God for guidance, who were asking for my help. Then I realised that the lack of faith wasn't on their side, after all. It was on mine.' The priest's voice came in a broken whisper. 'Somewhere down the line, I no longer had love in my heart. Perhaps there's no greater sin than that, detective. No greater loss.'

The old lady touched his forehead with her hand; the gesture was an odd one for a housekeeper to make.

'You're a good man,' she said softly.

Armando grew tentative. 'Believe me, Father, there are greater sins, greater losses. The man I'm looking for, he's no Catholic. And yet … this place must hold great importance to him. I just don't know why. Can you tell me about anyone –someone long ago perhaps – who might have come to this church, who might have made an impression on you at the time? Someone who stood out from the rest?'

The priest raised his head, looking up at him with haunted, haggard eyes.

Armando saw something behind them, a glimmer, some terrible recognition, only for a moment, like a spark perishing against a vast blackness. But it was there – a deep, awakened memory.

The priest looked away.

'Father, you said that somewhere down the line, you no longer had love in your heart. Did something happen way back then? Something specific? An incident, an event … a person? Did you see something? Did you do something?'

The priest flinched.

The housekeeper made to intercede. 'Detective, I must insist. The Father really isn't well. You have no right to—'

Armando leaned in towards the priest, his voice reaching and remorseless. 'I know you know something, Father. Tell me. For your sake – for God's, if you like – but most of all … for *her*. You remember her face, don't you? You remember how we found her that day.'

The old man was shaking. His eyes had grown glassy. He started to blink rapidly, and then he began to whisper rhythmically as though he were conversing with himself, as though reciting a mantra.

'And I saw a star fall from heaven unto the earth ... and He opened the bottomless pit, and there arose a smoke out of the pit, as the smoke of a great furnace. And the sun and the air were darkened ... the sun became as black as a sackcloth of hair, and the moon became as blood.'

He looked at Armando, his eyes gazing straight through the detective as though he was no longer seeing Armando at all. He raised one trembling arm as if to ward off a shadow.

'Enough, detective.' The housekeeper's voice had risen to a desperate shrill. 'Enough of this. I'm going to call your office. I will speak with your superiors, I will—'

Armando was on his feet. He backed away from the huddled old man and raised his arms in a gesture of placation.

'It's okay, I'm going,' he said and left the house.

***

Armando stepped out of the shadows just as the young man was about to unlock his car.

José Luis jolted in surprise before his soft, clean features darkened into a frown.

'Hello, partner,' Armando said gamely.

'I'm not your partner. You're not even a cop anymore. What do you want?'

'Need to talk with you. Just a few minutes of your time.'

'I don't have much time, Armando. Some of us have families to get back to, you see,' José Luis said bitterly.

324

Armando smiled a little. 'I deserve that. I know it. I let you down. I won't bore you with my excuses. The fact is: I need your help. There's no other way to put it. Just a few minutes, José. Please.'

José Luis stood there, blinking at him mutinously.

'Diego's?' he finally asked.

'No, not a cop bar. Let's go somewhere more discreet.'

They walked a couple of blocks, turned down a side street, and slipped into a bar named 'Smokey Joes'. It was dark and gloomy inside, and in a far corner was an old mechanical bucking bull clad with cobwebs.

The man behind the bar was wearing a wide cowboy's hat and barely glanced at them.

In the background, an old Yankee country music song was playing: Kris Kristofferson's 'Casey's Last Ride'.

They ordered a couple of beers and took a booth in the thick darkness. A single candle inside a large glass flickered, casting rings of soft light across the surface of the table.

'So, what is all this, Armando? Why all the cloak and dagger?'

Armando took a swig of his beer. 'You know I've been taken off the job. But it wasn't what you heard. I wasn't kicked out because of insubordination or complaints or incompetence, or any of those things, whatever they might have told you. I was kicked out for one reason and one reason alone.'

Armando took out his notebook and a folder thick with files that had been tucked inside his jacket.

'It was this case, José. It was this man. He's somewhere in these files. And they closed me down because I went looking for him.'

'Ah, the serial killer angle. You know what, Armando? I wasn't convinced by your argument at the time, and looking at you, looking at the state of you … I'm even less convinced now.'

Armando ran a hand over his face. 'Ever since we came across those corpses, the "ladies in the lake", they've been trying to dumb down controversial crimes – especially violence against women. The mayor is up for re-election. I know you know about the politics of this, José.'

'I do, I do. I know they didn't want the discovery of those bodies out there in the papers because of the bad PR, because of the elections. I agree with that. But none of that translates into the story you're telling yourself over and over, *hombre*. None of that screams monster.'

'They've had the *federales* following me,' Armando said in frustration. 'They destroyed evidence. They burnt a fucking building to the ground because it had links to *him!*'

José Luis leaned back in his seat and folded his arms. He took a drag on his beer. 'And you know what I'm hearing now, Armando? Paranoia. And along with it, a lot of white noise. But little in the way of any actual evidence.'

Armando opened the folder and took out Mercia's diary, flicking through to the back pages. He touched his finger to the symbols scrawled across them.

'What's this?' José Luis asked thinly.

'This is the diary of a girl called Mercia who went missing in the Santa Clara area. The same area we eventually traced that figurine to – the figurine found with the first body in the church. You remember the blind gringo who showed it to us?'

'Yeah, I remember him.'

'Maybe you remember, too, that he said that figurine was Aztec. Specifically, it corresponded to Mictlāntēcutli, the Aztec god of the dead.'

'And?'

'And I had an expert look over the symbols in Mercia's diary. He took one glance at them and identified them as Aztec.'

José Luis frowned. 'Even so, that's quite a stretch. The figurine and the symbols might both be Aztec, but so are a lot of stuff. It doesn't mean they're connected.'

'I agree. But now look at this.'

Armando took out one of the Polaroids he had taken of the woman's body at the church. It showed her belly and the symbols drawn on it.

'These symbols here … you see? They're the same as the ones in the diary.'

José Luis nodded a fraction, an assent.

'Mercia knew the man who did this.'

José Luis shook his head. 'It could still be something else. It might not be the one man. It could be a cult. Something like that. That could explain the connection.'

'I spoke to one of Mercia's friends from the time she was turning tricks in the Santa Clara district. She was very specific. Mercia told her about a man she had met. Mercia called him "the tall man". Mercia's friend showed me a place that Mercia had taken her to a long time earlier. I found more things there, more Aztec symbols … and other things. That evidence allowed me to go back further still. This guy, this "tall man", has been around, José. He's been doing what he does for a while. I traced him back to Las Asturias, an old copper mine – closed down now – just outside the Santa Clara district. In the *tierra*. Our guy had worked there as an itinerant labourer, and I got an eyewitness account of another body that turned up there, and the witness was certain our man was behind it.'

Armando leaned forward, his eyes shining intently in the light of the flame.

'Santa Clara, that whole area, man, it's one large killing zone. I went through the books of their local police. The records weren't great, but they were enough to show me in the past decade alone, the murder rate has been three times that of Puebla City as a whole. Most of the victims – prostitutes who—'

'But if one person is doing all of this, operating on such a scale, someone would have known, Armando. This guy would have been known to someone, would have been discovered, if – as you say – all the signs are there …'

Armando leant back in his seat. Took a swig of his beer.

'I've been thinking about that for a while now. The world we move in. It's like one great lake, and we've been wading through its water for a long time. Only that water is brown and dirty, and after a while, you can no longer see through it at all. You can't see the shadow of the shark circling underneath.'

José Luis bit his bottom lip and spoke to Armando in a low voice. 'By doing all this.' He motioned to the papers and photographs Armando had laid out on the table. 'Going after this one guy, you have lost everything.'

Armando began to gather the papers up very carefully, as though they were precious. He looked up at his young ex-partner, and his eyes flickered slightly. He glanced away.

And then he spoke quietly, 'José, I lied to you about something. A while back now, we were talking about Cynthia. I don't know if you even remember the conversation. I told you that she was out living out in Mexico City. But that wasn't true. José … Cynthia died a few years ago. After we split up, she became ill.'

'What? What are you talking about?' José Luis whispered.

'Not long after we separated, she got stomach cancer, a bad one. She was already living in Mexico City by that point. I … I'd messed things up pretty badly. I hadn't treated her good: the drinking, the arguments. After a while, she stopped answering my calls. I never even knew she was ill. I only found out … after she was gone.'

The younger man's face screwed up in consternation as he tried to process this information. 'You're …you're saying all this now? How … how do I know you're not lying about this? Reeling out a story to get me onside again.'

Armando looked at him openly, frankly. His face was haggard, and there was such sadness in his eyes. He gave a small smile, but there was no hope or light in that smile.

'José, I wish more than anything that I was lying about this. After I found out what had happened … I was gone. I went through the motions at work, of course, but for the rest of the time, I was pickling my brain with as much whisky and beer as I could get down me. Wandering the streets at night. Drinking into the early hours. It was like … I was drifting further and further away. But it didn't matter. Nothing mattered all that much.'

José Luis's forehead wrinkled. He went to say something but hesitated. He had never heard Armando speak in such a way.

Armando sighed and sipped the rest of his beer.

'When I caught this case, it meant something. I don't know how it relates to what happened with Cynthia and me. Or where my life was headed. But just … from the start, I had this feeling like I needed to follow it through to the end, whatever happens. Maybe because … because of some of the girls who've been killed, like

Mercia. Maybe because she was a good kid, and I think Cynthia would've liked her. And that, by me doing this ...'

Armando's voice slipped into a husky rasp.

'By me doing this, she might've been ... proud.' He put his hand to his mouth and coughed, a throaty sound. He blinked, rubbed his nose, and looked away.

José Luis looked at him and spoke gently. 'Tell me what you need from me, Armando.'

Without looking at him, Armando reached out his hand and patted his shoulder. 'You're a good man, José. And ... *a true detective.*'

Armando coughed again. He reopened the file on the table and slid a different photo out.

'I don't want you to worry. What I need from you isn't going to put you at any risk. I'm finished as a detective, I know that, but you're just getting started. The last thing I want is to ruin that for you. All I want you to do is run some information. When I went up to Las Asturias, I discovered some stuff that probably belonged to our man when he was working in the mine. This photo, in particular, caught my eye. In the background, you can just make out the letters – you see? They read: "St Cassian's Children's Home".'

Armando touched his finger to the image almost reverently.

'I looked into the place. It was around for decades. Existed before the revolution. And closed in the late 1970s. But I haven't really been able to find out who worked there and on what basis. I found out the director's name for those last couple of decades, one Manuel Angel Ortiz. But he passed away sometime after it closed. Beyond Ortiz, I can't find anything on the others who ran the place. I no longer have access to police records, but you do. I want you to find any names and addresses of people who might have worked there during the fifties, sixties, and seventies. It wasn't a big institution. Perhaps that's why the names have been so hard to come by.'

'You think our man was an orphan. You think he lived in this place as a child?'

'I don't know, but it's certainly possible. If not, he has some connection to this place somehow. One of the members of staff, maybe. José, I'm starting to see him, this man. I feel him … close.'

Nineteen

The sun was high above Puebla City, a white blaze of light filtering through the grey-blue of the hazy mid-afternoon sky. Parque Ecológico was packed full; children playing on the hills, families picnicking, and teenagers skateboarding down the paths that cut through the grass. It was *El Dia de Los Muertos* – The Day of the Dead – a public holiday.

Armando was crouching next to the water, trying to adjust the rudder of a large rowing boat. Esmeralda and Salome were watching a few feet away.

Suddenly, Salome turned to her mother. 'It was you. I know it was you!'

Esmeralda rolled her large golden-brown eyes, slapped a hand to her forehead, and gave a theatrical groan of agony. 'Oh, sweet mother of God, Holy Virgin of Guadalupe, Señora of the heavens … not this again. Please, don't put me through this again!'

Salome scowled up at her mother, watching her dramatics. 'I still know it was you!'

Armando looked up, curious. 'What happened?'

Esmeralda threw up her hands in a gesture of helplessness. 'Madam here has got it into her head that I have stolen her Monopoly money.'

'Well, it was there before. And it's not there now!'

'I understand that, darling. But, Salome, it doesn't mean I took it. Why would I take your Monopoly money?'

The child frowned. 'Well, perhaps you took it so you could buy chocolate and toys. Or perhaps you took it so you could buy a car. So you could go to the zoo to see the capybaras.'

Armando smiled at the kid's imagination.

'But, *princesa*, you're the one who's obsessed with capybaras. And I'm a bit old for chocolate and toys,' Esmeralda reasoned.

'Well, perhaps you took it so you could buy a castle and live far away. So you could leave me.'

Salome pronounced 'me' with stony seriousness, her top lip protruding slightly.

Esmeralda knelt down and looked into her daughter's eyes. 'Why would you say something like that? I'd never do that.'

Salome regarded her mother sceptically. 'This morning, when we were getting ready to see Armando, you said you were going to go and leave me, and you actually opened the door and went away, leaving me behind.'

'Darling, that was just something I said – because we were late. I was trying to hurry you up.'

The little girl carried on watching her mother with those large dark eyes.

Armando felt as if the sadness of the world was contained in them.

Esmeralda reached out and took her daughter's hands. 'Salome. I want you to listen to me very carefully. Because this is very important. I will never, ever leave you. Do you understand?'

'Okay, Mummy.' Salome smiled and blinked.

Armando looked at her fondly, awkwardly. He felt like he was seeing something private. A great and intimate love.

He mumbled into his hands. 'So, it's ready. We're ready to go!'

'Do you want to go, baby? Do you want to go on the boat?' Esmeralda asked her daughter.

Salome looked out over the sleek, shimmering waves of the lake with the same solemn gaze. It was as though she were about to set out across an ocean, never to see land again.

'Okay,' she said softly.

Armando pushed the boat out a bit and got in. It wobbled under his weight.

Esmeralda picked Salome up and handed her to Armando, who took her in his arms and placed her gingerly on the boat's wooden seat. Esmeralda peered at the boat with suspicion before holding her dress up daintily and trying to climb in with as much dignity as she could muster.

Armando shot Salome a wicked look.

As Esmeralda balanced herself on the wooden floor, Armando nudged her seat with his legs, causing the boat to wobble again.

Esmeralda shrieked in surprise. 'No, don't. No, Armando. I-I'm being serious … Don't!'

Salome giggled with delight.

Armando looked at her mischievously.

This kid's a rebel alright.

Once they were all secure, Armando took an oar and pushed out from the edge. The boat cut sinuously through the water, gliding forward. He rowed them towards the small island in the centre of the lake, where willow trees rose out of the lush high grass, sending their long sleek leaves sweeping upward to the sky before arcing over and flowing towards the surface of the water. Underneath, a gaggle of swans moved across the waves in a triangle formation, the mother gliding forward, right out in front, with the babies wobbling and paddling in her wake.

Esmeralda pointed at them. 'Look, Salome. Swans!'

Her daughter smiled. She repeated the word gently. 'Swans!'

The little girl watched them as they passed, watched as they moved away into the middle distance. Salome kept her eyes on them but didn't say anything more. She seemed lost in her own thoughts.

Armando had never seen her so subdued.

'Oh no. Oh no! Argh!' he cried out.

Both mother and daughter turned to look at Armando in shock.

He flexed one brawny arm. 'I've got a cramp. All the strength is gone from my arm. I can't do any more rowing. Kid, you are gonna have to take over!'

Salome looked at him with wide-eyed wonder and then gazed at her mother incredulously.

Esmeralda smiled at her daughter and nodded her encouragement.

Armando placed the oar so that it was pivoted by the side of the boat through the stock.

When Salome gripped it, Armando took his own oversized hand and placed it over hers as gently as he could. Then, he began guiding her motion, pulling the oar backwards and forwards. Gradually, he released her hand. The little girl's brow was furrowed in determination as she tried to sustain the rhythm of the movement, but she overcompensated, pushing the oar deeper down into the water, and at once, the movement became clogged and cumbersome. She used all her body's effort to hoist the oar out of the watery mire, but then it got dragged under again.

'This is stupid. I don't want to play this anymore,' Salome shouted.

'Hey, you need to—' Armando began.

'Don't tell me anything. You're stupid!'

'Salome! Don't talk to Armando like that!' Esmeralda said sharply.

'I will if I want,' Salome shot back mutinously, 'because … you're stupid, too, Mummy.'

Esmeralda's mouth dropped open in surprise.

Armando tried to smother a grin but failed. He looked at Salome.

'You can do it if you want, kid. It's just … up to you.'

Salome looked at him, those eyes impossibly serious once more. She spoke in a small voice. 'I can't, Armando. Because … I'm not big enough. I'm not strong enough.'

Armando moved closer to her. 'Listen to me. This isn't about strength. It's about savvy. You gotta use your head. When you move the oar, it's going in too deep, and the water on top weighs it down, so it's sinking.'

Her eyes never left his. But he could tell she didn't get what he was saying.

He frowned, thinking about it. Then, he began again. 'You know how when you comb your hair?'

She nodded.

'You don't press the comb too hard because if you do that, it hurts your skin.'

She nodded again.

'So, imagine the oar is the comb, and the water is your hair. You don't want to press down too hard because it hurts the water. You just want to comb across the surface. *Entiendes?*'

'*Entiendo,*' she whispered.

Armando helped her position the oar again and moved with her for a few moments. With his other hand, he moved the opposite oar. He gradually relaxed his grip and released her hand. Frowning in concentration, Salome manoeuvred the oar across the surface of the water. The first time she didn't quite make contact with it, but the second time, the oar cut the top of the water cleanly. Armando moved his oar in time.

Salome had her mouth slightly open, her eyes lit up. 'Mama, I'm doing it! Armando, I'm doing it!'

Armando grinned. 'Fuckin' A, kid.'

He looked at Esmeralda sheepishly – in his enthusiasm, the expletive had slipped from his lips. But when he caught Esmeralda's eyes, she was smiling softly, her face lit by the flickering of water riven with dancing light. He felt a moment of happiness as the boat glided across the lake.

He glanced up. From the other shore, he could see a tree, and beside it a figure. Perhaps it was a trick of the light, but for a moment, that figure seemed unnaturally tall in comparison with the tree – though, in the next moment, the boat moved into a sudden patch of gushing sunlight, and Armando had to blink. For a few seconds, there was nothing but blinding white.

When he looked again, the figure was gone.

Sometime later, they left the park and were in the city centre. The wrinkles of blue evening light had given way before the oncoming blackness of the night as they moved up a wide stone walkway. It led to the main plaza of Zocalo and the high vaunted bell towers of the old town cathedral, which were illuminated in a silvery gleam. The cobbled walkway was thronging with people, their faces rapturous, raised in the glow of the candles, which were everywhere, and the profusions of marigold flowers that spilt out from the balconies and benches.

Catrinas were gaping out from the rippling shadows, their white-boned faces stretched in expressions of pantomime horror, the mouths streaked in delighted grins of skeletal black. Clowns were prancing through the crowds, their ruby red costumes shimmering in the gloom, the orange plumes of their jester's caps streaking and curling from their heads. Floats were packed with partygoers on top, dancing and swaying to the traditional boleros, both joyful and melancholy. The air was warm and thick with the fragrant scent of jasmine and the more full-bodied aroma of cinnamon bread.

Salome was walking some feet ahead, with Esmeralda and Armando lagging back, watching her, their hands linked in the shadow.

'Did you see how she was today?' Esmeralda asked.

Armando thought about it. 'She seemed a little subdued. Usually, she's the nosiest one in the room. I don't think I've ever seen her that quiet before.'

'She misses her grandfather. He died when she was three. I thought that maybe kids, when they're that young, don't remember most stuff. For a while, I thought she didn't remember him at all. But children, the way their minds work … it's incredible. Years later, she would say something about him completely out of the blue. Ask me where he is. Or what he's doing. I think that's why she got … frightened before. When she was worried about the Monopoly money. She thinks … she thinks I might leave her. Because she can't really understand why her grandfather is gone.'

Armando nodded.

'Maybe today, in particular, she gets to thinking about him, even if she is not completely aware of it,' Esmeralda said.

A firework went off in front of them with a pop, lines of glittering blue fire fissuring through the darkness.

A couple of people whooped.

Salome watched the fireworks, a small figure in the crowd, her eyes wide, craning her head upwards.

Armando looked at Esmeralda. 'And what about you? Do you miss him? Your dad, I mean?'

Esmeralda gave a shy smile. 'Yes. Everyday.' She paused for a moment. 'When I was a teenager, we had a terrible relationship. He was very traditional, and I was partying, staying out all night, meeting friends … seeing boys.'

'I bet you were a real heartbreaker. You still are!'

Esmeralda shrugged, embarrassed. 'I don't know about that. But things were really hard. When Salome came along, it was the strangest thing. He hated the fact that I'd gotten pregnant, but once she was born, everything changed. Things actually got better between us. It was like, with her, he could be the way he never was with me – soft, open, playful even. Soon after that, he was gone. Then, sometime later, we moved here, to this city.'

She looked out at the bright colours playing against the black, but her face was sad.

'It was only when we first got here that I realised what my father had meant to me. I think that's one of the most stupid things in life – that you only realise something when it's too late. But I understood what he meant to me then.'

'What did he mean to you?'

Esmeralda frowned as though she wanted to get the words exactly right. 'Even though he said many horrible things to me, I realised that, while he was in the world, I'd always felt … safe.'

A single tear slipped from her eye. She brushed it away.

'For a while, after he was gone, I didn't feel safe at all. Only alone and in a strange place, a city where I knew no one. But then …'

She looked towards the little girl up ahead, who was now watching a troupe of dancers with fascination.

'But then I knew that all I wanted was to make sure *she* didn't feel alone. And to be in the world, so she could feel safe. She has me there to keep her safe. And now … she has you too.'

Esmeralda's voice was low, husky, but she spoke with almost ferocious determination.

'Yes, she does,' Armando replied softly.

He put an arm around her and squeezed. 'You're a great mum, Esme,' he added with feeling.

Esmeralda smiled as though it was the best thing anyone had ever told her.

They walked on for a few moments in silence, watching Salome as she danced up ahead, copying the movements of the adult entertainers, grinning maniacally as she did so.

Esmeralda's attention was caught by something else. 'Hey, Armando – that place over there, it was here last year. They do the best doughnuts, cheap but delicious. Chocolate bread ones. Special ones for Day of the Dead. Salome loves them. Can you watch her while I get us some?'

Armando nodded.

'I'll catch you up.' Esmeralda moved towards the hot food stall and disappeared into the crowd.

Armando focused on the small figure in front of him, bobbing as she walked. The people were flowing in the direction of the great cathedral in a stream of colour under the blackness of night. A large group of balloons floated past Armando, momentarily obscuring his vision. He moved to one side, but as he did, a figure, who was several feet taller than the others, and whose face was covered by a black mask with a long, crooked nose, lurched towards Armando, leaning into him on wobbly stilts and cackling theatrically. Something about the figure unnerved him. He shoved the man hard. The figure on the stilts almost went tumbling back into the crowd. Armando moved into the centre of the path again, scanning the area straight up ahead.

The small figure of Salome was gone.

It was as though something opened up in the centre of his being, a rippling crevasse of abject fear. Against the sounds of the tropical rhythms and the chatter of the spectators, he heard the rasping noise of his own breathing, the thudding of his heart. He swallowed, but his mouth had lost all moisture. He generated from his throat a dry desiccated croak. He threw his head to the side, first this way, and then that. The richness of burnished shadow and glittering colour seemed to spin and meld in one sickening blur of overripe images. Armando felt a familiar constricting pressure pressing down on his rib cage, swamping and crushing his lungs, and now he could feel the sudden desperate scrabble for oxygen playing out as the panic attack began to overcome him. He staggered forward, blinking desperately, fighting for breath.

'Armando!'

He turned to see the kid, a big grin on her face.

'Armando, here I am. I thought I'd lost you. Or that you'd lost me!'

Hot tears of relief gathered in his eyes, and then any feeling died cold. She was holding the hand of a tall man wearing a smart, low-brimmed hat.

Armando took in the grey, severe features of Hernando Martin, the retired detective who was now Juan Carlos's hired hand.

The older man smiled mirthlessly. 'Does this little lady belong to you, Armando? I found her wandering over there.' He indicated behind him. 'You really should try to keep a better eye on her. Unsupervised like that … something awful could have happened.'

Those grey predatory eyes were as cold as winter.

Armando reached out for Salome. She tottered towards him and curled her warm hand in his. When he turned to look at Martin again, Armando's eyes were dull hollows, bereft of everything but the blackest hate.

He tried to find the words, but all that arrived was an aborted whisper. 'You…'

Martin looked at Salome and winked.

The little girl winked back as though it was the funniest game in the world.

Martin touched a finger to his hat and edged a couple of steps back, his eyes still fixed on Armando.

Then, he turned and slipped into the crowd.

***

Some hours later, Armando was outside Septimecielo. He entered the club through the back door but could already hear the throbbing sound of the music. Several of the younger revellers from the Day of the Dead parade had ended up here, their faces painted up as skeletons, their eyes wide and dilated, the drugs and the drink helping turn the celebrations nocturnal and frenzied.

Armando pushed through the legions of swaying bodies and made his way up the stairs to the office. He slammed open the door.

342

Juan Carlos was in one corner, close to the wall. He didn't even flinch when Armando walked in. He just stood there, with his head slightly cocked and a lighter in hand. The flame lit his pallid features, giving Armando the impression that he, Armando, was beholding something dead.

Armando tried to contain the fury in his voice. 'What the fuck? You've got people following me. Why? What the fuck is wrong with you?'

'You ever looked at a cockroach, Armando? I mean, really looked at one?' The young man's voice was toneless.

'Huh?'

'There was one on this wall. A small one. But it's gone now.' Juan Carlos sounded sad.

Armando flexed his arms, feeling the anger pulse through them. He considered how easy it would be to …

Juan Carlos's voice arrived across the gloom, the music still thudding from below.

'I watched it for about half an hour, I think. It moved up and down this wall. I didn't hurt it. But I put the lighter close to it. Cockroaches are durable. However, eventually, it felt the heat. And when it felt the heat, it would scuttle further up the wall into the shadows. And then it would stop. I think once it was in the shadows, it forgot there had ever been heat. So, I put the flame to it again. And again, it moved.'

He turned to Armando.

Armando noticed the dark shadows under his eyes, the ghostly white of his complexion, the twitching nostrils, the vacant eyes. He saw the mound of cocaine on the table, accompanied by a half-empty tequila bottle.

'People are the same,' Juan Carlos said reflectively. 'They require that fire. The people down there, dancing – they take pills, they drink, the music plays, and they move. Take those things away, and they stop dead. Same with my employees, Armando. Same with you. You need the fire too. That's why I had you followed, so you understand. I know about the whore. I know about little Salome. I need you to know that.

'I'm not trying to hurt you. I don't want to do that. All I'm doing is bringing the fire close so that I can be sure that you'll move, too, when the time comes. Next Thursday, there's even more money at stake. I need you to make the same pick-up and delivery.'

Juan Carlos's eyes lost focus. He blinked several times and sniffed.

Armando spoke carefully. 'I'm not the person for this job. Not again. I did what you asked the first time. Why don't you just get Filippo to do it?'

'Filippo was loyal but incompetent – I had to let him go. You're the one who needs to do this.'

Those eyes were implacable; white glowing orbs with a dot of black set into their centres. There was an aspect of the young man that was both living and dead, a waxwork sheen set across a lifeless interior. Yet, something which was at the same time breathing, speaking, something that had been set into motion with the pure energy of malevolence.

Juan Carlos moved towards the table mechanically. His arm lurched out before he clutched the tequila bottle and brought it to his lips. Even by Armando's standards, Juan Carlos emptied a great deal of that pale opaque poisonous liquid down his throat.

Armando saw the large vein on the other man's neck throbbing violently against the pale skin. He thought there was a possibility he could overdose on the combination of tequila and cocaine. If that were to happen, some of Armando's problems would be alleviated. He wondered if there was some way he could hasten such an event …

Juan Carlos's black eyes shone. 'I know what you're thinking.'

'Yeah?' Armando asked cautiously.

'You're thinking I'm not really here. Sometimes, I don't think I am here either.' Juan Carlos's words slurred into the nonsensical.

He lurched forwards and then fell into the couch, still clutching the tequila bottle. He closed his eyes for a few moments.

Then, his voice returned.

'You know, when I was a little boy, I had a maidservant. An indigenous woman called Juanita. I remember that she was really fat and brown and funny looking. She smelt nice, though. And she loved me. She loved me a lot. Can you believe that?'

Armando was finding it difficult.

'She lived with us in the house, with me and Dad. He wasn't home much, so she looked after me. The other thing she loved was her pet cat. I don't even remember its name now, but I remember how it looked. Can you guess where this story is going?'

'You killed her cat?'

'Fuck yeah, I killed her cat. But not because I was jealous of the cat. Or because Juanita did something to upset me, and I wanted to hurt her. I don't really know why I killed it. I guess I just did it because … I wanted to see what would happen. What would happen when I put bleach, rat poison, and washing up liquid in its food. I mean, I wasn't a total retard – I knew the effects wouldn't be positive, of course. But I just needed to see. I needed to see … something die. To see what that would be like. Do you understand that, Armando? Kids are curious. I think it's in their nature. I think sometimes they need to see death. To … practise it. Do you get what I mean, *hombre?*

'Sure, whatever,' Armando muttered.

'I felt bad about it afterwards, though. Really bad. So bad that I couldn't sleep. But not because of the way the cat gurgled and rasped as its insides burnt out – actually, that was rather interesting. Nor because of the way that fat indigenous bitch screeched when she found her stupid dead fucking cat. What really frightened me was my father.'

Juan Carlos leant down. He took a bloody rolled note between his fingers and snorted a line of cocaine into one nostril. He gasped, laughed, and then became subdued again. He said nothing for a few moments, and then his face twitched.

He sighed. 'That's good. I need … I have to … feel something.' He looked up at Armando with bloodstained eyes. 'My father never laid a hand on me, Armando, but he was … is … very judgemental. He can make you feel …'

Juan Carlos stretched out one wobbly arm and extended his fingers, bringing them together in a crushing motion.

'My father could make you feel seven inches tall with just one look. And he's also severe – the type of parent who would make you stand outside in the cold for twelve hours at night. That doesn't sound that bad, but when you're a small kid and have to keep standing up, things go through your head. You start to think … strange things.' Juan Carlos's face was twitching again.

Armando noted the peculiarity of his language: sometimes he would speak of his father in the past tense; other times, in the present tense.

A spool of drool unravelled from the side of Juan Carlos's lower lip.

'Why are you telling me this?' Armando asked softly.

The younger man's eyes wavered. Came into focus again. 'She, Juanita, she went to him. She told him exactly what I'd done. I was only six or seven at the time, so I guess I didn't really know how to cover my tracks. I've learnt better since. Juanita was angry and sobbing. She told my father everything.' He blinked at the memory. Took another swig of tequila. His throat convulsed. He jerked forwards, on the edge of vomiting.

Armando knew from experience that it was hard to take alcohol straight after a snort of cocaine, especially given the quantity Juan Carlos had consumed.

'For nights, I couldn't sleep. I was waiting for my father to say something, do something. I was filled with dread. It seemed to last an eternity. But do you know what?'

Juan Carlos looked up at Armando, his face a ghastly mask. 'He never said anything at all. And he never punished me. Sometime later, Juanita packed her bags and shuffled out of the house – if someone that fat assed can be said to shuffle. It was at that point I realised …'

'Realised what?' Armando asked dully.

'I realised there were no consequences. Up until that point, I was frightened of my father, for sure. However, it was more than that – I was frightened by the universe itself. I was certain that if you followed through with the nasty thoughts inside your head, something or someone would always punish you for it. Maybe some people call that feeling God. But after that day, I understood that it didn't matter what I did, however bad it was, because there were no consequences. There … are no consequences.'

Those eyes flickered.

'At least not for me.'

Armando spoke quietly, 'Someone recognised me, made me as a cop, on that last job I did for you. They went after me hard. There are consequences for me.'

Juan Carlos's eyes faded to the point of unconsciousness but sharpened again. He wiped the saliva from his mouth before his face broke into a gradual smile, as if he were remembering a fond recollection.

Then, he released a hiccup of laughter. 'Niggers!' He chortled.

Armando felt the pulsing, beating ache against his temple. More than anything, he wanted to crush this man – or get away from him. 'What? … *What?*'

Juan Carlos regarded him, those coked-out eyes gleaming with fanatical enthusiasm. 'Don't you read *National Geographic*? Don't you know about the niggers in Africa?'

Armando felt the weight of exhaustion overwhelm him.

Juan Carlos blinked excitedly. 'They got a high rate of aids in Africa. The disease came from there – maybe that's why it spread so fast. But those niggers have happened on a cure. Do you know what that is?'

The young man's face contracted into a smile of concentrated malevolence.

'They find themselves a little girl, real young, and then rape her. They think that once they have done that, once they've violated some kid until she's bloody, then they're cured. Purified.'

Armando blinked. His words came out with halting disgust: 'What are you talking about? Why are you telling me … this?'

Juan Carlos's face was outlined by a slashing grimace of gleeful hate. Then his expression dimmed. He spoke softly, and yet, with such toxic menace.

'Because I have been thinking about doing that to young Salome. I feel diseased. Each day of my life. Only now, I think raping that little girl might cure me. Do you think that it might cure me?'

Juan Carlos raised those deadened, bloodied eyes to Armando's face.

Armando took a step backwards, his breath coming in violent rasps. He moaned the words in an agonized, guttural wheeze. 'Why … why would you say … something like that?'

'Because … because there are no consequences.'

Armando's head was pounding. Clenching his fists, he moved towards Juan Carlos, reaching for his neck, ready to choke him to death.

The young man giggled.

'Before you come and hug me goodnight, big man, make sure you smile for the camera. Our mutual friend, Señor Hernando Martin, had it installed only the other week.'

Juan Carlos indicated the corner of the office.

Armando blinked. He'd missed it when he came in; the blinking red dot, the camera angled at the corner of the ceiling.

He turned away at the very last moment, swung his body around, and made for the office door. He hit it as hard as he could, the frame folding and shattering from the impact. He gasped as pain ricocheted through his smashed knuckles.

Juan Carlos laughed all the more and clapped. 'Excellent, very good, big man. You never disappoint.'

But then the humour in his eyes faded. He slumped forwards onto the table and reached out his arm, propping himself up. His focus returned.

His voice was placid again. 'You will do the job next week, Armando. You know that now. And you'll do the one after that. And the one after that.'

Those coked-up eyes had suddenly achieved a definitive clarity.

Armando found himself stumbling out of the office, his whole body wracked with fury, his hands trembling.

Twenty

Armando pulled up in the city centre in the early afternoon. It was raining heavily, and José Luis got into the car, his coat pulled up high to protect himself from the rain.

Armando turned on the windscreen wipers, which swept across the glass, generating a smooth squishing noise, blurring the droplets of water with the lights of the city, creating a mosaic of bleary, glowing colour.

'How the fuck did you afford this?' José was scrutinising the interior of the sleek Beamer.

'Oh, this is just a rental,' Armando mumbled distractedly. Then, he looked at the younger man with earnestness. 'Did you manage to make any headway? Do you have some information for me?'

'*Si, hombre!* Just about. So, as you know, St Cassian's was an orphanage. The director, Manuel Angel Ortiz, passed away a couple of years after the place closed down. You knew that, too, right? Well, by all accounts, he was something of a hard ass. A real upright Christian who wasn't afraid of using the birch on the kids they took in. He would terrify them into discipline with stories of Hell and damnation. That sort of thing.'

Armando nodded. He knew the type. 'And the others?'

José Luis rifled around inside his jacket and pulled out a tattered piece of paper. He smoothed down the thick creases and peered at it through the darkness.

'Okay. So, here's the thing. Old Ortiz, he was in his late seventies when he popped his clogs, so it didn't come as any great surprise, but the other staff members who worked with him were all significantly younger. Yet, they don't seem to have fared much better.'

He stabbed at the paper with one finger.

'So, you got Maria Elena Vasquez, who worked there for seven years. She was thirty-five in 1972, at the time it closed, but died in a fire three years later. Then, Francisco Javier Miranda, forty-one at the time of closure. We don't know what happened to him. He's just registered as a *desaparecido!* Next is Leticia Rosario, another *desaparecida.* Then, Gerado David—'

'But did you find anyone living? A live connection to exploit?'

'Just getting to that, *hombre.* One Marco Antonio Cotto. He was the youngest of the group, but he is still alive. He's now in his mid-fifties. And, best of all, I have an address.'

'José …' Armando's tone was serious. 'I could kiss you! Whereabouts?'

'To the south, in the St Angel district.'

'That can't be more than ten minutes away.'

'There's some other good news too.' José Luis was playing with his hands.

'Yeah? What's that?'

The young man looked at Armando with full eyes – incredulous, childlike – and when his voice arrived, it came with a tone of soft wonder. 'Cristina … She's pregnant. We're going to have a baby!'

Armando leaned over and gripped his partner in a bear-like embrace. 'That's great, *hombre.* I'm really pleased for you both.' He relinquished his grip.

José Luis looked a little embarrassed but happy somehow, too.

'How's she doing? Cristina?'

'Yeah, she's really stoked about it.'

'And you?'

'I'm really happy, Armando. Only …' He hesitated.

'Only?'

'Only sometimes it doesn't seem real. And other times, it hits me all at once. I am going to be someone's father. I'm going to be the father of an actual human being. And it's almost … hard to breathe. It's scarier than anything that happens on the job. Because I can't be anyone's father. Because I was a kid myself only the other day, and I feel like I won't know what to do. That I'll end up messing the kid up.'

Armando looked at him shyly. 'Look, José, I don't have any kids, so I'm probably the last person who should give you advice … but you know what I reckon?'

'What?'

'I reckon every man who's about to be a father for the first time thinks the same as you're thinking right now. Every single one. But you can't know what to do in advance. You only learn how to be a parent by being a parent. You have to get into the water first before you learn how to swim!'

José Luis seemed to unclench, smiling a little more. 'Yeah. You know, that actually makes some sense.'

'What's more, you shouldn't even be here. Why don't you go home to Cristina, eh? I can handle this.'

José Luis looked at him thoughtfully. 'You're not doing this alone. Besides, you don't even have a badge. That'll make it harder to enter houses, to conduct interviews. Nope, I'm going with you. Let's get moving!'

'Thanks, José,' Armando said with feeling.

When they arrived at the district, the rain was falling in a grey drizzle, which caught the late afternoon light. Through it, the shapes of buildings were softened and blurred, and the figures of the people were as muted shadows.

As Armando and José Luis made their way through the streets, the rain stopped, leaving pools of liquid colour on the ground, while the warm droplets of dew clinging to the walls of the buildings evaporated in the heat. When they got to the address, they discovered a rather ordinary set of apartments. They opened the main gate, passed through a square courtyard, and then up several flights of stairs to a corridor, whose darkness was thrown into relief by a small window of pure throbbing light at the far end. They came to a hard, wooden door.

'This is the place,' José Luis said.

Armando unclipped his holster. 'Keep your wits about you.'

The younger man nodded and knocked on the door. 'Señor Cotto, it's the police. Open up, please. We need to talk to you.'

They heard movement inside and casually stepped to either side of the door.

'Show me ID, 'a high, querulous voice said from behind it.

José Luis presented his badge, raising it up to the peephole.

There came the sounds of keys turning and bolts being unlocked, a clicking and clacking sound that began high up on the door and gradually worked its way downwards.

The two men looked at each other. Whoever lived inside was incredibly security conscious.

Finally, the door opened with a creak. They saw a small man looking at them through half-moon glasses, a couple of grey hairs sprouting forlornly from a smooth bald head, lips held together tightly, eyes darting at them, taking them in with quick, shifting nervous movements.

It did not take a genius to figure out that whatever else, Marco Antonio Cotto wasn't their killer.

'Could you please take your shoes off?' Cotto asked.

The two detectives kicked off their shoes and followed the middle-aged man deeper into the apartment. The inside space was gloomy and sparse. He took them into a *sala* and bid them take a seat.

Armando sat down. On the far wall was a series of newspaper cuttings. Front pages of local newspapers. All perfectly arrayed. He caught the main headline of one:

'Leticia Rosario … missing presumed dead!'

Armando couldn't make out the features in the back-and-white photo underneath. But he did recognise the name as one of the people José Luis had identified as having worked at the children's home. In the dull light, the room's bareness, with the papers laid out across the wall, resembled Armando's apartment. The array of information, the way it had been set out, could have corresponded to a typical police investigation.

José Luis coughed. 'I am Detective José Luis, and this is my partner. We've come about—'

'I know why you've come. I've been waiting for you,' Cotto said.

'I don't understand, Señor Cotto?' That was often the detective's default position. To express bafflement and uncertainty to elicit a clarification from a civilian and thus glean more information.

The diminutive man took a seat between them and reached over to the table. There were six table mats laid out in a perfect rectangular formation. Cotto adjusted them, correcting their symmetry, but at the same time, returning them to their original pristine shape.

'You're here about St Cassian's,' he said, his voice soft.

'Yes,' Armando said.

Cotto looked at them with something like shy wonder. 'How did you ever manage to find me?'

'We have … certain resources.'

'How much do you know?'

'We know that your … friends …' Armando motioned towards the newspaper clippings on the wall. '… many of them have disappeared or died.'

'They weren't my friends. I haven't had any friends for a very long time.'

José Luis had climbed out of his seat discreetly. He moved towards the newspapers on the wall, but in standing up, the cushion that had been propped up against the back of the chair had fallen to one side, askance.

Cotto moved with surprising rapidity; he got up, walked over to the chair briskly, took the cushion, shook it twice, and then replaced it. However, as he did so, he carefully pressed it back so that its sides were adjacent to the sides of the chair. He spent several moments nudging the cushion this way and then that until he was assured it was perfectly straight.

He broke his concentration to glare at José Luis. 'Please don't touch anything, detective.'

José Luis turned, raising his hands.

Cotto's eyes were like pinballs, charged with movement, darting from side to side.

Armando made his voice as soft as he could. 'We're not here to interrupt your life. I don't suspect you of any wrongdoing, *señor*. And I'm certain you have better things to do than talk to us.'

Cotto looked at him, his eyes widening, his nostrils flaring momentarily, looking for the sarcasm, looking for the contemptuous insult. But Armando's gaze was even and direct. The other man's expression eased somewhat.

'I still need to talk to you, *señor*,' Armando continued in the same quiet voice. 'I think you might be able to shed light on the person we're looking for.'

Cotto looked at Armando shrewdly. 'I want to tell you something about myself, detective: I am a homosexual. A gay man.'

Armando's lower lip curled in involuntary disgust. He drew back in his seat just a fraction before he could regulate the movement. From the moment he'd stepped into this apartment – among all the strange disorientating elements about the place, about the man – Armando had realised that Cotto's voice had sounded kinda faggoty. But to have it confirmed like this, to have the man tell him something like that, was just … obscene. He tried to ease his grimace of distaste.

Cotto smiled. For the first time, he looked at home in his place. 'It's okay, detective. You abhor me. Me and my kind. That look on your face? I've seen it a million times before.'

'What you do … in your private life is none of my concern, *señor*. I just want to know about your work, in the home, with the *children*.'

He let the last word linger.

Cotto's face lost its smile. The older man just looked sad.

'I liked working with kids, for the most part. I started working at St Cassian's when I was seventeen. Not much more than a kid

357

myself. My parents never knew what I was. What I am. Not for sure anyway. I think they loved me in their way, but … they knew I was different. They were good Christians, and the director of St Cassian's was also a … good Christian. And a friend of my parents. They got me a job there. I suppose they hoped it would straighten me out. I was never a flamboyant teenager. I was … shy. Quiet. Yet, people … they sense if you are different. However much you try to fit in. They sense it in the same way a coyote can sniff blood.'

José Luis eased himself back into the chair.

Armando saw Cotto's expression darken. His eyes were focused on the cushion's position as José Luis sank into the seat. Once more, Cotto's fingers found the placemats on the table in front of him, rearranging them almost instinctively, ensuring they aligned.

'The director, *Señor* Ortiz, was a frightening man, detective.'

Cotto looked at Armando.

'I can see that you are repelled by me. And I can tell by looking at you that you are physically strong. I think you would even probably like to hurt me. But you don't frighten me, detective!'

Armando said nothing.

'*Señor* Ortiz, on the other hand, was a small man. And he was old by the time I was there. He was not physically strong, but I was terrified of him the whole time. We all were, in one way or another. All the staff.'

'Why?' José Luis asked, intrigued.

Cotto glanced at him briefly. 'He was a Christian, as I said. He was very big on that. He talked about responsibility a lot. He had these small, peevish eyes, and he always spoke about God and God's love in the moments before he was cruel. I think his cruelty knew little limits. For many of us, the carers – the people who put the kids to bed, got them up in the morning, cooked the food, organised them all – he was frightening. He'd have you in his office. He'd talk to you about infringements you had made, even if you hadn't known you were doing it. He'd make you understand that even the slightest mistake could not only cost you your wages and your room but you could be blacklisted, struck off. He'd suggest that other people had their doubts about you too. He'd say exactly the right things, even though he was a nasty, stupid, dogmatic man. He'd always know just what to say in order to make you feel helpless and inadequate. To feel like … like you couldn't even open your mouth. He made you feel ashamed without knowing why.'

Cotto's lips were curled in a bitter sneer. Then, the lines of his forehead slackened, and his expression grew temperate again and desperately sad.

'The effect he had on the children was a thousand times worse. He could … do more … there. A child who had infringed, who had committed some kind of infraction, would be locked in the cupboard in the basement for an hour, an evening, sometimes a whole day. The younger ones would scream. The newer ones … I can still hear that sound. There is something about the sound of a child screaming.'

The middle-aged man brought his fingers to the table and began to rearrange the placemats again.

'Sometimes he'd have Girado beat them with a stick.'

'Girado?' Armando asked.

Cotto looked at him with a smile, but the smile never reached his eyes.

'Girado David. I used to think of him as *Señor* Ortiz's general. A younger man. Must have been about forty at the time. Big, brawny, one of these guys who has a black hole inside them, and it can only ever be filled by humiliating and hurting the weaker people who are unfortunate enough to cross his path. I've met many like him since.'

Cotto's face was wracked with bitterness.

'I'm sorry,' Armando said. 'Would you care to continue?'

'Yeah,' the other man replied in a dull voice. 'Well, that was the thing. Girado was the one to physically hurt the kids. But to me, Señor Ortiz was the worst. He never, in as much as I saw, ever laid his hand on a child. But the punishments he meted out, the things he set into motion, and always with that never-ending talk about God ... There was something behind those glasses, those small grey eyes. He'd watch the fear and pain his orders inflicted. His face was grey, immobile. I never saw him take a drink. I never saw him even take his jacket off. He was ... rigid. But behind those glasses, those eyes ... I think that pain ... those screaming children ... I think he liked it. In fact, I'm certain of it.'

Armando looked at him. 'But the director is not the only person you want to tell me about.'

Cotto's face was ashen and immobile. 'No.'

'Who else? Tell us who else!' José Luis demanded in a sudden imperative whisper.

Armando shot his partner a glaring look.

But Cotto's concentration was not interrupted. The older man looked as though these events were playing out in front of him.

'In 1957. Perhaps you recall, there was a great flood.'

José Luis and Armando glanced at one another.

Cotto continued. 'Lots of people, houses, homes, whole families were washed away. Many died, but the survivors also arrived at Puebla City in large numbers. Children separated from parents. Some of them were returned to their homes, their villages. Some of them were shunted from police station to police station. We received several, but there was one in particular …' His voice had retreated into a whisper, his face utterly white.

'And …?' Armando prompted quietly.

'And he was famous before he even arrived, really. Or infamous, perhaps. The men who had brought him, the *policia*, had discovered him on the little lump of land he had washed up on, with a woman they presumed was his mother. Mother and child had evidently been there for some days. Weeks perhaps. The mother had expired. The boy had survived barely. But …'

'But?'

'The corpse of the mother had been … gotten at.'

'Huh?' José Luis frowned.

'The body had been eaten away. Now, various animals swarm through the water during any flood, feasting on whatever they can find. So, it could have been a case of lizards, snakes, and insects. But the police who found her and brought the boy back thought the bite marks on her body hadn't been left by those creatures – at least not exclusively. And given the fact that the little boy managed to survive and for so long …'

Cotto let the implication drain away like dirty water.

'So, the boy was brought to St Cassian's?'

'Yes, detective, yes he was.'

'And do you remember his name?'

'I never knew his real name. For the first few months that he was with us, he was as mute as the grave. The director himself tried to get him to speak, but nothing. Eventually, *Señor* Ortiz decided to call him by the one letter: "M". And we called him that, too.'

'M?' José Luis queried.

361

Cotto looked at the younger man. 'Yes. M for mute. Nothing happened in that place without *Señor* Ortiz decreeing it. So, after that, we all called him M.'

Armando noticed how, after all this time, Cotto still couldn't drop the title 'señor' from Ortiz's name. There remained some sense of deference towards the long-dead orphanage director that this middle-aged man could not rid himself of.

'So, what happened with M?' Armando asked softly.

'He was the strangest child. He didn't even seem like a child at all. All the colour had gone from his face. For a while, he looked like someone who had spent too much time underground. He had the waxy pallid skin of a doll. I remember I had to try to get him to eat. I could get the food into his mouth, and I'd watch as he would gestate it, and he'd even look at me as I poked him with the spoon. But when he'd look at me, I'd get the feeling he was looking straight through me. Like he wasn't seeing me at all. And touching him, even briefly, accidentally, with the back of my hand … it was like touching something cold, something clammy. Like seaweed.'

The older man rubbed his eyes.

'All my life, I've known what it's like to be different. To see the expression on the face of another. That faint but lingering sense of disgust. Over time, little things like that can make you feel exiled from the world. When you have a lifetime of people treating you that way, you can—'

'And the boy?' José Luis asked.

Cotto gave him a withering look. 'All I'm trying to tell you, detective, is that despite my repulsion, despite the feeling of strangeness he provoked in me, I reached out to M. I tried to speak kindly to him when I could. When no one else was listening. Because I also knew what it was like to be a stranger.'

Armando nodded. He used the other man's patronyms for the first time. 'Marco Antonio. Can you tell me how your effort worked out?'

The other man sighed. 'I think, maybe, it had some results, but who knows. He eventually started to speak. He spoke to me first, in fact.'

'That's something, no?'

The eyes of the older man were heavy, haunted. 'You don't understand, detective. It might have been better if he'd never uttered a word.'

'Why's that?'

'He looked at me with that strange, expressionless stare, like he was not really seeing me at all. And those first words ... not easy to forget. He spoke in a whisper. He told me that I was dead. He said that everyone in the home was dead. And then he told me he was dead too.'

José Luis blinked. 'That's ... fucked!'

Armando shot his partner another vicious look.

But Cotto seemed relieved. 'Oh God, yes, it was. Hearing something like that from a kid. I told him it wasn't true. I asked him what he'd meant. He looked back at me with those eyes! He told me that we'd all drowned in the flood. And now, we were living underwater – only none of us knew it.'

'And then?' Armando asked.

Cotto shrugged. 'From that point on, he began to talk. He didn't talk much, but enough to inform the other kids of this ... world view. Naturally, it didn't go down well. And eventually, it reached the ear of the director. Now, you gotta understand, *Señor* Ortiz's whole philosophy, the discipline, the cruelty – it was all papered over by this whole holier than thou Christian ethic. To have some eight- or nine-year-old come along and tell you that everyone was dead, that we were all living in some kind of drowned pagan underworld … it was not something the director wished to encourage!'

'What did he do?'

'He had M locked in the cupboard. At first, for some hours, then later, for a whole night, and eventually, for days. *Señor* Ortiz never laid a hand on him himself, of course – he was far too righteous for that. But he applied every pressure he knew how to get M to say that it wasn't the case, that there were no dead and drowned people here on Earth. That dead souls only resided above in the heavens or below in Hell – a place M himself would soon be burning in if he didn't recant his infernal testimony.'

'But the child didn't buckle?' Armando asked, but the question was more of a statement.

'No. Nothing the director did could make him change his story. But there was another boy. He'd been there for years before M. He was about twelve or thirteen at that time. However, he was one of those boys who mature very quickly. He already had the outline of a beard. His features, his bone structure, had hardened. He didn't look too much like a kid anymore. He was also angry. His name was Julián. He'd insulted the director and been brought up on disciplinary charges and punished harshly. He'd lashed out, hit other children, broken stuff, pissed on the beds of others, and it was known that he'd … interfered with some of the younger boys. We, the staff, had to restrain him on several occasions, and one time, he'd even broke Maria Elena's nose. She was the one person in that place who talked to me like a human being. So, you can imagine, I wasn't fond of this kid. This Julián. Yet despite that, I realised where he was coming from. We had a file on his life before he had

364

come to the orphanage. It didn't make for nice reading, detectives, to put it mildly.'

'Marco,' Armando interjected carefully, 'what does this boy's story have to do with M?'

'That's the thing.' The older man looked utterly haggard. 'Ortiz had been frustrated by M despite the petty tortures he'd inflicted on him. But there was this one room. It was cordoned off from the rest and had a bunk bed. Usually, a carer would have slept there, or maybe two, taking turns watching the kids for the night on the main corridor. But the director put M and Julián in that little room together.'

'And what happened?'

'I don't know exactly. I only know they were there, together, at night, for a while. And one day … one day when the kids were taking recreation …'

'What did recreation involve?' José Luis asked.

'A time wandering out in the gardens in front of the orphanage. They would have their lunches out there in the summers. But they would always go for walks, most days. Sometimes, the kids would break away and hide in the trees at the far back. When Julián didn't return, we assumed he'd done something like that. It was the kind of thing he did. Only then we heard a shout. But it wasn't from Julián. It was from M. He directed us towards Julián and said that some dogs had slipped through the railings and attacked him. So, he'd come running out to tell us.'

'But there were no dogs?'

'The bites on the boy's body – I am no expert, of course – but my guess was that they weren't canine in origin.'

'And Julián himself, was he killed?'

'No, he survived. He recovered … physically.'

'So, what was his explanation?'

'He never gave one. He never spoke again.'

'And M? What happened to him?'

'One of the things we used to do was take day trips – to churches, holy places, sanctuaries. As I said, *Señor* Ortiz was a devoted Christian. On one of those trips, some months later, I believe, M disappeared!'

'Is it possible, *Señor* Cotto, for you to give me some kind of physical description of M in the way that you remember him last?'

The older man blinked. 'I can do better than that. I have a picture from the field trip we took. The same day M up and vanished.'

Armando's heart felt like it had leapt into his mouth. This was more than he could have ever hoped for. 'That would be very useful … to us.'

Cotto left the room.

Armando and José Luis looked at one another, both primed, both on the edges of their seats, but neither said a word.

The older man was back moments later, with the picture in hand. He pressed it on the table and slid it towards Armando rather than put it into Armando's hand. Armando was relieved by that. As faggots went, Cotto was clearly not a bad person, but at the same time, Armando didn't want to be touched by him.

Armando took the picture and peered at it. Another black-and-white image. Not outside the orphanage this time. Somewhere else. Armando felt an odd sense of recognition, familiarity.

'Which one is M?' he asked, placing the photo back down.

Cotto touched a finger to a small face.

Armando peered at the boy. He seemed so … ordinary. His featureless white face was defined by two dull, dark eyes. He looked sullen rather than angry. Armando had no doubt that he was seeing the man he was looking for. The 'tall man'. Yet, it didn't seem quite real. This child was no taller or smaller than the others, just average. Armando had expected something more, but he was just a child.

He looked at Cotto. 'You have the clippings on your wall, the newspaper articles, and this photo so close to hand. What do you think happened to the other carers? The ones who disappeared. The ones you once worked with.'

Cotto answered with a single whispered syllable, 'M'.

'If he came for them, what's to stop him coming for you? Why do you stay here, in this city, holed up in this place?'

Cotto looked at him.

'My whole life, I've been told what type of job I can take, how I can dress, even the type of person I'm entitled to love. I feel so angry, detective. I feel I've had so much … taken from me. I don't suppose I'll be around all that much longer. But I will choose the place where I'll live the rest of my life out. That choice belongs to me.'

Armando nodded. This guy looked like the type who was always going to be bullied from pillar to post, but in his own way, he had eventually managed to man up, to make a final stand. Armando recognised a nobility in that – despite what Cotto was, no matter what he did with other men.

Armando glanced back down at the photo, at the image of the sullen child. All at once, something else hit him; he had to catch his breath.

At the side of the cluster of children stood a couple of carers and another man. The man had a thin goatee and was dressed in robes with a priest's collar. The face was much changed, it was true, but it was unmistakable.

Armando was looking at Father Diego Ramirez as a young man.

367

He knew now why the scene had evoked a sense of familiarity in him. The trees in the background, the wall behind them – it was the courtyard of the Parish of Our Lady of Refuge. The exact same spot where the first body had been discovered.

Armando looked up at José Luis. 'We need to go, now!'

The younger detective got moving at once.

Armando snatched the photograph from the table and stood up. But just before he headed out, he stopped and looked at the older man. Without even thinking about it, Armando placed a hand on his shoulder. The other man turned his face upward to look at him.

'*Señor* Cotto, the information you provided is very important. You just made a real difference here.' Armando turned away, almost running out of the door.

Once they were in the car, the words flew from his mouth.

'It's the priest, José. The priest, that church. I knew it was connected somehow. That motherfucker … I knew he was involved in some way. He's the lynchpin, the key. We need to get to him now.'

José Luis' response was lost in the sudden screech of the tires whizzing against the tarmac.

Some minutes later, the BMW pulled to a halt outside the Parish of Our Lady of Refuge. The men jumped out of the car. Armando was about to head in the direction of the priest's small abode, which was lodged next to the church, but then something caught his eye. From the church building came a flickering orange glow. The two men reached the main gates.

Armando pushed them open, and the detectives unholstered their weapons, moving swiftly through the shadows and into the church.

Inside, a series of flickering candles had been delicately arrayed in the fashion of a late-night mass. But the Christ figure suspended above the church altar looked wrong somehow, lopsided. At a glance, its paintwork seemed too vivid and slick, and its face was locked into the type of visceral agony that was quite unlike the holy, pristine suffering of a traditional religious icon. Also, there was no loincloth; the figure had its testicles exposed, with a shrivelled puckered penis and a rash of silver pubic hair. A sudden stench of faeces wafted across the dry air, and Armando saw the shit, which had dribbled down one of the legs. He felt his guts protest – the food he'd had that day pushing rancid flavour up through the piping of his body in a single hot belch. The figure had been raised in the classical crucifixion pose, but its chest had been peeled back, opened up in a single gaping hole – the shadowy lineaments of viscera draping and dripping within. At that point, the whole horror of the scene cohered, and Armando recognised the face of the priest, the face of Diego Ramirez – his eyes were rolled back, the pupils barely visible above unseeing egg whites, which had congealed like jelly. His mouth was slack, his tongue hanging out.

As Armando was taking all this in, he saw the figure of a man standing to one side, watching them. Someone in a pew, wreathed in shadow. Someone who was incredibly tall.

Armando peered and blinked. Only the mouth and eyes of the figure were visible. And the pale white skin. It was … grinning.

It seemed to happen in slow motion. Inside his head, Armando was already cursing himself for taking so long to draw. He reached for his sidearm and pulled the gun out, pointing it at the shadow.

He aimed his weapon. 'On the ground, now!'

The creature didn't move. Something rippled from within the darkness. Its voice arrived, an unnatural cloying sound, the sound of something that hadn't spoken in a long time, a gargling sound filled with mirth and rage.

'Noooaaa!'

It moved so fast.

In the same moment Armando fired, it flitted to one side and was gone.

The two men dashed down the aisle and through the door into which the figure had disappeared.

José Luis was panting. 'That's fucked up. That's so fucked up!'

'I know, José.' Armando rasped.

They moved into a dark space. Armando recognised it; they were in the kitchen. He could make out the rims of the saucepans, the pots in shadowy outline. He had been this way before.

They moved deeper in. There were two doors at the end. One to the courtyard on the left and one leading deeper into the back part of the building on the right.

Armando nodded at José Luis. 'Go that way. I'll take this way.'

Armando moved through the door on the right. He stepped into a corridor of almost complete darkness. He felt his way around using his free hand, the gun held out in the other. He hadn't even thought to bring a torch. But he couldn't go back now. He wouldn't risk losing this guy, not again.

His eyes began to adjust, and he saw the shape of the wall curling around. He was waiting for any movement, his finger so close. Usually, you wouldn't start to depress the trigger until you had aimed. Until you had sight of a target. But now, time was of the essence.

He allowed his finger to relax, to squeeze gently to the point at which he began to meet resistance. It was like any other machine. That point of resistance. Only a little more, and the contraption would be sprung.

He crept around the corner and felt something move in the gloom. His finger was on the verge of breaching the threshold.

The voice came out of the blackness. 'Armando.'

'José?'

'Jesus, *cabron*, I almost shot you.'

'Likewise. How the fuck did you lose him?'

'Are you shitting me, asshole? I came round. Must have been a perfect circle. You're the one who let him get away.'

Armando was about to say something more when they both heard the scream. It cut through the darkness, an agonized, mutilated, desperate sound.

Both men broke into a dash, moving back towards the church's main hall. When they stepped out into the steady glow of the gradually diminishing candles, Armando recognised the priest's housekeeper on her knees, gazing up at the flayed cadaver.

Armando looked at José Luis with desperation. 'I need to talk to this woman, José. Without the Father.' He nodded at the priest's suspended body. 'She might be our only hope.'

José Luis looked at him grimly and touched the walkie-talkie by his side. 'Do what you need to do. I can give you ten minutes, no more. And then I have to call it in. If a civilian calls this in first, and the police arrive to find me here, just scratching my ass, I'm finished. And if they know I'm helping you …'

Armando nodded.

He rushed over to the fallen *señora* and touched her head gently. He felt a sense of hysteria rising up from his belly. It was as though he, Armando, were blessing her, and all the while, the *Padre's* guts just went *drip, drip, drip.*

He tried to make his voice as compassionate and caring as possible. 'Don't look.'

'I won't … I won't leave him.'

He caught that in her tone – more woman than housekeeper. He had registered it before, but now it was confirmed.

He put his finger under her chin and raised her face up to meet his gaze. 'Isabel. I know you loved him very much. I know that. But you can't help him now. I'll make sure he's taken good care of, but I need to get you … home.'

He was praying that the solidity, the solemnity, he offered would be enough to curtail her screams and coax her away from the murder scene, back to her abode, giving him the one chance he might have to get the information he so desperately needed.

She let him raise her up and lead her out of the church. He looked back at José Luis and nodded ever so slightly.

When they were back in the small cottage-like building she and the Father had shared, Armando sat her down in the soft green mouldering chair where the Father had last sat. He took the liberty of going out into the small pokey kitchen. Found a bottle of brandy. His hands were still shaking. He knocked a third of it back, quickly. Swallowed hard. Then he took out two dusty glasses. He poured some brandy into one. Some water into the other.

He went back into the room.

'I'm not much of a drinker, myself.' He slid the glass of brandy towards her. 'And I'm sure you're the same. But I think you need to drink this now. It'll help calm your nerves after … what you have just seen. I know there's nothing anyone can say, but please … just drink this.'

The elderly housekeeper looked at the glass of brandy he proffered as though she couldn't quite make it out. Then with trembling fingers, she brought it to her lips and drank it in a single gulp. She stared out for a few moments before registering Armando's presence again. She looked at him vacantly.

372

'Why ... why would someone do that? His chest, his body, his ...?' She started to cry.

He watched her, thinking about the time, the little time he had, but he didn't press for anything yet.

Finally, she looked up at him, her large wet eyes forming a single question, credulous and childlike: 'What am I going to do? What am I going to do now?'

It was a question Armando had heard before, the same tone projected through a hundred and one different voices. Especially older married couples who'd spent their lives together, and then one had simply faded out, leaving the other alone. Sometimes death came suddenly, violently, at the hands of others – sometimes it was just time itself, the most artful and relentless of all butcherers.

He looked at the old lady and felt compassion for her. 'You were more than just his housekeeper, weren't you?'

She looked at him and went to say something. Her lips wobbled; she was on the verge of sobbing again.

She blinked the tears away. Spoke with dignity. 'We were man and wife. I knew Diego when we were both young. He was devoted to God and to the cloth. It hurt him to offer up our deception, but I never thought twice about it. I loved him. He loved me. And I know that love made God happy. I felt it. Whatever the priesthood might say.'

Armando chose his next words carefully. 'But Father Diego made other connections too. There was a child, a long time ago, from an orphanage. A poor child who possessed nothing ... not even a name. Something happened between him and the Father. Something the Father found difficult to talk about. Perhaps they got ... close.'

He let the last word linger in the air.

The old woman's expression changed; her ragged, grief-riven, tear-stained demeanour gave way before a sense of baffled incomprehension. Then her features hardened, sharpened, into an expression of anger and disgust.

'You … you would say something like that … now?' She was breathing hard, struggling for breath.

'I'm only trying to understand,' Armando replied softly. 'When I spoke to you both before, there was something that went … unsaid. Whatever happened, whoever this boy was, he eventually became a man. And that man is the reason why Father Diego … why your husband has been … hurt so horrifically.'

The old lady seemed to sink back into listless despair.

She spoke with a flat voice. 'I know about the child you speak of. Diego told me about him. And yes, that boy was a part of his life that he was ashamed about. But not for the low, sordid reasons you imagine. Diego would never, ever have … touched a child in the way you are insinuating. He loved children. He didn't hurt them. The boy from the orphanage – you're wrong about that too. He did have a name of sorts. I believe they called him "M". Diego said he was the most troubled child he'd ever come across. Things had … happened to the boy. Awful things. The orphanage, St Caspians—'

'Cassians,' Armando corrected but kept his tone gentle.

'Yes, St Cassians. The director brought the boys to the church as part of their education every few months. Sometimes this boy – he'd arrive showing bruises. He almost never said a word. Diego believed that the masters of the school were mistreating him. So, Diego would try to make an extra effort – to point out parts of the church to him, to show him the areas the other boys hadn't been permitted to see – to make him feel as though someone, at least, was interested in him, cared about him.'

'But respectfully, *Señora* Isabel, if that was all it was, why did your husband feel so ashamed?'

The old lady's expression was washed out and rueful.

'Diego was … the kindest person I'd ever met. He didn't think of himself that way, of course. Good people never do. But he felt a kinship with the poorest people. Ill people. Homeless people. People who dressed in rags and whose bodies stank. People who had done furtive, horrible things – in them, he could always sense a better nature, a kinder nature, albeit one buried deep inside. That was his gift. That was what God had gifted him with.'

'And M?'

She looked at Armando with haggard, haunted eyes. 'He told me that the boy had an effect on him. The way he looked out, the way the boy stared. His face. His features. Those eyes. Just looking at him – Diego said it made his skin crawl. Diego knew the child was being abused. Beaten. Who knows what else. I think for that reason, my husband made an effort. But he could find no love in his heart. Even though he knew the boy was one of God's creatures, he could find no love in his heart for him. And that day, when the boys from St Cassian's arrived and M disappeared, I think Diego felt something like relief. He never used that exact word, but I think that was what he felt. I think Diego was glad the boy was gone. And I believe he never forgave himself for that.'

Armando was leaning forwards. 'The boy, M – he disappeared while they were visiting the church, the Parish of Our Lady of Refuge?'

'Yes.'

'Do you think you could tell me—'

She hissed. 'You have what you came here for, detective. You've stuck your finger into his life, and you've moved it around until you have touched the shame and inadequacy of someone so much kinder than you'll ever be.'

Her eyes welled over. Her voice came out in a shell-shocked whisper.

'And … they haven't even cut him down. But why would you care about that?' The old lady stood up, her whole body trembling. 'You get out! Just get out!'

He raised his hands, stepping away; he had the sudden surreal feeling that the old bird was about to clock him with one of the glasses. In the same moment, he heard the sound of police sirens, a wailing that gradually grew louder. He nodded at her before backing away and hurrying out of the house.

He got into the car. José Luis was waiting for him.

'*Puta madre*! That was fifteen minutes at least.'

Armando stuck the key into the ignition, revved the car, and sped off. He caught the glint of blue in the rear-view mirror as the cop cars came sweeping towards the church.

Armando turned the car violently, and they were out of view. He drove down the street and then the next one before pulling the car to an abrupt halt in a darkened alley.

He rounded on José Luis. 'You must have seen him. When you were in the courtyard. You must have seen him go over the wall!'

José Luis blinked at him.

'Oh … you … *motherfucker*. Don't you even try to lay this on me. I saw no one. And those walls around the church – they're at least fifteen feet. He'd have to have been Spider-Man to scale those. There was no time. I would have seen him!'

'Well … then, maybe …' Armando said in desperation. '… maybe he hid in the trees, in the foliage of the courtyard. Maybe that's how you missed him.'

'I didn't miss shit. I circled the trees. I saw everything inside – every shadow, every movement. I know my job. You might wanna remember that, *civilian*.'

Armando banged his fist against the wheel of the Beamer.

'Okay, okay,' he muttered.

They both sat in mutinous silence for a few moments.

Finally, Armando submitted. 'I know you didn't miss anything. It's just … this is the second time I've come this close. We almost had him, José. I don't know how he got away. I'm starting to believe this guy might have supernatural powers after all.'

José Luis looked mollified somewhat. 'Did you get anything from the old woman?'

Armando rubbed his eyes. 'Difficult to tell, *hombre*. She was in a bad way after seeing … what she saw.'

Twenty-One

The evening had fallen. At this point, Armando would have switched on a couple of lights in the apartment, offsetting the dull gloom. Or perhaps he would have had the TV on to make him feel a sense of movement, of colour. To make him feel that he wasn't completely alone. The last shards of light thrown up by a sun, which had been swallowed by the horizon, were barely enough to outline the shapes and objects in his apartment.

Right now, he was looking at one object in particular. It was a twenty-year-old bottle of whisky that Cynthia had given him for their anniversary – the last anniversary they'd spent together before she departed the city and then the world. It must have been worth something; he knew that. She was always incredibly generous with her gifts – and her feelings. For whatever reason, he had decided to save it rather than drink it straight away. And once she was gone, he felt an almost superstitious fear before that bottle, as though if he were to open it and consume it, he might lose the last connection to her he had. It was absurd, irrational, and yet it was a feeling he could not shake.

Yet, as he stood in the gloom that evening, he was watching the bottle intently. He'd emptied his whole apartment of all remaining alcohol; bottles and bottles of whisky and tequila, some a quarter filled, some entirely drained. He'd gotten rid of them because, this evening, he needed to be sober. Had to be. Everything depended on it.

He was headed out once more at Juan Carlos's behest to pick up the first package, the cash, and return it to Septimecielo. There, he would pick up the second delivery, the drugs. The pure coke that the Sinaloa Cartel distributed through Juan Carlos and his father and their crime syndicate in Puebla City. Armando was to take the coke to the warehouse, where it would no doubt be cut and mixed before being distributed lower down the food chain.

He gazed at the whisky Cynthia had bought him. He wanted to take a drink, not just because his nerves were on edge but because, if he was killed this evening, the bottle would remain untouched, and no one would ever know that it meant something. Meant something to him.

Perhaps he should take a drink, for the memory of her …

Or perhaps that was the justification his alcoholism required.

He turned away in the gloom, left the apartment, and got into the Beamer.

He drove to the same estate, the same dilapidated courtyard with the single lonely basketball ring overshadowed by the gloomy tenement balconies. He saw the same lonely sentinel, got patted down in the same fashion, offered the same password – 'Septi' – and eventually returned to his car with another package of cash. Only, this one was a lot thicker, heavier. It was sealed, so Armando couldn't estimate how much money there was, but he was confident that it was more than he would earn in a lifetime.

When he arrived at Septimecielo, Juan Carlos wasn't around. Armando understood that. When these deliveries took place, Juan Carlos busied himself at 'La Casa Blanca' – the biggest casino in Puebla City and located bang at the heart of the city centre. There was no more perfect alibi. As sick as Juan Carlos was, the young man was cunning. He knew how to protect himself.

When Armando made his way up to the office, he was greeted by the grey figure of Hernando Martin. Armando handed him the cash package without meeting his eyes. The ex-detective went to the back of the office, opened up the safe, put the package in, and withdrew another – a much bulkier series of packages in a sack.

He handed it to Armando. 'Don't be a dumb bastard. Do this properly, get it out of the way, and things will be easier for you. You can have a real life. With that woman and her kid.'

Armando noticed that he hadn't called Esmeralda a whore. This time there was no threat in his words, just an appeal.

He looked at Munro briefly, nodded, and took the bag.

Armando made his way out the back entrance and got into the BMW. He took a breath. Started the car. What would happen in the next half an hour would determine everything. His mind span momentarily. His heart was pounding. He ached for a drink. He closed his eyes in the darkness. His palms were sweating. Perhaps he could pull over, buy just a small bottle. He tried to slow his breathing. He heard a voice, rich and throaty and wise. A friend's voice perhaps:

'*You play clever, Armando. You tink quick in the moment. But you don't have all dat much patience. You don't play a long game. In prison, the one thing you have is time. And from dat, you take patience. A day can feel like a month sometime. So, you have to learn to wait. And watch. Let life do its ting. Roll with dat. And then make your move. You hear me?*'

He saw the black man in his mind's eye, those eyes glittering with humour and swift, vulpine craftiness despite Cheese and Bread's great age. Armando saw the pieces on the chessboard laid out under the vast blue of an afternoon sky, and it was as though everything that had happened, and everything that would happen, was contained in those pieces, in that place – in the grin of withered lips, in the glint of an old man's eye.

He put the Beamer into gear and drove away from the club.

When he pulled up outside his apartment, he got out for a few moments, went over to the old, dilapidated Chevy sedan, did what he needed to do, and then returned to the BMW.

He put his foot to the pedal again, and the car pulled away. He headed towards the warehouse, the place where the drugs were to be delivered – the place where he'd been attacked with an axe and shot at, only to make it away in one piece, barely. It occurred to him his chances would be even lower this time around. But he never made it there. Instead, breathing hard, he parked and killed the engine not far from the city centre. There was that same feeling, that building sense of anxiety, of desperation, the feeling of fear spiralling out of control and running amok across the pathways of your body, flooding you, paralyzing you.

He looked at the sack in the back, laden with drugs. He took a piece of paper from his pocket; the number Juan Carlos had given him was on it. He picked up the car phone and dialled.

It rang for a few moments. His heart thudded. Then a crackle. And then Juan Carlos's voice. The single greeting: 'What the fuck?'

'This is Armando.'

'I know who this is, you fucking dimwit.' The young man's voice was a curt crackle.

Armando forced the words out. 'I'm sorry … boss. I can't do it. If I go there again, they'll fucking kill me. I just can't.'

Silence.

'I thought you were a man, but you're just as pathetic and frightened as everyone else. You're going to do this, Armando. If you don't, I'm going to—'

'Listen, Juan Carlos, please. I'm begging you. I've left the car and the package. It's on …' He looked at the quiet square he was parked in. 'It's on Plaza Royal! It's not far from the city centre. You can get that guy, Munro, to come pick it up. The bag is in the back of the car. I haven't touched any of the contents. I don't even know what they are. You win, okay? I don't want to fight. I haven't robbed you, boss. The car is intact. Your property is intact. Just get Munro to come now, and pick it up. I'm sorry. You won't see me again.'

Juan Carlos's voice crackled again across the phone, but Armando hung up. He took in another breath, a deeper one this time. The advantage was that the car and its contents were only two minutes from 'La Casa Blanca' – the casino where Juan Carlos was at that very moment.

Armando left the bag in the back of the car, grabbed the keys, and exited the vehicle. He left the driver's door slightly open and walked away with haste, his head down. He moved away from the square to behind a tree, where he tried to calm his breathing. Then he looked back.

It wasn't long before a black Porsche swung into the square. It sat there for a few moments before a figure got out of the vehicle. In the darkness, Armando recognised Juan Carlos. The younger man glanced at the BMW but did not approach it. He looked around. Scanned the streets, the buildings. Then he spat on the ground and muttered something.

Armando couldn't make out what Juan Carlos said, but he suspected it wasn't complimentary. Finally, Juan Carlos went over to the abandoned BMW. He tried one door cautiously and saw the driver's side was open.

He opened the door using the arm of his jumper to cover his fingers. Gazed into the vehicle.

A couple more seconds.

Armando's heart was pounding.

Suddenly, Juan Carlos snatched the bag from the back, returned to his Porsche, got in, and started the engine.

Armando watched the car leave the area before running back to the BMW and digging the keys into the ignition. Juan Carlos's car had already zoomed off, but Armando knew where the young man was headed.

When he pulled out onto the main freeway through the city centre, he caught sight of the Porsche up ahead. It was true that Juan Carlos had managed to apply pressure to leverage and gradually force Armando into doing what he wanted. The young man loved to exert power, more than anything else –this Armando had realised almost too late. And power was something Juan Carlos had. Armando couldn't report Juan Carlos's criminal activities to the Puebla police because Juan Carlos's organisation had long since infiltrated that same police, including Armando himself. Armando couldn't kill the abhorrent young man. Juan Carlos was too visible. Such an act would inevitably incite retaliation, not only against Armando himself but also Esmeralda and Salome – as Juan Carlos had already made abundantly clear. Most of all, behind Juan Carlos's father lay the shadow of the Sinaloa Syndicate, which was more powerful and terrible than any other. If you wronged them, you turned up dead, buried in the desert, mutilated, the insects swimming through the eye-sockets of your rotting skull. There was no real opposition to the Sinaloas.

No real opposition, that is, except one.

The *federales*.

The militarized state police force had been locked in bloody combat with the Sinaloas since the mid 1980s, when the *federales* carried out a sustained and brutal offensive, burning thousands of acres of Sinaloa marijuana fields, interrupting the planes that transported their coke from Colombia. A couple of years later, the *federales* had struck at the heart of the organisation, arresting the Sinaloa general *par excellence*, Miguel Ángel Félix Gallardo. For their part, the criminal organisation had reacted with unparalleled murderousness, targeting the *federales* and their allies, committing assassination after assassination. At times, it seemed nothing less than a civil war.

Armando pushed down the accelerator, and the BMW sped across the central freeway, following the Porsche some distance ahead. In the airless night, he heard that sound. A faraway rumble that echoed like a distant storm while the noise built and built until its thunder threatened to crack open the carapace of the world.

The motorbikes swept past him in formation – those dark-suited figures, their black visors strapped to their heads –roaring onward, honing in on the vehicle up ahead.

Armando watched as the *federales* bore down on the Porsche. Watched as Juan Carlos desperately tried to outrun the men on the bikes. Watched as one of the *federales* withdrew his machine gun. A second later came the sound of spattering bullets rattling briefly under the Porsche's wheels, sending the vehicle swerving and screeching to a stop at the side of the road. The bikes surrounded the vehicle the same way a group of lions might surround a buck.

As Armando slowed, drifting past in the BMW, he caught the image of the Porsche door being opened, and Juan Carlos, white-faced, his hands raised up in the front seat. Armando glimpsed him for a second, and then he was gone.

Armando had given the *federales* no reason to believe that he had discovered the tracking device they had placed under his sedan. Armando had left it where it was, clamped to his old battered car until a little time earlier – when he'd pulled up outside his apartment, removed the device, and thrust it into the bottom of the bag that contained the cocaine. He then left the bag in the back seat of the Beamer. He only needed to see if Juan Carlos would take the bait.

The *federales* had been trying to catch Armando in a compromising position. They wanted to put an end to his investigation, an investigation that threatened to reveal the horror just beneath the surface, an investigation that would prove damaging to the public image of the city and the career of its venerable governor. But any frustration that the *federales* might have felt about losing Armando would be more than made up for by finding Juan Carlos with twenty kilograms of the finest Sinaloa cocaine. Finding Juan Carlos – the son of the most significant criminal boss in Puebla City and a conduit to the cartel more generally – with drugs in the car would be like gold dust.

The *federales* were notorious for their extra-judicial activities. They would take members of the cartel – or people connected to the cartel – into dank underground places and apply certain methods of persuasion to their bodies. Juan Carlos was in for a rough few days. Armando envied them, those *federales*. He remembered the words Juan Carlos had spoken about Salome. He would have very much liked to have been there when the *federales* began their grotesque work on the body of that sick little shit.

But that wasn't chess. Revenge wasn't chess. It wasn't the key thing.

What was important was that Armando now had a window of opportunity. Hernando Martin would take some time to realise what had happened because Juan Carlos had not been arrested by local police. Given Juan Carlos's connections, it would eventually be established that he'd been taken by the *federales*, but it would take a little while longer.

Armando kept one hand on the wheel. In the other hand, he fingered a small miniature screwdriver.

This was chess.

For the screwdriver represented his next move. Cheese and Bread had told him he needed to play a long game, and Armando had taken that advice to heart.

Now, the game was unfolding just as he had intended.

***

The dark pall of cloud in the night's sky had broken again, unleashing a hard stream of black rain that threw up a misty veil as the black BMW glided off the freeway and into the suburbs. Armando's hands were trembling slightly; he needed whisky, if only to steady them, but there was much to do and little time.

As he drove down a central road, even though it was night, he hit traffic; a knotty string of cars honking and beeping, while the rain tapped out its relentless rhythm and wheels spun and sloshed in the gulfs of water that had so quickly formed.

As the BMW picked up speed again, Armando saw the bleary lights highlighting the scene of an accident: an overturned car with a body inside, its lifeless face bathed in that strange preternatural orange glow.

He shivered, though the weather was humid; he had a surreal, almost otherworldly awareness of his own exhausted, ageing body – the vulnerability of flesh, the interminable forces that pulled it towards death and decay. He suddenly felt older than his years, so very fallible, but he smothered the feeling, putting it to the back of his mind and forcing himself to concentrate.

He pulled up outside Esmeralda's block and made his way to her apartment. The air itself felt cloying; strange electricity seemed to trip across it, and he glimpsed the outlines of the mountains in the distance, their shape in the darkness hued in an eerie purple glow.

Esmeralda opened the door.

'Are you working?' he asked.

'No. I finished hours ago.'

'And the kid?'

'She's with the neighbour. Fell asleep round there. I'll pick her up in the morning.'

'Can I come in?'

'Of course, Armando.'

They went into the *sala*, the room that Esmeralda had shaped for Salome, decorating it with sea maps and the little girl's favourite cuddly toys – wide-eyed fishes, smiley octopi.

Armando closed his eyes for a few moments and imagined the sounds of the sea: the crashes of waves, the squawks of gulls. In the soft light, he realised how much he liked this room. It felt safe somehow.

He reached out and took Esmeralda's hands. 'Esme.'

She looked at him.

'I want you to stop working. I don't want you to do that job anymore.'

'That's not your decision to make, Armando.'

'I know that. But I have to leave the city, and I want you and Salome to come with me. We could go … to the coast. We could build a new life there. Is that something you think you might want?'

She looked at him, astonished. 'Are you serious?'

'Don't I look serious?'

She looked at him a few moments more.

'Is that something you might want, Esme?' he repeated, keeping his voice soft.

'Yes,' she replied. And then, 'No. I mean, I don't know. Salome … she goes to school here. She has her friends here. I have … I would have to think about it.'

'Okay. That's okay. But I don't have much time.'

'Why?'

He looked at her thoughtfully. He felt the screwdriver pressing against the inside of his pocket. He went to speak again but then closed his mouth. He put his hands to his temples and winced.

'What's wrong, Armando? What's going on?'

He smiled ruefully. 'When I was a kid, I'd wake up early in the morning and get this feeling in my belly. This feeling like something bad was gonna happen. And I was afraid.'

'I can't imagine you being afraid of anything,' Esmeralda said shyly. 'What were you afraid of?'

'That's the thing. It wasn't anything specific. Not a monster, or a bigger boy, or anything like that. Just a feeling without …' Armando searched for the words '… without definition. Just … something bad.'

He looked at his hands and frowned.

'I've been feeling like that again recently.' He looked at her and smiled. 'But with you and Salome, it goes away.'

He looked at her for a few moments longer. Then winced again. He brought his fingers to his temples and massaged the skin there.

'Esme, do you think you could make me up some hot chocolate and a little aspirin? My head's killing me.'

'Sure,' she said softly.

'In the meantime, I might step out onto the balcony. Get some fresh air. Give me a chance to see how the telescope's working.'

Some minutes later, he was standing outside, his face shining with warm rain, gazing up into the blackness. The strange purple hue behind the mountains had deepened, and the sense of electricity in the air was palpable. He heard thunder somewhere in the blackness. Then, another sound, a low-level rumble that seemed to come from the ground itself, seemed to come from inside his bones. For those few moments, it was as though he could feel the earth underneath him moving in its great, eternal rotations through the dark. And in the darkness, he saw Cynthia, and he saw Salome. He saw the little girl, and he saw the legions of dead women, and perhaps he would never stop seeing them. Even if he left the city, even if he managed to make it to the coast, perhaps they would always be with him, their faces, their dull still eyes – a silent reprimand from a world drowned in black. For, he hadn't managed to find the figure who had haunted them. He hadn't managed to give them their rest. That same figure had evaded him twice – once at the old mansion when Armando had pursued him and again at the church. Someone who had disappeared into thin air. A figment, a shadow. Someone he would now never find. The figure known as 'M'. M for 'mute'. M for 'Mictlāntēcutli'. M for ... 'Mictlān'.

His hand opened, and the small screwdriver he had been holding dropped to the floor, making a tinkling sound that barely registered as the rain streamed across the balcony.

A new set of images flashed across his mind with violent clarity. He saw the young professor in the classroom, speaking about the Aztec mythology; Armando heard the words:

'After the great flood, all the souls were sent there. Mictlān was the name of Mictlāntēcutli's domain ... Mictlān was his underworld!'

Then Armando saw the brutalised face of the stricken homeless prostitute, Kassandra, and he heard himself ask her, 'Mictlān? Can you tell me where it is?'

She had put her finger to her lips and then looked down.

Down at the ground.

Finally, Armando remembered the conversation with Salome. He recalled the little girl telling him, 'I am going to be an explorer ... I'm going to find the secret tunnels that run under Puebla City.'

In response, he heard himself saying, 'That's just a fairy story ... Look, kid, I heard those same stories when I was your age. But nobody has ever seen them. And do you know why? Because they don't exist.'

But what if they did exist?

What if Salome had been right all along? What if the stories he had heard as a child were true? What if 'Mictlān' was a reference to a real underworld, the network of tunnels that, as legend had it, ran underneath Puebla City?

Suddenly, Armando understood. The man he had been hunting ... Those two occasions when Armando had just missed him ... M hadn't disappeared into thin air.

He disappeared underground.

The bastard's using the tunnels!

The door opened.

Esmeralda was holding a small cup of hot chocolate and two aspirins. Her eyebrows were raised in consternation. 'I just heard over the radio. They're issuing flood warnings across the city. People are being told not to travel if they can avoid it.'

The rain was coming down in sheets now.

Esmeralda edged her way back inside. 'Do you want your hot chocolate?' she asked meekly.

He barely registered the question. 'Esme, do you have a phone I can use? It's urgent.'

'There's a payphone one floor up,' she replied, her eyes widening.

He moved past her back into the house. 'I gotta go. I'll be back as soon as I can. Think about what I said.'

He rushed upstairs and raised the payphone's receiver. There was a crackling dial tone. He pressed some pesos into the slot frantically and dialled the number. He took in a breath when he heard the smooth burr of the ringing.

Across the crackle came José Luis's voice. The young man sounded groggy.

'José, I know how he did it. I know how he got away from us. I think I can close this!'

'Armando? Do you have any idea what the hell time it is?'

'Meet me at the church. Be there in twenty minutes. I think we can close this. You and me, José. Tonight.'

Twenty-Two

Armando was driving towards the place where it had all begun, the Parish of Our Lady of Refuge. The rain was falling in torrents now, water rushing along the edges of the streets in streams of black, hitting the pavements and roads with a *slapping, splashing* violence. The air was heavy with its aqueous vapour, the night sky a blur of dark, dull shadow above. The lights of the BMW cut through the dark watery miasma, the windscreen wipers working furiously, sliding across the never-ending flow of liquid bucketing down from the blackness, and yet, Armando couldn't see more than a few feet in front of him, such was the force and ferocity of the deluge.

Eventually, he could make out the shape and contours of the old church. After he parked, he took his torch and unlocked the safety on his weapon. Things had come full circle; everything had led back here, to this point, now. He closed his eyes; the sense of inevitability swelled in him – the feeling that he was being pulled by some invisible force exerting its power from within the blackness of the storm.

Something slammed against the window.

Armando automatically reached for his sidearm. Beyond the glass, he could make out the dark shape of a figure. He wound the window down a little. He saw José Luis's face peering at him, aghast and slick with rain.

'What the living fuck, *hombre?*

Armando got out, trying in vain to shield himself from the rain as he walked around the front of the car, his feet already heavy with water, his socks squelching in his shoes.

José Luis looked at him. 'What the hell are we doing here, Armando? The flood warnings are all across the TV every fifteen minutes. People have been told to stay inside. Sounds like good advice to me. I fucking envy them.'

Armando could barely hear José's voice through the loudness of the rain. A peal of thunder opened up from the sky above, illuminating the old church and the yellow tape that had once again been placed around it.

Armando gripped José Luis by the arms. 'You were right, José, and I was wrong. You didn't fuck up. Neither of us did. He didn't go over the wall, and the bastard wasn't hiding in the trees!'

'What happened to him then?'

'You remember the story about the secret tunnels underneath Puebla City? The story kids used to talk about in school? The story our grandparents told us? I think that story might be real. I think, somehow, he went underground. Into the tunnels. That's why we missed him.'

'Are you shitting me? Are you actually shitting me? You brought me out here in the dead of night, in … *this weather*, all because of some urban legend?' José Luis blinked the water out of his eyes furiously.

'I know it sounds … fucked,' Armando admitted. 'But it's the only possible explanation. I almost had him before, at the old house I told you about. I followed him down into the cellar. I was sure of it. But when I got in there, he'd vanished. Disappeared. The mythology this bastard is constructing, all that Aztec stuff, remember? In his sick mind, everything revolves around that one place …

Mictlān. The underworld, José … *literally* the place under … our world.'

José was shaking his head. 'We can't go in there with that. We would be … disrupting a crime scene. The murder of a priest. They're going to be all over this place tomorrow.'

'One hour, José. Let's just take a look – one hour. You are already out here. You're already wet. Just give me one hour.'

Armando was gripping him in desperation. His voice came in a strained whisper.

'Please, José, I need this.'

The other man nodded.

After ducking under the yellow tape, they made their way into the church. The rain was pounding on the roof, thin lines of water streaming down, *splashing* against the corners and crevices of the main chamber. In the shadows, the old building had already begun to take on the aspect and odour of a slowly decaying ruin. The priest's body had long since been removed, but a stillness hung in the air, the lingering empty echo of the deceased.

The men shone their torches through the gloomy dark as they made their way down the central aisle, past the altar, into the back, and then through the kitchen and around.

'Same as before,' Armando whispered. 'You go that way, I'll go this way, and we'll meet in the middle.'

'I don't even know what I'm meant to be looking for.' José Luis hissed in frustration.

'Something. Anything that leads downward. A gap, a porthole, a stairwell. Something barely visible. In a place no one would think to look.'

José Luis sighed.

Armando watched as he walked away, the glow from the torch casting a bobbing beam of ghostly white light. Armando turned and went the other way, following the passage around from the kitchen, shining the torch over every inch of ground. The passage wound around the back of the altar; the ground was rough with uneven concrete that had never been smoothed out into a tiled floor. Every now and then, he came across an abandoned old cooker or a three-legged chair. There was the smell of dampness, not just from the heavy rain outside but something with a sour, more elemental tang –something that held peat and dirt, the flavour of mouldering earth.

Armando crouched down, following the cusp and contours of the low parts of the wall and heaving some of the discarded appliances to the side in order to see what was behind.

When he finally caught sight of it, he knew immediately this was it. A stone slab had been shifted to one side, and behind it was a heavy metallic grate. Beyond that, nothing but utter blackness. He leant down and put his hands to the cold metal; flexing his arms, he gripped the bars, pulling the grate out and sliding it to one side. At once came a blast of cold, stale air from underground.

He shivered.

Then, the sound of the rain on the roof began to quieten, and the shadows started to fade, and from the centre of his vision, a sunny brightness began to bloom. Now he saw the church as it had been, decades before, in the early afternoon, the parishioners lining the pews. He saw the murdered priest alive again – only this time as a young man with kind eyes and a faint moustache, his dark rich head of hair only just beginning to thin. Armando saw a couple of other figures. One of them was a shy-looking young man whom he recognised as a baby-faced Cotto – before the hardness of his life had set in. He saw the group of children gathered around as the priest talked. Children with mirthless quiet eyes. Children dressed in dour second-hand clothes.

And finally, he saw him. The sullen face, the dark shadows under the eyes, the mussy hair, and that dead stare. He remembered how M had come to believe he was living in a drowned world, living in a land of ghosts.

Armando watched the priest show the boys the new altar before leading them around the church. He watched as the boy with the strange eyes lingered at the edge of the group before slipping away into the back of the altar. The boy made his way into the corridor and peered into the shadows; for the first time, a glimmer of curiosity was in those dull-set eyes.

The boy walked up to Armando, passing straight through him before bending down to the vent. Armando watched the boy crouch, putting his weight into the effort. His taut body curled against the vent, using all the strength he had until finally pressing it free and sliding it to one side.

The boy looked up at Armando one last time and then moved into the gap. He disappeared into the darkness.

As the boy's image faded, thunder clapped from above, along with another peal of lightning, which illuminated the craggy passageway and returned Armando to the present.

'José,' he shouted. 'José!'

From somewhere, he heard the faint call back. A little later, the younger man arrived panting. He looked at Armando crouched by the grate.

'Take a look,' Armando said, shining his torch into the darkness of the open vent.

José Luis peered forward. The beam illuminated a wide underground tunnel carved out of rock. Across its floor ran a tumbling, rushing stream of water.

'*Jesús Cristo*,' José Luis murmured. 'I don't believe it. It's real. You were right.'

Armando grimaced. 'I'm going down.'

José Luis put a firm hand on Armando's arm. 'You don't know what's down there. You have no idea what you're walking into. We need to get back to the cars. Call it in.'

'I can't do that, José. He's been down there … for so long. He'll know the tunnels like the back of his hand. Thirty men marching through them … He'll hear them before they get near. And he will disappear for good. You go back. Call it in. But I need to see this through. Tonight. Now.'

José Luis gritted his teeth. 'You think I'm letting you do this on your own, *cabron?*'

Armando nodded and lowered himself through the vent and into the tunnel. It was hard to judge just how far down it was. He tried to get his feet as close to the ground as possible and then dropped several feet, landing hard, grunting under the impact, crouching in the cold flowing water.

He looked back up. 'It's about three metres down, José.'

The other lighter man dropped down, landing elegantly like a cat. He looked at Armando through the darkness.

Armando shone the light back up to the vent. Two, thin metal chains flowed down into the tunnel from the displaced grate and shimmered in the gloom.

Armando took one in one hand. 'This is him. He uses these to pull the grate back into place once he's come through it.'

Far above came another rumble of thunder.

José Luis was moving from foot to foot in discomfort. The water swirling around their feet was about three inches high.

Armando spoke in a whisper. 'The storm is flooding the tunnels. This water is going to rise. We need to get moving.'

José Luis made to move forward, but Armando stilled him.

'José. This guy … There's nothing … human in him anymore. And he's … strong. If he's down here, this won't end in an arrest. We're not looking to put the cuffs on him, *entiendes?*'

By way of reply, José Luis touched his sidearm.

The two men moved further into the tunnel, shining their torches in front of them.

'It's so cold. How could anyone live down here?' José Luis said.

Armando said nothing. His feet were soaked and numb. The hairs on the back of his neck were brittle and damp. It was as though the cold had soaked into his joints and bones; his movements felt heavy and sluggish.

They walked and walked.

His body ached.

The water was a little higher now. He had the urge to sit down, to prop himself up against the tunnel wall, to close his eyes for a few moments, but something told him he might never get up again. That he might simply float away in the darkness.

Up ahead, something rustled.

Both men reached for their pistols. Now they were creeping forwards as the cold water rushed around them, tickling the backs of their calves.

Again, another sound, this time a low growling rasp, an inhuman sound. Two glinting red eyes appeared in the darkness. They surveyed the men for a moment and then rushed towards them. The two men drew their weapons, but the speed at which it came, bounding across the wet streaming ground, took them aback. Neither man could peel off a shot before the snarling hound was on them, leaping high onto José Luis's chest. The younger man could barely raise his arm, and the dog bit into it with powerful crushing jaws.

Armando couldn't risk firing into the animal, but with an agonizing cry, José Luis was able to throw the dog back. His weapon had fallen to the floor, so he was backing away. But immediately, the dog crouched, coiled, ready to spring at him again.

But this time, shots rang out. The dog collapsed.

Armando lowered the pistol, his hands shaking.

'*Puta madre*! My gun. I dropped my gun,' José Luis said in desperation, shining the torch deeper into the tunnel.

'I see it ... I think I see it ...'

He broke into a run, splashing through the rushing water.

Armando, still panting, headed after him. He saw the figure of José Luis up ahead as the tunnel curved, and then he heard something else. An indistinct sound.

When he came around the bend this time, José Luis was gone. Armando felt the type of fear that begins as a small tingle deep inside your bones, gradually building towards an elemental sense of dread.

That dog was surely his – M's.

It would have alerted *him* to their presence, and the gunshots would have confirmed it. Everything was beginning to break down before Armando's eyes in the dark.

He broke into a run, trying desperately to catch sight of José again. He came to a point where the space expanded, and the tunnel forked into two directions. He didn't want to make himself known any more than he already had, but he was gripped by urgency, panic.

He called out into the blackness while at the same time muffling his voice, 'José!'

The sound echoed briefly before being swallowed by the constant noise of the rushing water, which was almost touching his knees now. It was that much harder to move; below the knee, he felt the cold and wet working its way into his skin. He had the feeling of someone close by. He turned, shining the torch, illuminating the space behind him, but there was only nothingness. He turned the beam forwards again, directing the light into the two tunnels ahead. He remembered that José was a right-hander. Right-handed people generally chose right when it came to direction. Armando knew such reasoning was flimsy at best. It depended on the assumption that José Luis was still standing, still capable of making a choice. It depended on the assumption – the desperate hope – that M hadn't already got to him. But that assumption was all Armando had.

He staggered onward into the right tunnel. The shadows thickened, and the air was heavy with aqueous vapour. Armando's torch blinked a couple of times and went off. The darkness was absolute. Nothing but the sound of that water. Nothing but the sound of his heart thudding within the black.

The image of Cynthia came to him again, the image from a nightmare he sometimes had; Cynthia, her eyes wide hollows of anxiety set into a skeletal bald head, lying on her back in a hospital gown, sliding into the dark opening of a hospital machine.

When you're in the prime of life, when everything seems to be going well, when you're young and in love, and at the start of your career, the future seems like this blazing light-riven space, like the

Parque Ecológico with its lake and its green hills on the most glorious of Saturday afternoons. But the truth is: the darkness is ever present, the creeping shadows at the edge of the grass, the gathering gloom in between the trees. It's just that somewhere along the line, you simply stop seeing it. But it's always there. Waiting.

He thought about the women who were at one with the dark, the young women who had been down here in the tunnels before him, and he imagined strange spectral forms rising up from the black water. All at once, the thought of the water, the thought of simply floating away, seemed darkly alluring; the exhaustion that crept across his bones was now perfuming through his mind.

He called out again, 'José!'

The sound echoed and disappeared.

For a few moments, there was more of nothing. And then a voice.

But it was not José's.

It was a thick, lugubrious drawling sound, strange and perverse, low and drawn out.

'Greetings … little … priest.'

The words resonated through the darkness.

Armando felt the hairs on the back of his neck prick up. The coldness seemed to fade as something kindled deep inside him; fear and a slow-burning rage.

He reached out into the gloom and shook the torch twice; small, precise hard movements. The bulb flickered as the beam stabilised and cohered once more. With one arm, Armando extended the torch; with the other, he drew his weapon. He rotated his body, sweeping the light around, but there was still nothing on either side of him except the swirling water, which had reached almost to his waist. Across the dark came that same disembodied voice, gleeful and deranged, thick with insanity.

'Come ... pay homage ... little priest.'

Armando did not reply. His concentration had narrowed to a single point, a cold, deathly certainty. If he was going to die down here, if he was going to be swallowed by the earth and water, he would kill this man first.

He shone the torch ahead and thought he detected movement, the motion of a shadow. He moved in that direction, wading through the water. Again, that disembodied voice:

'This is ... Mictlān!'

It echoed from all around.

'You have come to worship me with your life ... little priest. So many acolytes ... They pray for your soul in the realm of the dead. They watch over us ... little priest.'

'I'm going to enjoy shutting your fucking mouth!' Armando snarled under his breath.

He moved through an opening, shining the beam of light out across the ocean of darkness. He had arrived at a great room, a hexagon-shaped chamber with five openings. The sound of the water was rushing now as all its channels flowed into this one space.

Something flashed out at Armando from the blackness, and he shot his gun before swinging the torch around, glimpsing the fluttering form of a bat whistling into one of the adjacent tunnels. As he brought the beam back around, he saw a figure suspended from the wall, her black limbs reaching outwards, rickety and ossified. Her body was little more than a shell; the insides had collapsed, and the face was eyeless, with its jaw wrenched apart and set into that same demented scream.

Gasping, Armando spun around, churning the water and sending the beam of light sweeping over the chamber, illuminating the other side, where it exposed another figure, another hollowed-out woman, her dead limbs reaching forwards out of the wall, her jaw ripped apart in the same hideous shriek. He was fighting for breath now as he took a step forwards. And in all the commotion, he did not notice the bubbling in the water behind him, as the shape pushed itself out from the churning surface, rising up, slick and wet, morphing into a single figure, a crooked, demented grin streaked across a pallid face like a slashing wound.

At the very last moment, Armando sensed its movement and swung around with his right arm at the very last moment. Still gripping the gun, he pulled the trigger, releasing a single shot, but the man before him brought one impossibly long arm swinging across the space between them. He knocked the weapon from Armando's hand. Armando rolled his broad shoulders and threw his right arm forwards as hard as he could, his balled-up fist connecting with the other man's midriff. He breathed out, for the power of the punch was enough to take a man off his feet, any man, yet the other hardly moved. Armando heard him exhale before he stepped forwards again, and that was when Armando felt a blow smashing into his face, shattering his nose, turning him over into the water.

Suddenly, he was underneath, nothing but the blackness and the rush of bubbles. He felt the grip of vice-like hands as he was wrenched out of the water, one hand clutching his neck, the other grasping his head, raising him up; the power in those hands was cutting off his breath.

He kicked hard into his assailant, his legs flaying about, but the strength of the other man was like nothing he had ever known. In seconds, his body began to lose its impetus, and his head flopped

403

back. He began to hallucinate. In place of the formless roof of the chamber, he saw a night sky scattered with gleaming stars and a blood-red moon, and around the two men were the shadowy images of hundreds of dead women, draped in black, watching the tussle play out from the darkness of absent eyes. He felt his own eyes closing, those women melding with the night-time dark.

He heard M's voice from far away, that low drawling tone. 'Come, die for me, little priest.'

A last dying ember of resistance flared; instinctively, he moved his mouth towards one of the arms that were holding him, and with everything he had left, he bit down.

M released a single high-pitched scream.

Armando shook his head as hard as he could, cleaving away a large scrap of bloody flesh with his teeth. At once, the grip upon him slackened, and he fell back into the water. His head went under; the water rushed into his nose and mouth. He managed to raise his head up again, but he was choking. He had nothing left. He didn't even have the strength to lift his arms.

He saw the tall man lift his shirt to produce a jagged knife hooked on his belt. Then, another violent shout cut across the air. M was pulled back hard, the figure of José Luis behind him, clutching onto his back, trying desperately to drag him down.

Armando watched the scene as though he was seeing things from within the medium of a dream; the strange helpless floating sense of inevitability as M managed to grip José Luis, wrenching him over his head, flinging him down like a rag doll, his body hitting the water with an almighty splash. Armando watched as M bore down on José Luis, raising the knife, a single glint of steel in the dullness, which flashed as it fell.

No!

Armando managed to get to his feet, but M came lurching towards him once more, grinning luridly. Armando swung his arm, smashing his fist into the other man's chin, and this time, Armando felt the crunching impact, his body swinging around carried by the momentum of his punch. In the same moment, M had brought the knife down towards Armando's chest, only to be thwarted by Armando's twisting motion, and the jagged blade sliced across Armando's arm instead, shredding through flesh and muscle in a shuddering, scraping sweep. Armando tried to swipe with his left arm, but M sent a long leg out of the water and into his chest, the impact clean and unadulterated, lifting Armando off his feet, the breath driven from his body.

Before Armando had even hit the water, M was moving forwards again. However, this time, when Armando fell back, he did not fight it; he allowed his body to sink under the water. A long trail of murky blood rose from his wounded arm like a dark ribbon of cloud drifting across the night. He felt his back meet the ground several feet under, and a series of images flitted through his mind, broken and confused. He saw Salome's face and thought how much he would have liked to have been her father. He thought about José Luis, who could have been a father to a child he would now never see. A sadness passed across him and with it a sense of injustice. His mind cleared just enough that he was able to use his feet to push himself across the bottom, moving through the water. As he did so, he fanned out his arms, so they were skimming the surface of the ground, feeling and searching.

He kicked once, twice. The need to breathe, to gasp for air, was excruciating; his chest felt like it was bursting, his eyes bulging. There was nothing but that frantic biological urgency, every molecule in his body screaming for oxygen.

Armando could no longer stop himself from opening his mouth. But at the moment when he was about to draw breath, his right hand made contact with the hard shape of the gun, and with the little strength he had left, Armando propelled himself upward, taking the weapon with him and breaking the surface. M was about three feet away, and for the first time, he appeared surprised. Then, he lunged at Armando. Armando fired into the centre of the other man's chest until there were no more bullets.

The other man's body shook hard, but he remained standing. Then he looked down, touched a single finger to the holes that had opened up across the top part of his chest, and gazed at that finger. The ghost of a smile passed over his face before that tall, rigid body folded and collapsed, sinking under the water.

Armando didn't give him another glance. He let the gun drop and went over to the torch, which was still bobbing on the surface of the water. He took it and made his way over to where he had last seen José Luis.

He took in a breath, crouched, and went under the water again. He found the body of his partner and pulled it up. José Luis's shirt looked as though it had been put through a shredder. There was a single slug-like wound that had been opened up from belly to torso, hacking upwards into his heart. His mouth was slightly open. His eyes were wide. He didn't look to be in pain. He didn't look as though he was suffering; he looked indelibly childlike as though the world had whispered to him a question for which he had no answer.

Armando was suddenly aware of how young his partner was – had been. How he had always tried to win Armando's approval, and how that had eventually led him to a watery grave deep under the ground.

Armando felt his body convulse with a deep choking sob. He touched his fingers to the young man's eyes. And closed them.

José had been young and bright, but he had also been a warrior. He had fought down here to the bitter end.

Armando brought the body to rest in the water at the edge of the wall. Then he removed his own soaking jacket, ripped it into strips, and knotted one of those strips around his right arm, which was drenched in blood. He clutched the young man's body with his left arm and used the torch to find his way out of the chamber. He didn't look back. He dragged José Luis because he couldn't bear to leave him, because the young man had been a fighter and a police detective, and he deserved a proper burial.

But Armando was bleeding and depleted.

He pulled the body in his wake for as long as he could, but at some point, his hand, cold and numb, unlocked from it, the movement involuntary. He tried to grip the body again, but the stiffness in his fingers was too much.

Finally, with a gasp, he let it go.

He shone the torch on the body, the ghostly features of the young man's handsome face, solemn in death, fading into the shadows, disappearing into the water.

He turned and made his way deeper into the tunnel. The water was so cold, so high now, up to his chest. He walked some more. He knew he was still bleeding, but he could no longer feel it. He could no longer feel … anything.

Not long afterwards, the torch died. He shook it, but it didn't return to life this time.

He kept moving through the blackness. For how long, he couldn't say. The water was up to his chin now. His eyes were almost closed. Drowsiness had settled over him, a thick, heavy, dampening feeling, which had merged with the wet and the cold, slowly turning him to stone. From somewhere ahead, he thought he saw a light. Though perhaps it was the misfiring of neurones in his brain, the loss of blood, the strange hallucinations thrown up by a flickering existence on the verge of perishing in the black. He moved towards it on instinct. Now he was tilting his head upwards to take in oxygen from the rapidly disappearing gap of remaining air.

All at once, he was underwater.

He pushed himself forward, swimming towards the thinning slant of light. He got closer. Finally, he met the gap, crawling through it into a small, tight tunnel, which was just wide enough for his body. He slid his ragged, bloodied body upwards with everything he had, only to come up against hard bricks: a sealed-off exit.

The water was still coming, rapidly filling the small cocoon of space, forming a watery tomb. He pushed his fist against the bricks as hard as he could, his breath rasping in the black.

Come on, dammit.

Although he had little strength in his arm, the bricks gave way. They had not been cemented but merely stacked over the opening.

Armando crawled out into a dark room and laid on the floor as the water dribbled out around him. He had no idea how long he stayed that way, but when he began to move again, he felt his body sliding across a thick dusty substance.

Ash.

He raised himself up onto one knee and then managed to stand. He hobbled out through the darkened room towards the beams of light that shone down from a staircase leading out. He climbed the steps and stepped out into what seemed like another world, the charred, blackened architecture of some long-lost civilisation with a thin mist creeping across it.

All at once, he realized where he was. He had emerged at the point of the old mansion, the hacienda, the building the *federales* had burned to the ground all those months ago. He moved through the blackened remains of the garden, where the mist lifted, dispersed by the long sleek slats of sunlight.

Armando made his way out onto the road. It was early morning, so a few people were out. The rain had stopped.

Eventually, he limped his way to a bus stop. The bus was a 29, which crossed the city close to his own *barrio*. As he climbed aboard, the driver blinked at him in astonishment and went to say something but then closed his mouth again.

Without paying for the fare, Armando walked down the aisle. Some indigenous workers had already taken many of the seats – their eyes found him briefly from underneath those wide-brimmed black hats, but there was no malice in their expressions, only a sad curiosity.

Armando made his way towards the back and sank down into an empty seat. He looked out of the window and saw the sun on the horizon, climbing higher into the sky, marking the start of the new day. As the bus *sloshed* through a wide pool of floodwater that came up to its wheels, the passengers looked and pointed and laughed. That sense of expectation, that sense of the passing of the storm, and a new beginning …

But for José, there would not be that. There would never be … that.

Armando thought about the young man somewhere underground, beyond pain or hope. Something moved inside him. A phrase came to him, from where he did not know:

Let the dead bury the dead.

And he thought about Esmeralda and Salome – most of all he thought about Salome – and realised, as the sunlight fell on his face and arms, drying his clothes and tingling against his raw skin … He realised that, for him, Salome was the new day.

Tears of grief and relief pricked his eyes.

A few minutes later, he got off the bus and limped to his street. He would get cleaned up and then go to the hospital and get stitched up. He would also go to Esmeralda and do whatever it took to persuade her to leave Puebla City tonight, and through the clarity of his determination, he understood something else: for the first time in as long as he could remember, he didn't feel an urge to drink.

And just like that, he knew the time had come to quit.

His red-rimmed eyes blinked incoherently as the massive figure of a man approached.

Filippo.

It was the ex-bouncer who appeared dishevelled and ragged, almost beyond recognition. He was swaying, heavily drunk.

'What are you …?'

Armando was interrupted when the other man punched him in the belly. He gasped and blinked up at Filippo.

The ex-bouncer muttered in a drunken slur, 'Fuck you … to hell.' He blinked at Armando with a rueful, rage-filled gaze.

Then the repetition, the same toneless voice: 'Fuck you to hell.'

Armando breathed in hard as the fat bouncer lumbered away, swaying dangerously along the street. He couldn't quite make sense of what had just happened. He put his hand down to where Filippo had struck him. It was hot and sticky. He brought his fingers up;

410

they were smeared with blood. That was when he realised he'd been stabbed.

He gasped again; for a moment, it didn't seem quite real, and then he felt a shuddering weakness at the core of his being. At once, his adrenaline kicked in, and he scrunched up his shirt and pressed the material into his wound, holding his hand there, gripping it, trembling, stemming the flow of blood. There was no real pain, yet something about how his body felt told him it was really bad; the feeling of his consciousness slowly starting to detach itself from itself.

He thought about Esmeralda again. And Salome.

He staggered off in the direction of their building, clutching his belly. The distance was some two blocks, and he nearly passed out several times along the way, but he made it to the building, to the buzzer, and then to her door. It was perhaps the strangest journey he had ever made, stranger still than the journey he had undertaken with José Luis under the ground, for this time everything around him was completely familiar –the buildings, the streets, the texture of the daylight, the hue of the sky. And yet he realised he was seeing these things for the very last time. He knew there was nothing to be done, but he knew he had to see her. He had to see Salome.

To say goodbye.

Esmeralda opened the door, and Armando saw, as though he was seeing her for the first time, how beautiful she was; the open smile that so easily lit up her face, despite the suffering she had been through, despite the poverty and the hardship. Those dark golden eyes shone with joy. She was artless in this way; every emotion she felt passed across her beautiful, beautiful face with the clarity of water. At the same moment, she saw him, and her face fell. Her lips began to tremble as tears formed in her eyes so instantaneously. He

411

reached out one hand and touched her cheek with all the tenderness he knew.

'What's … happened to you?' She was crying.

He looked at her and gave a sad smile. 'It's going to be okay, Esme. I need to come in. Can I come in?'

Shaking a little, she helped him through into the *sala*, into the room that he had fallen in love with somewhere along the line, and in the middle was Salome with Lucillia, the old lady who lived on the same floor.

When Salome looked at Armando, her large eyes shone, but then the little girl's face fell. She looked at her mother and then at Armando again.

'Hey, kid,' Armando said with an awkward smile. He suddenly realised that in his desperation to see Salome, he hadn't really figured out what he would say to her. 'I just wanted to—'

The image of the room dulled. Salome's face, those wide eyes, faded into a distant shadow as he felt himself slump downwards. He felt hands on him, touching him, and the feeling of them was pleasant because in some strange way, even though he knew he was dying, he knew at the same time he was safe.

He blinked himself into consciousness again. When he opened his eyes, he saw the soft expressions of the toys gazing down at him, those goofy sea creature faces, and he felt the touch of the little girl's hand gripping his arm as tightly as she could. It occurred to him that this was the only heaven he would ever see. And he felt okay about that, not just okay, but a strange happiness, which bloomed from the midst of his fear and his disorientation.

Esmeralda had recovered herself. He was aware of that now. She was speaking to the old lady in an urgent voice.

'Lucillia, please, go. Call the ambulance. Go now!'

412

He was vaguely aware of the old lady shuffling out of the room. He focused again on the kid, on Salome, and felt himself smile.

He reached up and pinched her cheek affectionately. 'Hey … kid …' The words just made it out through the burble of blood rising in his throat.

Her eyes were wide, so impossibly wide, shimmering with tears, but she was stubborn; she was trying so hard not to cry.

She's a fighter, he thought.

Just like him.

'Armando,' she whispered, a voice so slight he could barely hear it. 'Armando!'

'Yeah … kid.'

'I … love you.'

He reached for her hand. It was so small. So slight. It occurred to him that everything precious, all human life, was exactly like that.

She looked at him. 'Do you … do you love me?' she asked with that same halting whisper.

He felt something unfurl inside him, a letting go. The words came so easily. So naturally. 'I do, Salome. I love you … very much.'

'Then you can't leave. That means you can't leave.'

Finally, it was too much for her. The little girl was crying.

He touched her chin. 'Look at me,' he rasped.

He felt his vision fading out again but willed himself to remain conscious. The feeling in his gut sent a sudden spasm through his arm.

He spoke as gently as he could. 'I'll still be with you, I promise.'

'How?' The word came out in a plaintive sob, which verged on anger, betrayal.

413

His eyes were closing.

He opened them again. Smiled. Touched his finger to her chest, to her heart. 'Here. I'll be with you here.'

She wrapped herself around him, clasping him to her.

He sighed from the pain of her body against his and the sense of loss he felt from losing her.

Lucillia had come back into the room. She nodded at Esmeralda, who looked utterly stricken.

'The ambulance is on its way,' Lucillia said.

Armando didn't hear those words. As Salome hugged him, a sudden gush of blood spilt out of his mouth and trickled down his chin. He raised his weak right hand, desperately trying to wipe it away. He looked at Esmeralda helplessly.

'I've said ... what I needed to. She doesn't need to see this ... next part,' he whispered.

Esmeralda nodded at him and looked at Lucillia. 'Lucillia, would you take Salome to her room?'

The old woman put her arms around Salome, gradually moving her away from Armando. 'It's okay, *princesa*,' she whispered.

But when Salome realised what was happening, she beat her hands against her babysitter's back.

'No, no. Let me go. No. No. Armando. PLEAAAASEEE!'

Her words dissolved into desperate shuddering sobs as the old lady rocked her in her arms, taking her down the corridor.

As Armando watched her go, an involuntary shudder caused another sudden deluge of blood to bubble out of his mouth, dribbling down his chin and chest.

Esmeralda leaned into him. 'You're going to be alright. You're going to be fine. The ambulance is on its way.'

He looked at her through hazy eyes, unseeing eyes. He slipped into unconsciousness.

Seconds later, he saw her again. She was pushing her hands against his chest.

'No! You are strong, Armando. You're not going to go away. I won't let you go.'

He smiled one last time before his expression grew fearful. She had to lean in to hear his whispered words.

'Esme ... The telescope. Look through ... the telescope.'

She gripped his head. 'I will. Every night. Me and the kid. I promise.'

Armando's eyes closed.

She watched as that great chest rose once more; his body shook hard, and then, subdued, he died.

Esmeralda heard the wail of the ambulance. She kissed his lips. She cried.

Epilogue

Hernando Martin hated chaos. Hated imprecision. He was a violent man, for certain, but he regretted violence, took no joy in it, utilised it only when necessary to achieve a particular and practical end. That was why he loathed the young man he worked for. Juan Carlos III was impetuous, arrogant, rich and spoilt. Beyond that, Martin had come to realise that his client was a sadist of the sickest type.

Juan Carlos's father was a different type. Also a killer, but someone who had come from poverty, like Martin himself; someone who liked to remain grey and non-descript, someone who sheltered in the shadows. A brutal person, *sí*, but the tortures the father carried out had nothing in common with personal pleasure. They related only to the extrication of information, the physical pressure applied to another in order to generate a certain outcome – not always savoury and certainly corrupt, but always to the point.

Juan Carlos *fils*, on the other hand, had little regard for such a work ethic. Juan Carlos Junior's appetite for suffering was something in and of itself. The pain he inflicted was bound up with his pleasure and rage, the sudden bouts of vicious euphoria, the strange subdued gloomy silences; the young man spent time with his captives, his victims, his employees, his subordinates, and on occasion, did certain things, which –despite his forty years on the police force, despite all the horrific things he had seen – caused Martin to draw in breath.

The older ex-detective suspected that was why the young man's father, the boss of the organisation, had placed him with his son in the first place. To curtail his more … creative urges. To rein him in. Easier said than done. He had succeeded up to a point. He had helped bury the bodies of those women with whom Juan Carlos Junior had become a little too excitable. He had tried to wean the young man off his pattern of blatant sadism and murder, but the young man was a cunt. And a loose cannon. It was only a matter of time before he crashed and burned. And even Martin couldn't prevent that.

He'd kept him out of prison, of course, because the ex-detective had contacts high up in the police hierarchy. And then suddenly, the whole thing had blown up. That Armando – the detective Juan Carlos had developed something of an obsession for, determined to bring him into the fold – had seemed a little too savvy, a little too independent. When it had all gone down, Martin had not been surprised to discover that Armando had been in some way at the centre of it all. Juan Carlos had been taken the same night Armando had disappeared along with a large quantity of cocaine.

It had taken a few days for these events to become clear, but once they had, Martin was sure that somehow Armando had engineered it. Had orchestrated the whole thing. He'd taken some men to Armando's apartment, but then they had discovered that Armando had been killed only a couple of days after Juan Carlos himself had disappeared. A death was hard to fake, especially when you had access to police reports. They had paid a cursory visit to Armando's whore, but she and her kid had left the neighbourhood.

Eventually, it transpired that Juan Carlos had the drugs and not Armando. Martin couldn't figure out how any of this had played out. But Juan Carlos had been taken by the *federales*, sucked deep into their system of 'justice', and Martin doubted whether the young man would ever see the light of day again. He didn't feel too bad about that. But now, he needed to cover his own back. He'd already had several calls. The *federales* had raided a number of Juan Carlos's father's establishments. He knew that Septimecielo would be next. So, when he heard the screeching sound of the police sirens, he was already primed to leave via the back exit. He opened the safe and grabbed the bulging envelope of cash. It was enough so that he would never need to take any of these low, dirty assignments again. And the father's empire was crumbling all around. The son would never return; the money was Martin's and his alone. He felt certain about that.

He slipped out into the night, turned down a side street, and got into his car. He could see the flashing blue glow of the police in his rear-view mirror. His days of work, of risk, were over. He ripped open the envelope and flicked through the thick pile of notes. As he did so, his face changed into an expression of incomprehension. And then disbelief. The first few notes were 1,000 peso bills, but the others had changed colour – orange, red, pink, and purple. He gripped them hard and then took in a breath before releasing a bitter cursing snarl.

The envelope had been packed out with Monopoly money.

***

Esmeralda was watching her daughter playing on the beach.

Salome was fascinated by the sea. She had been here years before, when her grandfather was alive, but the young girl didn't remember much about that time. Not anymore.

The tide had retracted, the sun was setting, and the wide beach seemed to stretch into the distance, shimmering and glistening under the gentle glow of the dying light. The little girl was moving across the sand, turning, spinning her body, and then she would grow still, kneeling, peering at some crustacean or shell that had caught her eye.

Esmeralda had the impression that Salome was gradually healing in this place. She would watch her daughter, who had always been imaginative, but she had changed. Before, she had been loud, a bundling bursting profusion of energy; now, she was more subdued, a child who had seen more than any child should.

Esmeralda would watch Salome on the beach, and she would see her daughter's mouth moving, conversing with the images of people and things Esmeralda could not make out. After what happened, Esmeralda had brought Salome to Las Esmeraldas, the beautiful seaside village where she herself had been raised. Esmeralda remembered the village as a constraining, awful place; the place that she had been named after also seemed like the place that had held her down, trapped her into a definition of herself that she simply didn't recognise. She had broken away long ago. But now, coming back, she felt a sense of well-being she had not known for a while. And Salome seemed to enjoy it. She had tried to talk to her little girl about what had happened with Armando, but Salome would simply nod, politely almost (which was so strange for her) and look away. Esmeralda knew her daughter didn't want to touch the subject of what had happened that day.

And yet, every night without fail, Salome demanded one thing: that her mother tell her the one story, over and over; the story about the bad-tempered bear who banged his head too much, who saw shadows, and who one day met a small little monkey with dark eyes. A monkey with whom that bear became the best of friends. Salome couldn't fall asleep until she had heard that story, and that was all right with Esmeralda because she was grateful her daughter could sleep at all.

Sometimes, after Salome went to bed, Esmeralda thought about Armando. Her client. Her lover. And eventually, she had come to believe ... her friend. She wasn't idealistic about men. She had known that Armando was a violent man; she had also suspected that he'd been a corrupt policeman and that his death had, in some way, resulted from that. Nevertheless, Esmeralda had seen a seam of goodness within him, a great kindness; she knew that about him, even if he hadn't understood that about himself.

At the same time, sometimes in the night, she would wake up and feel angry. She would wonder if it might have been better if he had just disappeared from Salome's life rather than putting her through the trauma of what she had seen. Sometimes she was glad that her daughter had the chance to say goodbye to a man whom, Esmeralda felt, had loved her child absolutely. Sometimes her anger was hot and petulant, and she felt selfish. Something in her had seen Armando as a father figure, a great protector, someone whose strength would ward off all the bad things, someone she and Salome could shelter under as life unleashed the one awful thing after another. And sometimes, she felt mad because she wanted him to hold her in the night, and she hadn't been touched for a while.

These thoughts, and others, flitted across her mind. Her father's house had long since been sold. She and Salome were staying in a rented house, and the savings she had were being drained every week. They wouldn't last much longer. But she knew her child needed this change of scene; they both did, and when the time came, when she had to return to her job, she wouldn't do it in Puebla City. She would never go there again.

She thought about Armando once more, a combination of bitterness and loss. He had left them alone, even if he hadn't wanted to.

It doesn't matter, she told herself.

Once the money ran out, she would do whatever she had to do to keep that little girl out there talking to her imaginary friends, playing, and dancing on the beach.

Another memory came. Those last gurgled words from Armando:

'Look through the telescope.'

Of all the things, this was something that continued to hurt her. She knew it was so horribly petty on her part. He'd told Salome that he loved her.

But would it have been too much to ask? That he might have said the same to me?

Perhaps Esmeralda had always been a whore in his eyes. But that didn't matter either. His relationship with Salome was the important thing. She knew, without a doubt, how much that man had loved her child. She felt it.

What could be more important than that?

She looked out towards the beach again. The tide was drawing in. The first premonitions of night were beginning to prickle on the horizon, and still, Salome danced and ran and crouched and dug her fingers into the sand.

Esmeralda thought about her father. And then Armando again.

Those last words …

She watched her daughter as those words turned over in her mind.

'Look through the telescope.'

Then, that blood-clogged gurgle. But more than that, those words … had seemed strange.

On an impulse, she went to the back of the room, where the boxes were still laid out – the unpacked things that they had salvaged from the apartment in Puebla City when they had left early in the afternoon after the ambulance had gone. She hoisted out the telescope, one of the few things they had been able to bring with them in the van, and one of the things that Salome – wide-eyed, grief-stricken, and exhausted – had screamed that they take.

Esmeralda fiddled about in the same box. She found something she could use, an old screwdriver. She didn't recognise it, but she must have bought it at some point in the past.

'Look through the telescope.'

Having rested the heavy base of the telescope on the floor, Esmeralda applied the screwdriver to the screws, her arm twisting wildly. This was not something she was good at. But she persevered and eventually pulled away one metallic panel from the base of the telescope.

Finally, she could look *through* the telescope.

Inside, she found a thick brown envelope. She ripped it open. It contained more money than she had seen in her lifetime. More money than she could ever have imagined.

Her eyes welled with tears, and for the first time since Armando had died, she shuddered and began to sob with abandon. She would never have to work again.

She tried to pull herself together only to cry again, a sound wrought from happiness but also grief. The feeling of missing him resonated through her, but there was a feeling of joy, too, the sense that he had loved her and was determined never to let her go.

Trying to contain the gulf of emotion that had so suddenly opened up from inside, Esmeralda stepped out and onto the beach. The air was warm, and the sky was riven with deepening colour. In the distance, the vague outline of storm clouds began to attain definition.

Esmeralda raised her hand to her daughter and called out.

Salome raised her head, looked back at her mother, and waved.

Miles and Miles of Ancient Tunnels Discovered Underneath Puebla City

December 12, 2014
Written by Gabriela De Las Fuentes

As a citizen of the world, you might well have heard about the catacombs that lie underneath Paris or Rome, a subterranean complex of tomb and tunnel. But I bet you have never heard of the ten kilometres of underground passageways that sneak beneath the Mexican city of Puebla.

That is partly because these underground tunnels have only just been discovered – and not by an intrepid team of archaeologists with bullwhips and Indiana Jones hats. Rather, a construction crew came across them when digging up the ground to create the basis for a new underpass.

This rather magnificent but macabre discovery – the workmen discovered a scattering of old bones in the more general detritus of the flooded subterranean tunnels – has led to teams of archaeologists working night and day to discover clues concerning the tunnels' origins. Some of these specialists believe that the tunnels date back to the founding of Puebla itself in the early 1500s, providing a means by which nuns and priests could travel quickly and swiftly from the churches to colonial outposts without detection when the city was under siege.

But others speculate that the tunnels have older origins and that the Aztecs created them as some kind of netherworld to which their blood sacrifices might be sent.

Of course, such a sinister explanation very possibly disguises a more prosaic reality. The tunnels were more likely to have been an attempt at an early water or sewage system, and what has been discovered in their mud – along with bones – has included antique guns, forks, toys, and even marbles.

Some of these items are ancient, but some date right up to the nineteenth century, which suggests that, for a long while, Mexicans were aware of the existence of these tunnels. However, at some point, this awareness faded. The location of the tunnels was forgotten as they fell out of use and eventually became the stuff of Puebla folklore – more myth than fact!

But now, their existence has been definitively revealed once more, and the citizens of Puebla are beginning to take an active role again. Walk down the Cinco de Mayo Road, and you will see a large opening leading underground as if to a subway. However, it is much more than a subway; it's a gateway to the city's subterranean history! And in the years to come, with the right renovations, these tunnels will become Puebla's greatest museum: a place for tourists to come and soak in history, away from the heat of Mexico's burning sun.

About the Author

Tony McKenna is a writer whose work has been featured by *Counterpunch*, *Al Jazeera*, *The Huffington Post*, *Salon*, *New Statesman*, *ABC Australia*, *TRT World* and many others. His books include *The War Against Marxism: Reification and Revolution* (Bloomsbury), *Angels and Demons: A Radical Anthology of Political Lives* (Zero Books), and a novel, *The Dying Light* (New Haven Publishing).

Printed in Great Britain
by Amazon